WATCH OVER ME

JANE RENSHAW

Revised Edition 2019
INKUBATOR BOOKS

www.inkubatorbooks.com

First published as "Risk of Harm" by Jane Renshaw (2019)

ALL SCOTTISH DIALECT AND SLANG TERMS ARE EXPLAINED IN THE GLOSSARY AT THE BACK OF THE BOOK.

PROLOGUE

She thought at first that it was a cruel practical joke. That the blood must be tomato ketchup from the kitchen cupboard. That the shaft of the arrow must be a stick-on plastic fake from Bonzo's, that awful shop in Edinburgh, just off the Royal Mile, where you could buy itching powder and whoopee cushions and disgustingly realistic dog mess.

Her daughter lay on the grass in the orchard, on her back, her arms flung out to either side. Her favourite yellow T-shirt was spattered with red spots and the collar area was saturated – that was going to need a good long soak. Her hair, especially at the left temple, was sticky with the stuff, and it was streaked all down her face. They'd really gone to town with it around the eye, presumably to hide the place where the fake arrow was meant to penetrate. The whole of the socket area was concealed under gloopy red goo, which was very silly and dangerous. She hoped they'd covered the eye with something first.

'Oh for goodness' sake!' she exclaimed.

The girl who had summoned her was still sobbing convincingly. The other sat on the grass, ignoring the bow lying next to her, watching a blackbird that was hopping about on a coil of old rope under a tree. She didn't say a word. Didn't make a sound.

And the first, sickening shiver of doubt ran through her.

'For goodness' sake,' she said again, briskly, dropping to her knees in the long grass, clutching her daughter's upper arms and shaking them a little. 'Come on now! This really is going too far.'

The thin arms flopped in her grip like a rag doll's.

She recognised the arrow. It was made not of plastic but of splintery wood, with green flight feathers slotted into the end. Her husband, against her wishes, had bought six arrows and a bow last Christmas. It had been the only one of the presents he'd wrapped, sitting at the kitchen table complaining about the awkward shape while she fumed inwardly. A bow-and-arrow set, for a child?

How stupid.

How irresponsible.

But she hadn't stopped him. She hadn't snatched it from him, ripped the paper away, snapped the bow in half and put the arrows in the fire.

It was blood.

The red gloop concealing the eye was blood, starting to clot in the fierce July sun.

With fingers that did not, miraculously, shake, she carefully wiped it away so she could see what was underneath, all the time repeating, steadily, 'All right, darling, all right.'

The splintery wooden shaft had gone straight into the open eye. Watery jelly had leaked out with the blood, and she thought suddenly of the bull's eye she had had to deal with in physics class, long ago.

Okay.

Okay.

All her mother's instincts screamed at her to get it out, to get that thing out of her daughter's eye, but she knew that that would be the wrong thing to do.

Only maybe two-thirds of the arrow shaft was visible.

The rest of it was inside her head.

They needed a doctor. They needed a surgeon.

They needed an ambulance.

She shouted, finally, she emptied her lungs, she roared at the bright blue summer sky that was just a sky, a wide, bright, indifferent sky, because there could be no God. She roared until her husband came, until he came running, with the awkward gait of someone who never ran, to where their daughter lay dead in the orchard.

1

Ruth stood at the gate looking up the path to the cottage, trying to see it with Deirdre Jack's eyes. Deirdre would be here in forty-five minutes. She was only maybe a decade or so older than Ruth – early to mid fifties – but Ruth was always conscious of a great gulf between them, like the gulf that had separated her from the teachers at school when she was a child, a great moral gulf that she had no hope of ever crossing.

No.

No.

Ruth had been a quiet little mouse of a girl at school. A sweet little mouse who scuttled about the classroom doing good deeds, like helping the slow ones with their reading, and slipping her pocket money and toys into poor children's desks. Sweet little Ruth had been conscious of no such gulf because none had existed. And adult Ruth was completely at ease with Deirdre. They had a lot in common.

But it didn't help that Deirdre looked like a Botticelli angel. She had a long delicate face, a full bottom lip and pale, wistful eyes. Short, neat, greyish-gold hair that curled a little on her forehead.

A Botticelli angel in crumpled linen and Fairtrade cotton scarves.

Hopefully she would like the idea of a cottage in the middle of nowhere, just a mile from the bonnie banks of Loch Lomond, with half an acre of garden and a paddock crying out for a pony. Hopefully she would like the rather unkempt garden, with its long grass and lichen-covered apple trees, its tangle of hawthorn and wild roses, dotted now with glossy red hips. Ruth would have to remember to say that they left it wild to be ecofriendly.

And she would have to prime Alec so he didn't guffaw at this and say something like, 'It's called wilful neglect.'

Alec, of course, wasn't in the least overawed by Deirdre. Deirdre was an idealist-by-proxy, he'd decided, having discovered – by simply asking straight out – that she didn't have any adopted children herself. Her excuse, as Alec called it, was that one of her own children had Asperger's. He said Deirdre was the type who banged on about the state of society but assiduously avoided her neighbours; who bewailed the fate of the rainforest but hadn't a clue where her garden furniture came from; who shook her head over the lack of adoptive parents but had never for one moment contemplated becoming one herself.

Okay, so maybe he was right, and maybe there was no reason for Ruth to be at all worried, but she couldn't help it.

Deirdre scared the shit out of her.

And she was so tired, her brain dangerously sluggish. She'd lain awake most of last night while Alec had slept like a baby next to her and high winds had howled round the cottage, groaned in the chimney, whispered in her head:

They're going to find out. They're going to find out.

But why should they?

How could they?

Deirdre wouldn't be coming at all today if Ruth hadn't passed their suitability tests with flying colours. All the screening had already been done. Every time she'd stepped into that aggressively cheerful little room at the Linkwood Adoption Agency, all red walls and big Impressionist prints, she'd braced herself for Deirdre to greet her not with a smile but with a look of barely concealed disgust and a cold 'I'm sorry, but something has come up in the background checks' – but that had never happened.

Of course it hadn't.

There was no way they could possibly know that the Ruth Innes who had married Alec Morrison fourteen years ago had died in a house fire in Melrose, along with her mother, stepfather and two brothers, when she was six years old. Not unless they'd taken the details off her birth certificate and used them to trawl through the death records.

And they obviously hadn't done so, or this wouldn't be happening. The home visit was just the final step in the process; the rubber-stamping of the approval of Alec and Ruth Morrison as potential adopters.

She looked down the little single-track road. After the night's high winds, the tarmac was carpeted with a fresh fall of coppery beech leaves – all colours of copper, from newly polished to dull and tarnished. The huge old beech trees along one side of the road arched their pale, thick branches up and up against the bright china blue of the sky, and on the other side a stubbly field rose from the hedge up the slope to the plantation. There was no sound, except for a bird somewhere in the wood, chattering a complaint.

It was beautiful.

It was going to be fine.

Deirdre Jack could have no concerns about Ruth or she'd already have voiced them. Her main worry was probably the carbon footprint she was leaving in coming all the way out here from Glasgow – although Alec would say she probably felt carbon footprints didn't apply to people with socially responsible jobs. Maybe she was enjoying the drive. Singing along to Emmylou Harris or Nanci Griffith. Looking forward to spending a pleasant morning in pleasant company.

Deirdre was coming not to interrogate them again but to check out their home, the environment in which they were proposing to bring up a child.

Which was beautiful.

Which was perfect.

Wasn't it?

It was going to be fine?

She looked up at the sky, an unbroken blue apart from one high wispy little cloud.

Did all this baseless worrying have at its root her desperation to adopt a child, her fear that she was going to be knocked back at the final hurdle, or was it her brain's way of telling her that this wasn't right? That this wasn't what she wanted at all?

She walked a little way along the road. Amongst the beech leaves were scatterings of crushed beech nuts where tyres had run over them. All the trees that would never be. She stooped to pick up an intact nut and close her hand on it, its spikes prickling her palm.

And now she was there at her side.

Ruth had known she would come, her face turned up to her with a smile – rosy cheeks, a woolly red hat, blue and green stripy-gloved hands full of the brightest leaves for the collage they'd make later at the kitchen table.

'Darling,' she whispered, like a madwoman. 'No. No more.'

She had only ever confided in one person about her daydreams of this unborn, unnamed child – and that one person had been Sara, the woman she'd been paired with by the agency, who had adopted three children through them.

She'd been so lovely, Sara, a woman made to be a mother if anyone was, and Ruth had found herself confessing that she fantasised, regularly, about an unconceived, unborn, never-to-be child.

Sara had smiled, and nodded, and told her she used to do the same.

'I'm so scared,' Ruth had gulped. 'I'm so scared I won't love the little girl we adopt as I would have loved my own.' Scared about other things too, of course, but those fears she would never, ever blurt out to anyone, let alone a virtual stranger.

Sara had grabbed Ruth's hand. 'Oh *no no no*, you mustn't worry about that! *She will be your own*, and you'll love her *so much*. You'll love her as you've never loved *anyone* in your *life*. You'll love her just as much, maybe even more than if she'd been biologically yours.'

But those were just words, a politically correct recitation of what you were meant to feel.

Maybe it was fifteen years of living with Alec, or maybe it was the pragmatism that nurses seemed to have inbuilt or to develop, but she had a horrible suspicion that blood ties mattered. They were the basis of life, after all, of evolution, of animal behaviour. Human behaviour. Her own experience of the neonatal unit had shown her just how strong, how primeval, was the bond between a mother and her child. Her *own* child. Her own flesh and blood child.

The little stranger who was out in the world somewhere waiting for Ruth, waiting to be loved as every child deserved to be loved, was counting on her to love her like a flesh and blood mother would.

'Go,' she said. 'Go.'

She threw the beech nut to the verge. And her never-to-be little girl flung out her arms and ran, full tilt, red wellies kicking through the leaves, running away from her down the road without a backward glance.

'Go.'

Stupid stupid stupid, to be crying. To be thinking that if there was a heaven, if by some remote chance it existed, surely there must be a place in it for her own child, a place where all the never-to-be children waited for their mothers.

So stupid.

But as the little figure blurred and faded, as she found a tissue in her pocket and blew her nose and laughed at herself, as she looked back at the road, at nothing, she let her never-to-be mother's love fill her heart and spill over and speak itself aloud, just once, to the empty air:

'I would have loved you... I would have loved you mo–'

But before the last word had quite left her lips, she had put a hand to her mouth to stop it. The woman Deirdre was about to meet would never think that. Ruth Morrison would be horrified at the very thought that an adopted child could be any less loved than a biological one. Less wanted. Less valued. Less worthy.

Such a possibility would never even cross Ruth Morrison's mind.

2

'Right, let's make a start, then,' goes the sheriff woman. 'Ladies and gentlemen. This Court of Session is sitting to determine an application for a permanence order, with authority to adopt, by Glasgow City Council in respect of the child Bekki Johnson. The application is opposed by the child's grandparents, Jed and Lorraine Johnson.' She takes off her glasses, looks right at me and starts on about what a permanence order is, like I'm a daftie, like I dinnae even know what it is I'm fucking fighting.

I know what a permanence order is. It's the fucking system saying Bekki's gonnae be adopted by fucking randoms and there's nothing we can do about it.

Our fucking Bekki.

The sheriff bumps her gums, blah fucking blah, and then Mair gets up, in her white silk shirt and wee black skirt and I'm-so-down-with-the-kids nose stud. If it wasnae for Bekki, I'd swing for her so I would.

She goes to the box thingmie like a sheep pen in front of the sheriff's bench. She sits on the chair inside it and puts her papers down in front of her, like she's so fucking professional.

'Ms Mair.' The lawyer who's for the Council gets up. The lawyers have this big table in the middle of the courtroom court room with computers and that. 'Could you describe for the sheriff what your role has been in this case?' Bastard's English. *Fwah fwah fwah.*

'I'm the social worker assigned to Bekki Johnson's case. I'm the author of the permanence order report, Lady Semple, which I think you have there...' The smug face on her, like Bekki's an exam question she's aced.

Sheriff goes, 'Yes, thank you, Ms Mair. A very clear, comprehensive report it is too.'

Aye, a very clear, comprehensive load of shite.

Fwah: 'Perhaps you could give us some brief background on Bekki and her family situation, Ms Mair?'

Mair: 'Bekki is now two years and eight months old. She's a bright, healthy child, but I would also describe her as unusually quiet and undemanding for her age. She has been assessed by medical doctors and a psychiatrist – I think you have also had those reports, Lady Semple. They found her to show no signs of physical or cognitive impairment, but there were some indications of impairments in developmental functioning and emotional well-being, in particular symptoms of anxiety, excessive shyness and withdrawal. Immediately following her removal from the family, she was found to be malnourished and was diagnosed with a vitamin C deficiency. There were also some dozen or so cuts and bruises to her arms, legs and torso. She's now living with foster parents. There has been no contact with her mother, Shannon-Rose Johnson, or any of her biological family, under the terms of the emergency child protection order granted by this court in July of this year, following Bekki's removal into Local Authority care, as there was felt to be a significant risk of harm.'

I dinnae lose it.

I give Bekki's Shrek a cuddle and shake my head, like I'm that disbelieving the bitch has the brass neck.

Fwah moves back to the table and leans over his computer screen. 'The mother is a paranoid schizophrenic, I believe?'

Mair sits back with a put-on sad face. 'Yes, Bekki's mother, Shannon-Rose Johnson, suffers from paranoid schizophrenia. Before her arrest for murder, she had poor adherence to medication, which, coupled with substance abuse, resulted in frequent episodes of psychosis. While experiencing such an episode on the twenty-fifth of June this year, she fatally stabbed her partner, Dean McGillivray, with a kitchen knife. She has pled guilty to murder and is currently awaiting sentencing in a secure psychiatric unit.'

Fwah: 'And these tragic circumstances resulted in Shannon-Rose's parental responsibilities and rights – PRRs – in respect of her two-year-old daughter Bekki being removed and granted to the Local Authority?'

'In the immediate aftermath of Shannon-Rose's arrest, Bekki was taken to stay with her grandparents, Jed and Lorraine Johnson. In such cases there is always a presumption in favour of PRRs being allocated to the child's biological family, with or without a formal adoption. But in the case of Bekki Johnson it was, sadly, clear from the outset that this would not be in her best interests.'

Mandy goes, 'Was it fuck,' and Carly goes, 'Wait a wee minute.'

I goes, 'Shut it yous.'

Sheriff eyeballs us.

Jed wanted the whole lot of us coming down but I wasnae having it. One look at Jed, at his bust nose and scars and the manky tattoos up his neck, one look at Ryan flashing his fake Rolex and gold chains, like he'd a big sign on him saying 'Drug Dealer', and the sheriff would be all *Christ on a cheesy biscuit* and checking security. Goodbye Bekki. Even if Jed and Travis didnae lose their shit.

So no Jed, no Ryan, no Travis. Just me, Carly and Connor, and Mandy.

It was maybe a mistake bringing Mandy but. My big sis. We've both of us got a cleavage on us you could smother a fucking babby in, but at least mine's under cover, eh? Mands is putting it all out there and she's wearing a bra two sizes too wee – her daft budget version of a Wonderbra – and she's having issues, got her hand down her top wammling like a fucking ferret.

Aye, thanks a lot, doll, why don't you give the court the whole fucking floor show while you're at it? She tells folk she used to be a modern dancer, but she was just one of they fat lassies used to jiggle their bits in the back room at the Anchor Bar.

Mr Lyall told us how to act when we got here.

No eating or drinking.

No swearing.

No shouting out.

'You have to show the sheriff that you're the kind of people a child would be secure – safe and happy with,' says Mr Lyall, looking down his long neb, like I wouldnae know what *secure* means. 'You need to let her see you as a nice, loving family. Maybe you come from a bad area, maybe you have problems, but you love each other. You're reasonable people. You know how to behave. All right?'

Like the only way we'll come across as decent fucking human beings is if we're faking it.

I put an arm round wee Connor. 'It's okay, love.'

Connor gives me evils.

I squeeze his shoulders. 'It's okay. It's okay, son.' I squeeze him and he wrinkles up his face but he doesnae look like he's upset, he looks like he's shat his fucking pants. Connor's got my brains but he's a wee diddy so he is. The other week Ryan's like that: 'Connor. I wish you all the best and every success in your chosen career, aye? But you are a dowfie wee fuckwit.' And he's pointing a finger like the fucker in The Apprentice. *'You're fired.'* And that's Connor's arse out the business.

Ryan says the coppers went and stopped them up the High Street and Connor's all 'We've no got nothing on us, Big Man, so we havenae,' and he turns round and eyeballs the bin where Ryan's just dropped his blade.

The boy's a wee diddy.

I give him a nip.

And another.

And there we go. It's a wee shame so it is, the effect it's all having on Connor.

Fwah: 'Not in her best interests to remain with her biological family? Could you explain why this was felt to be the case?'

Mair: 'Following an assessment of the household, Social Work concluded that kinship care was not appropriate for Bekki, and we applied for an emergency child protection order to remove her from Mr and Mrs Johnson's home.'

Fwah: 'And why was this done?'

Mair takes a big sad breath. 'On my initial visit to Jed and Lorraine Johnson's home, I found the family situation to be chaotic. The Johnsons have five children: Shannon-Rose, Ryan, Travis, Carly and Connor. They share their home with three of these children – Travis, Carly and Connor, plus Travis's girlfriend Mackenzie, and Travis and Mackenzie's baby Corrigan. Their eldest son Ryan and his girlfriend Shannon... this is another Shannon, obviously, not Shannon-Rose... they and Shannon's two children from previous relationships live across the street, but they were all there at the time of my visit. The house was in a poor state of repair, with several internal doors missing or off their hinges, and holes in the plasterboard of the walls and, in one place, the ceiling... It was also very dirty, with no attempt to clean seeming to have been made for some time. The air was foetid and thick with the smell of chip fat and cigarette smoke – the family are all smokers, with the exception of youngest son Connor, and Mr and Mrs Johnson permit smoking throughout the house. There were dirty nappies in the living room, one of which a Rottweiler puppy was chewing. There was a used condom on the carpet by the side of the sofa. I was subjected to threats and verbal abuse from several family members from the moment I entered the house. They also verbally and physically abused each other in my presence. Jed Johnson told his son Travis to –' She makes like she's consulting her notes '– "Go off and take your face for a shite, you wee fucker" and attempted to strike him on the back of the head. Travis Johnson took evasive action, called Jed Johnson a "fucking old alky bastard", and pushed him against the door frame.'

Mandy's pissing herself laughing, and she's no the only one.

Sheriff goes, 'Please, ladies and gentlemen.'

Fwah: 'I see. And had the situation improved on your subsequent visits?'

Subsequent visits?

'Unfortunately not.'

The brass neck of her!

'And as to the child, on that initial visit?'

'Bekki at first could not be located. I found her myself in the back garden, where she had been left unsupervised. She was curled up in the corner between the shed and the wall of the house. It was raining. The back garden seemed to be a dumping ground for a variety of items that would present a hazard to a child, including two old fridges, a mattress with its springs exposed, and a car engine. The ground was covered in dog and possibly human excrement. Bekki was dirty. Urine was leaking from her nappy. There were cuts and bruises on her arms, legs and back.'

With the hand that isnae on Connor, I grab Mandy's arm.

'I was subjected to continued threats of violence from Mr Johnson and his eldest son Ryan. Ryan Johnson then physically assaulted me. I left the premises, called the police, and applied immediately for an emergency child protection order. Bekki was removed from the house later that day.'

Fwah: 'And what happened subsequently?'

Mair: 'A series of meetings – arranged by the Social Work Department of Glasgow City Council in conjunction with other stakeholders – and LAC reviews and children's hearings were held to determine what the next steps would be. Lady Semple, the reports and minutes from all the meetings and hearings that have considered the child have also been supplied to you. Although Mr and Mrs Johnson were informed of the dates and times of the meetings and hearings they were entitled to attend, they only attended one, and on that occasion unfortunately had to be ejected from the room for disrupting proceedings and making threats against myself and others. This is all detailed in the report.'

Fwah: 'Thank you, Ms Mair. That's all very clear.'

Fucking bitch.

Mr Lyall gets up and goes, 'Ms Mair. You must, in your daily round, see a lot of households living in less than ideal conditions. In poverty and deprivation.'

'Well, yes –'

'And would you say that this alone would be sufficient cause for removal of a child from his or her family?'

'No, of course not.'

'Of course not. Otherwise half the sink estates and housing schemes in the city would have to be emptied of their children, I suppose?'

'This wasn't just poverty, this was – the conditions were insanitary. Dangerous. The household was clearly one in which relationships were characterized by aggression and casual violence. Bekki was obviously being neglected and probably physically abused.'

'In which case, presumably Corrigan Johnson has also been removed?'

'What?'

'Little Corrigan Johnson. The son of Travis Johnson and his girlfriend Mackenzie Smith.'

Ya dancer! Get it up ye!

'No. He's on the at-risk register, but I understand he's still living there. That's out of my control.'

'I see. Thank you. I think that's all for the moment.'

Mair bolts out the pen like there's a Rottweiler hanging off her arse.

Fwah: 'Dr David Reid, please.'

Oh here we go. Trust-Me-I'm-a-Fucking-Doctor Reid. Old bugger with a comb-over and a big red alky's nose.

He goes on about Jed being an alky, a chain-smoker and maybe a junkie. Then he starts in on me. 'Lorraine Johnson is also a very heavy smoker. Her lung function is poor. Her BMI is thirty, placing her in the obese category. Insulin concentrations in her blood were found to be elevated, indicating that she is prediabetic. She has problems with mobility and has difficulty rising from a chair.'

Fwah: 'In your opinion, Dr Reid, would these medical problems impact on the ability of Mr and Mrs Johnson to care for a two-year-old child?'

'Most definitely, yes.'

I squeeze Shrek.

I breathe.

I count in my head, like Connor said.

One. Two. Three.

I jump up and point at Reid.

'*Difficulty rising from a chair*, is it? Aye?'

'Mrs Johnson, please sit down.'

'I. Am. Not. *Fucking obese*. Excuse my language, My Lady. Okay I'm heavy, but that's down to a wee bit podging – comfort eating, you know? – after Shannon-Rose got put in the jail and Bekki got taken off us. I'm a fff – a *wreck* so I am, thanks to the fff – *system* doing nothing to stop Shannon-Rose killing Dean and then turning round and taking her babby off of us. Aye we're all chain-smoking, and Jed's back on the drink – because of *that bitch!*' I point at Mair.

'Mrs Johnson,' goes the sheriff, 'if you do not sit down and *be quiet*, you will be ejected from this court. You will have your chance to speak in due course.'

I sit.

Mr Lyall's giving me evils.

I take a hud of Connor's hand. He tries to pull it away but I dig in my nails.

Next up: Trust-Me-I'm-a-Fucking-Doctor Fernandez. Big red lips on her and a wee short skirt like she's away to shake her fanny up a Drumchapel close. Doctor my arse.

Fwah: 'Dr Fernandez, I understand you accompanied Ms Mair on a subsequent visit to the Johnson home to carry out a psychological assessment of Jed and Lorraine Johnson.'

'I did, yes.'

'Gobshite!' yells Carly. 'She never came near! She never!'

I goes, 'Shoosh.'

'Please, Miss Johnson.'

Fwah: 'In your report, you state that in your opinion Mr Johnson may be suffering from a number of undiagnosed conditions, including early-onset dementia, bipolar disorder, borderline personality disorder, and substance dependence.'

'My interview with Mr Johnson was necessarily cursory, but from his answers and behaviour generally, those would definitely be among a number of possibilities. I would also estimate him to have an IQ below the normal range.'

'And Mrs Johnson?'

'Again, the interview was brief, but she displayed some signs of a mood disorder and showed depressive symptoms. And also low IQ, possibly to the point of learning disability.'

'And in your opinion, would there be any issues with this couple being the primary carers of a two-year-old child?'

'Such a responsibility would present a significant challenge, in my opinion, to both Mr and Mrs Johnson.'

'Thank you.'

Mr Lyall gets up. 'What form did these "interviews" take? Were they structured interviews? The Bipolar Spectrum Diagnostic Scale? The Hamilton Rating Scale for Depression? Some other recognised scale?'

'No... They were informal interviews, given the circumstances, but –'

'Are you a medically qualified psychiatrist?'

'My degrees are in clinical psychology. I'm qualified to make such an assessment.'

'And yet you did not use any of the accepted standardised interviews for diagnosing the conditions with which you have labelled Jed and Lorraine Johnson on the basis – let us be clear here – of a brief chat, in stressful and, dare I say, very trying circumstances for the Johnsons? Dr Fernandez? You did not follow even the most basic standard protocol for such diagnoses, is that correct?'

The bitch goes, 'In the circumstances, that was not possible.'

'Thank you. That's all.'

Like Carly says, she never came near. She's never even met me and Jed, never mind 'interviewed' us. And Mair never showed her face neither after that first visit. All that about *three subsequent visits* is a pack of fucking lies but we cannae prove it. I asked Sonia McLeckie to gonnae give us a wee deek at her CCTV footage to try and maybe prove neither of those bitches had been at the house after Mair that first time, but Sonia McLeckie told me to fuck off.

The lawyers and the sheriff go on some more and then Mr Lyall's eyeballing me and going, 'Mrs Johnson, please?'

Jesus Chutney.

I feel like I'm gonnae piss myself, and my heart's going like the clappers. What if I go and piss myself? What if I go and throw up? Like a right daft cow?

Mandy goes, 'Gie them hell, Lorraine-hen.'

Connor goes, 'Maw, dinnae swear, aye?'

'Do it for Bekki, hen,' goes Mandy.

Aye, do it for Bekki. *Get a grip, Lorraine.*

I get out from the row of seats and pull my jacket down over my arse where it's ridden up. I'm in my funeral suit. Fucking appropriate, I'm telling myself. Fucking appropriate.

It's gonnae be someone's funeral if we dinnae get Bekki back.

You can do this, Lorraine.

You can do this for Bekki.

With a hold of my statement in one hand and Bekki's Shrek in the other, I pull in my stomach and get my fucking arse in that sheep pen.

3

Ruth examined herself in the hall mirror. She'd dressed in the sort of clothes Deirdre favoured: beige jeans, boots, a long indigo shirt and two dangly necklaces with colourful glass beads and wooden elephants strung on them. Minimal make-up. The long shirt did something to disguise her fat hips and waist.

She would have to remember to mention to Deirdre that she was successfully losing weight. She'd lost a stone and a half so far on the Atkins diet, but needed to lose as much again to be down to a healthy size. Maybe she shouldn't mention Atkins to Deirdre, though – it was a bit faddy, wasn't it? And Deirdre was probably vegan and would be horrified by the thought of the vast quantities of meat involved. All the additional slaughter and environmental damage required to keep Ruth in steaks.

This was something Ruth worried about herself, although admittedly usually as she was passing the junk-food aisles in the supermarket en route to the raw animal section. And really, could eating so little carbohydrate actually be good for you? She was feeling a bit light-headed now, in fact.

Maybe she should eat just a little something sugary.

After she'd had another quick check round.

She stood at the front door and looked at the hall as if she were Deirdre: at the Victorian pew with their shoes lined up under it, the waxed floorboards, the new jute mats, the fresh off-white walls (she'd persuaded Alec to give the whole cottage a new lick of paint last week) on which she'd carefully arranged some framed photographs of animals and a watercolour of a tranquil river scene.

It was a little gloomy, necessitating the lamp on the table being on despite the bright sunshine outside. She should open the sitting room door to let in more light.

First impressions were important.

The sitting room itself was perfect. Every surface gleamed – the old bureau which had belonged to Alec's parents, the coffee table, the TV, the little side table – with a careful selection of books stacked on it, on things like the Scottish Colourists and ancient Egypt – the windowsills, the bookcases. They'd gone through their selection of books last night, removing all the grimmer crime novels and *Of Human Bondage* by Somerset Maugham. Just in case Deirdre hadn't read it and got the wrong idea.

There were windows to the front and side, so although they were small, the room was nice and bright. She had lit the wood-burning stove and it was crackling merrily.

Perfect.

Leaving the door open, she crossed the hall to the study. She had made Alec have a major tidy-up in here and then had deep-cleaned it herself.

He had pulled the curtain across the window to shade his PC screen. She pulled it back. There were shelves floor-to-ceiling on one wall, crammed with books and folders. On top of a battered metal filing cabinet was a shallow glass tank filled with soil in which three bonsai trees grew, which Alec called Pinkie, Perkie and Podgie.

Three bonsai trees and Mimi the Mycorrhiza.

The glass sides showed the roots of the trees branching through the soil and the white threads of the disgusting fungus thing that was Mimi, a sinister net that looked as if it was smothering the tree roots, the soil, the tank itself, forming a fine, ghostly, filigree pattern on the glass, like something from a sci-fi nightmare.

Alec would have to explain Mimi to Deirdre. Tell her it was a mutually beneficial thing for the trees and the fungus. To grow successfully, in nature most plants tapped in to the network of fungal mycorrhizas in the soil which provided them with water and nutrients in exchange for sugars.

But Ruth found it creepy. She didn't like to think of the soil under her feet being infected by thousands, millions, trillions of those ghostly white threads. A single individual fungus could cover more than two square miles, apparently.

Maybe better tell Alec not to say anything.

Poor Alec. She'd made his life a misery these past few days, obsessing and nitpicking and nagging and generally being an OCD nightmare.

On the wall above the desk were the grotty old prints of fungi that Ruth had banished in here, and the framed Gary Larson cartoon of two man-eating crocodiles relaxing on a riverbank. She imagined Deirdre's wistful angel expression going even more wistful, disappointed wistful, if-only-Alec-hadn't-been-a-bit-of-a-sick-bastard wistful.

She removed the cartoon and shoved it in the top desk drawer.

But the empty hook was a dead giveaway that something potentially compromising had hung there.

On the hall table was a collection of photos of their families. The biggest one in the A4-sized frame, of Alec and his sister Pippa and their parents, had a little metal loop on the back. Pippa at ten had already been taller than Alec at twelve.

She was gangling in a short dress, long pale legs crossed self-consciously one behind the other.

Ruth took the photo to the study and hung it up.

Hmm.

Was it a good idea to remind Deirdre that both sets of parents were dead? That they had no extended family network apart from Pippa, who was currently backpacking in Nepal with two random men she'd met on a beach in Cambodia?

Both their fathers had died when they were children. Ruth's mum had been killed in an accident when Ruth was at university – the driver of a milk float, of all things, had reversed without looking and run her over. A witness had testified that Mum had just stood there, as if in a daze, that she hadn't seemed to see it coming, but how was that possible? What they'd meant was that she hadn't tried to get out of the way. Quite apart from the guilt – because Ruth had no illusions that this wasn't down to her – she hated telling people about it because of the comic element. Not everyone was able to suppress their natural reaction to laugh. Red faces and awkwardness all round. Sometimes even hysterical choked giggles, and the person having to make an excuse to leave the room. She always felt so bad for Mum, that her death should be a source of amusement.

Of course, for a candidate adopter, a parent dead in an accident was far preferable to a parent dead from a heart attack or stroke or cancer. No red lights flashing 'genetic risk of early death'.

Alec and Pippa's mum had died of lung cancer last year, but she'd been a heavy smoker, and Alec had never so much as taken a puff behind the bike sheds.

God.

She had to stop this.

It was going to be fine.

The study was fine. It said *Alec is a clever academic*.

She walked on down the little passage to the kitchen.

Hopefully it wasn't too much of a cliché that she'd baked scones. They did smell amazing, six appetising cheesy hummocks cooling on the rack.

Or rather, five.

Alec, sitting at the table with his laptop, gave her a sheepish grin.

He hadn't even used a plate. There were crumbs on the keyboard and on the table and, yes, on the flagstones under his chair.

She opened the cupboard and grabbed the dustpan and brush.

'Up. *Up.*'

He closed the laptop and tucked it under his arm and stood, backing away as she pulled out the chair to get under it.

'I don't believe this.' She swiped at the flagstones, reaching under the table for the outliers, feeling her face going red with the effort.

'Sorry.'

As she straightened, he put down the laptop and reached to take the dustpan from her, but she pulled away. He was liable to tip the contents over the floor again while emptying it into the bin.

He raised his eyebrows. 'Don't you think you're going a bit overboard with the Stepford stuff? We don't want the place to say *We're too uptight to be parents.*'

She replaced the dustpan in the cupboard and scanned the kitchen. Maybe it was a bit unnaturally pristine. She had decluttered, banishing even the toaster, temporarily, to a drawer. She had sanded and oiled the wooden worktops and arranged a careful collection of objects on them – a matching set of tea, coffee and sugar cannisters in a tasteful sage green enamel, a miniature trug with apples from the garden, a wire-fronted shabby-chic egg cupboard with posh blue, white and speckled-brown eggs inside. She had used baking soda on the Belfast sink after making the scones, so its white porcelain was hospital-bright. The ironed tea towel hanging over the rail of the Rayburn was red and white gingham. There was a basket by the door to the utility room with pine cones in it, for no good reason.

She imagined Deirdre standing here, looking around her, blinking her wistful-angel eyes. Shaking her head. And then turning to Ruth and sighing: *Oh, but you see, I'm afraid we know.*

She took a long breath, in and out.

She had to pull herself together. Get a grip and concentrate.

The kitchen. Was it okay?

No, actually. Alec was right. It wasn't a kitchen any child would be comfortable in.

'Oh God. It *is* Stepford!'

'It's fine. Here...' He opened the fridge and took out the butter. Then a side plate from the neat stack in the cupboard, and a knife from the drawer. He smeared the knife across the butter and set it on the plate, and the plate on the worktop next to the sink, as if someone had just had a scone and left the plate there.

'There would be crumbs on the plate,' she said.

He picked a few off the bottom of one of the scones – she'd have to remember which one, so she didn't give it to Deirdre – and scattered them on the plate.

'And maybe you could get some papers from the study and leave them lying somewhere in the sitting room? And maybe here on the table...'

'Ruth. Relax, for God's sake. I don't know what you're so worried about. It's going to be a breeze. What more perfect mother is there than a paediatric nurse?'

For a long moment she couldn't say anything. She just couldn't.

And now he was looking at her oddly, questioningly, a little anxiously.

She puffed out a big exasperated sigh. 'It's not *me* I'm worried about.'

Of all the lies she had ever told him, this might just be the biggest.

But, as his mum would have said, that put his gas at a peep.

And he really had been a bit of a liability from the word go, from the very first session of the Preparation Course, in that airless little room with the fluorescent lighting and the awful faded posters – a close-up of a child's hand held in an adult's; a blurred child playing in a garden; a sad-faced boy sitting on a step with lost-waif eyes lifted to the camera...

Alec had found that one particularly amusing. He'd said to Ruth, without bothering to lower his voice: 'Reckon the same outfit does the SSPCA and homeless stuff – add a bald dog and a Big Issue seller and you've got the set.'

There had been four other couples on the course. They'd all sat in a circle on moulded red plastic chairs while Ben the tutor, a whispery, I'm-so-caring type, made them introduce themselves.

While the others spoke, often tearfully, about why they were there, to gentle nods of encouragement and '*Mmm, mmm*'s from Ben, Ruth had found her gaze returning to the poster of the little waif. Which was ridiculous. He was a child model. He had a family, a family who were perfectly nice, probably, when they weren't exploiting his Oliver Twist qualities to make a quid or two. But she knew, if she and Alec 'got through' and ever had to make 'the choice' (she was already picking up the jargon), that she was going to be forever haunted by the faces of the children they didn't take. How did you turn the page on a desperate child? How did you decide that you didn't want to love him, consigning him to God knows what?

Because she already knew that she wanted a little girl.

She hadn't told Alec, but their child was going to be a little girl. She was out there somewhere, a little lost soul, waiting for Ruth to find her. Waiting for Ruth to love her.

Ben had started murmuring at them about how the children could be expected to have developmental delays and challenging behaviour because of what they'd been through.

'How do you think you'd address that?'

No no no don't ask Alec, she'd prayed.

But of course he'd asked Alec.

People always warmed to Alec. There was a gauche friendliness about him that lulled them into a false sense of security. And his skinny little childlike geeky frame, thin arms poking from his T-shirt, made people feel protective.

'Alec?'

Alec had sat back in his chair and pushed his feet out and frowned, considering, and then he'd come out with it: 'Well, I don't know that there would be much I could do to *address that*. Developmental delay and behavioural problems are likely to be down to things like foetal alcohol syndrome, foetal complications of heroin addiction, genetically inherited conditions... the list goes on. Just for instance – up to a fifth of adopted children have some sort of foetal alcohol disorder, which can produce a small head and brain, learning disabilities, epilepsy... autism, ADHD, horrendous behavioural issues... And as for genetic conditions, it's been estimated that about half of single parents with serious psychiatric illnesses lose custody of their children. That means that a high proportion of children up for adoption will be at risk of having inherited a mental health condition from one or both parents. Bipolar disorder has a heritability of seventy-five per cent. Schizophrenia, eighty-one per cent.'

Ben opened his mouth.

Alec held up a hand. 'Now, when I say *heritability*, that doesn't mean that a child of someone with schizophrenia has an eighty-one per cent chance of inheriting it. It means that eighty-one per cent of variation in the presence or absence of the condition can be attributed to genetics.'

Ruth could feel her face going bright red. She made her voice light. 'Alec... I don't think anyone is interested in a lecture on genetics?' And she giggled; a high, nervous, slightly manic sound.

Maybe they would think that *she* had a mental illness? Maybe they would think that was why Alec knew so much about it? Maybe Ben would pass on his concerns to his boss and they'd decide to look at Ruth a bit more closely?

'No, but...' One of the other men was rubbing his chin with the back of his hand. 'I hear what you're saying, Alec. These mothers who give up their kids, or have them removed... You gotta wonder what's at the root of that. You gotta wonder whether – You know, they're often not the sharpest pencils in the box either...?'

His partner, a neat corporate type in a grey designer trouser suit, was staring at him in horror. He gave her a placating grimace.

Alec nodded enthusiastically. 'Yep, mothers who lose custody of their children also tend to be of below-average intelligence, which is also massively hereditary. So I reckon, quite honestly, that if the child is backward or shows *challenging behaviours*, there's probably nothing much we can do about it. The heritability of IQ is around eighty per cent. And you can't cure bipolar disorder or schizophrenia or foetal alcohol syndrome by putting the kid on the naughty step.' And he'd flapped his hands in that dismissive way of his, as if to say *I don't expect any of you to understand, though, so what's the use.*

But then he'd smiled, his wonderful, bashful, infectious smile, and laughed, and said, 'So should *I* go on the naughty step, then, Ben?' and all of them, even Ben, had laughed too, and the women had given him the indulgent maternal looks that women tended to bestow on Alec, while Mr Chin-Rubber had beamed at him in something close to awe.

But she was pretty sure Deirdre wouldn't appreciate a repeat performance.

'Don't mention anything to do with the child's probable gene pool. Don't say you dislike children. Don't say you were quite happy that I couldn't have any, and that at least adopting a toddler will cut out the earliest years of maximum noise and mess. Don't say you feel like a bit of a mug for volunteering to bring up someone else's child, like reed warblers would feel about cuckoo chicks if they had brains bigger than a pea, but you're hoping your own preprogrammed nurturing neural pathways will kick in if and when the child is dumped on us.'

Alec opened and closed his mouth.

Pippa said Alec was socially incontinent, like a child, blurting things out regardless of context or appropriateness – and Ruth had to agree, but she also liked to think it was a sort of social courage, a refusal to compromise himself to fit in with what was seen as acceptable just to be popular – and, ironically, it was this very quality that *made* him popular. That, and his self-deprecating sense of humour, and a sort of quiet exuberance that had attracted her to him straight away.

He wasn't in your face, he didn't dominate a room, he listened more than he spoke, but he had an air of childlike wonder that she loved, an eagerness to be told about the world, a way of being fascinated and delighted by what people were telling him about quite ordinary things; an awareness that he was a hopeless novice at life and needed to be schooled in it by those more capable than he. At the same time he came across as quite confident, opinionated, prickly at times, easily exasperated by stupidity – but that just seemed to make people want to please him all the more.

As he laughed shame-facedly at himself now – the sound a cross between a donkey braying and a seal barking – she found herself laughing too, and apologising for being such a pain, such a Stepford nightmare; and felt all the tension that had been lodged in her body, in her brain, in the sore place behind her eyes leaving her as he pulled her to him and kissed her on the lips she'd so carefully made up an hour before.

It was going to be fine.

4

'Now, Mrs Johnson,' says the sheriff. 'I realise that this is a difficult and emotional time for you. But please keep your language under control and respect the court, or I'll have to ask you to stop and sit back down. Do you understand?'

'Yes, My Lady.' I set Shrek on the wide bit of the sheep pen in front of me. 'I'm sorry about before. I'm just that wound up, you know?'

I cannae look at Mair or I'll lose it. I concentrate on Mr Lyall's eyes behind his glasses as he goes, 'I believe you've prepared a statement to read to the court.'

'Aye. And it's all my own work by the way.' I fold out my statement and give a wee cough. 'Our Bekki means the world to us. She's our wee angel and we all love her to bits. She should be with us, her family, where she belongs. We may not have much money but we have plenty of love to give. Bekki has had a difficult time with Shannon-Rose and she needs the security of her family around her, not strangers who don't know her and don't love her, and who can never love her like we do.' Oh God. Oh *fuck*. I've got to stop. I cannae even breathe.

'You're doing very well, Mrs Johnson. Just take your time.'
He's a nice wee man, Mr Lyall.

'Aye. I'm sorry. This is a bit hard.'

'Of course it is.'

'Every grandma loves her grandkids, but Bekki and I have a special bond because of Shannon-Rose being the way she is. I always stepped in when I could, but often Shannon-Rose wouldn't let me in her flat and when I went to her social worker she said there was nothing they could do about that.' I heave in another breath. 'We aren't in the best of circumstances financially and as a family we've had a hard time of it lately, but we are turning our lives around. I've got a wee job at the Co-op, and my manager Mrs Shaughnessy has written me a reference which Ms Mair said she never got, but it was sent recorded delivery and Mrs Shaughnessy has the tracking document to prove it... She'll give it you if you want, the document that proves the receptionist at Social Work signed for it, so she did –'

'Please just continue with your statement, Mrs Johnson,' goes the sheriff.

Mr Lyall's nodding at me, so I take another breath.

'The reference says: "Lorraine Johnson is a valued and well-liked member of the Co-op team. She is a very conscientious worker and can be relied on to perform any task in the store to an exceptional standard. She is particularly popular with the older customers, sometimes even helping them carry bags to the bus stop, and with children, with whom she has an obvious connection, never too busy to chat and raise a smile. I join with the rest of the staff in hoping she will be successful in gaining custody of her granddaughter Bekki."'

Mr Lyall nods. 'Well... That's a glowing reference if ever I heard one. So, Dr Fernandez's assessment of your IQ as low enough to put you in the category of "learning disability" is perhaps wide of the mark, given your success in your new job?'

'"Dr" Fernandez never visited us. This is the first time I've laid eyes on the bitch.'

'*Mrs Johnson*,' goes the sheriff.

'Sorry. On the *lady in question*. She never interviewed us. *Ms Mair* never visited us except for that one time. That's a pack of lies in her report about three more visits by the way. And she must have turned round and told "Dr" Fernandez a pack of lies about us, and "Dr" Fernandez put them in her report, making out she'd interviewed us. She never.'

Mr Lyall frowns. 'I see.'

'My neighbour's CCTV proves it. Sonia McLeckie's CCTV. That proves Ms Mair only came the once, and there was no one with her. On the other dates she *claims* to have come, and the date she *claims* to have come with "Dr" Fernandez, she never.' And now I do eyeball Mair, and the bitch sitting next her. Mair's bright red, and Fernandez's got a face on her like she's chewing a wasp.

Gotcha.

They're not to know Sonia McLeckie wouldnae piss on me if I was on fire.

'I also sent Ms Mair a reference from one of the teachers at my old school, which she also *apparently* never got. I've got that here an' all?'

'Please read it, Mrs Johnson.'

I cough. 'Mr Ingrams taught maths at my school. He's been retired for years and he's eighty-odd but he still remembers me. "Lorraine Johnson, or Slorrach as she was then, was a bright and likeable pupil who, despite many difficulties at home, more than managed to keep up with her peers in class. She was in the top stream for maths, and it was hoped that she would stay on for her Highers and perhaps apply to university. Sadly, in S4, due to unfortunate circumstances, she missed a lot of school and ended up leaving without any qualifications. However, this was in no way a reflection of Lorraine's ability or potential."

Aye? Let's get that wee windae-licker in the top maths class for a wee joke, is it?'

Mr Lyall goes, 'My goodness, Mrs Johnson – I wonder how many of us in this court can say they were in the top maths stream at school? Personally, I never did get to grips with quadratic equations... So, I would venture to suggest that it has never – until now, that is – been suggested that you might have a "learning disability"?' And he turns and eyeballs Fernandez.

You didnae need to be Albert Einstein to get in the top maths class at Govan High, right enough, but I goes, 'Just because I'm fat and that and live in a council housing scheme doesnae mean I've no got a brain on me.'

'Well, quite... Now, Mrs Johnson. If we might address the medical assessment carried out by Dr Reid...'

Old bugger was jakied by the way – drunk as a fucking skunk. Bell's Original syping out every fucking orifice. Here's me up on the couch and here's this old jakie coming at me with a massive fucking needle giving it *Let's try again, shall we?*

But what bastard's gonnae believe that?

'*Medical assessment*, is it? Medical assessment? Weighed and measured and jagged like we was ffff... like we was animals, and not so much as a *How is you?* I'd "difficulty" getting off the couch because I'd a swalt knee from tripping over the dog and cracking it off of Captain America that the kids had left lying, not because I'm too *obese* to get off my arse.'

I get up, sit down, get up.

'Aye? If *Dr Reid* had asked I'd have telt him I'd a bad knee, but he never. And that's a lie an' all, what Mair said about the cigarette smoke. I dinnae let anybody smoke in the front lounge. Or near the bairns.'

'I see. And Ms Mair's other remarks about your household...'

'Pack of lies! Jed and the boys never threatened her or "assaulted" her. They were raging and they might have been swearing and that, but they never touched her! The condom by the settee, aye there maybe was one, Travis and Mackenzie are a pair of wee mingers but at least they use condoms, aye? Most young ones wouldnae be that responsible?'

'I fear that's only too true.'

'And Bekki had run off into the garden because *Ms Mair* came in all confrontational and Bekki was feart. Ran off and hid. The cuts and bruises on her were down to Shannon-Rose. She might have been malnourished, maybe, but that's because Shannon-Rose didnae feed her nothing but bacon rolls and chips. She'd been getting plenty peas and carrots and that at ours, and she liked a wee banana mashed up with blueberries in yoghurt before she went her bed.'

'So the injuries and malnourishment had occurred prior to Bekki's arrival in your home?'

'That's correct.'

'And as for the – um – dirty nappies in the living room...?'

'That Rotty was a right wee rascal. He'd pulled them out the bin, is all I can think. The dog's dead now so it is. And the state of the place, aye it was bowfin' but I was incapacitated with my knee and none of those ones bother their arses, but now I'm back on my feet that house is f-spotless.'

'I'm sure that's the case, Mrs Johnson. And I'm very glad to hear that you're restored to health. Now, if I could turn to the meetings and hearings Ms Mair alleges you failed to attend?'

'We was never told! Well, aye, twice we was. One time we did attend a meeting but that load of bastards widnae listen to what we was saying so we may as well no have been there. The other meeting we got told about, we got to the place, right, and here they'd only given us the wrong time! The meeting was over. We didnae know anything about the other meetings. Ms Mair never let us know about them.'

'Ms Mair says letters were sent to you.'

'Aye right.'

'You never received them?'

'She's at it! We never!'

'I see.'

'She. Gives. Me. *The boak*, so she does.'

'I'm sorry?' goes the sheriff.

'She makes me sick.' I turn and give Mair evils. 'How you can live with yourself hen, coming in here giving it *I did this* and *I did that* when you never, and *It's in my report* like that makes it fucking gospel –'

'Mrs Johnson!' goes the sheriff, and at the same time Mr Lyall goes, '*Thank you, Mrs Johnson.*'

Mr Lyall sits down, and *Fwah* gets up and takes a look round about like he's saying *Can yous believe this gobby cow?*

'Mrs Johnson.' He says my name like it tastes bad. 'When Ms Mair – a social worker with almost twenty years' experience – said your household was "chaotic", wasn't that the truth?'

'No it wisnae. Aye we've a big family, but we get by fine so we do.'

'Isn't it the case that your household is one in which casual violence has been normalised?'

I goes 'Eh?', which makes it sound like I dinnae get what casual violence being normalised means, but I cannae think what to say.

'Your husband Jed, your sons Ryan and Travis, and of course your daughter Shannon-Rose all have criminal records and have served or are serving time in prison for murder, other violent crimes and/or drug dealing. Is that not the case?'

'Aye, but –'

'Isn't it the case that your husband Jed has been convicted of numerous crimes of violence? In one particularly disturbing case, didn't he keep his victim, a rival dealer, locked in a dog's cage for a week in his own filth, sever three of his fingers and both earlobes, and make him eat them? He enjoys torturing his victims, doesn't he, Mrs Johnson?'

'Aye, when he was young he was maybe a mad bastard right enough, but now he's sakeless so he is.'

'Sakeless?'

'Harmless, aye?'

'In 2010, the police were called to your address – 34 Meadowlands Crescent – that is your address, is it not? – a total of fifty-four times. Jed and your son Travis are both currently subject to ASBOs, and Travis wears an ankle tag. There have been numerous complaints to both Glasgow City Council and the police about you and your family from your neighbours, one of whom has described you as a "family from hell". Do you think that's a fair description?'

I open my gob, but nothing comes out.

So help me I'll swing for him.

So help me I'll swing for that cow Sonia McLeckie.

'All right. If we could turn to your daughter Shannon-Rose, who is currently awaiting sentencing for murder. If and when Shannon-Rose is returned to the community, how do you propose to keep Bekki safe from her? From her own mother?'

'Shannon-Rose is a mentalist. You think we'd let her anywhere near Bekki?'

'I'm afraid I've no idea, Mrs Johnson, what you'll do. And that, I would venture to suggest, is the whole problem.'

I cannae think of a fucking thing to say.

Not a fucking thing.

'Thank you,' says *Fwah*.

'You may step down,' says the sheriff.

I feel like I'm gonnae boak. I snatch up Shrek. As I step out the sheep pen I catch my heel against the edge of it and I nearly fall over. I cannae breathe. I cannae look at Connor or Carly or Mandy.

I've let Bekki down.

I've let that English bastard kick my arse from here to fucking Christmas.

Then *Fwah* goes, 'My Lady, if I might recall Ms Mair for a moment.'

Mair gets up, and as she goes past me she gives me a wee smile.

I get to my chair and sit with my head down. Connor pats my arm. 'That was ace, Maw. You were ace.'

'I was shite.'

I shouldnae have let the bastard get to me. I should've kept the heid, eh? Should've got my brain in gear and not just stood there with my gob hanging open like a fucking schemey retard.

'Ms Mair,' goes *Fwah*. 'Mrs Johnson claims that she never received notification of the meetings and hearings held to discuss Bekki's future.'

'That's not the case. Mr and Mrs Johnson were sent invitations to all the meetings they were entitled to attend. I can produce copies of the letters...?'

'That won't be necessary. As for the character references...?'

'I never received any character references. I can assure you that if I had done so I would have followed them up and, if appropriate, included them in my report.'

'Now, as to the injuries that are detailed in the doctor's report on Bekki when she was first removed from the Johnson family home. Mrs Johnson maintains that they were old injuries inflicted by her daughter Shannon-Rose. Is this, in your view, a plausible explanation for the injuries to the child that were documented?'

'I'm afraid not. If you look at the doctor's report, you'll see he talks about "fresh bruising" and says that he'd estimate most of the injuries were inflicted less than twenty-four hours previously.'

'And Bekki was last with Shannon-Rose...?'

'Two weeks beforehand.'

'I see. That seems clear-cut... Now, another allegation of Mrs Johnson's is that in fact you only visited the Johnsons' address on one occasion, not four, and that neither you nor Dr Fernandez visited the property on the twenty-second of August.'

'The dates in my report are correct. I visited the Johnsons four times, and was accompanied by Dr Fernandez on the twenty-second of August visit. The suggestion that we would collude in falsifying evidence... My professional reputation, I think I can say, is unblemished. As is that of Dr Fernandez.'

'Am I correct in saying that you have an impeccable fifteen-year record of employment in the Social Work Department of South Ayrshire Council, followed by an impeccable four years in your current position with Glasgow City Council?'

Blah fucking blah.

'I'M SORRY TO SAY,' says the sheriff, 'that I found Mrs Johnson to be a somewhat unreliable witness, in marked contrast to Ms Mair, Dr Reid and Dr Fernandez. In particular, I would like to commend the professionalism shown by Ms Mair in what has evidently been a challenging and upsetting case. Although I have no doubt that the Johnson family's affection for Bekki is genuine, I am persuaded that there is a significant risk of harm should Bekki be placed in their care, and in such cases the safety of the child must always be the paramount concern. I am persuaded that it is in Bekki Johnson's best interests that the permanence order, with authority to adopt, be granted, with the recommendation that neither Shannon-Rose Johnson nor her parents or siblings have any further contact with Bekki and, should she go on to be adopted, that it should be a closed adoption with no contact between the child and her biological family. Under the terms of the closed adoption, when she reaches the age of eighteen Bekki will be given information that will enable her to resume contact, but this will be entirely Bekki's decision.'

Out in the lobby, Mr Lyall goes, 'We'll appeal of course, but... You mustn't hold out too much hope, I'm afraid.'

'We've lost her,' says Mandy. 'We've lost our wee darlin'.'

'I'm very sorry. Mrs Johnson, you spoke most eloquently on the stand, but...' He lifts his skinny shoulders.

'Aye, no so eloquent though, eh, when that bastard started in on me? If I'd been all "I can assure you", if I'd been a snobby bitch like fucking Mair, the sheriff might have taken a wee bit notice of what I was fucking saying, eh? I was daft so I was, thinking playing it straight was gonnae get us anywhere with these bastards.'

Mr Lyall's thinking *Thank fuck these fucking schemies are outta my hair.*

I hold out Shrek. 'Here's her wee toy. We were keeping it for her, you know? Can she have her Shrek? She takes it with her to her bed.'

'She needs it,' goes Connor in a wee choked-up voice. 'Bekki needs her Shrek.'

Oh aye, now he's giving it Disneys, now it's too fucking late.

Mr Lyall angles the top half of his body away from Shrek. 'I'm sorry, but that won't be possible. You can rest assured that she'll be well looked after. I'm sure – I'm sure she'll have plenty of – of other, um, cuddly animals... to, um, take to bed with her...'

I take a hold of Mandy and she takes a hold of me.

As we leave the court building and the wind hits us, I've still got fucking Shrek cuddled in to my tits. Stupid fucking thing. Stupid cheap fucking toy that needs a wash, and Mr Lyall's right – Bekki, wherever she is, will have a nice dolly or teddy to take to her bed, not a cheap knock-off from the market that's probably got illegal fucking chemicals in it.

But in my head I'm going, *It's okay, wee Shrek. It's gonnae be okay.*

5

Ruth and Pam leant side by side on the gate, sharing a sneaky packet of smoky bacon crisps while they watched their daughters. Although the sun had finally appeared and the Met Office was promising high pressure for the whole weekend, it seemed to have been raining for most of September, and this corner of the paddock was a dubby mess.

Which was why Ruth and Pam weren't venturing in there.

In the middle of the paddock, Emma slithered to a halt as Beckie and Hobo trotted up to her, Alec floundering along at their side, mud spattered all up his jeans. Emma threw her arms round the pony's neck and flopped against him, wailing: 'I surrender!'

Beckie kicked her feet from the stirrups and slid off Hobo's back.

Pam shook her head. 'Beckie, sweetheart!' she yelled across at them. 'Have a longer go! Don't let Emma bully you!'

'I'm not!' Emma, indignant, yelled back. 'Beckie wants to be hunted!'

Beckie, grinning, dashed across the grass towards them while Emma waited impatiently for Alec to lengthen Hobo's stirrups. At eight, Emma was a year older than Beckie and several inches taller, a raven-haired girl with long supple limbs and a dancer's grace.

Which was where any resemblance to Tricia Fisher began and ended. Ruth would never have let the two families become so close if she'd had any doubts on that score.

This new craze of theirs, 'Hunting', involved one of them chasing the other down on horseback. Well, ponyback, and with Alec running alongside and grabbing girl and/or reins at the first sign of trouble.

The paddock was ideally situated between the two cottages. Opposite this gate was another they'd made into the paddock from Pam and James's back garden, so the girls could nip across it without having to go on the road.

'Look at him running,' said Ruth as Emma, Hobo and Alec trotted after Beckie. Alec had an exaggerated, uncoordinated, John Cleese-ish running style, managing to look gawky and stork-like at five foot six.

Pam was trying not to smile. 'I'd swap James's athletic ability for Alec's willingness to spend his whole Saturday morning running about a muddy field any time.'

'He is pretty good that way.' Ruth dived in for another handful of crisps. 'He never really wanted kids, you know, in the abstract. When it was just a generic child we were talking about.'

With most people, she rarely if ever referred to the fact that Beckie was adopted, as if it was something she had to keep a secret, as if one day someone was going to look at her and narrow their eyes and say, 'Oh my God. They let *you* adopt a child?'

Pam was different. She'd never had a friend like Pam. For

the first time in her adult life, she felt she had a friend she could trust. She had even, in her madder moments, wondered if she would some day be able to tell Pam.

But of course she wouldn't.

If she told her, Pam wasn't going to nod sympathetically and say 'But you're not that person any more.' She was going to be straight on the phone to Social Work.

They'd take Beckie away.

Or Alec would leave her and take Beckie with him.

Pam was looking at her now with comically wide eyes. '*Really?*'

'As soon as he saw Beckie, of course, that was it. Adoration at first sight.'

Pam scrunched up the telltale empty bag and shoved it in her pocket. She linked her arm through Ruth's. 'Who could help but adore Beckie?'

Who indeed?

She'd been such an adorable little thing, standing there in the middle of a roomful of toys looking so lost and scared, dressed in a green and pink smock and white tights, a wooden train clutched in one plump little hand. Deirdre had warned them that Bekki might not respond to them at this first meeting and that they shouldn't be downhearted or alarmed if they 'failed to engage' or Bekki appeared 'distressed or fearful'. For all her training and experience with children, Ruth had frozen, a fixed grin on her face, and it had been Alec who'd hunkered down to Bekki's level and given her a quick, easy smile before turning away to pick up a wooden carriage.

'Now then Bekki, I think I'm going to need some help here. Does this fit onto... this?' And he'd picked up a Duplo brick.

Bekki had just stood there.

Alec had tried fitting the brick onto the carriage. First one way, then the other. He'd sat down and frowned, not looking at

Bekki, speaking as if to himself. 'Hmmm. This isn't going too well. It's got a little hook on it, so it must attach to something... *Something* must go on here...'

'Thith one,' Bekki had finally whispered, squatting down next to Alec and holding out the train.

And Alec had turned and smiled at her and said, 'Oh, thank you, Bekki. Just right!'

Just right.

Pre-Beckie, the idea of Alec running about a field with a pony and two little girls would have been laughable. The idea of Alec at a Family Fun Day at a National Trust for Scotland property, or at a pantomime, or in a soft play area, or doing anything at all, frankly, involving children would have been something Ruth struggled to imagine.

But he was a great dad. The best. It had brought out a whole new side to him she hadn't even suspected was there. He just loved being with Beckie. He loved everything about her. He even looked forward now to *Strictly* and *Bake-Off*, programmes on which he'd previously heaped vitriol, because he loved watching Beckie watching them.

And who knew he was so good at stories?

Ruth couldn't help being a little bit jealous of this. It was hard not to feel rejected when Beckie sleepily requested 'a Daddy story' in preference to the book Ruth had selected. Her favourites were Alec's stories about the Wanderers, a family who lived on a boat in Viking times. It was, Alec assured them, based on fact, or at least on stories handed down through the generations on the west coast, and from his grandma to Alec and Pippa, and now to Beckie.

'And I'll tell my children if I have any,' Beckie would promise, snuggling down with an anticipatory smile as Alec started the next instalment with a recap.

'So last time, Fiona and Donald were sheltering in the cave on Wild Dog Island. Left behind when the others set sail.'

'Their mum thinks they're asleep in the cabin, but they're not!'

'Yep, and Fiona's really angry with Donald now.'

'But it's Fiona's fault too! She should have said *No, it's really dangerous and stupid. We mustn't.*'

'Mm. Probably if she had, Donald wouldn't have gone sneaking out to the cave on his own, you reckon?'

'No. He wouldn't. He'd have been too scared.'

Beckie loved playing Wanderers whenever they went to the Loch, pretending that she was Fiona and one of her toys was Donald, and Alec was maybe a Viking chasing them, or their dad, or their annoying older brother Kenneth. She wanted nothing more than to be allowed to have sailing lessons so she could be like the Wanderers. This was good leverage to encourage her to keep attending her hated swimming classes – you can only have sailing lessons, Alec and Ruth had told her, when you can swim well enough for it to be safe.

In the oral histories of the west coast, the Wanderers were families displaced by the Vikings, running from them, or rather sailing away in their boats, but never settling on other shores, always hankering after their own beach, their own turf house, their own lost lives. Their homes had become their boats. They might land on a lonely island or come in to a harbour for a day, a week, a month, but sooner or later they'd be back in their boats and away. Everything had happened in those boats: babies were born, young folk were married, old folk sickened and died and were buried at sea.

Alec had never told Ruth any of his grandmother's stories.

He had never told her a lot of things – although those omissions hardly even registered on the scale compared with hers. Alec's weren't really omissions at all. It was more as if Beckie had made him more completely himself, as if the complete Alec – the whole, rounded, wonderful man he was always meant to be – was only now emerging.

It helped, of course, that Beckie was Beckie. She had proved Alec wrong in his stereotyping of adopted children in that she was very bright, with a particular aptitude for puzzles and games – even chess, at the age of seven! – and shared Alec's curiosity about life, the world and the Universe. And she was very sweet and good, although Ruth worried a little, still, that she was too eager to please.

She worried that, with her compliant nature, she might be a target for bullies. But so far so good. She loved school, and her little group of close friends were cheerful, easy-going girls Ruth trusted. That being said, Emma could be a feisty little thing, especially in the face of a perceived injustice, but this was a positive in Ruth's opinion: Emma could be counted on to protect Beckie from the other children if need be.

'I don't want to ride,' Beckie was insisting now, even though riding Hobo was her favourite thing in the world. She was leaning back on the fence getting her breath, one arm hugging a post, as Emma, Hobo and Alec trotted up.

'Are you sure?' said Emma.

'Uh-huh.' Beckie undid her pink riding helmet and balanced it on the fence post. 'Absolutely sure.'

Absolutely was a new favourite word.

Ruth looked at her daughter, drinking her in, feeling her stomach plummet and a shiver run through her. It was as if love for your child was a terrible physical force that swept through you and left you weak, frozen on the edge of a terror you couldn't name.

Sara had been right – Ruth had never felt love like this before.

Or hatred.

How could those people have hurt her? How *could* they?

'Aren't you tired out?' Alec asked, doing a comical stagger. 'Personally, I'm knackered.'

Beckie laughed. 'We can have a rest if you want? I'm not,

like, *really* tired. But my head's hot. I don't need to wear my helmet if I'm not riding, do I?'

'Yes you do, Beckster.' Alec picked it up and plonked it back on her head. 'What if you tripped up and Hobo stood on your head?'

Both girls for some reason found this scenario hilarious. For several minutes all they could do was laugh, Emma staggering to the fence and supporting herself on it and then on Beckie, the two girls clutching each other as they shook, eyes streaming.

All three adults laughed with them.

Then: 'Now, come on, girls,' said Ruth when it had gone on long enough and showed no signs of abating.

'Sorry Mum,' Beckie gasped, leaning back on the fence and trying to make her face serious.

'Emma,' said Pam.

The girls were both gasping, more exhausted by their laughter than by any amount of running around the field. Ruth remembered how it had felt, this hysterical prolonged hilarity with friends, the agony of trying to stop. There was something almost desperate about it, something not really enjoyable at all.

'Come on now,' she said again.

But they couldn't stop. They would sober for a while but then erupt in fresh paroxysms of mirth whenever they looked at each other, made all the worse by Alec's, 'It wouldn't be so funny if it actually happened.'

When they seemed finally to have laughed themselves to a standstill, Alec looked over at her. 'Mum, Beckie needs to wear her helmet, yes?'

In fact, Ruth considered this unnecessary – Hobo wasn't going to step on Beckie if she fell over, the pony was far too sensible – but she said, 'Yes. Let your head cool off a bit and then put it back on. Better safe than sorry.'

Beckie's mouth twitched.

And then Emma was gasping, 'Imagine you all *sorry*,' and Beckie was making a sad head-squashed-by-Hobo face, and Emma was wailing '... wee myself!' and running for cover in the broom.

6

J ed rolls over on the settee when I put on the telly and goes, 'Load a pish.'

But I'm having my *Bargain Hunt*. I've been sweating on that fucking exercise bike for a fucking hour while that prick's been swadging on the settee wasting space as fucking usual.

'Get to your bed if you're wanting to sleep,' I says, getting comfy in my chair with my wee bit scone and my cup of tea. The Rotty comes and shoves his gob at me, slavers swinging, and I says, 'Beat it.' The kids feed the dug crap and that's why he's in your face twenty-four-seven.

I get my tablet on my knee and navigate through to FAF: the Forced Adoption Forum. I cannae post after that wee fucker EagleHasLanded got me banned, and I cannae open the 'Members Only' section, which is the best bit, but I can still read the other posts. I can still see how my pal Big Bertha's doing trying to stop her lassie's bairn getting taken off her. I dinnae have an email or nothing for Bertha, so I cannae get in touch with her. I registered again under a different email and username and sent Bertha a wee PM asking for her email, but then I cannae help myself, I'm getting sucked in to a thread on hearings, and some bastard goes 'CoopyBird is Bekki's Gran back' and that's Coopy-Bird's arse banned before Bertha's had a chance to reply to the PM.

I dinnae want on their fucking forum anyway.

Fucking bastards banned Bekki's Gran the first time for telling MrMan to get his babby's photy on Facebook like we've got Bekki's, and get the media involved and try and find your wee laddie. Fucking FAF is meant to be *helping* folk who've had their bairns taken off them, and I get my arse banned for that? All the other bastards were just giving it 'I know it's hard, but at least you're allowed to send your son birthday and Christmas cards and get photos three times a year' like MrMan was gonnae turn round and say 'Aye that's fine then thanks very much'. The poor guy has lost his wean because the wean's ma wanted it adopted, and she got pregnant by MrMan when they were both jakied, and the court says the poor guy isnae fit to look after the babby, even though he's at uni and that, and his ma and da are gonnae help, because he's on the sex offenders' register because that wee hairy was fifteen? When I says about Facebook and the media he's all 'But I don't want to get in trouble and have them stop the little contact I do have' and I'm 'Couple of fucking cards a year?' and he's 'Yes, you're right, Bekki's Gran, what have I really got to lose?' and I'm 'Go for it, MrMan,' and my arse was banned for that?

I open the section 'Contact with the Child'.

The latest thread, 'Help! Council mistake gives contact details!!!', was started by JennyPenny.

```
Hi all, got a bit of a strange one here, the
County council (not going say which one)
sent our son's Ex-Partner a copy of the
adoption order for their child after she
wrote them to ask them to send it because
```

she's entitled to see it by Law but they've
made a mistake and the details of the couple
our GD is being placed with havent been
sensored.
So… We now have their names and address!!
What to do? Obv we're not going to alert the
council that we now have this info, my son is
all for making contact but I'm worried this
might be held against him. My son's Ex
doesn't want to do anything.

Thoughts, anyone?

Thanks, JennyPenny

EagleHasLanded was straight in there:

JennyPenny, you MUST NOT do anything with
this information, you must send the documents
back to the Council, alerting them to the
problem, and forget you saw this. Any attempt
to contact your granddaughter will have
serious repercussions for you and your family
and could compromise your prospects of
contact at a later date.

Then all them that always sook up to EagleHasLanded:

Fran: JennyPenny, Eagle is right, you must
forget you saw this. Hard I know. Hugs.

KJ: God Almighty, what next? Bloody idiots. But
yes, you can't do anything with the info.
Sorry if that's not what you want to hear,

but I have to say I'm a bit worried by your
reaction:
Obv we're not going to alert the council
Why 'Obv'? This sounds like you're intending
to take some kind of action. Just because
they've made a mistake doesn't give you the
right to make contact if the courts haven't
said you can.

Stitcher: Oh dear. I have to agree with the
others, Jenny. You don't want to jeopardise
anything by using this. You don't want to
alienate the APs by hassling them or trying
to make contact with your GD. Also, think
about your GD — could really upset/traumatise
her. You are making a big mistake IMO which
could hurt a lot of people. Please think long
and hard about this.

Then in comes Bertha: Hey, am I missing something
here or has JennyPenny done nothing wrong?
Get off her case, people.

JennyPenny: Thanks Bertha :) Everyone, I'm not
going to do anything, it's my son I'm worried
about he is an adult and I cant stop him
going round there if he wants. But what would
happen if he did? Could he get arrested?

EagleHasLanded: Yes he could get arrested.

Bertha: Yes he could get arrested. And get a
slap on the wrist.

EagleHasLanded: Big Bertha, I hope you're not
suggesting that JennyPenny's son SHOULD make
contact with his daughter and/or her adoptive
parents. He should NOT!!!
And you need to be very careful what you say
on here. Suggesting that someone should defy
the courts is dangerous and wrong. Please
remember what happened to Bekki's Gran when
she posted similar advice.

Bertha: Bekki's Gran, if you're reading this,
miss ya babe :)
OK Eagle, pull your horns in. Am I allowed to
say that JennyPenny and her son and his ex
could use this info to look on Facebook etc.
and see if the APs have anything up on the
net? That way they could maybe see photos of
their girl and find out how she's doing etc.
without breaking the court's conditions. How
would anyone know you were doing that anyway?

Miss ya too, babe. Bertha's spot on, as ever. What a woman.

I read out the posts to Jed and Connor, who's just come in to get the end of *Bargain Hunt* before his shift at PC World. He looks like he's back at the school in that fucking uniform, black trousers with a belt and a short-sleeved blue shirt with 'Currys PC World' in red over his tit.

Jed goes, 'Ya beauty' when I read out Bertha's first post. Jed's Bertha's number one fan so he is.

I goes, 'Mair might have made a mistake an' all. Left those bastards' details on a document.'

'Naw,' says Connor. 'Me and you've read through that shite how many times? I think we'd mebbe have noticed a minor detail like the folks' names and address?'

'Aye, well, we need to check again. And we need to check we're no missing any documents – anything where Mair *might* have left crap uncensored. We need to check we've been sent everything we're entitled to. Connor son, get all the shite out, aye?'

He goes to the sideboard and gets out the pile of papers and dumps them on the table next my chair. 'Right then. See yous later.'

'Throw a sickie, son, and gies a hand here. Get on the net and check what all we're entitled to get sent.'

Connor sighs but he gets out his phone.

On top of the pile there's my scrapbook with our articles. While Connor's coughing down the phone, I take a wee look at the *Daily Mail* one with the big photy of me and Jed on the settee. Settee looks dead nice. That was right after we got it and it's like something out a showhome, pure white and shiny. I'm in a black Laura Ashley top with lacy bits and Jed's washed and shaved and in a brand new black cashmere jumper that covers his tats, most of them, and we've both got our sad faces on us. The caption says: 'Devastated: Lorraine and Jed Johnson.' The article goes on about how our wee angel was torn from our arms, just because our daughter was mentally ill, and quotes me saying how Social Work failed to inform us of meetings and that.

Media campaign turned out pish but.

And brought the nutters out the woodwork, mad bastards giving it *You people should all be sterilised*, and there was this Holy Mary kept posting on the Get Bekki Back page on Facebook wanting to know if we'd been saved by Jesus and saying we should pray for Bekki and trust in the fucking Lord.

I sort out all the letters and documents sent us by the Council, and Connor gets a list of what all we're entitled to, and we read and cross-check all through the *One O'Clock News* and

Reporting Scotland. I dinnae even bother turning over for *Home and Away*. I dinnae even stop for my lunch.

'Looks like we've got everything, Maw. And there's no address or that on any of this. That's for definite.'

I goes, 'Fuck it.'

'Worth a try though, eh?'

'Aye. Fuck it, but.'

Jed wakes back up and turns over and reaches for his fags, effing and blinding. Was a time, eh, when he'd no just limit hisself to mouthing off – he'd come at me. I was a fucking doormat by the way, daft wee bint that I was, but the first time he made to raise his hand to a babby I told him – you fucking touch that wean and we're outta here. Aye he maybe skelped them when they was older, but only when they was out of order. Anything more than that and he knew I wouldnae stand for it. And any road, most of the time the kids were growing up, thank Christ, his arse was under lock and key in Barlinnie.

'Wait a wee minute,' I says to Connor. 'Wait a wee fucking minute! This could still be the way to go. Forget Facebook. Forget the press. It's the fucking system has what we want, aye? It's the fucking system can tell us where Bekki is?'

Jed flicks his lighter, and says round his fag: 'Like they're gonnae go, "Oh aye Lorraine-hen, here you go, here's Bekki's address, you only had to ask, hen."'

'Shut it, you! What I'm saying is, we can get it out them if we're a wee bit sleekit-like.'

'Aw Christ, Maw.' Connor's sitting on the carpet with the Rotty, pushing his fingers through the dug's hair. 'Next time it'll no be just a caution, eh?'

A couple years back I phoned up Mair pretending to be those bastards who've got Bekki, all *Hello Ms Mair, sorry to bother you, it's Bekki's mum, I just wanted to check you've got our current address.* But Mair goes *To whom am I speaking, please?* and course I didnae know their fucking name. And they traced the fucking call.

Jed goes, 'Never mind all that shite. Give me five minutes with Mair. Five minutes. I swear to God.'

'Aye, and that's Mair got another excuse to get the polis on us.'

'She'll no be making any calls to the polis after I've paid her a wee visit.'

'You cannae touch her, Da,' says Connor.

'No wonder folk cannae credit he's a Johnson, eh? If he didnae have your fucking ears' – I point at Connor – 'I could maybe fantasize I'd been Rohypnol-ed by some fucker on this scheme whose DNA's half way to fucking normal.' I eat a bit scone. 'Right then, listen up. The most successful scams, they Nigerian email scams and that – what is it they're counting on?'

'Folk being eejits,' says Connor.

'Aye, *and*? This is the *best* ones I'm on about, the ones folk fall for.'

Connor shakes his head. 'Maw, you're no –'

'They use. The fact. That *every bastard is feart o' scams.*'

And now Connor's got a wee smile on his face. He cannae help it.

He's a Johnson right enough.

'They're all *This is an urgent message from the Bank of Scotland. There is a possibility there may have been fraudulent activity on your bank account, and we need you to transfer all your funds to a new, more secure account immediately to prevent their misappropriation...* They're getting the bastards panicking, aye, and no thinking straight, they're no giving them time to maybe be a wee bit sensible and check it's for real.'

'Belter!'

'Right, son. Get me the phone numbers of all the adoption agencies in Glasgow. I'll call some and you call some, making out we're from the Council doing checks. Auditors or that –

what's the name of that fucking committee I sent my complaint to about Mair?'

'Scrutiny and Audit Committee.'

'We're on the Scrutiny and Audit Committee and we're needing all the names of the case workers who've had anything to do with Bekki Johnson. If they say *Sorry, that's not one of ours*, we try the next agency, and the next, until we get the name of the bint at the adoption agency who's been the main one on Bekki's case.'

'Aye, and then?'

'And then, we've got Adoption Woman's name and number. Let's say she's called Bunty. We wait a few days. Then I'm Mair, right? I'm shitting myself because I've just telt the Johnsons where Bekki is. The fucking Johnsons have been and scammed me for real this time –'

'But how would we –'

'Naw naw. We *dinnae*. But I calls up Bunty. I goes, "Oh, hi, Bunty. It's Saskia from Social Work."'

Jed and Connor are pissing themselves.

'That's Mair,' goes Connor.

'"Bunty, I'm just checking, sorry if I'm being paranoid here, but you just called me ten minutes ago, yes?" Bunty goes, "No." I goes, "Oh shit. I've just had a call from someone saying they were you… saying you were checking that all stakeholders had up-to-date details for Bekki Johnson's adoptive parents, and asking me which address I had on file, because some mail from the Council seems to have been sent to the wrong address. That wasn't you who called me just now?" Bunty: "No." "In that case, we may have a problem. I – I'm afraid I read out the address we have in the database…" "Oh my God. Saskia!" "Well I thought it was you! It *sounded* like you!" You know how Mair would, she'd make out like it was Bunty's fault for having a voice any fucker could copy. "Shit. I think we've been scammed. I think it could have been Lorraine Johnson." Bunty's thinking, *You stupid fucking bitch.* But she just goes, "Oh God." Mair's up shit creek and she's like that: "I'm going to have to call the police. There's a real possibility the Johnsons will try to snatch Bekki. I'll alert the parents too. The mobile number I have for them is oh-blah-blah-blah. Is that right?" Bunty checks her files. "No, it's oh-blah-blah-blah." Mair goes, "And do you have their landline number and a current email address?"'

'Belter,' goes Jed.

'Then you can use the phone numbers and email to find out their names and their address on the net, aye Connor?'

'If they've got any kinda web presence, aye.'

'And if they dinnae, we just phone them up and scam their names and address out them.'

'Aw God Maw, that's *fucking* wicked! You are a *fucking* evil genius!'

'You watch your mouth, son.' But I'm that made up I chuck the rest of the scone to the dug. 'Gies the phone.'

7

'Beckie?' Ruth peered over the hedge to scan the paddock.

No sign.

Surely she wouldn't have gone over to Emma's without telling her?

'Beckie?' She turned and pushed her way through the knee-high grass between the apple trees, wading round the side of the house to the front.

There she was, still in her blue and yellow school uniform, trying to balance Fat Bear in the branches of the gean tree. The camera they'd got her for Christmas was carefully placed on the study windowsill. Hildebrand, the sinister cross-eyed lemur, was already in position, long legs hooked over a branch, leering upside-down at Ruth.

'Mum!' Beckie came bounding over and jumped up at her, hugging her arm. 'Can I take a photo of you? Pleeeease? You look so pretty in that top. I mean, you always look pretty, but that top's really *really* nice.'

Beckie knew how much Ruth disliked having her photo taken and was under the impression that it was because she was insecure about her rather full figure. Hence the flattery. But Ruth found herself looking down at the top she was wearing – a gypsy blouse in a floral print – and thinking it did rather suit her.

'If you must, I suppose...' While Beckie ran for the camera, Ruth stood under the tree. 'Here?'

The little paparazza considered the composition. 'If you move a bit that way, I can get you in the middle more.' She was squinting at the screen on the back of the camera.

'I'm not sure I want to be in the middle... Remember to hold the camera straight, Beckie.'

'Oh yeah.' A smile. 'I'm so rubbish at photos. But I can delete them if they don't work out, so it doesn't really matter.'

'You're not "rubbish" at photos. That's a lovely one of the sunset Dad has in the study.'

'It's so not! It looks like a monkey took it, or maybe you know that elephant who paints pictures? Maybe him. If I took a blurry photo of a big poop, you and Dad would still be like "Oh Beckie that's lovely" and putting it on the wall.'

'We certainly would not!'

'Oh, hold it there, that's good.' Beckie started snapping. 'Work it, Mum, *work it!*'

Where did she pick this stuff up from? Emma, presumably. Ruth put her hand on her hip and made a pouty face at the camera.

Beckie frowned through a smile. 'Don't make me laugh or it'll be all shaky.'

'That's the general idea.'

Ruth posed and pouted and made faces for what seemed an age.

'Come on, darling, that's enough, surely? I'll take some of you now.'

Beckie handed Ruth the camera, then pulled her hair out of her ponytail and fluffed it round her face. She had become self-conscious about her slightly protruding ears after a boy at school had started calling her Wingnut.

Ruth had gone straight to Miss Barbour, her class teacher, and it had been nipped in the bud. And then she'd had a big row with Alec about the possibility of an operation to have Beckie's ears pinned back.

'Why would you want to change her?' Alec had said, dangerously quietly.

'I don't! I'm thinking of *her*! Of how it might just make her life a bit easier if she didn't have to worry about her ears.'

'Why should she have to worry about them? There's nothing wrong with her ears. I love her pixie ears.'

'So do I, but *she* doesn't.'

'What message would it send, bringing up the possibility of an operation? That we think she's defective and needs fixed? How's she going to feel about that?'

He had a good point, of course, but Ruth wasn't going to give up on this. She'd revisit it in time. Let the idea sink in; let him get used to it. She loved Beckie's ears too, but Alec just didn't understand what it was like for girls these days.

Beckie had already picked up from somewhere how to pose for a photograph like a little cheerleader, one leg in front of the other, nonexistent chest pushed out, big false smile plastered on her face.

Ruth took three photographs. As she was lining up the fourth, her phone rang.

'Hi, Ruth, it's Deirdre Jack.'

'Oh, hi Deirdre!' She handed Beckie the camera and walked off back into the house.

'Have the police been in touch, Ruth?'

The words sucked the breath from her lungs. She froze, gripping the phone so hard she could feel the muscles contracting, painfully, all the way up her wrist and forearm.

'The *police*?'

'Or Social Work? Saskia from Social Work?'

She sat down on the pew, her heart starting to gallop. 'No. Why would they?'

'I'm afraid we've done something very stupid. There's a possibility the Johnsons have found out your address.'

'The Johnsons? Beckie's –'

'Beckie's biological family. Yes. I've just had a phone call from Saskia Mair, the social worker on Beckie's case who –'

'Yes, I remember Saskia Mair.'

'She's in a bit of a panic. It seems the Johnsons may have scammed your address out of her. Lorraine Johnson – we think it was Lorraine Johnson – phoned her up pretending to be me, wanting to check that Saskia had an up-to-date address for Beckie's adoptive parents, and like an idiot Saskia read it out.'

'Oh God.'

'The police and someone from Social Work are going round to the Johnsons' home now, to warn them not to try to contact you or Beckie and not to come near you, but you should just be aware that they may try to do so. It might be an idea to have a little chat with Beckie and explain the situation. Keep an eye out for them.'

'Oh my God. But the Johnsons are dangerous, aren't they?'

'No, look, I'm sure you're not in any danger from them. They may try to contact you though, which is obviously in breach of the court order specifying a closed adoption, so –'

'But it's a closed adoption *specifically* because they *were* thought to pose a significant risk of harm to Beckie!' Her head was suddenly swimming.

This was her punishment, then.

This was the Universe punishing her.

Her, and Alec, and Beckie.

There were little grey blotches in her vision. She swallowed; blinked.

'If she was living with them, yes, but it was more a case of neglect than physical abuse.'

More. 'Oh God.'

'I'm sorry, Ruth, I've scared you – Shannon-Rose is thought to have physically abused Beckie, but Shannon-Rose isn't getting out any time soon, if ever, and the rest of the family don't really pose a threat to her –'

'Jed Johnson's a murderer! He served sixteen years in prison for murder!'

'A gangland killing's a different kettle of fish from hurting his own granddaughter. Even Saskia had to admit that the grandparents seemed genuinely to love Beckie. I'm sure she's in no danger from them.'

'But there were fresh bruises on her arms and legs and back when Saskia had her taken away!'

'Yes, but they could have been caused by rough play with other kids. Which again could suggest neglect, but –'

Breathe. 'So they know where we live and they could be on their way here right now.'

'Ruth –'

'I'll call you back.'

Ruth was aware of herself, as if from outside her own body, snatching up her car keys and going back outside and saying to Beckie, 'Okay darling, I'm sorry, but you'll have to resume the photo shoot later. We have to go.'

'Go where?'

Beckie had a way of looking at you, her expression somehow primed, anticipatory, wary, ready to assume any number of variations according to your response.

'To the shops.'

Beckie smiled.

Always an acceptable option.

'I need to wee.'

'Okay. Be quick.'

Ruth grabbed the soft toys from the tree – she was never sure quite why she did that – and ran to the car parked on the gravel area beyond the outbuildings. She threw the toys in the back seat and started the engine and then ran back to the house and upstairs to the landing. The bathroom door was shut.

'Come on, darling.' She put her shaking hand on the door.

'Coming!'

The door clicked open and Beckie was smiling at her.

If anyone tried to take her darling she would kill them.

If she could, she would kill them.

'Right, let's go.'

Down the stairs, through the hall. At the door, though, she stopped. The Johnsons might be out there now. Shouldn't they just lock themselves inside?

No.

The Johnsons could smash a window. Batter down the door.

They had to get away.

She took Beckie by the hand and together they stepped out into the sunlight, too bright in her eyes so she couldn't see properly, she couldn't see if there was anyone there, but she didn't stop to scan around her, she started to run, pulling Beckie.

'Mum!' Beckie half-laughed, half-wailed.

'We need to hurry, darling.'

'Why?'

'The shop will be closing soon.'

'You didn't lock the door!'

'Well, never mind.'

'You didn't even shut it!'

Past the end of the old byre with its rusty corrugated iron roof, past the mill stone she'd planted up with thyme, into the dappled shade of the sycamore and onto the gravel, their feet sending little stones skittering.

She hauled open the back door of the car and bundled Beckie inside and onto her booster seat, fumbled with the belt, shut the door and jumped into the driver's seat and slammed her own door, wrenching the wheel round in almost the same movement.

And then they were accelerating away down the road, and Beckie was saying:

'Mum. What's wrong? Mum?'

SHE DROVE them not to the shops but to the car park at the start of the walk round the loch shore, busy at this time on a sunny autumn afternoon with families and hikers. To make the call, she got out and stood looking at the white horses on the water while Beckie sat locked inside the car.

'I'm sorry to have scared you, Ruth,' Deirdre said at once. 'The situation's not quite what we thought it was. It's okay, they don't have your address after all.'

Oh thank God. 'So it wasn't Lorraine Johnson who called Saskia?'

'Actually, it seems it wasn't *Saskia* who called *me*. It's all a huge cock-up, I'm afraid, and it's all my fault. I'm so sorry. I – I was so sure I was speaking to Saskia. She said she'd just been scammed into giving out your address to someone pretending to be me. She said she'd tried calling you to warn you, but the number wasn't being recognised and she wondered if you'd changed your mobile number... So I gave her your current one, like an idiot, and Alec's, and your landline number and email address... I should have followed procedure, which in those circumstances – where someone phones up purporting to be a colleague wanting sensitive information – the procedure is to *phone them back*, just to make sure it really is them. But the thing is, I know Saskia quite well, and I was sure it was her.'

'But it wasn't.'

Far out on the water a yacht was tacking, white sails flapping then filling as it changed course. Two birds flew above Inchmurrin, and then three more, and soon there was a cloud of black specks in the sky. Rooks. She could hear them now, faintly, cawing in concerted bursts across the water.

'No,' said Deirdre. 'Saskia never called me.'

'So –'

In the car, Beckie wasn't looking at Ruth. She had Fat Bear under one arm and Hildebrand under the other and was speaking to them. Ruth could see her lips moving.

'It was Lorraine Johnson pretending to be Saskia.'

'But this means they don't have our address, just our phone numbers and email?'

'Yes. I guess she rightly figured that I'd smell a rat if "Saskia" asked for your names or your address. Pretending she'd got an out-of-date phone number, on the other hand, reeling it off for me to confirm it was right – that didn't ring any alarm bells. And it was an emergency, or so I thought, there was a time pressure... I'm sorry. I'm so sorry.'

'Deirdre, it's okay. We're really careful about not putting our phone numbers or email addresses online. There's no way they can find us from those. Our email addresses don't have our names in them either. We can just change our phone numbers and dump that email address, whichever one it is you have.'

'No one's called you trying to get your name or address out of you?'

'No.'

'Can you phone Alec straight away and alert him? I couldn't get through to him on the number I have.'

'Yes. Right. I'll do that now, but I'm sure he wouldn't give out that kind of information over the phone.'

She couldn't get through to Alec either – he was probably giving a lecture or in a practical – so she left a message saying to call her back urgently, the Johnsons might have their phone numbers and an email address, and if someone contacted him trying to find out his name and address, for God's sake don't tell them.

She went over to the car and opened Beckie's door. 'I'm sorry, darling, that was a bit weird, wasn't it?'

'There *is* something wrong, isn't there?'

'That was Deirdre.'

They had been more or less honest with Beckie about her adoption and her birth mother, telling her that Shannon-Rose had something wrong in her brain and had done bad things and was now in prison – although they hadn't told her yet what Shannon-Rose had done, and she hadn't asked.

Beckie looked up at her with that guarded expression she hated. No seven-year-old should ever look at anyone like that, least of all her own mother.

Ruth gently stroked back the strands of hair falling over her face.

'It's nothing to worry about. Deirdre has made a mistake and your birth family, the Johnsons, have found out our phone numbers. But it's okay because we can easily change the numbers right away, and they won't be able to phone us.'

'I don't want them to phone us.'

'No, darling, they won't. You don't need to worry about that.'

'I don't want to see them.'

They had told her that the Johnsons were bad people and that was why Beckie wasn't ever going to see them again. They didn't know where Beckie was and never would. She could just forget that they existed.

Did she remember them?

Did Beckie remember what they had done to her?

Memories weren't laid down at that age, of course. But subconsciously – yes. Beckie knew what had happened to her. Ruth had no doubt about that.

'They might hurt us.'

'Oh darling, no!' She scrabbled with the belt, lifted Beckie out and pulled her into a hug. *Oh my darling girl, don't be frightened, don't be frightened.* 'Daddy and I will *never* let them hurt you. *Never*.'

'They might – h-hurt – *you*.'

Ruth hugged her close. 'No. They're not going to hurt any of us.'

How typical of their sweet, loving girl that her main concern should be for them and not herself. How could that family possibly have produced a child like Beckie? It was as if they had nothing to do with Beckie at all, as if by some accident she'd found herself living amongst them, a changeling in a fairy tale, until Saskia Mair had come along and rescued her.

She made her voice light and bright. 'Let's go for a walk, shall we?'

'Can I take Fat Bear and Hildebrand?'

'Of course you can.'

'Can we play Wanderers?'

'Yes, let's!'

'Fiona's being chased by a Viking.'

As Beckie ran ahead on the path and Ruth juggled Fat Bear, Hildebrand and her phone, she reflected that she should have known Saskia wouldn't make that kind of mistake. She should have known it would have been Deirdre's cock-up.

At long last she got through to Alec.

'Did you get my message?'

'Um? No. What's up?'

'Nothing to panic about, but Deirdre's cocked up and given the Johnsons our phone numbers and an email address – the Gmail one. So we're going to have to change them. You haven't had any dodgy calls or emails, have you, trying to get your name and address out of you?'

Long, terrible silence.

She stopped walking. She dropped the animals. 'Alec?'

. . .

ALEC REACHED FOR HER – then hesitated, his fingertips just touching the denim of her jeans. She smiled at him and took his hand. What was the point in wasting anger and energy on recriminations? The important thing was what happened next.

They were sitting at Saskia Mair's kitchen table. Beckie was in the sitting room, watching TV with Saskia's partner and kids, two sweet little boys with big brown eyes. Beckie had shown polite enthusiasm when offered a pot of yoghurt and the opportunity to catch up on the latest doings of Shaun the Sheep, but she hadn't seemed too sure about Saskia's partner, a tall, lean Scandinavian type who had obviously been about to head out on a bike ride and was rather sinister in neck-to-knee black Lycra and those weird little cyclist's shoes.

But he was obviously as lovely as Saskia. When he'd whisked the kids away to the other room, Ruth had protested weakly, 'Oh, but you're obviously just heading out...' and he had assured her, 'No no, just back actually,' hustling the two boys away as one of them had started: 'But Dad, you're not –'

Thank goodness for people like him and Saskia.

Deirdre had been useless.

Kevin Patterson, the director of the Linkwood Adoption Agency, had been useless.

The police had been useless.

The only person in the world Ruth trusted right now was Saskia Mair.

'I'm sorry,' Alec whispered.

She shook her head. 'It's okay.'

Although, of course, it wasn't. It wasn't okay that he'd blurted out his name and address to Lorraine Johnson when she'd called him pretending to be someone from Argyll and Bute Council chasing unpaid council tax. It wasn't okay that he'd practically foisted the information on her.

He'd related the conversation to her word for word, as she stood with her eyes open on the picture-perfect view across Loch Lomond, seeing none of it.

It had been a woman's voice.

'Mr McAllister? This is Ann Thomson from Argyll and Bute Council. I'm calling about your council tax account. We've sent out three reminders, but your account is still in arrears to the sum of –'

'No no,' Alec had protested. 'I'm not McAllister.'

'This is the mobile number in the database for Mr David McAllister.'

'My name's Alec Morrison.'

'This is the contact number associated with the account. If you're having difficulty paying, we can arrange for you to pay in –'

'But it's not *my* account! I don't owe any council tax, we pay by direct debit. My name is *Alec Morrison*. My address is Back-hill Croft, Arden...'

Candy from a baby.

'Okay,' said Saskia. 'I know they've given you a load of crap about balancing your need to know with the rights of the biological family. But I'm guessing you've Googled them. You'll have found out a bunch of stuff about Jed and Ryan and Travis?'

Ruth nodded. 'We Googled Shannon-Rose as soon as Deirdre told us her name, while we were still going through the process of adopting Beckie. And we found out all about the Johnsons and their convictions.'

Saskia made a face. She had a plain face anyway, with rather prominent eyes, and that big nose stud like a huge black-head. Her hair was streaked with pink. 'The official stuff, the stuff in the press – that's not the half of it.' She took a gulp of hot coffee. 'I'm sorry. I should have laid it all out for you from the get-go, but to be honest... When I met you, I just wanted so much for you to take Beckie, I knew you'd be perfect for her and – I was worried that if I told you everything I knew about the Johnsons you might back out.'

'That wouldn't have happened,' said Alec.

'I realise that. I'm sorry. I'm really sorry.'

Ruth shook her head. 'None of this is your fault, Saskia. You mustn't think that. We really appreciate what you've done for Beckie. And all the other kids like her. You're their lifeline – literally – and I can't begin to imagine what it must be like, what a toll it must take, fighting their corner the way you do, all those poor little...' She took a long breath. 'You're amazing. You're completely amazing – and we can never thank you enough. But you need to tell us now. You need to tell us all about the Johnsons. We have to know what we're dealing with.'

'Thank you for saying that.' Saskia reached out to touch Ruth's arm. 'I'll help you in any way I can.'

'I know you will.'

Ruth jumped as the door clicked open behind her. Turning in her chair, she saw one of Saskia's boys standing holding on to the door handle.

'Hello, sweetie,' said Saskia, and the boy came round the table and into her arms. 'What's wrong, little one?'

Ruth smiled. This was the older of the two boys. How nice, she thought suddenly, to be called 'little one' by your mother when you were the big one to everyone else; the older sibling who was expected to be more stoical, more sensible, more grown up.

'Nothing,' he muttered into Saskia's fluffy mohair jumper. 'I just wanted to see you.'

Saskia pushed away the blue file that had been sitting on the old pine table next to her coffee cup, as if to put distance between its contents and her own child. As she took him out of the room with her, Ruth reached over and opened the file.

On top was a photograph. A mug shot of an elderly man

with protruding ears, a gaunt, grey face, tattoos on his neck, and cold eyes; literally cold, an almost colourless icy blue.

'That's Jed Johnson,' said Saskia from over her shoulder. 'Fifty-nine but looks at least a decade older. He did sixteen years for murder a while back, a gangland killing, and he's served shorter sentences for GBH, false imprisonment, armed robbery and drug-related crimes. That's only what they've managed to do him for, of course.' She came back round the table and sat down, pulling her coffee cup towards her and cradling it. 'He was charged with a second murder but got off on a technicality after the procurator fiscal missed a statutory deadline. No mystery where Shannon-Rose gets her tendency for violence. This didn't come out at the Court of Session hearing for the permanence order – I guess they felt there was enough ammunition against the Johnsons without applying for the release of confidential medical records – but in the course of his many incarcerations, Jed was assessed by two different prison service psychiatrists on the Hare Psychopathy Checklist. On a scale of zero to forty, one of them scored him as thirty-seven and the other thirty-nine. That means he's right at the top of the spectrum for psychopathy.'

She took a slug of coffee. 'Jed gets off on other people's suffering. I could tell you a dozen horror stories, but the best documented is an incident that happened in prison. It seems Jed's sidekick, who was also his cellmate, made the mistake of standing up to Jed when he started victimising a young prisoner. When the warder opened the cell door in the morning he found Jed sleeping like a baby, the floor awash with blood, and the cellmate close to death. There were two hundred and thirty-six separate cuts found on the man's body. Fifty-two of which were on his penis, which was almost severed. The weapon had been the edge of a laminated sheet of tumble drier instructions taken from the prison laundry, where Jed worked at the time. The man claimed to have inflicted the injuries himself, so no action could be taken against Jed... I'm sorry, but I think you have to know this.'

Ruth, a hand to her mouth, nodded.

Saskia passed across another photograph. 'And this is the eldest son, Ryan Johnson.'

This was another hard face, but much younger and startlingly handsome, with long dark lashes and dark eyes, dark hair slicked back 1950s-style. It could have been an actor's press shot.

'Ryan was still relatively small fry five years ago, but these days he's a bit of a kingpin on the Glasgow scene – drug-dealing and prostitution, mainly. He's extremely violent. He's served sentences for drug-dealing and GBH. He's been implicated in at least three murders, but there wasn't sufficient evidence for a prosecution; what witnesses there were wouldn't talk or, in one case, couldn't. Not after falling to their death from a tower block.'

Ruth couldn't speak.

Another photograph came across the table at them. 'This is a press photograph of Ryan, Lorraine and in the background that's Travis, the second son – this was them going into court at the start of one of Jed's trials.'

She stared at the photograph. Lorraine Johnson was a burly woman in a black suit with badly dyed blonde hair falling over a doughy face half turned from the camera. Travis was bodybuilder hefty, with a ned's fringe plastered to his forehead. 'I think Beckie needs to see these too. In case –'

Alec squeezed her hand.

She pulled the photo closer. So this was Beckie's grandmother. 'What's Lorraine Johnson like?'

Saskia grimaced. 'Foul-mouthed, aggressive, volatile, self-righteous and self-deluding. But there's another side to her – she's a victim too in a way, had a horrendous childhood – abused physically and sexually – and I think she's probably in an abusive relationship with Jed. She holds that family together, such as it is. I think she really did love Beckie. But...' She sighed. 'I always come back to those fresh injuries... I'm not saying it was Lorraine, I very much doubt it would have been, but Lorraine must have been aware of them. She must have known someone in the family was still hurting her. Probably Jed.'

Ruth pushed the photograph away.

'And when Beckie was removed, she was neglected. Her nappy hadn't been changed all day, I suspect, and she needed a wash – who knows what was going on in that household? It's possibly the case that Lorraine was incapacitated at the time and had been relying on other members of the family to take care of Beckie, but even so...'

Rage rushed through Ruth, adrenaline surging, so she had to close her eyes and breathe and try not to imagine Beckie, as they'd first seen her as a toddler, in that little smock dress and white tights, with Lorraine or Jed or Ryan Johnson... On the day Saskia had visited the house, dirty and scared and with the signs of their abuse on her little body –

When Beckie had first come to them, that first night, she had been so quiet, so stiff in Ruth's arms as she had carried her up to bed. She had obediently grasped the white rabbit Alec had offered her, but mechanically, without even looking at it. She had let Ruth stroke her hair back from her forehead as if it were an ordeal to be endured.

It had been months before that had changed. She would always remember the first time Beckie had initiated contact. It had been a cold January afternoon and she and Beckie had been cosy in the sitting room with the wood-burning stove roaring, and Ruth had suggested a story. Beckie had nodded. So the two of them had gone to the bookcase to select a book from Beckie's section, Beckie sitting on the carpet, Ruth kneeling next to her, reading out the titles of the choices from the spines.

'Well, let's see... There's *Meg on the Moon*; *I Want My Hat Back*; *The Tiger Who Came to Tea*...' And as the familiar litany had continued, very, very gradually, her eyes still on the books, Beckie had leant in to Ruth's side.

Ruth said, 'We need to make sure that none of them ever come anywhere near her again.'

Alec nodded. 'But how are we going to do that?' He turned to Saskia. 'I mean – what do you think they'll do? Are they going to try to take her, or...'

Saskia grimaced. 'Honestly? I think they will.'

Alec suddenly stood, dropping Ruth's hand, and walked to the sink. He ran the tap and splashed water on his face. 'Sorry.'

Saskia got up and handed him a towel. 'This is where the justice system falls down. These people are violent convicted criminals, Beckie suffered in this family, and they *are* – I'm not going to beat around the bush here – they *are* a danger to her and to you, yet there's nothing the police or the courts can do about it.'

'So what can *we* do about it?' Alec was gripping the towel in both hands. 'What do we do about it?'

Before Saskia could answer, Ruth said, 'We go. We just go. We disappear.'

She'd done it before.

She could do it again.

8

There's plenty room on the grass by the roadside, eh, but when I says, 'Just stop here, son,' Ryan keeps on going and pulls the Audi into the proper parking bit by the old wrecked farm buildings. It's a fucking off-road vehicle that's never been off fucking tarmac.

The place is a right mess, weeds and that all over. This is where Bekki's been for five years? Ms Adoption Woman comes out and sees the place needs knocking down and goes *Aye that's fine then*?

'Right,' says Jed, and he and the boys get out. Ryan leaves the engine running and the headlights on.

I get out the car.

Christ. If it wasnae for the headlights it'd be pitch black.

Safe for a wean? Out in Teuchterland in the middle of fucking nowhere?

When I get to the cottage, the door's lying open and the lights are all on, and Jed's raging.

'You stupid fucking cow!' he's in my face. 'I telt ye we needed to get her! I telt ye!'

Fuck it.

We're in the front room. I can hear the boys through the house, ripping the place up, smashing stuff. It's just an empty room we're in.

The fuckers have gone.

Jed goes and kicks the wall.

I goes, 'Fuck it.'

'Aye, *fuck you!*' Jed's back in my face. '"Naw Jed, this needs planning but, we cannae just roll up and get her but." Planning, is it? *Planning?*'

Aye, planning.

A wee flat rented away the other side of the city. Couldnae just take her to our bit. Jed was 'Fuck that, let the polis come and try and take Bekki off of us again, just let those fuckers come and try it,' but Ryan and Travis and Carly and Connor were like that: 'Naw Da.'

Plan was, me and Carly'd disappear and stay in the wee flat with Bekki till the villa on the Costa Brava's finished. It's gonnae have white walls and big glass windaes and doors, and a brand new kitchen and bathrooms and en suites – Bekki'll get the best room, mind, with a sea view and her own wee en suite – and brand new furniture, black and white and grey, all matching, and outside a massive infinity pool. Bekki and the other weans never out the sea. Life of fucking Reilly.

We'll tell Bekki the Morrisons stole her off of us, and we didnae know where she was, but now she's safe home and no fucker's taking her off us ever again. If she starts with *I want Mummy and Daddy*, we'll be like that: *They don't want you hen, they gave you back. They're no your real mum and dad. We're your real family.*

'Stupid fucking bitch!' He pulls his head back and spits right on my lips.

I spit it right back at him and he takes a hud of my shoulders and slams me back against the wall. I knee him in the baws.

He doubles over. 'Ah fuck. Ah fuck.'

'Maw,' says Travis. 'They're no here.'

Travis, God love him, was at the back of the queue when they were handing out the brains in the Johnson family.

It's another fucking wee Teuchterland hovel, roses round the door maybe, but Christ, the windaes and the door are from nineteen-canteen. Like they think they're in a fucking stately home preserved for the fucking nation, draughty shite windaes an' all.

Needs gutting.

I ring the door again. It's 6:30 in the morning. They cannae be out.

Door opens and a woman's standing there. She's up herself, long shiny hair and long legs in designer jeans.

'I'm sorry to bother you so early in the morning,' I goes with a polite wee smile. 'I'm hoping you can help me. I see Backhill Croft is empty now, and I'm just wondering if maybe it's for sale?'

'Oh. Well. I imagine it will be. But it's not on the market yet or anything...' She's got a voice like she's Scottish, aye, but she wishes she wasnae.

'You wouldn't happen to have contact details for the sellers?'

'No. Sorry.'

'They've moved away, have they?'

'Yes. Sorry, I can't help.' And the bitch goes to shut the door on me.

I breenge against it and go, 'Come on yous,' and Jed and the boys are in and through the house.

I push the bint down on the floor and she's all 'Oh, oh, oh' and I'm 'Tell us where they are and I'll no touch you,' and then Jed and Travis are back with a man in boxers and a wee lassie in her jimjams, eyes like saucers, poor wee bairn, and Travis dumps her down on a chair and I'm 'Tell us where they are and they'll no hurt your bairn' and she's 'I don't know where they are, they've just gone, they never told us they were going even, men with a removal van just came and took all their stuff but they wouldn't tell us where they were taking it or why the Morrisons had left so suddenly or anything, and I've tried calling them but their mobile numbers are unobtainable –'

Shit.

'What's their names? Alec Morrison, aye, and what's his wife called?'

'Ruth,' says the man. 'And their little girl's Rebecca. They call her Bekki.'

They call her Bekki?

'You're friends with them, aye?'

'We thought we were,' says the bint. 'But they just up and left without a word –' And she clamps her mouth shut and stares at me, and it's pure comical so it is.

'Aye. The explanation? You're looking at it, hen.'

'Oh my God.'

'*Oh my God,*' goes Travis.

I goes, 'Right. You're going to tell us all you know about your good pals the Morrisons, aye? Where they work. Where their friends and relations stay at. What they have for fucking breakfast.'

'And if you tell anyone,' says Ryan, leaning against the wall, 'if you tell the polis or Social Work or that, if you tell *anyone* and I mean *anyone* that we were here...'

'*We'll be baaaa-aaaack,*' goes Travis.

THE KITCHEN's like something out a museum. The sink's one of they old china ones and there's no even any proper units, there's shite like my grannie had, one of they cabinets with a front you pull down for a shoogly wee worktop, and cupboards and that that dinnae go, all chipped and stained. There's a nice big dresser but, like something off of *Antiques Roadshow*, and bonnie cups and plates on it.

Table's massive, with chairs round it that are no even the same, some wood and some painted sweetie colours like sherbet lemon and candyfloss. Ryan pushes the man at one of them and goes, 'Anyone fancy a wee bit breakfast?' and he's opening cupboards.

The lassie suddenly turns round and runches her teeth down on Travis, and he goes 'Ah ye bass!' and she's legging it out the door and Jed's 'Fuck' and going after her, and Ryan's got the bint against the cupboard and she's yelling, 'Emma, Emma!'

Then Jed's dragging the bairn back in by the hair and she's greeting and he's shoving her at the bint and going 'Keep that fucking wee animal under control, aye? Fucking went and tried to get the fucking phone,' and he throws the phone at the dresser and some of the cups and that smash, and the bint's going 'Oh *God*!' and she's backing into the corner between the Aga and the cupboard coorying her bairn and going 'Leave her alone! Leave her alone!' and hubby's just sitting there with a big glaikit face on him.

'Fucking wee bitch,' goes Travis. He's running the tap on his hand. With the other hand he points at the bairn. 'Needs a fucking muzzle on her.'

Ryan's pissing himself.

'Please don't hurt her,' the bint's going, and Jed's in the wee lassie's face going, 'Any more shite from you and you're getting more than a wee nip and a slap, aye?'

God's sakes. The fucking prick. He's got that radge look in his eyes like he'd get when he used to go for me. He's loving this so he is.

'Get away from her!' goes the bint, and she's pulling the

bairn round into the corner, she's got her back turned to Jed, and the wee lassie's got her face pushed in her maw's chebs.

I go, 'What's the wee lassie's name – is it Emma, aye?'

Bint doesnae say nothing. She doesnae turn round.

'You come here to me, Emma-hen. I'll no let they buggers touch you, eh? Come here to me. My name's Lorraine.'

Wee lassie huds on to her maw. Jed grabs the bint and Travis pulls the bairn off of her and round the table, and the bint's going 'Do as they say, darling, just do as they say' and then I've got my arm round the bairn and I'm going 'It's okay hen, it's okay wee Emma,' and Jed's got the bint's arm up her back.

Emma's standing staring at her maw and Jed. I pull her closer and I go, 'Come and sit on my knee, hen,' and I sit down on a chair and pull the bairn down on top of me and smooth her hair. She's got awful bonnie hair. Dark and shiny.

The bint's still going, 'Do as they say, darling, do as they say,' and Jed gives her arm a yowk for no reason, the mentalist, and she's 'Oh God oh God please.'

Hubby's no said a fucking thing.

I goes, 'This's your bairn, by the way? That's your bint? You gonnae just sit there giving it *Whatever*? You. Are. A fucking disgrace.'

He goes, 'What do you want?'

Wee Emma's shaking. I give her a coorie. 'Dinnae you worry, hen, dinnae you worry. Maybe your da's a gutless fucking wonder, but no one's gonnae touch you. Ryan son, take a seat, aye? Travis, get us some coffees.'

'Please –' goes the bint. 'Please let her come to me.'

'Och, she's fine where she is, eh, wee Emma? What's *your* name, doll?'

'Pam.'

'Take a seat, Pammie. We'll be out your hair soon enough.

Soon as you've telt us all about your pals the Morrisons. Let's us start with where they work at and where they're from, eh?'

'Do yous take milk and sugar?' goes Travis.

'And get the lassie a juice, son.'

Emma goes, 'I don't want any juice!' She's sitting on my lap with her wee toes pressed against the chair next us and her legs lifted up off of me, balancing on her wee arse like she's no wanting any more of herself touching me than she has to.

'A nice wee glass of milk, then.' I chuckle. 'Bairns, eh?'

'It's all right, darling,' goes Pammie, sitting down across the table. 'Just sit and be good and they'll soon be gone.'

The man goes, 'Alec is a scientist. A botanist. He works in the Botany Department at Glasgow University. Ruth is just a housewife.'

'Aye? Where did she work at before?'

'I think she was a nurse?' He turns to Pammie.

Pammie's hudding her sair arm and smiling at her bairn. 'She was a paediatric nurse at Glasgow Royal Infirmary.'

Ryan's got his phone out and he's keying it all in. Like he's taking the minutes at a fucking board meeting.

'And where are the fuckers from?'

'Alec's from Perth,' goes Pammie. 'That's where he grew up.'

'What bit?'

'What?'

'What bit of Perth?'

'I don't know.'

'It was near the big park,' goes hubby, 'I don't know what it's called – he used to talk about how his house was near it and these boys used to hide and ambush him – he used to joke about it, he said it was like Inspector Clouseau...'

'He got family there still?'

'His parents are dead,' goes Pammie.

'But I think he has some cousins might still live there.' Hubby's the class fucking swot. 'His sister Pippa is working in

India, I think... He had family on the west coast as well. Torridon.' Travis puts a mug on the table in front of him and he goes, 'Thank you.'

Twat.

'Whereabouts in Torridon?'

'I don't know. But it's not exactly a populous area, and I'd imagine it's a close community – I wouldn't have thought it'd be hard to find the family...'

'And what about Ruth?'

The bint goes, 'She's Australian, originally. After her dad died, she and her mum came to live here. When she was small.'

'Aye, and?'

'And what?' She's giving me evils.

'Where did they live when they came to this country?'

'St Andrews.'

'And whereabouts in Australia is she from?'

'I don't know. Sydney, I think. She never talked about her childhood.'

'Aye right. Yous were best pals, and she never telt you about her childhood?'

'No, really, she didn't. I always thought it was odd that she didn't. I said to you, James, didn't I?' She turns to hubby and he gives her a wee smile. 'We assumed Ruth must have had an unhappy childhood and that was why she never talked about it.'

'Ruth was weird,' goes hubby. 'I always thought there was something weird about Ruth.' Mr Brown Nose is that far up my arse he could lick my fucking tonsils.

'In what way?'

'Ruth wasn't "weird",' says Pammie, and she's eyeballing him like she's thinking *Who is this gutless fuck?*

'Okay Pammie. Let's just see what hubby here has to say about your pal Ruth, and then when he's done we'll hear from you, aye?'

Hubby's right in there. 'She used to overreact to things.' He turns to Pammie. 'Like when Emma tied a scarf round Bekki's wrists when they were playing prisoners? It wasn't even tight. Ruth screamed blue murder at Emma. Remember?'

Pammie nods but she's no saying nothing.

'And that time they were jumping on our bed, and Bekki fell off and bruised her shoulder, and when you took her home, Ruth went ballistic, called you an irresponsible parent? Even though you'd told them to stop? And Bekki wasn't even hurt really. It was just a very small bruise.'

'It's called being a good mother,' Pammie raps out. 'She was right, I should have hauled them out of there and not just told them to stop. That bed's really high. Bekki wasn't badly hurt, no, but she could have been.'

I'm pissing myself. 'Okay, let's no have a domestic here, let's keep it civil in front of the bairn, aye? What else was "weird" about the bint Ruth?'

Hubby's practically got his hand in the air. 'She never wanted her photo taken. She didn't even have a passport – we had this idea of the two families going on holiday to France, but we couldn't because Ruth didn't have a passport and for some reason was resistant to getting one. Alec used to joke it was because she didn't want to get a photo from one of those booths – at least I assumed he was joking, but maybe that really was the reason.'

I eyeball Pammie. 'Right hen. Now *you're* gonnae tell us all about your weird best pal Ruth. You're gonnae tell us what she likes and what she doesnae. You're gonnae tell us about her friends and family and where she said she always wanted to go and bide. We need to know all this shite, cos that mad bitch has got our wee lassie. Bekki's our wee lassie, see? And if we dinnae get her back, we're gonnae be coming for *your* wee lassie. Wee Emma here. That's a fucking promise.'

'Mum!' goes wee Emma. 'They can't get Bekki! Don't tell them anything!'

'It's all right, Emma. We don't know anything to tell, do we? We don't know where Bekki and her mum and dad are.'

'I know, but maybe their family...'

'Ruth's parents are dead,' goes Pammie. 'She doesn't have any siblings or cousins. She used to be a nurse, but she gave that up when they adopted Bekki. She worked in Glasgow Royal Infirmary. She's still in touch – or was in touch – with a couple of the other nurses, Donna and Claire... I don't know their surnames. They used to meet up for lunch in town and go shopping.'

'Mum! Stop it!' goes the bairn, and she's greeting, the poor wee sweetheart.

I bounce her on my knee and go, 'Now now hen.' She tries to wriggle off but I've got my arms round her.

Pammie goes, 'Shoosh, darling, shoosh, it's all right. It's going to be all right.' She reaches for her bairn and grabs wee Emma's hand.

Jed's lunging, but I goes, 'Beat it you!' and he backs off.

'These bints still work at the Infirmary, aye?'

'Claire does.'

'Right. And who else?'

She's stroking wee Emma's hand and smiling at the bairn. 'Ruth didn't have many friends... There's Laura, who's got a son in Bekki's class. They live in one of the cottages at Hinksfield... But... I think I was her only close friend. Or I thought I was.'

'Aye, so what else "weird" is there about her?'

She takes a big breath. 'Well. When I – we were in a café one day and I said *I'm so lucky to have a friend like you* or something like that, *You're such a lovely friend*, and Ruth just stared at me, and then she said *No I'm not! You don't know anything about me!* and got up and ran off to the loos. I guess that was weird. When she came back to the table, she said she was feeling bad about shouting at me that time Bekki fell off the bed, but I don't know if that was really it, or if...'

'There was something off about the bitch.'

'No! All I'm saying is that she was secretive about her past. So I can't tell you anything much about it. I really can't. I really didn't know much about her.'

'You must be able to think of something,' goes hubby.

'Jesus Chutney!' I chuckle. 'You've got a real diamond there, hen, eh? But aye, you must be able to think of something. Starting with where you think they'd go.'

'Italy,' goes hubby. 'Alec spent a summer in Italy when he was a student, and Ruth always fantasised about a villa on the Amalfi coast. Didn't she? Pam?'

Pammie nods.

'She doesn't have a fucking passport,' goes Ryan.

'Maybe she's got one now.'

Aye, fuck it.

'And what all else? What about when she was living in St Andrews? What all's she told you about that?'

'I'M LIGHTIN' it,' goes Jed.

We're in a KFC on the way back to our bit. I'm on the low-cal ginger and a chicken wrap – fucking diet. The boys have both got Big Daddy Box Meals and Jed's got a Zinger and fries.

I'm in his face. 'You light it and what's there for them to fucking sell? A burned-out fucking ruin?'

'Aye Da,' says Travis. He's got a plaster on his hand and he keeps rubbing his finger on it. Getting bit by a wee lassie? He's no a happy bunny.

'You're back *planning*, aye?' goes Jed.

'Aye, so shut it.'

Ryan gets up for another Coke. He's in his Armani and among all the wee neds he sticks out like a Rolex on a scabby dug. Folk look at him as he walks by. All the wee hairies going *Gies a slice o' that.*

When he gets back, I says, 'Right yous, listen up.'

'Is it a belter, aye?' goes Jed.

'Shut it. This is what we do, right? We don't do *nothing*.'

'Here we go.' And Jed puts on the daft voice that he thinks is him talking posh: 'Why – am – I – not – surprised?'

'We wait till that wee house goes for sale. We make like we're maybe gonnae buy it. We get the Home Report sent us, to an email address Connor will set up that's no traceable. We get them thinking we're that interested in buying. But we've a shitload of questions and the estate agent cannae answer them so we're like that: *Gonnae gie us the seller's details so we can ask them about the septic tank.*'

I lean back and pick a bit chicken out the wrap.

'But Maw,' goes Ryan. 'Even their best pals havenae a fucking clue where they're at. Are the bastards gonnae give the estate agent their details so they can get them scammed out them? That's no happening. They'll have done it all through their fucking brief.'

'Aye, it's a long shot, son. But in the meantime we check out they places, eh? Perth. Torridon. Fucking Amalfi, wherever the fuck that is. Fucking Australia if we have to.' I bite the chicken. 'First up, Torridon. Teuchterland Central – they'd think they're safe enough there, eh? But we dinnae go in all confrontational. Me and Mandy'll hire a shite wee car, one of they new Fiats maybe, and go and book in a B&B. We're there because our pal Pippa Morrison telt us all about it and we thought it sounded right bonnie, and where are the Morrisons living at now so we can go and say hello to Pippa's folks?'

Travis is eating with his gob open, and when he goes 'Fucking belter!' a bit chip falls out onto his Rangers top and then it drops on the table right next Ryan's Coke.

'Jesus,' goes Ryan. 'Get that out my fucking space. Fucking chimp.'

'What?' goes Travis.

Ryan gets a serviette and, all delicate like, picks up the bit chip, and Travis makes to get up out his chair but Ryan grabs him by the tit and shoves the chip up his neb, and Travis is 'Ah fuck, ah fuck!' and tipping back in his chair. The chair cannae take it, Travis is a big lad, eh, and a leg breaks under him and he's couped out it on the floor.

Jed's pissing himself.

'Quit it!' I yell. 'God's sakes!'

Travis gets another chair and Ryan goes, 'We're gonnae need our ain place for Bekki till we get Spain sorted. Flat's fine aye, but we're shitting money up the wall there renting. And Bekki might like a garden, eh? She's been living out in that wee cottage with a garden and nature and that, how's she gonnae like being stuck in a fucking flat in fucking Nedland? Naw. I'll buy us a wee house with a garden, a wee newbuild someplace nice. Bearsden maybe. Plenty trees and that. I'll put it through the holding company so there's no any paper trail.'

Shannon-Rose is Ryan's twin, eh, and her wee lassie means the fucking world to him.

'But can you stretch to it, son, with Spain an' all?'

'Aye Maw, nae worries. Can sell it on after, eh?'

'That's barry then, son. Barry.'

Ryan's eyeballing me.

'Barry,' I goes.

'What?'

'Nothing.'

'You're thinking we're no gonnae need heehaw for Bekki, and we're no gonnae need to fuck off to Spain. You're thinking we're no gonnae get Bekki back?'

Ryan's got my brains right enough. 'I'm no gonnae lie, son,

I'm getting a bad feeling about this bint Ruth. A bad fucking feeling.'

'Aye?'

'Why's she never telt Pammie nothing about her childhood?'

Jed, Ryan and Travis gowp at me. The Three Fucking Stooges. 'They're best pals, aye? See each other every fucking day for five fucking years?'

Not a dickie bird.

'She's a fucking *woman*.'

Nada.

'Every fucking woman on the planet tells her best pal about when she was wee. Every fucking woman. This Ruth bint's a clever bitch, I'm thinking. Maybe she's had it at the back of her heid that maybe we'll find them, that maybe they'll have to disappear, and she's got an ace up her sleeve – she's got somewhere to run to, somewhere she lived when she was wee, and she's no giving away *nothing* about it to any fucker, not even her best pal Pammie. I'll bet a million fucking pounds she's no even from Australia.'

'No bastard can stay off the radar these days,' goes Ryan. 'Dinnae you worry, Maw. We'll find them. Torridon and they places, aye we'll check them out, but if the bastards arenae there, we get looking into Ruth Morrison and where she was at before she was married. There'll be records, digital footprints. We'll get Connor on it. Get the wee fucker earning his keep, aye?'

I bite another bit wrap and take a swally ginger and say 'Aye son,' but I've still got that bad feeling.

There's something no right about that bint Ruth.

There's just something no right.

And she's got Bekki.

9

EIGHTEEN MONTHS LATER

'Could it have been slugs?' said Beckie, squatting on the path to poke at one of the holes that marked where the tulips had been.

Flora kept her voice light. 'Would have to be very hungry slugs.'

Did Beckie do it? Did she sneak out here last night, when they thought she was upstairs asleep, and rip out all the tulips? To punish Flora for losing it at her yesterday? But then she'd have to somehow dispose of them. Maybe under the hedge?

Flora couldn't accuse her, not without evidence. She mustn't overreact. At least, she mustn't overreact any more than she already had done. She mustn't start blaming Beckie for everything.

This was probably just random bored kids intent on some easy vandalism. They always locked the gates at night, but the small one at the end of the path from the front door to the pavement was only three feet high. Easy enough to climb over.

And Mia had been staying next door with Ailish and Iain last night. Flora wouldn't put it past that girl to sneak out in the small hours for some 'fun' making all the tulips mysteriously disappear.

She looked up, over the hedge that divided the front gardens, to the first-floor windows of Ailish and Iain's house. Maybe Mia's bedroom was at the front. If so, the tulips would have been in full view if she'd been looking around deciding on her next 'project', as Ailish called her niece's schemes.

'Is it time *now*?' said Beckie. She'd been looking forward to this damn barbeque for weeks. A barbeque in early May, for God's sake – Flora had been hoping for rain, but of course it was a lovely sunny day, perfect for an outdoor party. The thought that Mia was just next door was driving Beckie nuts – every minute they remained apart was a minute wasted, apparently.

When Flora had suggested to Neil that there might be a link between Beckie's behaviour at school and her friendship with Mia, he'd laughed.

He'd actually laughed.

'Poor Mia's getting blamed for this as well now, is she?'

This. *This.* As if it was nothing.

She looked at Beckie.

What was going on in that little head?

Beckie didn't seem in the least bit worried about the 'mediation discussion' Mrs Jenner had arranged for Monday after school, when Beckie and Edith and their respective parents were going to 'sit down and talk through the issues and agree on resolutions'. This apparently was going to involve an 'acknowledgement of wrongdoing and harm' by Beckie and 'restorative gestures'. In other words, she would have to say she was sorry.

But *was* she sorry?

'Mum?'

'What?'

Beckie bit her lip.

Flora made herself smile. 'Sorry, darling, I was miles away. What is it?'

'Is it time yet?'

'Almost. Go and put on a fleece or a jumper. It's not that warm out of the sun.'

Beckie ran off back inside and Flora followed her, looking up at the elegant sandstone façade of their own house. Or rather, the house they were living in. Despite all her efforts to make it theirs – the kitchen extension to make a 'family room', the frantic redecorating, the fact that they'd taken every single stick of furniture with them, even the things that really could do with replacing – it still didn't feel like home.

It felt like somewhere they had washed up, the three of them: a strange shore.

Gardens Terrace was, of course, a wonderful place to live. It was one of the nicest streets in one of the nicest cities in the world: a single row of big Victorian and Edwardian houses looking across a quiet road to the Botanic Gardens and backing onto their own huge gardens, and beyond them the huge gardens of the street behind. The houses all had relatively generous front gardens too, most with mature hedges and trees.

They were very lucky to live here.

At certain times of day when there wasn't much traffic, it was almost like being in the country. You heard bird song, and the wind in the trees, and squirrels chattering. Sometimes, to Beckie's delight, ducks from the pond in the Botanic Gardens flew over the house.

They had only been able to afford Number 17 thanks to their inheritances, thanks to both sets of parents being dead. They had paid an obscene price for a semidetached house. But it had been worth it, she kept telling herself, for the location and the garden and the beautifully proportioned Victorian rooms with shutters on the windows and deep skirting boards and cornices, and a working fireplace to sit round on a winter evening watching *Strictly* or an old film or, when Beckie was in bed, a Scandi noir box set.

They were very lucky to live here.

Did Beckie think so?

Was she happy?

Or did she still secretly miss Arden, and their old lives, as much as ever?

The problem was that Beckie was always so eager to please, so concerned about 'bothering' them, that trying to get her to reveal her true feelings was always a challenge. 'Yeah, it's great here,' she'd say, whatever she felt about it.

The leaves were coming out on the little silver birch tree by the gate, and there was a smell of new shoots and cut grass and freshly turned soil: the promise of summer.

She took a deep breath of it.

Surely Beckie was happy?

She seemed happy, didn't she?

This problem at school – it was probably just a blip, as Neil said. Beckie had always been such a good child that any bad behaviour was always going to be magnified, to seem a much bigger deal than it would have been in any other child.

No one was perfect, as Neil kept saying.

But it was just so hard to believe that she'd done it.

Beckie?

Their Beckie? Their sweet little girl, their popular, easy, laid-back little girl who made friends effortlessly wherever she went, who had so many invitations to birthday parties it was getting to be a logistical nightmare? Their Beckie, held up by other parents as an example to their own kids?

When Flora had arrived in the playground yesterday after-noon, the headmistress, Mrs Jenner, had come over and asked if she could have 'a quick word'. Flora had gone with her quite happily to the little office overlooking the playing field at the back of the school. It hadn't even crossed her mind that Beckie could be in any sort of trouble.

Mrs Jenner had sat down at her desk and waved Flora to one of the comfortable chairs in front of it. Flora had still been relaxed, reflecting that there was something not right about a headmistress who looked younger, rather than older, than her actual age. Mrs Jenner, who was in her early sixties according to one of the other mums, wore a bright cerise blouse under her fitted jacket, which was low enough to show cleavage. Her hair was a tumble of honey curls on her shoulders.

She looked Flora straight in the eye, as she'd presumably been instructed to do on some training course or other, and said, 'I'm afraid it seems Beckie has been bullying another girl.'

Flora had repeated, stupidly, 'Bullying another girl?'

'I'm afraid so. I witnessed her hitting Edith myself. Beckie has denied it, but I saw her with my own eyes.' She gestured at the window, from which there was a view of the playing field with its miniature goal posts.

'Edith?' Flora couldn't remember an Edith.

'When I spoke to her, Edith at first refused to admit there was a problem but then broke down and revealed that Beckie has been bullying her for some time. Physically, and in other ways. Beckie has told the other girls not to play with Edith. She makes fun of her and encourages the others to do so too. She has instigated a particularly cruel ruse which involves getting two or three other girls to pretend to Edith that they now want to be her friends, not Beckie's, and are going to play with her, and then, at a signal from Beckie, they run away at top speed. Poor Edith falls for it every time. She tries to run after them, and then they all turn and shout insults at her and laugh. Some of the name-calling has been disablist, although Edith isn't technically disabled, just... a bit uncoordinated. Spastic, mong, et cetera.' She said the awful words in a brisk, businesslike tone that somehow made them all the worse.

Flora felt the room recede and fade.

Mrs Jenner's voice was very faint, and then suddenly very loud.

'Mrs Parry?'

There were grey spots in front of her eyes.

And then Mrs Jenner was round the desk and pushing Flora's head down past her knees, pushing a plastic cup of water into her hand.

Flora found herself repeating weakly: 'I'm sorry, I'm sorry.'

She brought the cup to her lips and gulped at the luke-warm, synthetic-tasting water.

'Now, Mrs Parry,' Mrs Jenner said briskly, like a nurse would speak to a difficult patient. 'There's no need to work yourself up.' *How pathetic*, she was probably thinking. *No wonder Beckie's out of control.* 'It's really nothing to worry about – children can be very cruel to each other, you know, and this sort of thing will happen from time to time. I've known far worse, believe me. I'm sure we can nip it in the bud.' And Flora felt a quick pat on her back. A little rub between her shoulder blades.

'But...' She sat up and looked into the other woman's bright blue, heavily mascara-ed eyes. There was a big clump of mascara sticking together several of the upper lashes of her right eye, like the lashes were melting, like this was a face in some surreal dream, melting away as soon as you got up close. 'Are you sure?'

This wasn't Beckie. It just wasn't.

Beckie was so good with children with problems; so kind. At break and lunchtime, she and her friends always passed by the Buddy Bench, where children could sit to indicate they needed a 'buddy', and asked whoever was there if they wanted to join them.

Mrs Jenner nodded, and retreated once more behind the desk.

'I've spoken to Beckie, of course, myself. She's unrepentant.

She denies that she's been bullying Edith – says it's Edith who's the problem and "everyone hates her". A common justification, I'm afraid. She maintains that people run away from Edith because they hate her.'

'I'm sorry, I'm just –' Flora gulped down more water. 'I'm having a really hard time believing that Beckie would do that.'

'I realise it's a shock. We're all very surprised. Beckie has always been a pleasure to have in the school. There hasn't been anything... Any problems at home...?' And the bright blue eyes scanned Flora up and down.

Flora could only shake her head as all the statistics gleaned from furtive late-night Googling flashed through her mind, about schizophrenia and bipolar disorder and their age of onset and possible triggers. Was that what this was? Was this her nightmare coming to pass? Was this the monster Beckie carried inside her, in her genes, awakening, stretching and yawning and flexing its muscles, because of something Flora had done? Something she'd done to trigger it?

Of course not.

As bullying went, this was pretty mild, really. Every child went through phases of being naughty, difficult, acting out. As Mrs Jenner had said, this wasn't anything out of the ordinary. And it could be nipped in the bud in this 'mediation discussion' she was talking about, asking Flora if Monday after school would be convenient.

'Yes, of course,' Flora had said. 'Of course. Monday would be fine. Obviously, we'll make sure – we'll make sure Beckie stops it. That she stops bullying this poor girl. Poor Edith.'

When they'd got home, Flora had chosen her moment to broach the subject with Beckie. They'd got out Beckie's favourite jigsaw, featuring a litter of Labrador puppies, and knelt opposite each other at the coffee table in the family room to work on it.

When she'd gently told Beckie what Mrs Jenner had said

about her being unkind to Edith, Beckie had looked from the piece of puzzle she was holding to Flora's face in indignation. 'It's not *my* fault Edith's horrible.'

'Oh Beckie. I'm sure she isn't "horrible". And even if she was, that's no excuse for bullying.'

'But I didn't bully her! She's twisting it all round, Mum. I've never *hit* her.'

'Beckie, Mrs Jenner saw you.'

'But I was just pushing her away after *she* tried to hit *me!*'

Oh God.

'So you're saying *Edith* is bullying *you?*'

'No! No one's bullying anyone, Mum. Edith is just so stupid and horrible that she spoils everything.'

'That's a really silly thing to say.'

Beckie shrugged.

'Darling... Is there something wrong at school? Is there anything... Maybe some other girl or boy is bullying *you*, or... getting you to do things you don't want to do?'

Beckie shook her head in what seemed like genuine puzzlement.

'Did another girl or boy make you be unkind to Edith?'

'No. *Edith* made me be "unkind" to Edith.'

Flora sighed. 'Darling... Nobody wants people to be unkind to them, do they? Just try to imagine for a second what it must be like to be Edith... Yes, I know, but just try to imagine. The bell goes and you run out to the playground and everyone's having fun, and you see some girls from your class that you'd really like to chat to and play with, but then they start calling you cruel names and laughing at you and telling you you're horrible. How do you think you would feel then?'

Beckie shrugged. 'Edith's not like that. Edith doesn't care what we say.'

'How do you know that? If it were you, how would you feel?'

Beckie, looking at her sideways, muttered reluctantly: 'Lonely?'

'Yes, you would feel really lonely, wouldn't you. And upset? Maybe even scared, when the girls all start ganging up on you?'

Beckie had nodded, and her lip had trembled. 'Can you not tell Dad?'

'Dad will have to know, Beckie – it's too serious not to tell him about it. And we have to go to a meeting with Edith and her parents after school on Monday, and you're going to tell Edith you're sorry and you won't be unkind to her any more.'

And just when Flora had thought she was getting through to her, Beckie had wrinkled her nose and said, 'Do I have to?'

'Yes you do.'

And Beckie had sighed, in that way she had, as if to say: another adult stupidity I have to go along with to humour the poor deluded souls.

She'd got that sigh from Mia.

Mia, Mia, Mia.

Flora shut the front door behind her, eased her feet out of her shoes, and stood leaning back against the door. Sometimes she wished she could shut out the whole world. Keep Beckie from it. Like the Wanderers in their own little boat, adrift. Apart.

Safe.

But Beckie had been looking forward to this damn barbeque for weeks.

BECKIE WAS WEARING her favourite leggings with tiny daisies all over them, and a furry blue fleece on top of her T-shirt. In one hand she swung the little silver gift bag with the present for Mia in it – a fart machine, which Ailish was really going to be thrilled about – even though, as Flora had reminded her, it wasn't a birthday party and a present wasn't necessary. Beckie would have spent all her pocket money on presents if Flora had let her.

She'd always been a kind little girl.

She ran ahead down the path to the gate, but then stopped and waited for them.

A good little girl.

'Okay, Beckie,' said Flora.

Beckie opened their gate, skipped along the pavement ten metres, and opened next door's, which was identical to their own, right down to the twists in the Victorian wrought iron.

'Can I ring the bell?'

'Of course you can, darling.'

Beckie skipped to the door and reached for the pebble-like pottery bell-push with 'PRESS' on it, set in a metal disk – identical to their own bell.

Neil said, 'How long do we have to stay?'

'Two hours minimum.'

The door opened on a blast of noise: ABBA, overlaid by the shrieks and howls of what sounded like women in pain. Dozens of them. Flora had a sudden image of Ailish's head flung back, mouth open, cackling in glee as she skipped about the kitchen from one instrument of torture to the next – coordinating thumbscrews, maybe in Cath Kidston prints, for all her guests, and more elaborate offerings for her special friends: a cage fashioned from shabby chic wirework swinging above the hob for Katie, who'd be pretending to be enjoying it and doing her utmost not to drip sweat on the Rayburn; a rack rigged up on the kitchen table for Marianne, spread-eagled, her bouncy curls full of bits of scone and cake and broken pastel crockery, gasping an apology to Ailish for the mess...

Flora smiled at Jasmine, who was standing at the door looking up at them through her hair.

Jasmine, Ailish's fifteen-year-old daughter, was an androgynously skinny little thing, looking utterly ridiculous in a black boob tube, tiny red shorts and high clumpy black shoes. Her fake-tanned, stick-thin legs with their bony little knees were those of a child, but her blonde hair fell in shiny sheets on either side of her face, which was plastered in foundation and dominated by huge black caterpillar-like eyebrows she must have spent forever pencilling on.

Without looking at him, Flora knew Neil was staring at the eyebrows.

Jasmine didn't respond to Flora's smile.

'Hello, Jasmine!' she persevered. 'You look nice!'

'Your hair's amazing,' said Beckie.

Jasmine, ignoring them both as usual, muttered to Neil: 'Mum's in the kitchen?'

'I don't know,' said Neil, deadpan. 'Is she? I, like, *really* don't *know*, Jasmine? I've only just, like, *got here*?'

'Dad!' said Beckie, rolling her eyes at Jasmine, whose mouth might have twitched at the edges before she turned away.

The noise was even worse inside. Leaving them to shut the door behind them, Jasmine clumped her way through the hall ahead of them. The house was a mirror image of their own, with the stairs on the right of the hallway rather than the left. It always unsettled Flora, being here in this skewed, out-of-kilter version of their own home. Ailish had painted the oak panelling a soft dove-grey, and in place of Flora's beloved scruffy antiques were the 'pieces', as Ailish called them, sourced from interiors shops: a too-chunky, clumsily carved cabinet finished in pale pink chalk paint and inexpertly 'distressed', which had none of the charm of the genuine antique it was trying to emulate and probably cost five times as much; a tub chair in pink and yellow tweed; a huge mirror with fairy lights strung around it.

The whole house looked like a boutique interiors shop.

In the kitchen, Marianne was standing at the sink shrieking and flicking her hair, and dabbing at her cleavage with a cloth.

Katie and Ailish each had one of Mia's hands and were bopping to the beat, swinging the child's arms encouragingly, while Mia, standing stock-still, had a 'this too shall pass' expression on her face. The two other women in the room Flora didn't recognise. They were fussing with the candles on the table.

'Beckie!' Mia yanked her hands free and came rushing across the room to them.

Flora made herself smile down at her.

It was hard to believe that Mia was related to Ailish. She was a little tomboy with no interest in how she looked, her hair cut in a strange mullet, short at the sides and long at the back. The child cruelty aspect of this haircut featured regularly in Ailish's Facebook posts. Mia herself was presumably not meant to be aware of this, but, 'Auntie Ailish hates my hair,' Mia had told Flora with satisfaction the other day. 'She wants me to grow out the sides. But I like it. No long bits falling in my face, but long at the back to show I'm a girl.'

How frustrating for Ailish, although possibly it suited her not to press too hard to make Mia over. Mia was naturally pretty and, particularly as she grew up, would be in danger of putting Jasmine well and truly in the shade.

There were studies showing that pretty girls got away with bad behaviour more easily than their more ordinary-looking peers. Flora had read that on the internet, and had immediately thought of sparkling green eyes and an oval face and long raven hair.

'Floraaaaa!' Ailish came tottering round the table and gave her a hug. 'Hiii-yiiii! How are *you*?'

Ailish always wore heels. In her bare feet she'd have been about five foot nothing. Her hair was streaked blonde and cut in a feathered crop, her eyes carefully made up in purples and greys as if to match the kitchen. In fact, this was possible. She had a small mouth and nose and slightly upward-slanting eyes all close together in the middle of her face. Neil called her the Toxic Chipmunk.

'How about this *weather*?!'

This was a dig at Flora's suggestion, when Ailish had first mooted the idea of a May barbeque, that it was a bit risky.

'I know!' Flora beamed back at her. 'Perfect! We haven't even brought the umbrellas I had lined up!'

'I think May often *is* the best month in Scotland, isn't it?'

Mia grabbed Beckie's hand and they ran to the door and out into the sun.

Flora wanted to run after them, to pull Beckie back inside.

Neil thought her reservations about Mia were ridiculous. And they probably were. Mia was no doubt just what she seemed – a funny, rather naughty little girl who had no real malice in her. A girl who loved playing outside and using her imagination, who loved creating all sorts of worlds to run around and get grubby in.

It *was* ridiculous, to jump to conclusions about Mia being a bad influence on their daughter and being responsible for what Beckie had done to Edith, when Mia didn't even go to the same school; and neither one of them, as Neil had pointed out, had ever witnessed Mia being unkind to another child. To ban Beckie from seeing her best friend, for no good reason, *would* probably just make things worse.

Neil was right.

Annoyingly, he usually was.

But Flora couldn't help worrying about what Mia might do, unsupervised, when there were no adults watching. She was Ailish's niece, after all – and, let's face it, she was basically feral.

She set the Tupperware container with her mini-quiches on the worktop. The table was shabby-chic-ed to within an inch of its life, all vintage china and pastel plates and scented candles in moulded green glass holders.

Neil was standing staring around him as if he'd just landed on another planet.

'Iain and the boys are out there' – Ailish waved a hand at the open door – 'burning a range of meats he hunted down last night in Tesco.' She had a high, little-girl voice. 'They could probably do with another of the tribe to stand looking at it while it burns to a crisp.' Giggle.

Men Are So Funny And Hopeless was one of the themes of The Chipmunk Show, as Neil called Ailish's Facebook posts, and no doubt there'd be some photos up there tonight of Iain grinning hopelessly at a charred burger.

Neil scuttled outside. Not that he'd relish the prospect of two hours with 'Iain and the boys', but anything was presumably preferable to *this*.

And he'd be able to keep an eye on Beckie out there.

'Take a pew,' said Ailish.

At least the coffee was always good. Flora glugged it and shovelled up macarons amidst the giggles and shrieks as Ailish held court, relating the latest outrage perpetrated by her ex-sister-in-law, Mia's mother, who had an important role as the villain 'She' on The Chipmunk Show. It seemed She had thrown away the tap shoes and unitard Ailish had bought Mia a fortnight ago, last time Mia had been staying. Mia usually stayed with Ailish and family rather than with her father, Ailish's hopeless brother, on the weekends on which he was supposed to have her.

And now She was refusing to take Mia to tap dancing classes.

Marianne: 'Why do people like Her even have children, if they can't be bothered with them?'

The faces round the table were flushed, bright-eyed, eager. A pack turning on their prey. A mob at a witch's trial.

It was what Ailish did. What women like her had always

done. *She's strange, She's weird, She's a freak. Compare and contrast Her with amazing Me.*

It was at times like this that she most missed Pam. Her old life. Ruth's life.

'I could *sort* of understand it if Mia was running around going to a load of other activities, if taking her to tap once a week was going to be a problem because She couldn't fit it into their packed schedule. But the only organised activity She can be bothered taking Mia to is blooming *rock climbing!*'

Intakes of breath and pained faces.

'It's like She really is trying to turn her into Arya Stark. Next Christmas it'll be a sword called Needle! Stick 'em with the pointy end!'

Flora felt a shiver go right down her body, from shoulders to thighs.

No.

No.

This was just Ailish being Ailish.

She had to try to keep a sense of perspective here. What would Pam have said?

Pam would no doubt have agreed with Neil that Mia's mum was doing a great job, giving Mia a free-range, old-fashioned childhood, letting her play outside with her friends most days after school in their village, not caring if she got muddy or ripped her clothes, and resisting all the pressure there was these days to do so many organised activities that there was no room left for kids to do their own thing and use their imaginations.

And Pam would probably also have agreed that Mia was good for Beckie, who might come back from playing with her with a graze on her hand or a cut on her chin, but bubbling with excitement as she related their latest adventure.

But surely Pam, as a mother, would see the dangers that Neil couldn't?

Flora was going to have to speak to Neil again. Insist that she really wasn't happy about Beckie playing with Mia unless they were closely supervised.

'I – actually, I did a bit of rock climbing myself as a kid,' admitted Katie, flushing. 'It's meant to be good for... for coordination and suppleness...'

'Well, maybe if it's properly organised and safe,' Ailish conceded. 'On one of those indoor walls or whatever. But the place She takes her is just some Clampit's farm. Probably not even certified or licensed or anything – it's just this farmer who's got a quarry on his land and has decided to make a fast buck by getting a load of kids dangling off it on ropes.'

'You know,' said Katie, flushing all the more, 'I sometimes think we wrap them in cotton wool to an extent that's – in its way – *more* of a problem than letting them take some risks.'

Ailish looked at Katie as if she'd just suggested they take their offspring to the nearest motorway and turn them loose on the hard shoulder.

But Katie, for once, wasn't backing down. 'Like we did when we were their age – going out playing on our own and getting into scrapes... climbing a drainpipe, or being chased by the parkie, or swimming in a river... Never did us any harm. Quite the opposite.'

'Maybe you were lucky,' said Flora, and she couldn't quite keep the edge from her voice.

Ailish looked at her.

She hastily invented: 'A boy... in my class at school... this boy, he was drowned in a river. A group of boys were messing around one lunchtime, and he drowned.'

Ailish raised her eyebrows. 'Were you there?'

Flora could feel her face flushing. Her heart pumping. 'Not when it happened, but... I was in the playground when the other boys came running back, soaking wet and crying, and... I've never liked being in the water since. I think that's why

Beckie doesn't like swimming – she's probably picked up my feelings about it.'

Had that been convincing?

Ailish was looking at her oddly.

As the conversation turned to Jasmine and her general wonderfulness, Flora muttered something about checking on how the incineration was going and slipped through the open doors to the garden.

Ailish and Iain's garden was even bigger than theirs, as they didn't have an extension on the back of their house. But it wasn't as nice. Fewer trees and no wild areas – an expanse of perfectly mown grass and a huge area of patio, on which the men had set up the barbeque. There were three large outdoor tables with chairs round them, and one of these had been appropriated by Jasmine and her friends, all with their phones out.

The younger kids were at the end of the garden playing a game involving a lot of rushing around, hysterical laughter and shouting. This was fine, though, as the manicured nature of the garden meant there were no overgrown areas in which they could conceal themselves from adult view. They seemed to be playing harmoniously, but at the first hint of discord Flora would have no qualms about stepping in. She didn't care how many other parents she offended.

Mia, of course, was doing most of the shouting. Her cousin Thomas seemed to have been cast in the role of an animal of some sort, crawling around on all fours, mouth hanging open.

Thomas was a mouth breather.

He was pretty much airbrushed out of The Chipmunk Show. But Flora liked Thomas a lot. He was a good influence – as easy-going as Beckie but much more cautious, much less adventurous. 'Mia, *don't!*' he was often heard to exclaim when the three of them were playing together. He could be surprisingly stubborn and forceful if he felt his cousin was going too far. And Mia, equally surprisingly, would always back down when that strict note came into Thomas's voice.

If Thomas was there, Flora could maybe relax.

The men were clustered around a woman she recognised as a neighbour from a couple of doors down. She was in mid-anecdote, waving a glass of red wine and laughing, and the men were guffawing and striking poses and sucking in their bellies.

She was very attractive, but cleverly attractive, attractive in a way that looked casual and effortless, but which Flora knew was not. Her glossy hair was caught up loosely in a clip at the nape of her neck, and strands of it were coming out, caressing her bare neck and shoulders. She wore a simple khaki sweater with a low, wide neckline, dark skinny jeans and pink trainers.

She reminded Flora a bit of the girls in The Apprentice – the hard, efficient ones, all sleek suits and heels and hair, rather than the poor quirky souls Flora identified with who were obviously just there for the entertainment value. She seemed to remember Ailish saying that this neighbour was an HR consultant, whatever that entailed, always jetting off to London and Birmingham and Belfast. A single career woman with no kids, and therefore suspect in Ailish's eyes.

She was striking rather than conventionally pretty, with a strong jaw and wide mouth, and had the kind of figure Flora had always envied: slim and leggy but curvaceous. Flora had seen her out jogging in the mornings. She was the kind of woman who regarded her body in the same way as she regarded any other aspect of her life, as something in which she would achieve the highest standard possible within the bounds of a robust cost–benefit analysis.

And what was wrong with that, for God's sake? It was commendable.

Jasmine take note.

Jasmine was sitting staring expressionlessly at her phone.

There was a blank quality to her that Flora always found disturbing – it was more than the usual sullen teenage thing. It was as if the real Jasmine, whoever she was, had shrivelled up and died inside the carapace Ailish had constructed for her.

Princess Jasmine, Ailish called her with the faux-critical humour she specialised in when talking about her daughter. Jasmine, ran the subtext, had the life of a princess thanks to Ailish being a super-mum, and had an aura of royalty about her, a sheen, a polish, a butterfly beauty, for the same reason. Well, that and Ailish's genes.

Poor Jasmine. A very ordinary girl under relentless pressure to be extraordinary.

Ailish's main brand.

Stop it. She had to stop this habit of judging she seemed to have fallen into, whether it was Beckie's friends or the mums at school or her neighbours. It was as if she didn't want to make friends, as if she didn't even want Beckie to have any. As if she was determined to see the worst in people so she'd have an excuse to keep them at arm's length.

Mrs Jenner had asked if there were problems at home.

What she'd meant was: What are you doing that's messing with Beckie's head?

She crossed the patio to where Neil was standing with a glass of beer. He was the only man not in Apprentice Woman's group of swains, preferring instead to examine the contents of the small raised pond.

She sighed. 'What time is it?'

Neil looked at his watch. 'Almost 12:30. Hour and a half to go.'

'Hour and a half to go until what?' said an amused voice. It was Apprentice Woman, standing raising her eyebrows at them.

'Oh...' Flora couldn't think.

'Till we can escape,' said Neil.

'Neil!'

Apprentice Woman looked behind her, to where the other men were gathered now around the barbeque, and whispered, 'Is there a tunnel or what?'

Neil didn't lower his voice. 'Not for want of the kids trying. They've excavated about eight inches so far on our side of the wall.'

'Well, they need to get a bloody move on! So you live next door?'

'Someone has to.'

'*Neil!*'

A grin. 'Lucky for you I'm not Ailish's sister or something.'

'Lucky for *you*,' said Neil, on a roll, beaming in smug wonder at his own wit as Apprentice Woman threw back her head and laughed, clutching Flora's arm for support.

Flora couldn't help smiling too.

'Oh God,' said Apprentice Woman, 'can you imagine being actually *related*?'

And they all looked over at the teenagers' table.

'I try not to,' Flora found herself saying. 'I don't think Jasmine...' But no, she couldn't say that. She didn't even know this woman. And who was she, anyway, to criticise the way someone else was bringing up their daughter?

'Oh God, I know! Surely there must be laws she's breaking? *Seriously?* I mean, what is she thinking? Putting the poor girl all over Facebook and Instagram practically in a thong, like she's pimping her own daughter?'

Neil guffawed, spraying beer onto the flagstones.

Apprentice Woman looked behind them again to check there was no one in earshot. 'Apparently Mia's mum has started calling Jasmine "Princess Prozzie".'

Jasmine, it had to be said, did look like a prostitute.

And she must be freezing.

'Oh, so *that's* what those posts were about?' Neil grinned. 'The inspirational quotes...'

'"You can mess with me but mess with my kid and I'm coming after you with fifty shades of crazy"?'

'Where does one actually get those things?' Neil was loving this. 'Is there a website specifically catering to offended parents of fifteen-year-old girls dressed up for a walk round Leith docks?'

'Some of those posts aren't even private.'

Flora grimaced. 'I don't think she feels there's anything wrong with the way Jasmine dresses. I think she just considers it teenage culture... All the celebrities are doing it. She's desperate for Jasmine to fit in and be popular; to be an object of desire, I suppose. It's kind of sad, really.'

Good. That had sounded like Flora was trying to understand rather than judge.

A big part of the problem, she suspected, was that Jasmine wasn't pretty enough for Ailish's purposes. And so, to achieve the 'stunning' accolades Ailish was always fishing for on Facebook, a lot of work was required. The girl was always heavily made up, with those thick eyebrows, huge false eyelashes, heavy smoky eye make-up, lip-liner and glossy lipstick. Her clothes were designed to showcase her figure, which, thanks to being on a diet since she was eleven, was straight up and down with little in the way of breasts or hips. Flora suspected that the calorie restrictions may have prevented her going through puberty properly.

Neil and Apprentice Woman had assumed suitably serious faces, like kids who'd just been told off by the teacher.

'Oh oh, here she comes,' said Flora, feeling herself flushing as Ailish tottered out onto the patio with her retinue, Marianne screaming with laughter, her arm hooked through Ailish's. But then she found herself muttering at Apprentice Woman:

'Phone at the ready to get a Facebookable shot of Princess Prozzie.'

'Shot into the sun. With maximum soft-focus. God, we're such bitches.'

Flora couldn't help grinning. 'This is going to sound really bad, but I can't remember your name.' Somehow it was okay to admit this to her.

'Caroline, right?' said Neil.

'Give the man a cigar! Caroline Turnbull. And you're Flora?'

'You could at least have pretended to get it wrong.'

'Yeah, sorry, I forgot to mention I'm also irritatingly anal, so I know your daughter is Beckie and she's eight going on nine and in Thomas's class at school, and she's quite the chess champ and is teaching Thomas the finer points. Now, that's impressive, you have to admit, given that Ailish hardly ever refers to Thomas – or, for that matter, to the accomplishments of other people's children.'

'That *is* impressive,' said Neil, sitting down on the low wall of the raised pond, crossing his feet at the ankles and smiling up at Caroline. 'Being anal is a very underrated quality.'

'It is! Thank you!'

'Okay, so you can tell us all about our fellow guests, then?' said Flora, keen to divert the conversation from Ailish and her parenting shortcomings.

'Probably the only one of any interest is that guy.' Caroline tipped her head in the direction of a man standing on the edge of the barbeque group, who was looking beyond them to the table of teenagers. 'Mr Rapist.'

'Mister *what*?'

'Or Mr Serial Killer. Or Mr Rapist-hyphen-Serial Killer. Not sure. Need a few more months probably to decide. He lives upstairs from me, so I'm likely to be a target at some point.'

'And here was I,' said Flora, 'berating myself for being judgemental.'

'Hey, you're playing with the big girls now. But actually I think I could be right about him. Maybe being judgemental's not such a bad thing? Could actually save your life?'

'Yes!' Neil was really enjoying this. 'It could be that humans have adapted through natural selection to living among rapists and serial killers and what have you – only the judgemental have stayed out of their clutches and passed on their genes.'

'Looks like we're all safe then,' said Flora drily. 'So what's his real name?'

'Tony Hewson.'

'Just a rapist then,' said Neil. 'Hasn't got the serial killer ring.'

'Anthony Hewson?'

'Better. But he calls himself Tony to throw people off the scent. But okay, I'll bite – what makes you think he's either a rapist *or* a serial killer?'

'Oh... The usual. Stands too close when he's talking to you... Weird whispery voice... Stary eyes... Obsessed with the outflow pipe.'

'The what?'

'Or whatever it's called, the waste pipe thing that goes down the outside of the building? Which the baths and sinks and loos feed into? He's obsessed with it. Keeps asking me if I've had any problems with it getting blocked.'

'Body parts?' Flora mused.

'Yep, I reckon he's flushing body parts and he's worried they might back up into my bath –' Caroline broke off as a football came sailing across the pond right at her. She did a sort of hop and a jump and stopped the ball dead with her foot, then turned and flicked it up over her back to send it arcing back onto the grass.

Beckie and Thomas came running up.

'Sorry!' panted Thomas, mouth hanging open as he stared at Caroline.

'How do you do that?' said Beckie in awe, going to the ball and trying to flick it up with her foot like Caroline had done.

'Easy-peasy,' grinned Caroline, setting down her glass and jogging round the pond and onto the lawn. 'I'll show you...'

The other kids were soon gathering round. Flora heard, somewhere behind them, Marianne saying, 'She's probably in a women's football team or something,' and Ailish: 'Or just hangs around men's ones a lot,' and shrieking.

'Mr Rapist-hyphen-Serial Killer at nine o'clock,' Neil muttered.

'Shh!'

The poor man seemed more like victim material: thinning, greasy hair that looked like he cut it himself, stary eyes as advertised, and a shuffling walk. He was carrying a tray of burgers in buns.

'Hi. Tony... Can I interest you in one of these?' His voice wasn't so much whispery as very soft, so you had to lean towards him to hear.

'Oh, no thanks, I've been stuffing my face with macarons,' said Flora. 'I'm Flora and this is my husband Neil.'

Neil wiggled his fingers over the tray. 'Come to Papa!'

'You're from Number 17, yes?' mouthed Tony.

It wasn't good that they'd been in the street over a year and didn't know anyone properly apart from Ailish and Iain – although maybe that was just urban life rather than a consequence of Flora's reluctance to get involved. When they'd lived at Backhill Croft, they'd known everyone within a mile radius, whether they'd wanted to or not.

'Yes, that's right,' said Flora as Neil chomped down on the burger. 'Have you been in the street a while?'

'Yeah, a while. Over ten years.'

'Great street,' Neil mumbled with a full mouth.

'Suits me fine. I don't have a proper garden – mine's an upper flat, so I just have the little bit of ground at the front of the building –' Flora lost the rest of the sentence as it was drowned out by Mia shrieking. 'But with the Botanics right across the street, I don't feel the lack of it.' He dropped his voice still further. 'I'm in there most nights.'

'Nights?' said Flora.

'Yes, just before it shuts, you have the place pretty much to yourself.'

She had an image of him stalking his victims in the shrubberies, through the glass houses...

'And it's a great place for kids.'

Beckie suddenly intruded into Flora's imagined scene, happily skipping along a path, Tony lurking wolflike in the trees behind her.

'Do you have kids?' she asked.

'No!' He chortled, as if the idea was utterly ridiculous. 'I like kids...'

Oh here we go.

'... but I couldn't eat a whole one.' The punchline proudly delivered at normal decibels.

At this point Caroline appeared at his elbow and grabbed a burger from the tray. She had beautifully manicured hands, Flora noticed, with little shell-pink nails. 'Maybe a premmie?'

While Neil choked on his burger, Tony smiled uncertainly. Flora imagined her own smile was just as unconvincing.

'A premmie?' queried Tony, turning to stare at Caroline. He did have rather an alarming stare, it had to be said. A hungry stare.

'A premature baby,' Neil explained.

'Ah. Right. Ha, yes, maybe a premmie! Ha ha!'

Eventually he moved away, and Caroline said, 'You see?' and then she was back on Ailish again, going on about how Ailish had posted a scan of a certificate Jasmine had received at school for 'Performance Above Expectation' in her mock exams.

Neil assumed a bright, Ailish-esque smile. '"Beauty *and* brains! Super-proud mum!"'

Caroline raised her eyebrows.

'Yep,' said Flora. 'He can practically recite the posts word for word. He's obsessed.'

'Oh God, me too!' Caroline grinned at Neil. 'But doesn't she get that a certificate like that's the equivalent of a prize for taking part? Doesn't she get that posting it on Facebook is a major embarrassment for Jasmine?'

'You could basically say the same thing about the whole Show,' said Neil. And as Caroline raised her eyebrows: 'Her page. We call it The Chipmunk Show.'

Caroline smiled. 'But seriously, what about all that nasty stuff on there about Mia's mum? What if Mia read that? And wee Thomas hardly even mentioned, like she doesn't even have a son?'

'I know,' said Flora. 'She doesn't seem to spend any time with Thomas beyond the basic requirements of taking him to and from school and feeding him. As far as we can tell, the only photograph of Thomas ever to have appeared on The Chipmunk Show is that one of the whole family at Hallowe'en where Iain's a zombie, Ailish is Marilyn Monroe –'

'The scariest of the lot,' put in Neil.

'– Jasmine's a sexy fairy and Thomas is a pumpkin, with only his eyes and feet showing. Other than that, he hasn't featured. I suppose the problem is that she can't put make-up on him.'

'Although if she shot him in *really* soft focus... God, we are bitches. And whatever the male equivalent is...'

'Hey, I'm happy with bitch,' said Neil, and he and Caroline giggled away as Flora felt the smile stiffen on her face. Yes, she realised: Caroline *was* a bitch. And the worst of it was, Flora was enjoying her company. Vying with her, even, as to who could be meaner about people.

You're playing with the big girls now.

She had to get away from this woman.

She had to get out of here.

She turned to put her glass down on the wall, and caught Ailish's eye.

Oh God.

Had she heard that?

She was near enough to have heard, sitting down at a table just a few metres away, although the group of people she was with were making enough noise, hopefully, to have drowned out their conversation.

10

'Well that was a lot better than expected,' Neil said as they headed up the path to their own front door. 'Caroline's quite a character, isn't she?'

'Mm.' Flora removed the massive original key from her bag and unlocked the door, and they filed into the spacious vestibule between the front door and the inner door with its original stained-glass panels in the upper section. There were two narrow stained-glass windows on either side too, and on the floor Victorian terracotta tiles in black and brown and ochre and white.

Beckie slipped off her trainers, lined them up neatly with the others under the pew, pulled on her pink slipper socks, danced through to the hall and grabbed her tablet from where she'd left it on the stairs.

'Half an hour screen time max, Beckie!' Flora called after her as she disappeared upstairs.

Neil kicked off his shoes – literally, sending them thumping into Beckie's. 'Didn't you like her?'

'Yes, she was fun.'

'There's a *but* coming.'

'No there isn't.'

Why was it always so cold in here? His feet must be cold on the tiles, with only those thin socks on. One blue and one green, she noted, with a surge of such tenderness that she had to blink back sudden tears.

She sat down on the pew, felt under it for Neil's scabby moccasins, and chucked them over to him. Then she bent over her own shoes, taking her time with the laces, breathing long breaths.

'Flora? What is it?'

She looked up at him and he looked down at her, his eyebrows slightly raised in enquiry, his eyes so kind, so full of puzzled concern.

'Is it this stuff with Beckie at school? Listen, don't worry about it. All kids go through these phases. Pushing boundaries, they call it, don't they? I was a right little bastard to Pippa when I was Beckie's age.'

And she wanted to get up and throw her arms round his neck, to rest her head on his shoulder and cry.

She wanted to tell him.

She wanted him to hold her and say that it was all right. That she wasn't Rachel, and nor was Beckie. That Caroline wasn't Tricia. That Mia wasn't Tricia.

She looked back down at her shoes. 'But I *am* worried about it.'

'Look, I'll come with you to the meeting on Monday. I'll see if I can get Stephen to cover my honours class...'

'No, I don't mind going on my own. It's not about the meeting, Neil. It's not that.'

'Okay.' He puffed out a breath. 'I know I'm not much good at this. You... It'd be good, wouldn't it, to have a female friend to talk this stuff over with? Don't you think that maybe Caroline...? You could ask her over for coffee sometime?'

Whenever she was upset or worried, Neil's response was

always to try to come up with a solution, which usually involved her doing something, as if the problem was quite easily resolvable if only she would think it through; as if there was always something she could and should be doing about it.

So: Neil realises he's no good at talking about 'stuff' with her. Solution? Neil tries harder? Neil sits down with her and just listens? Nope. The obvious solution is that Flora needs to find someone else to talk to.

She swallowed the hysteria rising in her throat.

'Well. I could, yes. But Caroline's not the kind of woman who has many female friends, I don't think.'

'Why on earth not? Because other women feel threatened by her?'

'And why should I feel threatened by her?'

He started to splutter, 'No no. I don't mean –'

She took pity. 'I don't feel *threatened* by her, thanks very much.' Not in the way he meant, anyway. 'But I very much doubt she's got any interest in being friends with a boring old fogey like me.'

'But you must be about the same age?'

She smiled. 'Nice try. But I doubt she's even forty.' She pushed her feet into her sheepskin slippers. 'And, more importantly, she's obviously horribly indiscreet. And – well, we were as bad, weren't we?' She stood, and made herself look him in the eye. 'Two seconds into talking to her and you've regressed to Mr Tourette's and I'm not far behind. What do you think will happen if we make friends with her? We'll probably get drunk and blurt out all about Beckie and the Johnsons and having to change our names and everything.'

'No we wouldn't. And even if we did let something slip, she's hardly going to go looking for the Johnsons to tell them where we are.'

'She wouldn't have to. She'd just have to spread it about a

bit, and before we knew it someone would be tipping the John-sons off. I wouldn't put it past Ailish to do it anonymously.'

'Okay, so now you're being ridiculous.'

'Do you think she heard?'

'Do I think who heard what?'

'Ailish! Do you think she heard me saying –' She felt her face flushing all over again. 'That stuff about her not being able to put make-up on Thomas? She was right behind us. And she had this look on her face... I'm sure she heard!'

'So what if she did? Serves her right!'

'We have to live next door to these people, Neil.'

If Ailish took against her... If Flora was ever to warrant, in Ailish's eyes, the same treatment as Mia's mum, what lengths might she not go to? And Ailish was sharp. Flora could just imagine her picking up on tiny little things she had said, tiny mistakes, and sitting up into the small hours on Google.

Although, if the Linkwood Adoption Agency hadn't picked anything up, surely Ailish wouldn't?

Neil shrugged. 'Doesn't mean we have to be bosom buddies. God, I hope she bloody well did hear, if it means no more having to socialise with that lot.'

Flora felt some of the tension leave her shoulders. 'There is that. Although you realise she'd probably defriend us? No more Chipmunk Show?'

Neil stared at her. 'Christ, Flora, *what were you thinking*?... Although maybe Caroline will give us continued access to The Show, if she's not defriended by association.'

But we can't be friends with Caroline! Flora wanted to shout. *I can't be!*

Instead, she gave him a thin smile and went ahead of him into the hall.

As NEIL SLUMBERED at her side, Flora lay awake, staring at the strip of yellow streetlight in the gap between the shutters, wanting to get out of bed and draw the curtains across it but somehow not managing to summon the energy.

Every time she tried to stop thinking about Tricia her brain went crazy, whirling random thoughts around so fast that she couldn't catch hold of any of them long enough for them to be a distraction.

Tricia.

All she could think about was Tricia.

Tricia Fisher, the new girl in the last term of Primary 6. She'd been such an exotic creature, all the way from Toronto in Canada. In the little rural school near Peebles, whose windows looked out on nothing but a field of damp, windblown sheep and the bleak hillside beyond, any new child had been an excitement, but a girl from *Canada*...!

And Tricia had lived up to all their expectations.

Flora remembered her that first day, standing by Mrs Stewart's side in front of the blackboard as she was introduced to the class. She'd had long black hair, and skin that was a lovely pale brown colour, and she'd been wearing a dress with a fringe along the bottom. She'd been slim and very graceful, with a smiley face, pretty green eyes and a long nose, which somehow made her look older.

After the class had chanted, 'Hello Tricia,' and Tricia had done a funny little wave and said, 'Hi!', Kenny Scott had said, 'Are you a Red Indian?' and Mrs Stewart had gone mental at him and given them all a lecture about (a) shouting out and (b) shouting out personal questions.

Tricia had smiled and said no, she wasn't an Indian, 'I just tan real easy.'

She'd proved to be even more of a rebel than Kenny. This had become obvious that first day. They'd been doing pond life. They'd all had to look down a microscope at a smelly Petri dish with water boatmen and horrible larvae and shrimps in it doing disgusting things like eating each other alive and mating. Mrs Stewart had told them to draw one of the creatures they'd seen, but then she'd caught Tricia doodling on her jotter instead, and when she'd told her to get on with what she was supposed to be drawing, Tricia had said, 'Bugs! Who wants to know about bugs? Count me out.'

Count me out!

Rachel had thrilled at those words – so casually dismissive – and repeated them to herself in her head over and over. *Count me out.*

Imagine actually saying that to a teacher!

Mrs Stewart had seemed similarly shocked. For a long moment she hadn't said anything, just stood over Tricia's desk, blinking her pale eyelashes and putting a hand up to smooth her already smooth, neatly cropped sandy hair. 'Tricia, I don't know how things worked in your school in Canada, but in this school you don't give teachers cheek. And you do as you're told.'

'Oh, I'm sorry.' Tricia had paused in her doodling to smile up at her angelically. 'In my old school, it was okay for the kids to talk like that, you know? And if we didn't want to do something yucky, we didn't have to.'

'Well, that's not how things are here. Please take your turn at the microscope and make a drawing of one of the creatures you can see.'

Everyone had wanted Tricia as their friend, but to Rachel's amazement it had been to her own group that the Canadian girl had gravitated.

Rachel had been standing with Gail and Susie in the porch, sheltering from the rain, although by rights they weren't allowed in the building at break time – if it was raining, they were supposed to shelter under the trees or the canopy of the annex, or just get wet. But the porch was sort of half inside and half outside, a space about five feet wide between the outer and inner doors of the side entrance.

There was no heating in it, but at least it was out of the weather.

Rachel, Gail and Susie had been doing hairstyles – braiding and unbraiding each other's hair, and adding the multicoloured clips that Rachel had given Susie for her birthday. Gail was good at doing French braids. Rachel had been standing with her eyes closed as Gail's gentle fingers worked methodically down the back of her head. She loved people playing with her hair. Even the constant traffic through the porch – P7s were allowed inside the lobby during break – hadn't bothered her. They had been in their own little world.

Until the door to the lobby had crashed open and Tricia had been shoved through it by one of the prefects.

'Chrissakes! It's a school hall, not Buckingham Palace!'

Rachel had opened her eyes.

Tricia had made a face at her and grinned, and Rachel had grinned back and said, 'Yeah, but the P7s think they're royalty or something.'

It hadn't really been all that funny. But Tricia had yelled with laughter, and come and stood with them, leaning against the wall and chucking her rucksack down on the floor.

Fifteen minutes later they'd all four of them been standing in the headmistress's office, trying to explain what they thought was *funny* about putting their bags in a row in front of the porch door – which for some reason opened outwards – so that people coming in, unless they happened to glance down at their feet, tripped over them.

'Didn't you realise how dangerous that was?' Mrs Campbell had snapped at them.

Gail and Susie had been crying.

It was the first time any of the three of them had ever been in real trouble.

But Rachel had caught Tricia's eye and copied her insouciant expression. And on the walk of shame back to their classroom, Tricia had jumped up and flicked a hand at the catch on a window, punching it open to the rain, and said: 'Hey Rache, wanna come back to my place after school tomorrow? My parents don't get back for maybe two hours. And my brother can't stop us doing whatever we want.'

'Oh!' she had squeaked. 'That would be... yeah, that would be great!'

Susie had looked at her expectantly but she had turned away, watching Tricia's fingertips trailing along the wall. Tricia had had elegant fingers with long nails which made a shishing sound against the wall. Rachel later found out that her mum let her have long nails for playing the guitar.

Tricia had walked very slightly in front of the others, the hand trailing in front of them like she was marking an invisible line for them to follow.

Not *them*.

Her.

Rachel.

Rache.

'Can we come?' Gail had asked.

Tricia had pretended not to hear, talking over her.

Rache had pretended not to hear, laughing at what Tricia was saying.

Why couldn't she have smiled, and said that sounded like fun, but could they all come? Why couldn't she have told Tricia that she couldn't make it?

She hadn't even looked at Susie and Gail, she'd looked only at Tricia, at her long dark hair slapping her back as she walked, at those long nails trailing on the wall.

She still remembered the smell of those corridors: smelly gym shoes and polish and boiled beetroot.

11

I've got one of they microcloths and I'm going round Bekki's room wiping the plastic Elsa and Anna and Sven the reindeer figures, and the castle, and the sparkly brush and hairclips and jewellery box on her wee dressing table, and the lamp that's a toadstool with animals keeking out the windaes, a badger and mouse and that. Me and Mandy did the whole room over before Christmas in a *Frozen* theme, like all the wee lassies are still wanting even though the film's been out a while, but we left the toadstool lamp because what wean's gonnae care it doesnae go, eh?

Before *Frozen* we'd went for a jungle theme because Pammie had said Bekki loved animals and was into that film *Madagascar* and lemurs. I found this wallpaper with trees on it, and got Connor to fix up some real branches and dangle wee stuffed animals off of them. Looked magic. The duvet cover was called Cheeky Monkeys and had cartoon monkeys and chimps and gorillas on it, although Connor was like that: 'Chimps and gorillas arenae monkeys.' Like Bekki was gonnae care.

But all the lassies are into *Frozen* now, eh?

I go to the wardrobe and open the door and take out the

Elsa and Anna costumes. They're no Tesco shite, they're from the Disney store. One's all shiny, ice-blue, with glittery sequins on the bodice and a see-through snowflake cape. There's two skirts, a see-through one on top of a shiny one. Like it's made of ice.

The other one's even bonnier. It's got a wee red satin cape and a black velvet bodice with bonnie flowers all embroidered on it, and gold trim, and a satin blue skirt with more bonnie flowers at the hem. And at the neck there's a wee gold brooch.

When Carly saw them she went, 'She's eight, but? Too old for dress-up.'

But I'm minding me and Mandy and they princess dresses. I was eight year old and Mandy was ten, and we wasnae too old for dress-up. We loved they dresses. Maybe our lives were shite, but when we put on they dresses we were wee princesses. Mandy was Princess Vicky and I was Princess Sarah.

We called ourselves for Vicky and Sarah Ramsay, the doctor's daughters. After school this time, Mandy was crying in the lavvies because she'd lost one of her gloves and she was feart to go home, and Sarah Ramsay finds her and goes, 'Don't cry. Here, have my gloves,' and she asks Mandy if she'd like to come to her birthday party. Sarah Ramsay was in another class and Mandy didnae even know her.

Mandy goes, 'Can my wee sister come an' all?' and Sarah goes, 'Yes.'

That birthday party was pure amazing. There were sausages and miniature pies and sandwiches and salty biscuits with cream cheese and cucumber, I ate my weight of them so I did, and a shitload of crisps and nuts, and strawberry and vanilla and mint choc chip ice cream, and a big chocolate cake with 'Sarah is 11!' on it in white icing, and bowls of all different kinds of sweeties you could rake in whenever you wanted and Mrs Ramsay just smiled when you put a handful in your pooch. The Ramsays' house was a fucking mansion and all us wee lassies was allowed to go mental, running through the rooms and up and down the stair, and when Mandy was sick on the carpet Mrs Ramsay just went, 'Aw Mandy, it's okay, don't worry about it. Are you all right? Come and get a glass of water.'

The best game was sardines – one of us hid, maybe under a bed, and the other lassies had to find that first one, and then hide with her, until the last one found all the others and we'd all jump out and shout 'Sardines!' so loud it hurt your throat.

Magic.

When it was my turn to hide, Vicky went with me because I was scared in that big house on my own. Vicky was older, maybe fourteen. She could have been a model she was that bonnie, long blonde hair on her and a right bonnie face. She opened a door in Sarah's bedroom and it was like one of they stories Miss MacGregor read us at school, it was a whole other wee room that Vicky called a cupboard, and there were all these bonnie clothes on hangers all round the walls and my gob was dropping open, and I touched one of the dresses and I went, 'Are yous princesses?'

That was a right daft thing to say.

I wasnae a babby, I was eight year old.

Vicky laughed, but not in a mean way, and she went, 'Actually Sarah's too big for that dress now. Would you like it?'

When we went home we each had a carrier bag with a princess dress in it and we couldnae believe it. Mandy hid them up her coat when we got to our bit. We kept them under the bed in our room and at night we'd put them on and pretend we was Princess Vicky and Princess Sarah and we'd go to our servant: 'No they diamonds, *they* ones, you stupid fucker!' Mandy's dress was too wee for her and one of the seams ripped but it still looked dead nice. It was purple with shiny blue stripes on the skirt and a blue frill round the neck and on the ends of the sleeves, and tiny wee buttons down the front of the bodice that looked like maybe they were jewels, all sparkly blue. Mine was pink with a white lacy layer over the top and if you looked close at the lace you could see there were the shapes of flowers and that in it, and I'd stand and birl round one way and then the other and the pink skirt under the lace would swirl like it was water.

Magic.

Then one day the dresses were gone.

Must be Ma or Billy found them.

Next year we stole a wee present for Sarah from Woolworth's, a box of fruit jellies, and we were that excited counting down the days to her birthday, and even if we didnae get dresses we would get to be in the princess house with the real Vicky and Sarah.

But she never asked us.

We never went in that house again so we didnae.

No reason Sarah Ramsay would ask us again, eh? She wasnae even in Mandy's class. Sometimes she would say 'Hi' in the corridor or in the playground, but we werenae friends or nothing.

Fruit jellies were nice but.

And sometimes still, me or Mandy will go, 'Mind they dresses?'

I smooth down the skirts of the Elsa and Anna costumes and hang them back in the wardrobe.

I sit on the bed and give Shrek a coorie and imagine Bekki here, all cooried down under the duvet with Shrek. The duvet's got Anna and Elsa on it. I can never mind which is Anna and which is Elsa, but the frozen one with the blonde hair, her dress, the icy one with sparkly snowflakes and crystals, it covers half the duvet it's that long.

'She'll be back soon,' I says to Shrek.

Bekki loved her Shrek. She was that funny, all them would come in to see her chubby wee cheek pressed against Shrek's, beauty and the beast right enough, and Bekki would hold up

Shrek for them to kiss, and they'd all do it, even Ryan. Then when they'd gone, I'd sit on the floor and stroke her hair and her wee face and I'd sing that song 'It Is You' out the film. I knew all the words so I did. Each verse ended the same way.

It is you I have loved all along.

And I'm wondering if that bitch Ruth, or Flora she's calling herself now, is putting Bekki to bed and reading her a story like Bekki's her fucking wean.

Does Bekki still have that lemur?

Is she coorying down with the lemur and that Flora bitch is stroking her hair?

But I cannae think about it.

I cannae think about they fuckers or I'll go mental so I will.

I put Shrek back on the pillow. The pillow's baby-blue with a giant white snowflake and 'Like a snowflake I'm one of a kind' on it. If Bekki likes all this shite we can take it with us to Spain. Weird but, snowflake bedding and mobiles and that, when it's thirty fucking degrees.

I go down the stair and get my coat. I leave the heating on low and a light on in the hallway. Then I pick up my bag and lock up and head off down the wee lock-block drive to the street. It's a cul-de-sac with landscaping and grass and bushes and a blossom tree on the corner that you can see from Bekki's windae. All the houses in this street are brand new newbuilds, some double-fronted detached like ours and some semidetached, all matching in with white walls and red tiles and wee porches. Dead nice.

I cannae wait, so I cannae, till I'm in the house with Bekki and Carly and Connor. We're bringing her here when we first get her, and Jed and them will stay at our bit. Then it's *Viva Espana*!

I power-walk to the bus stop and when I get there I get out my phone and take a deek at the photies Ryan took last time he was out there. The windaes are in, and the glass doors out to the patio round the pool. Rooms are massive by the way. Ryan's getting a sound system put in through the whole house, and the heating's gonnae be remote-controlled.

It's raining and I'm all bumfled up in a scarf and my big coat and boots. There's no wee neds at the stop like there would be at our bit, bevvying and yowling and chucking Minstrels at the motors from packets they've robbed from the shop. There's just an old couple with a wee laddie, and they're reading the timetable up on the shelter and the wee laddie keeps going, 'What does *that* say, Nana?' and when she reads out 'Bearsden' he goes, 'Are there *real* bears in Bearsden?' like he's hoping, and the old guy goes, 'Aye, Christopher, there's one there look driving that bus' and the woman's like that: 'Silly Granda.'

Nana smiles at me.

I goes, 'There was once a bear in Bearsden, but that was hundreds of year ago. The laird's sons kept a bear cub in a pit.' I looked it up on the internet in case Bekki asks. The bear died, but I'm no gonnae tell Bekki that bit. I've a wee story ready. 'But that was cruel, eh, and the poor wee bear didnae like it. It wasnae a proper den, it was just a hole in the ground with nothing for the wee cub to coorie down in. He was cauld. The laird's sons couldnae be doing with him and hardly ever came to play with him any more. They were more interested in drinking fancy wine and that. The bear cub was lonely. He didnae like it in that pit, so he didnae.'

'Oh, the poor wee bear!' says Nana. 'What happened to the poor wee soul?'

Christopher's looking up at me with big blue eyes. He's pure gorgeous so he is, with that soft creamy skin bairns have, and I want to pick him up and squeeze him and pinch his wee cheeks.

I give him a big smile.

'Did he escape?' he whispers.

'Oh aye, he escaped all right. He got out the pit one night

and ran away, and after lots of adventures he found a nice fisherman with a cottage by the sea who had always wanted a bear for a wee pal, and he lived there in a cosy den lined with wool from the man's sheep, and he went swimming by the man's boat when he went out fishing, and just had a rare time altogether.'

'He lived happily ever after,' goes Christopher.

Aye, in the version I'm telling Bekki, that's the happy ever after.

But now I'm thinking: wee fucker, everything's happy ever after for wee Christopher, eh, and Nana and Granda, off home for tea and fucking crumpets. While my Bekki doesnae even know who the fuck I am. I'm no her nana, I'm just a fucking random.

So aye I shouldnae, but I cannae help it, I goes, 'He's happy aye, but then this big fierce mad dug comes along, and it fights the wee bear and gies it rabies so it does, and the bear goes fucking mental.'

Christopher's wee face!

Nana's and Granda's!

'Fucking mental, and when the nice fisherman comes and goes, "Here, wee bear, let's us go for a swim, aye?" the bear opens his gub like that!' I pull back my lips and give Christopher a good long deek at my molars. 'And he jumps on the man and rips his fucking head off!'

Nana grabs Christopher and wheechs him out the shelter, and Granda hyters after them, but the bus is pulling up. I go and stand at the door but I dinnae get on, I pretend I'm looking in my purse for change, so they have to come back past me. Christopher's greeting and Nana flings him up the steps and as Granda goes past me he's like that: '*Bitch.*' And then: 'You need help,' like that's me telt.

I goes, '*Excuse me?* I think you should maybe watch your language in front of the bairn, aye?' real loud. As they move on down the bus I goes, 'You heard that, Driver? You heard that man giving me verbals, calling me a bitch and that, just because I wasnae quick enough looking out my change? That's sexist. That's misogynistic so it is. Are you gonnae respect my right to get on a bus without being fucking abused by a sexist prick or are you no?'

The driver sighs and gets out his seat and goes down the bus and says to Granda:

'Okay sir. *Aff.*'

And that's their nice wee day out turned to pish.

12

The corner shop was literally on a corner, the door across the angle of the block, with fresh fruit and vegetables displayed on stands to either side – although Flora never bought any of them because she worried about them soaking up pollution from the busy road. Inside, though, one whole wall contained shelf after shelf of wonderful old-fashioned sweets in big glass jars, all with natural colours and flavourings.

On a Monday after school she and Beckie always came this way rather than taking the quieter, more scenic walk through the leafy back streets, so that Beckie could get her treat. Compensation for it being a Monday. She usually chose jelly babies. They weren't the usual kind, they were smaller and sharper and 'more diverse', as Beckie put it. They had counted nine different flavours in total. Beckie's favourites were the purple ones, and Jennifer, the girl who usually served them, always tried to get as many of those on the little shovel as she could.

Flora was partial to the jelly babies herself – Atkins was

ancient history. They always got a little bag each and ate them as they walked home.

But today, Flora had come this way on automatic pilot.

She had no intention of going in.

She turned and looked at her daughter, who'd been walking a couple of paces behind her all the way rather than bouncing and chattering at her side as usual.

'Are we getting jelly babies?' Beckie muttered.

'No.'

'Is it my *punishment*?'

'Well Beckie, don't you think you *should* be punished?'

Beckie shrugged.

She'd done a lot of that in the mediation discussion. A lot of shrugging and sighing and saying 'Yeah,' while little Edith had sat so still on her chair next to her mum, and kept aiming pathetic little mini-smiles at Beckie, identical to the ones her mum, Shona, gave Flora. As if it were Edith and Shona who were at fault here.

Mother and daughter were both very petite, almost malnourished-looking, with pale, thin hair pulled back from their bony faces, pink scalps prominent along their partings. Like old photographs of Victorian slum-dwellers. Flora had wondered if maybe Shona was anorexic and Edith didn't get enough to eat at home. Maybe she could give Beckie some nutritious snacks to take to school, with strict instructions to give them to Edith? Falafels or some of those mini-rolls with chicken salad, or houmous and avocado. And dried fruit and unsalted nuts. It could be part of Beckie's reparations.

Beckie's so-called apology had been just embarrassing. 'I'm sorry I pushed you, Edith, I –'

'Uh, Beckie, I don't think it was just a push, was it?' Mrs Jenner had interrupted.

Beckie had sighed. 'I'm sorry I "hit" you, Edith.'

And Edith – little Edith had smiled and said, 'That's okay.'

Now Beckie was kicking at a crisp bag, not looking at her.

Flora said, 'You're not getting any jelly babies, and you won't be until I see a big improvement in your behaviour generally, and in particular until I hear from the teachers and Mrs Jenner that you've stopped being so nasty to Edith. Now come on.'

Flora started walking.

At the end of the block she looked back to make sure Beckie was following. She was scuffing along with her head down, the picture of martyred dejection.

She fixed a smile to her face. 'Come on, darling.'

Beckie looked up. She wasn't crying – Beckie rarely cried. But she didn't return Flora's smile.

Flora walked back to her and pulled her against her side. 'It's okay. I'm not angry. I'm not *happy* about it, and yes, you *do* need to be punished when you do something so wrong, but I'm not angry, and neither is Dad. But you have to talk to us and tell us the truth, so we can sort it out and work out why you've been doing this.'

If there was a *why*.

There hadn't been a *why* for Tricia and Rachel.

They hadn't been acting out. Neither of them had had problems at home.

They'd done it because it had been fun.

It had been fun to scare little Adrian Drummond in Primary 3 so much he skittered in his shorts – she could still see the brown stream of it running down his leg; remember the feeling of amazement that she had such power over someone else's bowel movements. It had been fun to chase poor Gail round the bike shelter, after they'd found out she'd been born on a Wednesday, and chant: 'Wednesday's child is full of woe! Wednesday's child is full of woe!' until Gail broke down crying: 'I am *not* full of woe!'

Beckie was glaring up at her. '*I* haven't done *anything*. But you don't believe me.'

'We can sit down and you can tell us your side of it.'

'And you still won't believe me.' Beckie wriggled out from under her arm and began to run away up the pavement, rucksack bouncing on the back of her maroon sweatshirt.

'Beckie!' Flora ran after her. 'Beckie, stop right there!'

As it became obvious that Beckie wasn't going to stop, and that Flora wasn't going to catch up, she yelled: 'Be careful of the traffic!'

God, Flora was unfit. She had to slow to a walk within two blocks, chest heaving.

Beckie was out of sight.

She was almost nine. She had good road sense. She'd be fine.

Flora had handled this so badly.

Okay, so, despite what Neil might think, it was pretty much cut and dried that Beckie was guilty as charged, given what Mrs Jenner had herself witnessed, but Flora should have heard Beckie out properly. When she'd first broached the subject of Edith on Friday over that jigsaw, she should have said something like, 'Are you having a problem with a girl called Edith at school?' and let Beckie talk, let her give her side, and then carefully bring up the hitting, and if Beckie denied it, gently point out why she knew Beckie wasn't telling the truth – pulling Mrs Jenner out of the bag as star witness – and encourage her to own up to what had really happened.

At last she was crossing the road and turning into their street, breathing in the fresh green smells, relaxing a little, as she always did, at the sight of trees and hedges and grass and flowers. In the garden of the Tudor-effect house there was a carpet of bluebells on the raised grassy area in front of one of the mullioned windows.

Rather spoiling the ambience, though, was the man walking a hundred metres or so ahead of her. He was in dirty jeans and a football top which revealed tattooed arms, quite sinewy for a man in, what, his sixties? He looked like he might be drunk, walking with a sort of rolling swagger.

Further down the road she could see Beckie. She was standing by the privet hedge that belonged to one of the other semidetached houses a few down from theirs, plucking leaves off it. Flora waved, but Beckie didn't respond.

Flora increased her pace.

The man had weaved across the pavement, putting himself on course for a collision with Beckie.

'Beckie!' she called, and started to run.

The man stopped a few paces from Beckie and said something to her.

Beckie shrugged.

'Beckie, come here!' Flora shouted.

The man turned.

He had protruding ears, a long, gaunt face with a stubbly chin and stubbly close-cropped hair.

It was the face that had stared out at her from the mugshot Saskia Mair had shown her, from the photographs in the press she'd dredged up about his convictions, from her own imagination in recurring, half-remembered nightmares.

It was Jed Johnson.

She was running full tilt now, her bag bouncing on her hip.

'Beckie!'

But Beckie just stood there.

'Get away from her!'

As she came running up he lurched towards Beckie, and Beckie whimpered and dodged past him to clutch at Flora.

'I'm calling the police,' she said, her arms tight round Beckie.

'Aye, call the fucking polis!' He staggered and half-fell

against the hedge. 'I need to report a fucking theft! Fucking theft of *my fucking granddaughter!*'

Flora edged round him, Beckie clinging to her.

'There y'are hen! Wee Beckie!' He pushed himself upright. 'I'm your granda! I'm your granda, hen!'

'No you're not!' Beckie wailed.

Flora pulled her along the pavement in the direction of Number 17 and safety, but suddenly there were two more men in front of them, a grinning thug and a handsome man in a suit, and oh God, she recognised them too, they were Travis and Ryan Johnson, and then Flora was screaming, stupidly screaming:

'Help! Please help us!'

She pulled Beckie towards the road but there was a huge four-by-four parked tight up against the kerb, close up to the car in front. She turned round but Jed had moved up behind them. Beyond him, she could see Ailish and Thomas coming along the pavement.

'Ailish!' she screamed. 'Help! Ailish!'

Beckie was clutching Flora's arm so hard it hurt. Flora pressed her to her chest. 'Get away from us! Get *away!* You'd better go before the police get here!'

'Oh I'm so scared!' Travis Johnson tittered.

'She *fucking stole you off of us!*' Jed suddenly roared in Beckie's face. 'You want to stay with her? You want that?'

Beyond him, she could see Ailish's rapidly retreating back. She had Thomas by the hand and was trotting away in her high-heeled boots. Thomas was staring back at Flora, mouth open.

'Help us!' Flora yelled, hugging Beckie.

Across the road there was an elderly couple on the pavement that ran alongside the high hedge of the Botanic Gardens. They had stopped and were staring across.

'Please help us!' she yelled at them. 'They're trying to take my little girl!'

And then suddenly someone else was yelling, a woman was yelling, 'Flora! It's okay, the police are coming!' and Caroline came running out at a gate and barging past Jed Johnson to stand between the two thugs and Flora and Beckie, phone held aloft like a weapon. 'I'm filming this! Back off!'

'They're trying to take Beckie!' Flora gasped, and now Beckie was properly crying, wailing, shaking against her. 'It's all right, it's all right,' Flora kept repeating, stupidly. She could see wee on the pavement by Beckie's feet.

'It's okay Beckie, they're not going to touch you,' said Caroline.

And it was a miracle, because the thugs *did* back off.

'Come on, Da. Leave it.'

The one in the suit, the one she was sure was Ryan Johnson, pointed a fob at the four-by-four and it flashed its lights. He opened the back door and half-threw Jed into the back seat. Then he turned to Caroline, and then Flora, aiming his hand at them like a gun.

'See yous later.'

He jumped up into the driver's seat and the four-by-four was reversing, and then roaring away almost before he'd closed his door.

Caroline still had her phone pointed at it.

'Oh thank you thank you,' Flora babbled.

'Number plate,' said Caroline briskly: 'RJ MAG16.'

'I don't know how to thank you.'

'You *saved* our *lives*!' Beckie sobbed.

Caroline smiled. 'Oh, I don't think so, sweetheart. They were just cowards, weren't they? Amazing how many people are, when they realise they're being recorded. Right. I didn't actually have time to call the police. I'll do that now. I can show them this footage... You get inside. Lock the doors. Or actually, no, you'd better come to mine. Yeah?'

'Thank you.' It was all Flora could find to say.

'No problem.'

'Mum,' whispered Beckie.

'It's all right, darling. It's all right now.'

'I've wet myself.'

Flora hugged her tight. 'Oh Beckie, don't worry about that, silly.'

Caroline ushered them back along the pavement and in at the gate to Number 13.

'I can't go into her house all wee,' whispered Beckie.

The Victorian hallway of Number 13 had an ugly 1970s partition across it, in which were set two frosted-glass doors. Through the left-hand one she could see the distorted shape of the stairs which must lead to the upper flat. Caroline unlocked the door on the right, saying:

'I don't know about you, but I could murder a cuppa.'

'Mum!' said Beckie, desperately, pulling back against Flora's arm, standing carefully on the mat.

'Beckie's had a little accident,' said Flora. 'Would it be okay if we cleaned up...?' She hunkered down and started to unbuckle Beckie's shoes.

'Of course, don't worry about it, sweetheart!'

Shoes and socks off and stuffed into a carrier from Flora's bag, Beckie clutched onto Flora again. The two of them moved crab-like through the doorway. Beckie's bare feet, very white against the parquet floor, were small in relation to the rest of her, as if the growth spurt of last year hadn't reached them yet, still little and chubby and babyish.

'Bathroom's just in there.' Caroline gestured. 'Come through to the kitchen when you're ready, okay-doke? There're clean flannels and towels and that in the cupboard in there.'

They joined Caroline in the kitchen five minutes later,

Beckie with her arms held stiffly at her sides against her skirt, mortified that underneath she wasn't wearing any pants. The kitchen was at the back of the house, like theirs was, but there the resemblance ended. Caroline's kitchen was a 1980s country 'oak' monstrosity. It was neat as a pin, though, with the minimalist look that younger people seemed to favour. No fridge magnets, no colourful oilcloth on the table, no bits and bobs. No 'clutter', as Caroline would probably refer to the stuff in their kitchen.

'Here's some socks and slippers – they'll be a wee bit big...' Caroline indicated a pair of socks with dogs all over them and some fluffy slippers which she'd set on one of the kitchen chairs. 'Tea? And what about you, sweetheart? The only juice I've got is apple. That do you?'

Beckie nodded as she pulled on the socks. 'Thank you.'

Caroline went to the fridge, brought out a carton of juice – the stuff made from concentrate, but who the hell cared – and turned back to Flora. 'Tea, coffee?'

'Whatever you're having.'

'Tea with sugar's meant to be good for shock, eh, according to *Coronation Street* anyway?'

Flora smiled.

Caroline made the drinks and shook some plain digestives onto a plate. 'Sorry, haven't got anything more exciting. I'm a crap hostess at the best of times, but I'm just back from a week away with work and the cupboard is bare. Ish. Let's go through to the lounge, yeah, and relax? Till the police get here anyway. I think they'll probably class this as non-urgent – they asked me whether the situation was "ongoing" and like an idiot I said no. So it could be a while.'

'Oh, but we won't hang around – I mean we won't take up your time. I'm sure you're busy.'

'Nothing that can't wait.'

Translation: *I am busy, but I'm being nice. Yeah?*

The lounge was a depressing room decorated in beige and brown and silver. Flora and Beckie sat on the sofa and Caroline took one of the armchairs.

'Thank you so much for what you did,' said Flora.

Caroline was offering Beckie a biscuit. 'Honestly, Flora, stop it, it was nothing. It wasn't any more than anyone else would have done.'

'No – that's not true. Ailish was there. I shouted to her and she couldn't run fast enough in the opposite direction.'

Caroline made a face. 'Why doesn't that surprise me?'

They both smiled.

'They were the Johnsons, weren't they?' said Beckie suddenly.

Flora hugged her. 'Don't worry darling, they're not going to come anywhere near us again. The police will sort it all out.'

'But it was them?'

'Yes.'

'That man – he's really my – grandad?'

'No. The only connection you have with them is genetic.'

'But he's my genetic grandad?'

Caroline was pretending she wasn't hearing this, sipping her tea and looking out of the window. There was a lovely view over the privet hedge of the cherry blossom across the street in the Botanics.

'He's genetically your biological mother's father. Yes.'

Beckie's lips trembled. 'He's horrible. They're all horrible. They're *evil*. That's why I was taken away from them, isn't it?'

'Well darling, they weren't able to look after you properly, and maybe some of them aren't very nice people, but I wouldn't say they were *evil*.' Wouldn't she? 'They've had – difficult lives, I should think, and when people –'

'They might come back. They probably will. How can the police stop them?'

Oh God.

'Beckie,' said Caroline. 'You saw how they reacted when all I did was point my phone at them, didn't you?'

Beckie nodded.

'I mean, look at me. Okay so I do kick-boxing and karate, and I once punched my big brother's nose and made it bleed... But really? There were three of them, two of them big strong guys, but when a skinny wee woman stood up to them they legged it out of here, didn't they? You don't need to be scared of them.'

'But you might not be there next time.'

Shame flooded through Flora. She should be the one Beckie looked to to protect her, not some random neighbour they hardly even knew.

Caroline, she saw, was looking at her. 'Well, how about I teach your mum some self-defence moves so she can kick their arses, eh? Oops, sorry, bad word slipped out there.'

'That's okay.' Beckie was grinning now. 'Stress of the moment.' It was what Neil said when he accidentally swore in Beckie's hearing. 'Could you teach me too?'

'Sure thing. It's mainly a matter of confidence –'

'And my dad?'

'Hey, let's throw in the dog while we're at it, let's ninja up the whole family!'

Beckie laughed. 'We don't have a dog, but we have a hamster.'

'Ninja-hamster? Works for me.'

'You're so cool. You're like Xena Warrior Princess or something. Although actually no, she's not that cool. Not as cool as you.'

'Why, thank you. You're pretty cool yourself. You're being a very brave girl, I reckon.'

Beckie flushed. 'No I'm not. I was useless. I just – basically I just cried. And peed my pants.'

'Well of course you did. It was horrendous for you both.

Really horrendous.' And she set down her mug and reached over and touched Flora's arm. 'How are you doing?'

There was so much kindness in her voice.

All Flora could do was nod.

SHE'D KNOWN it was going to be bad, telling Neil, but she hadn't expected this.

He was shaking.

He was looking at her with repressed fury in his face.

They were standing facing each other in the cramped, bleach-infused en suite of the hotel room. Beckie was finally asleep. She'd been hyper for the last few hours, insisting on exploring every inch of the hotel 'to make sure it's safe' and insisting on both of them coming with her. Trekking after her down one endless corridor after another, each the same, each with a synthetic blue carpet, magnolia walls and row after row of identical veneer doors, Flora had muttered to Neil that it was as if they had somehow become trapped in *Minecraft*.

And then they'd turned a corner and Beckie had almost walked into the big belly of a man coming the other way, and she'd screamed, clutching Neil, and burst into tears. The poor man had stood there blinking and saying, 'Sorry. Sorry, is she okay?'

She wasn't okay. Of course she wasn't.

Back in the room, she'd sobbed into Flora's chest, this little girl who never cried, and gulped out, of all things: 'I'm sorry I was so horrible to Edith.'

'Oh darling, never mind about that.'

'Do you think I'm horrible?'

And Flora had squeezed her tight as she felt it again, that sick weight in the pit of her stomach that she'd carried around all her teenage years, the weight of knowing that her mother didn't love her any more. That she'd forfeited her love.

At the time she hadn't blamed her mother, only herself. But since Beckie, she could no longer understand it.

How could a mother's love not be entirely unconditional?

'There is nothing you could do, my little Beckie,' she had said, 'that would ever make me think you were horrible. There is nothing you could do that would ever make me or Dad love you even a millionth trillionth bit less.'

'My turn for a hug,' Neil had said then, in a choked voice, and then they'd bathed her together, like she was a toddler again, and brushed her hair, and snuggled with her in the big bed with packets of crisps, Beckie's tablet and the usually forbidden *EastEnders* on the big TV.

And now she was finally asleep.

'How could you let it happen?' Neil said now.

'What do you mean, how could *I*?'

'She's eight years old! How could you let her go off on her own –'

'I didn't *let her go off on her own* – she ran away from me!'

'Well she's never done that when I've been with her.'

Flora took a breath. 'Okay. I'm sorry I didn't stop her running away from me. She flounced off in a huff because –'

'And how did they find us?'

'That's my fault too, is it?'

'I don't know. Is it?'

He was lashing out because he was scared. She took another breath. 'Maybe it is. I don't know, Alec, because I've no idea how they found us.'

'*Neil!* It's *Neil!* Although what the hell does it matter now?'

'Shh. You'll wake her.'

He sat down, suddenly, on the loo.

She leant back against the cool tiles. 'They've found us. It doesn't matter how. What matters is what we're going to do about it. The police are obviously not going to take effective action. We have to try to discuss this calmly and sensibly and decide what we're going to do.'

There was a long, heavy silence, and then he lowered his head. 'Yes. I'm sorry.'

Tentatively, she touched his shoulder. 'Maybe I should have called you. But there was nothing you could have done.'

He took in a long breath. 'No, it's okay.' He put his hand over hers. 'It must have been... terrifying.'

He stood, and for a long, still moment, they held each other. Then Neil said, 'So what exactly did the police say? Did they take a statement from Caroline too?'

She pulled away from him and ran a hand through her hair. 'Yes. We both gave statements, separately, and they took the footage off her phone. I told them I'd recognised the Johnsons from photos in the press – I didn't land Saskia in it by saying she'd shown us photos. Caroline says she told them she heard Jed Johnson shouting about how we'd stolen Beckie from them –'

'Did he actually say he was going to take Beckie?'

'No, not in so many words, unfortunately. And my statement... when it was written down, what they did say didn't sound that bad. Not as... threatening as it actually was.'

'But Caroline's footage...'

'There's no audio on it.'

'Couldn't you have made something up? Said they said "Beckie's ours and we're taking her back" or something?'

'Well, in hindsight, maybe, but Caroline and I would have had to collude...'

'So they're not going to do anything, basically?'

'They're going to question the Johnsons about breaching the court order prohibiting contact with us or Beckie, and depending on what they say, they could be charged.'

'And then what? A few hours' community service? It was

practically an assault! If Caroline hadn't been there... Isn't it classed as an assault, or threatening behaviour or...'

'Apparently not. The footage shows they made no move to touch us.'

'Attempted kidnap?'

'There's no proof of that.'

'Harassment? Is that a thing? Stalking?'

'Apparently a single altercation in the street doesn't constitute harassment or stalking. It needs to happen at least twice.' She took a deep breath. 'We have to go. We have to disappear again.'

'How many times?' And suddenly Neil was shouting at her: '*How many fucking times, Flora?*'

What did he mean? What did he mean by that?

With a guilty look at the door, he lowered his voice: 'How many times are we going to have to run from them?'

She breathed. 'We'll make sure, next time, that they can't find us.'

'And how are we going to do that, if we don't even know how they found us this time?' He shook his head. 'It's not fair on Beckie. She's only just stopped asking when she's going to see Emma. And crying about Hobo. She's made new friends. She's settling in –'

'And how *not fair on Beckie* is it going to be if the Johnsons snatch her?'

'But is that their intention?'

'Of course it is!'

They lapsed into silence. Neil sat down again on the loo.

'This doesn't make any sense,' he said slowly, as if offering some profound insight.

'Well, that's life,' she said impatiently. 'As you keep telling me. Life isn't supposed to make sense. It doesn't have any *meaning*. We're all just trying to survive as best we can.'

'No,' he said, with a faint smile. 'I don't mean life generally. I mean the Johnsons. If they're such desperados, if they're so determined to get Beckie back, why didn't they take her? There was just you there, at first, before Caroline arrived on the scene – and even then, two women against three Glasgow toughs? If they'd wanted to take her, they could have done.'

'The police would have acted, though, if they had. They'd have got Beckie back.'

'Only if they knew where to find her. Think about it. If the situations were reversed – if the Johnsons had Beckie and you had an opportunity to snatch her – you'd do it, wouldn't you, you'd take her and disappear? We've shown it can be done.'

'Maybe they don't want to disappear. And even if they did... I can't imagine they'd be too good at blending into the woodwork. Assuming new identities – it takes a bit of doing.'

'They'll have all kinds of dodgy contacts. Disappearing would be far easier for them than it was for us. No. I'm thinking... Maybe they don't actually want her back. Maybe they just want to cause trouble. Maybe they just want to...' He shrugged. 'Punish us.'

'*Punish us*? For what?'

'For giving her what they couldn't?'

'But that's... mad.'

'I don't think they're the most mentally stable people in the world.'

Suddenly she was just so tired. It was vitally important that they thought this through, that they made the right decisions, decisions that would determine the rest of Beckie's life, but she felt as if they were both floundering, adrift, the two of them and Beckie in this hotel room, while all around them the sharks circled in a vast, indifferent ocean.

No one was going to come to their rescue.

It was down to them.

'Whatever their intentions, running away again isn't the answer,' said Neil.

Flora opened her mouth to argue, and then closed it.

The idea of yet another identity standing between her and Rachel – was it a dangerously appealing idea she was too eager to embrace? Was she thinking more of herself than of Beckie?

It had been so hard for Beckie to leave her old life behind, to sever all ties with it. And she'd been so scared when they'd told her the reason why.

But not as scared as she was now.

'So what *is* the answer, then?'

Neil sighed. 'We need to know what exactly it is we're up against. Didn't Deirdre say the Johnsons didn't actually pose a danger, to Beckie or to us, in her opinion? What happened today supports that. They didn't actually physically hurt you, did they? That supports what Deirdre's said all along. But we didn't listen to Deirdre. We listened to Saskia.'

'You weren't there. It felt like a pretty dangerous situation to me.'

'Yes, I know. I'm sorry, I didn't mean –'

'And Deirdre never even met the Johnsons. Saskia knows much more about them than she does.' She shook her head. 'But you're right. We have to know what the Johnsons are likely to do before we make any decisions.'

'Yes. Yes.' He sounded bone-tired too.

'We need to talk to Saskia.'

13

I'm raging so I am.

I've got the Three Stooges in the front room, Travis and Ryan on the settee and Jed on the La-Z-Boy, but I cannae sit, I'm moving to the windae and across to the door and back to the windae. I cannae look at them.

I'm fucking raging.

'What did you say to her?'

'I didnae say shit!' goes Jed.

'Aye?' goes Ryan. 'How was she greeting her face off then, Da? How was she pishing herself?'

'Aye she was feart, any wee lassie would have been feart. But I didnae say nothing to her.'

Jed's back chain-smoking and the air's minging with it.

'You're no smoking round Bekki,' I goes. 'Put that fucking fag out.'

'Bekki's no here.'

I'm in his face. '*Put*. That fucking. Fag. *Out*.' And I'm snatching it from his gob and stubbing it out on the fucking La-Z-Boy, and he's jumping up and in my face:

'Get off my case Lorraine!'

'Oh, I'm no on your case! When I'm on your case, you'll know about it!' I push him back down on the La-Z-Boy.

What did I ever see in the fucking prick?

But I'm stuck with the bass. He'd no last five minutes out there on his own, so he wouldnae, the fucking loser.

He's the reason Shannon-Rose is the way she is – fucking mentalist DNA.

I sit down in my chair and go to Travis, 'Get me a rum and Coke, son.'

While he's up at the sideboard, I eyeball Jed. 'You're no going near Bekki again. You're outta this.'

'Am I fuck.'

'Aye, you are fuck. You want Bekki so feart that when we get her she's gonnae go running off to the fucking polis first chance she gets? We cannae keep her locked up the rest of her life!'

'Aye Da,' goes Ryan. 'Keep your neb out, aye?'

Jed goes in a huff, sitting like a big bairn in the La-Z-Boy with his arms folded, eyeballing the carpet.

Travis hands me my rum and Coke and goes to look out the windae. 'Polis.'

Through the nets I can see them pulling up in the street. 'Right,' I goes. 'Yous were at the Botanic Gardens and then you –' I point at Jed '– saw Bekki. Aye she's a lot older but you'd know her anywhere. It wasnae an intentional breach of the court order. Aye?'

Jed gives me evils.

'You never touched they bitches. You never touched Bekki.'

'We didnae,' goes Travis.

'But you've got to keep on about it, aye? We dinnae want no trouble, we're just that upset. Seeing Bekki was hard for yous. But we're no gonnae do nothing. We're no gonnae snatch her. She's best off where she is, aye? We're no gonnae make contact again.'

The doorbell rings.

Ryan gets up, a wee smile on his face. The local polis are all shit-scared of Ryan. He goes out to the hall and I hear the door opening and Ryan going:

'Gentlemen! What can we do for yous?'

Travis sits back down on the settee. 'What if they flit again, Maw?'

I lean forward. 'They're no flittin'. They're no going nowhere.' I lean back. 'Now shut it.'

FLORA AND NEIL were shown into a room dominated by a large table. The surface was some kind of cheap veneer, scuffed and scratched and lifting in places. There was a tray in the centre with mugs, a cream jug and a bowl of coffee-stained sugar. A plate of biscuits.

The tall man asked: 'Tea or coffee?'

Neil shook his head. Flora asked if she could have a glass of water.

The man went to a cooler in the corner of the room.

The others sat down at the table, and the woman who'd introduced herself as Yvonne Richards smiled and said, 'I'm so sorry this has happened.'

'I don't know how they can have found us,' said Flora as she sat down and the tall man placed the water in front of her. 'Thank you.'

'Is Saskia not going to be here?' said Neil. 'Even if she doesn't work for you any more, would it not be possible for her to be here?' They'd been told that Saskia Mair no longer worked for Glasgow City Council. 'She knows more about the Johnsons than anyone. We need to talk to her. We need to know how much of a danger they actually pose to us.'

Yvonne exchanged a quick look with the other woman, Frances someone, then sat down at the table, placed her forearms on it and leant towards them. She was about Flora's age, with a round face, big eyes and a Cupid's bow mouth, like a child's drawing of a woman. 'Saskia Mair doesn't work here any more because she's been suspended. It's – I'm afraid it's a very sensitive matter and not yet in the public domain.'

'She's under police investigation,' said the man.

Yvonne flicked him a look. 'We feel that it's necessary, given the circumstances, to tell you what's happened, but I do have to stress that this is confidential. Any media attention could jeopardise a future prosecution.'

'Prosecution? For what?'

'I'm afraid this is going to come as a shock.' Yvonne looked past them to the door, as if wishing she could make a break for it. 'Saskia Mair has been accused of harming a child to whose case she was assigned.'

Neil grabbed Flora's hand under the table. '*Harming a child? Saskia?*'

'I don't believe it,' said Flora. 'I'm sure Saskia would never do that.'

It was as if some evil god was playing with her, with her life, with the people in it. Taking everything and twisting it out of shape.

Yvonne sighed. 'There is video evidence.'

The man said, 'Saskia Mair was assigned to the case of a family with a small child, a boy of three, on the at risk register. She reported that she felt he was at imminent risk of harm. After a visit to the family, she applied for an emergency child protection order, saying she'd found unexplained cuts and bruises on the child's body.'

'That's what happened with Beckie,' Flora said numbly.

'Yes, I know.'

'The family are saying it was Saskia? Who hurt the boy?'

Yvonne nodded. 'They're not just saying it. They have video

evidence. They'd set up hidden cameras in all the downstairs rooms because – well, it's not relevant, but the child's father suspected his partner's brother of stealing cash from them. Anyway. The camera in the back bedroom, where Saskia was examining the child, caught her hitting him with a rolled-up umbrella and cutting his skin with nail scissors.'

Flora gripped Neil's hand tight. 'Oh God.'

'Saskia has admitted it,' said the man. 'She said she did it to enable the child to be removed from the family. She said she needed evidence of harm, and there wasn't enough.'

'So she supplied it,' Neil said hollowly.

'She supplied it.' Yvonne closed her eyes briefly. 'Which is a terrible thing to have done. But Saskia – she was under a tremendous amount of pressure. The well-being of these children was in her hands. Their lives, in some cases. The strain of it evidently just got too much and she... I'm not excusing her. But what she did... She only did it because she thought, mistakenly of course, that it was the right thing to do for the children.'

'She did it to Beckie,' Flora said. 'She hurt Beckie.'

'She's denying ever having done it before or since,' said the man. 'But there is a possibility – we feel it's unlikely to have been an isolated incident. The police investigation will include Beckie's case, I'm afraid. There are photographs of the cuts and bruises that were found on her. They'll be compared with the injuries found on the boy...'

'She's going to be taken away from us,' said Flora. 'She's going to have to go back and live with the Johnsons.'

I SKEDADDLE through the door from the lounge to the kitchen. When the polis come round the house for Jed or one of the boys, it's best if I'm no there, so they're no looking at me thinking, *Lorraine willnae let them touch us so she willnae.*

I leave the door open and stand with my eye to the crack at the hinges.

Ryan's all: 'Take a seat, gentlemen, take a seat,' waving at the settee.

One of them looks about twelve year old.

Ryan goes, 'Can I get yous a tea or a coffee?'

'You're all right,' says the adult one. He's got his notebook out. 'Now, Mr Johnson... We've had a complaint regarding a breach of a court order. We have witness statements to the effect that three white males, matching the descriptions of yourself, your father and Travis here, confronted the adoptive mother of your niece Bekki, and the child herself, yesterday afternoon in Edinburgh.'

'Aye,' goes Ryan. He sits down in my chair and leans forward towards the polismen. 'Hands up, that was us right enough. I'm no gonnae lie to you. But it was a pure accident so it was. My brother, he's starting a market garden business and we'd gone for a deek at the Botanic Gardens for a wee bit inspiration. Took the old guy along because he doesnae get out much these days.' He nods at Jed. 'But he was "tired and emotional", if you get me, and we have to leave him in the motor while we're in the Gardens. Then when we get back, he's only gone and clocked Bekki, and he's out the motor giving it: "Wee Bekki-hen!" and aye, maybe he's out of order. But he's no all there. He's a vulnerable adult so he is. And God, you can maybe understand the shock of it, aye? Here's this old jakie wakes out an alcoholic stupor and there's his wee grand-daughter that was taken off of him six year ago standing right there on the pavement? He's looking for the pink elephants and giant fucking bunnies, but naw, it's Bekki and she's fucking real. No one with her, mind. Eight-year-old lassie on her own in the street? That's no right.'

Ryan sits back in the chair.

The adult polisman goes, 'So, Mr Johnson. You're admitting the breach of the court order?'

'Aye. But it was unintentional, like. We're no out to make trouble for Bekki or her new family. We dinnae want no hassle. Even Maw and Da have accepted it now, so they have, that she's better off with they folk. We're no going to go hassling them again. Aye? Could you tell them sorry like, it was just the shock, eh, after all these years? Da maybe was out of order, but as I say, he's a vulnerable adult.'

The two polismen eyeball Jed.

'Right. Yes. I see.'

'Aye,' goes Ryan. 'Forty year on the bevvy will do that to you. Take a good look, gents. There's a walking public health warning right there, eh?'

'And is Mr Johnson able to understand why we're here and what we're saying?'

'Course I'm fucking able to –' goes Jed.

'Okay Da, okay.' Ryan smiles. 'Kids call him Father Jack. Wee rascals.'

'Ah... Hmmph. Well. I think, in the circumstances, we'll be able to offer you the option of a caution rather than involving the courts. Now, you don't have to accept the caution, which will be entered into the record, including the Police National Computer. You can go to court if you so wish. And you don't have to decide right now. You may wish to take legal advice.'

'Naw naw,' goes Ryan. 'You're fine. Caution's fine.'

'Mr Johnson?' He looks at Jed.

'Aye,' goes Jed.

'That's barry,' goes Travis. 'We have to sign it, eh? God, I could recite what's on that form so I could –'

'Aye, I think we're all fine with cautions, thank you,' goes Ryan. 'And please pass on our apologies to the family and wee Bekki. We're hoping when she's eighteen maybe she'll get in touch, but we understand that's her decision.'

'And you understand that the court order prohibits any contact in the meantime?'

Ryan's nodding. 'It wasnae that we were intending making contact. It just happened, eh? We hold our hands up but. Da shouldnae have spoke to Bekki. God, I wish he hadnae, causing trouble and that. Poor wee lassie. We only want what's best for Bekki, you know?'

Belter.

And as the polismen are getting out their forms and that, and Travis is going, 'Naw, I dinnae need to read it, I've seen it afore,' Ryan turns and gives me a wee wink.

That boy's something else so he is.

When it's his turn to sign, he squeezes onto the settee next the twelve-year-old and goes, 'Cosy,' and signs the form and then he goes, 'You're Raymond Bain's laddie, eh? I was at the school with your cousin Isla. Went with her a while. What's Isla up to these days?'

The laddie's got a beamer on him so he has, and the other polisman is getting up and giving him evils, and the laddie jumps up off the settee and goes, 'She's fine, aye.'

'God I was mad for Isla. Right clever wee bint. She went the university?'

'Aye.'

'Computer sciences, aye?'

'Naw, geography. She was gonnae do comp–'

'Thank you, Mr Johnson,' goes the other polisman. 'We'll see ourselves out.'

I give it a wee minute and then I'm out the kitchen and high-fiving Travis and going to Ryan, '*Vulnerable adult*, oh God, *vulnerable adult*,' and me and Ryan and Travis are pissing ourselves and Jed's like that: 'I'll give you fucking *vulnerable*, ye wee bass, I'll give you fucking *vulnerable*.'

And aye, you can see it in his bangstie wee eyes, he's going radge, but he's no fit for the boys and hasnae been for years, and Ryan's in his face giving it 'Oh aye, Da, go on then, you fucking old *vulnerable* bastard,' and Jed's raging so he is, kicks the door on his way out the room, and Travis is giving him the finger.

What goes around comes around, eh?

14

Saskia's house looked different in the daylight. It was a 1960s semi in a nice area in the north of Glasgow, on a housing estate circling a wooded hill. There were lots of grassy areas and a small park across the road from the house, complete with a children's assault course. A view of the distant hills of the Highlands from the front door. You'd be able to hop in the car and be climbing a Munro in less than an hour.

But the white paint on the wood cladding was peeling, there were weeds all up the path, and the doorbell didn't seem to work.

Neil tried it again, then pounded on the frosted-glass door.

'Try to stay calm,' said Flora.

But it was so hard, having to rethink everything they'd believed. The way Beckie had been when she came to them, that traumatised, withdrawn little girl – had she been nothing more than a child wrenched from the people she loved, a child who didn't understand why they didn't come for her, why she had been abandoned to yet more strangers?

A figure appeared behind the glass. The door was opened by a tall thin man in bare feet, with an incongruous little beer gut nudging at his T-shirt. He had the pasty, spotty complexion of someone who never saw daylight.

She barely recognised him as Saskia's husband.

'Hello. Is Saskia in, please? It's...' Flora realised that they'd had different names last time they'd met. 'It's Alec and Ruth Morrison.'

His shoulders slumped. 'Beckie's parents.'

'Yes. Look.' Neil grimaced. 'We're not here to make a scene. We just need to talk to her. Please.'

'She's not here. We're not together any more.' He reached behind him. 'She's renting a flat in Haghill. This is the address.'

A DANK, deeply shadowed close led from the street between a warehouse and the high wall of a tenement. The concrete underfoot was slimy with algae and slippery, and littered with wrappers and Lucozade bottles and cigarette ends. Flora's foot crunched on a piece of broken glass. On the wall was a grubby sign with an arrow on it and 'Nos 34a–h, 35a–h'.

The close ended in a tiny courtyard surrounded by high tenements which must never get the sun. There were two doors faced with hardboard and painted blue. The one on the right, Number 34, was tattered along the bottom as if a large animal had been gnawing it.

What an awful place to have to live. But Flora couldn't summon any pity for Saskia.

She pressed the buzzer for 34g.

After a long moment: 'Hello?'

'Hi, Saskia? It's Flora and Neil. Parry. We need to talk to you – is that okay? Can we come up?'

As the door buzzed open, Neil said, 'I guess we could go back to Alec and Ruth Morrison, couldn't we? Now they've found us, now they obviously know who we are –'

Flora shook her head. 'Let's just leave it for now. Beckie

doesn't need any more upheaval. She's just got used to being Beckie Parry.'

The stairwell was lit by a flickering fluorescent light. The windows on each half-landing were so grimy it was impossible to see through them. But the stairs themselves were clean enough, and on the first landing someone had put a sad little loop of fabric bunting above a door painted a tasteful powder blue.

Flora looked up the stairwell. It spiralled up and up, several more stories. A lot of these high old tenements had been demolished in the Glasgow slum clearances, but many remained. When this tenement had been built in the Nineteenth Century, each household would probably have had just one room – 'single ends', they'd been called, with a range and a sink and a bed recess, with communal toilets out the back or, later, at the bottom of the stair, to be shared among them all.

Now the single ends had been put together to make flats, just two households on each landing rather than six or eight.

Saskia's flat was on the top floor. She stood in the doorway watching them ascend to the landing, and any thoughts Flora had had about Saskia choosing to live here because of an interest in social history vanished. She looked terrible – hair greasy and in need of a cut, fleece and leggings wrinkling on a frame that had shrunk several sizes since Flora had last seen her. Her feet looked huge in matted brown faux-fur slippers.

'Hi,' she said flatly. 'If you've come for an apology – I'm sorry. Really I am.'

'No,' said Flora. 'That's not why we're here. I understand why you did it. We both do.'

Not true. Neil was completely baffled and outraged by what Saskia had done.

'Can we come in and talk?'

'Place is a mess.' But she held the door open for them.

The smell hit Flora as soon as she entered the living room –

an open-plan kitchen and sitting area with a large flat-screen TV opposite a sofa on which Saskia had evidently been sleeping. There was a yellow-stained pillow on it and a duvet cascading onto the floor. In front of this was a coffee table with an ashtray full of joints. The sickly smell of cannabis and sweat and mouldering food was so overpowering that Flora wasn't sure she was going to be able to stand it. Dirty dishes were piled up all over the worktops.

Flora turned to Saskia. 'Are you – are you all right?'

Saskia gave a mirthless laugh. 'Fine and dandy.'

What about her children? Did they come here, or did she meet her husband at a café or a park or the zoo to spend time with them? An image came into Flora's head of a tousle-haired little boy in Saskia's arms.

I just wanted to see you.

She couldn't ask her about her children. She couldn't afford to have Saskia break down and be unable to tell them what they needed to know.

'We'll not stay long,' she said, perching on one of the chairs positioned on either side of the sofa.

Neil didn't sit and Saskia also remained standing, near the door, as if she was expecting to need an escape route.

'Please come and sit down, Saskia,' said Flora. 'Neil.'

Neil perched on the other chair, while Saskia went to the sofa and folded up the duvet, shoved it to one side and sat. She still hadn't met Flora's eye.

'Did you hurt Beckie?' Neil said. She could hear the strain in his voice, the effort it was taking for him to remain calm.

Saskia didn't respond.

'We're not going to repeat what you tell us to anyone,' Flora said. 'We just need to know. We need to know the truth about what you did, and what you made up, and what the Johnsons really did and didn't do. Because they've found us again.'

Saskia looked up. 'Oh God... I'm sorry.'

'Yeah,' said Neil. 'Right. You're sorry.'

'Neil.' Flora wanted to just get up and leave, to run out of this stinking flat and down the stairs and forget Saskia Mair existed. But they needed to hear the truth from her. 'Please, Saskia. I mean it, we won't go to the police or anything with what you tell us.'

Saskia shook her head and, finally, met Flora's gaze. 'I did it for the kids. And you know what? I'm *not* sorry. I'd do it again in a heartbeat. A few seconds of discomfort weighed against a life-time of abuse and fear and misery and deprivation?'

'That wasn't your call to make,' said Neil.

'Oh, but you see, it was. I knew those kids. I knew those families. You're really saying Beckie's not better off today than she would have been if she'd been left to grow up in that family?'

'If they weren't actually doing her any harm, if she wasn't really in any danger from them – you had no right to take her away. No wonder they're angry. No wonder they moved heaven and earth to find her. My God, in their position I don't know what I'd do.'

'Of course they were doing her *harm*,' Saskia almost spat. 'Most of it was true, what I put in my report.'

'What bits, exactly?' said Flora. 'We need to know what you made up and what was true.'

Saskia shut her eyes.

'*Saskia!*' Flora bunched her fists.

Saskia breathed out, opened her eyes, and stared off. 'The house was filthy. There were holes in the walls and doors miss-ing. The place was full of cigarette smoke. The dog was out of control. There was a used condom lying on the carpet. Dirty nappies were spilling from the bin and the dog had hold of one. Beckie really was outside in the rain. Okay, she didn't have a dirty nappy. She wasn't dirty. She was in clean clothes. And there were no signs she had recently been physically hurt, although there were old bruises. But she was obviously not happy. She was obviously frightened of something. And Ryan and Travis and Jed really did threaten me. They didn't actually assault me, but only because Lorraine stopped them. Jed Johnson really is dangerous – he's a psychopath. A truly evil man who gets off on torturing people. Ryan's more subtle, more sophisticated maybe, but he's a killer too. As is Shannon-Rose. Travis is just a violent thug. That isn't a family any child should have to grow up in.'

A long silence.

Neil was looking out of the window, his face expressionless. If you didn't know him, you'd think he'd lost interest in the conversation, but Flora knew it was taking all he had not to lose it.

'And that's the truth?'

Saskia nodded. 'The courts won't take Beckie away from you. Not now. No court in the world would deem that to be in her best interests, after all this time with you. You're her parents as far as she's concerned. You're her family.'

This was what Yvonne Richards had told them. That there was no need to worry on that score.

'So they never actually harmed Beckie,' said Neil quietly. 'They were looking after her well.'

'I'm sure they *did* harm her! I just didn't have the evidence.' Saskia's voice caught. 'Surely you must know that yourselves, surely you've seen the effect living with them had on Beckie? You're not going to tell me she's not been affected by it?'

'No, I would certainly never claim she hadn't been,' said Flora. 'She's –'

Neil cut through her: 'But that could have been down solely to Shannon-Rose! Who was a schizophrenic and not responsible for her actions – and the rest of the family certainly can't be held responsible for what she did. Whatever Beckie suffered before she came to us might have nothing to do with them.'

'Oh, believe that if you want to!' Saskia reached for a roll-up. 'Go ahead and get the adoption changed from closed to open if you want and see what happens. The courts would probably look favourably on such an application, in the circumstances. If you're so confident they're no threat to Beckie, go ahead and let the Johnsons back in her life.'

'We've no intention of doing that,' said Flora.

But Neil didn't look at her.

15

'What the fuck's up wi' you, doll?' goes Mandy.

'Aye,' I goes, 'excuse me if I'm no maybe wanting to bankrupt my arse on a wean that's no even out the fucking womb.'

We're in the TK Maxx on Argyle Street, me and Carly and Mandy, and I'm pushing the trolley because Carly thinks being pregnant means she cannae do nothing. Doesnae stop her shopping for Scotland, mind.

I goes, 'Next time you go for a check-up, hen, you should maybe ask if there are no any procedures, like maybe they can get a pair of Swarovski earrings onto one of they keyhole whoogies and shove them up your fanny into the bairn?'

Mandy cackles.

Carly's chuckling an' all. 'My Big Fat Gypsy Bairn.' The wean's da's that wee fucker Ryan calls Gypsy Bob, but he's no really a traveller, he just keeps getting evicted by the Council. 'Aw is that no gorgeous?' goes Carly, and she breenges past another bint – She's pregnant, aye? So get out her fucking road – and shakes a baby-gro in my face. It's pale yellow with wee bunnies and bees and that. Soft as anything.

'Aye go on.'

She chucks it in the trolley. 'Aw, and look at they wee sundresses! Would Bekki no look bonnie in one of they?'

'We dinnae even know her right size.'

Carly's holding up the dress. It's turquoise with bonnie white flowers.

'That's adorable,' goes Mandy.

Carly eyeballs me from under her big false eyelashes. 'She's like average size for her age, aye, give or take? Six to eight's gonnae be too wee. Nine to eleven? If it's too big it'll do for next year?'

'Aye go on,' I huff.

'What the fuck's up wi' you, doll?' Mandy willnae let it go. 'It's no like there's gonnae be a TK Maxx in Spain by the way. Or any shops that are any fucking good. Eh?'

I cannae fool Mands.

When Carly's off looking at bibs and that, I go, 'Buying crap for a wean that's no born... for Bekki – it's like... like the fucking Universe is gonnae go *Fuck off, Lorraine.*'

'That's mental.'

'Aye, but.'

Mandy puts her arm round me. She's no the freshest after a day trauchling round town, and I get a big whiff of BO off of her. 'It's gonnae be OK. Scans are all normal, aye? And we're gonnae get Bekki back. We're gonnae get our wee lassie back, Lorraine.'

'They bastards... they're smart, aye? They're maybe gonnae rumble it.' I get my arse moving, pushing the trolley through the lines of bairns' clothes to the tills.

In the queue, Mandy starts back in. 'Bastards gave it their best shot, disappearing and that, but they havenae a fucking clue. Have a wee bit faith in yourself, hen.' She puffs. 'God, would you listen to me giving it Pollyannas?'

When we were wee, any time any good shite happened, like

we were in the park with our pals and we all had cones, and we were lying on the grass licking them, and the sun was shining and that, and I'd go, 'This is barry,' Mandy would go, 'It's just a fucking cone' and 'Fucking Pollyanna' and I'd be all, 'Shut your face Misery Mandy.'

Felt bad, when I got old enough to work out what all had gone on. No wonder Mandy wasnae a laugh a minute, eh? She kept letting that fucker Billy do that shite to her so he wouldnae go all the way with me, and she got infections and that, and that's why she couldnae have bairns.

I go, 'Thanks doll.'

'They're smart, aye, but you're smarter than ninety-nine point nine per cent of the population. Just you mind that, Lorraine.'

Connor got me doing this IQ test he found on the net and I aced it by the way. Came out my IQ's a hundred and sixty-seven. And Connor's like that: 'Christ on a cheesy biscuit! You should be the fucking Prime Minister!'

Mandy goes, 'You're one smart cookie.'

'Aye, okay I've got a brain on me, but near enough two fucking years to find Bekki? It's like we're no meant to get her.'

'That's mental.'

'I've got a bad feeling, Mands. A bad fucking feeling.'

Thought it would be easy to find them. Once we'd got photies of them off of Pammie, all we had to do was go to all the places they could be – Torridon, Perth, St Andrews, fucking Amalfi, fucking Australia – and go round asking folk if they'd seen them because they'd kidnapped a wee lassie. Get Connor searching for Ruth and Alec Morrison on the net and checking out folk's blogs and sites and that from they places. Checking out nurses and botanists. Every botany department in the English-speaking fucking world.

Nada.

Fucking two years wasted.

'Two fucking years,' I goes.

'That's nothing,' goes Mandy. 'Look at all they fuckers on FAF. How many of them are gonnae find their bairns *ever*?'

Right enough.

I'd been all out of ideas, sitting on my arse watching this daft TV show with Connor, *The Big Bang Theory*, about a load of dowfie wee fuckers in a university, and then I'm jumping up out my chair and I'm like that: 'Oh my God' and Connor's: 'What?' and I'm: 'Alec Morrison's one of they, aye? One of they boffins? How's he gonnae survive outside a fucking university, out in the real fucking world?'

Connor's nodding. 'Aye! Like pandas and that. They can only eat bamboo, aye? They cannae survive in any other habitat. They're too specialised.'

'Aye, he's like one of they fuckwit pandas. He cannae do a normal job. He cannae transfer his skills. Maybe he's no working in a botany department, but he has to be in a fucking university. He's maybe just moved departments, eh?'

So me and Connor get searching the net: all they university department web pages, any department to do with biology, looking for his face, because it's ninety-nine per cent he'll have changed his fucking name.

Nada.

Then we try web pages for conferences, press stuff, boffins' blogs and that.

And bingo.

There's his geeky wee face in the background of a photy showing some professor retiring. At the Microbiology Department at Edinburgh University.

Two fucking years, but.

Mandy's pulling her heid back into her chins like she's up for a rammie, like she's gonnae belt any fucker gets in her road.

'They're that arrogant, they think moving a wee bit west to

east and changing from bot-logy to bile-ogy's gonnae stop us finding them? They're that fucking complacent, Lorraine?'

Aye.

Fucking Alec moves from Glasgow to Edinburgh University, from botany to microbiology, and the fucker thinks that's him disappeared? He's all: *They wee windae-lickers willnae even know what the fuck a university is.* Fucking arrogant wee fuck.

Thought he'd been smart not putting a photy on his profile page on the departmental website. All that meant was Ryan and Travis had to park up on campus and wait till they saw him coming out the front door of the Microbiology Department. Follow the fucker home.

'Aye,' I goes. 'Fucking complacent.'

16

Having spent an hour lovingly constructing 'Jed-Bag' from a pair of old jeans of Neil's, one of his old shirts, a pair of Flora's tights, Caroline's make-up and some rags, Beckie and Caroline had hung him by the neck from a branch of the sycamore.

Now Beckie was doubled up, hysterical, as Caroline aimed another kick at his crotch area, which she followed up with a jab to the eye, sending Jed-Bag spinning on the rope.

They'd made his head by stuffing old pillowcases into Flora's tights and used make-up to do long-lashed, wide-open eyes and a manically smiling mouth like Mr Blobby's. They'd tied up the ends of Neil's jeans with string, so Jed-Bag's sausage-like legs ended like Christmas crackers. And at his crotch Caroline had hung one of those orange mesh bags you bought onions in, inside which she'd arranged a carrot and two onions which were now receiving heavy punishment as the targets of Caroline and Beckie's ninja skills.

Was this appropriate, really?

But Beckie was having such fun. Flora didn't have the heart to object.

'Who needs a blender,' grinned Neil, sitting back in his favourite lounger with a cold glass of ginger beer.

Flora stood behind him, arms folded, watching their daughter over his head. That was all she seemed to do now – watch Beckie. Whenever Beckie was out of her sight she felt twitchy, unable to settle to anything. Instead of walking to and from school, she now drove Beckie there and back. And she'd started arriving at the school half an hour early to pick her up. Which was ridiculous. It wasn't as if the teachers were going to let the Johnsons take her, was it?

She no longer let Beckie play in the garden on her own.

This morning Beckie had begged to be allowed to ask Thomas over – 'And if he's here, you don't need to be hovering round me all the time, do you, Mum?' – and Flora had gone next door to issue the invitation.

Ailish hadn't even let her over the threshold.

'Sorry Flora, he's Skyping his gran.'

'Well, maybe when he's finished? You could bring him over?'

Ailish had smiled mechanically and started closing the door. 'Sorry Flora, I've got to...'

She couldn't even be bothered making up a believable excuse.

Ever since the incident with the Johnsons in the street, Ailish had been treating Flora and Beckie like lepers. Flora had tried to explain what had happened, but, unsurprisingly, the information that Beckie's delinquent birth family had found out where they lived hadn't seemed to help.

Ailish was just looking out for her son. Of course she was.

And now on top of everything, when Caroline suggested swapping mobile numbers, Flora had been unable to locate her phone. Where was the damn thing?

'Sit down, Flora,' said Neil. 'Relax for five minutes.'

She made herself sit on one of the other loungers and lean

back, but she couldn't relax. She seemed to have lost the knack. She found she was gripping the chair's wooden arms as if she was on some sort of terrifying fairground ride.

She caught Neil's eye, and returned his smile half-heartedly.

He got up and came round behind her; put his hands on her shoulders. 'Nothing bad's going to happen to her.' He started to knead the muscles at the base of her neck. 'You're blowing this up into something it's not. If they were going to do anything, they'd have done it by now.'

It was over two weeks since the incident in the street.

'They haven't had the chance. Wherever she goes, I go.'

'They haven't even tried, though, have they?' His fingers pushed into her flesh, into the tension across her shoulders, and finally she allowed her muscles to relax, the tension to drop through her shoulders and down her arms.

She released her grip on the chair.

'Mm. I guess not.'

'I think their apology was genuine.'

The police had said that the Johnsons had asked them to pass on an apology for what had happened – it was all down to the alcoholic father, apparently, and they were really sorry if she and Beckie had been frightened. It wouldn't happen again.

She closed her eyes.

Neil seemed determined to take it at face value. But he hadn't been there. He hadn't seen the looks those thugs had given her. The way Ryan Johnson had made his hand into a gun and mimed shooting her and Caroline...

It hadn't all been about the alcoholic father.

She snapped her eyes open and sat up, away from Neil's hands.

Beckie was jabbing her fingers into Jed-Bag's face, bouncing in front of him, and Caroline was bouncing next to her, whooping encouragement.

Flora pushed herself out of the lounger and turned to face Neil, who was regarding her with a wariness that might have been funny in other circumstances.

'Of course it wasn't genuine! God! You're so *gullible!*'

'No,' he said, obviously choosing his words, as he'd started to do, as if she were some sort of mental case he had to be careful not to upset. 'I don't think I am. I'm looking at the facts here, Flora, and so should you.'

'I *am* looking at the facts!' She belatedly lowered her voice, although, given the amount of noise Beckie and Caroline were making themselves, they were unlikely to notice if she started screaming like a maniac. But she kept her tone as reasonable as his. 'The facts are that the Johnsons know where we are, and that they're psychopaths. What does your evidence-based approach to your daughter's safety have to say about that?'

'They're not "psychopaths" – other than possibly the old man, and he's hardly a threat any more. They're a disadvantaged family, yes –'

'They're drug dealers and murderers.'

How was she going to get through to him? She'd always loved this live-and-let-live attitude of his: no matter how cynical-scientist he might be when talking in the abstract, in practice, in his actual dealings with actual real-life people, he would always give a person the benefit of the doubt. Which was fine, provided that that person wasn't a danger to their child.

He threw up his hands. 'Even Saskia had to admit that they loved Beckie.'

'So? They're still dangerous, Neil, and the fact that you won't admit that is putting Beckie's safety at risk. Okay, maybe I'm going over the top, maybe I'm being ultra-paranoid, but that's partly because I feel I'm on my own here. Because you're not taking it seriously.'

'Of course I'm taking it seriously. It's just... You have to admit, Flora. Jed Johnson – when he said we've stolen Beckie from them... Well. There's some justification to that. Beckie was removed from their home in a horrendous miscarriage of justice.'

Flora put a hand to her mouth as she felt the bile rise in her throat.

'Think about it from their point of view. Isn't it incumbent on us to at least let them have some contact with her? Supervised contact?'

Oh God.

She swallowed. She groped for the nearest lounger and sat on it. 'No,' she got out. 'It isn't *incumbent* on us to do anything that could put Beckie in danger.' A shiver ran right through her chest and up into her shoulders. 'How can you even say that? God, Alec!'

'But –'

She had to hold it together. She had to make him understand. 'Beckie's safety has to come first. Surely we agree about that?'

'Of course we agree about that. I'd do anything to keep her safe – you know I would. The question is, how do we achieve that?'

'Not by letting the Johnsons back into her life!'

'You think I actually *want* to? But this isn't about what *we* want. It's about how to minimize the harm done to Beckie. Do we do that by making enemies of the Johnsons? Or by acknowledging what's happened and being reasonable about it?'

'Oh, you think they're *reasonable*? You think they're *reasonable* human beings now, do you? Murderers? A "family from hell"? That's what their neighbours call them. That's why Saskia did what she did, to get Beckie away from them.'

'They obviously have problems...'

'No, Neil. They *are* the problem. You're so naïve! Poor family from hell, it's society's fault they make the lives of everyone around them a misery, they can't help it...'

'There are usually two sides to any neighbour dispute. We don't know what's been going on there, maybe the neighbours are equally to blame, maybe there's some sort of vendetta against them –'

'Okay.' She took a long breath. 'Okay. So you want to go and tell Beckie she has to see the Johnsons? The people she's so terrified of that she's learning martial arts to protect herself?'

They both looked over at Beckie, who didn't at that moment look exactly terrified. She had collapsed against the tree in hysterics.

Neil said, 'That's because you've told her that the Johnsons are bad people.'

For a long moment, Flora could only stare at him. When she spoke, she couldn't keep the fury from her voice. She felt like she was choking on it, that it was all she could do to force the words through it. 'No, that's because they assaulted us in the street and scared her so much she *wet herself*.'

'They didn't *assault* you.'

Flora stood. She walked past him and through the open doors to the family room.

He followed her.

'Flora.'

She walked past the two big blue sofas facing each other across the coffee table. In the kitchen, she ran water into a glass, then turned to face him, leaning back against the cool porcelain of the butler's sink, gripping the glass in her hand.

He didn't say anything. He came and stood in front of her, and then he smiled, just a little, and gently, gently, pushed his fingertips into the hair above her ear, smoothing back a sweaty tendril that had become stuck to her skin.

She felt her face collapse.

He took the glass from her, set it on the draining board, and pulled her into his arms.

'I'm sorry.'

She pulled back. She groped behind her for the glass and took a sip of water, all she could force through the tightness in her throat.

'It was horrible, what happened, and I'll never forgive them for it,' he said. 'For putting you and Beckie through such a terrifying experience. But... I really think you're wrong about them. I think I always knew there was a disconnect between what we were being told about the Johnsons and the way Beckie is. Intrinsically... She's so... she's just so naturally *sweet*, Ruth. That's not just down to environment, that's not just down to us.'

'That's down to her genes?'

'In large part, yes, I think so.'

'Nature versus nurture?'

'Obviously nurture plays a part, obviously she's having a much easier time of it than her biological family...'

'You're saying the lovely but disadvantaged Johnsons have produced a child whose nice middle-class environment is revealing the true genetic Johnson saintliness?'

He smiled. 'Yeah, I guess that's –'

'Have you forgotten that she's been bullying a disabled child?'

Okay, the disabled bit was maybe an exaggeration.

He gaped at her.

'Your little paragon is a *bully*!'

He was looking at her as if at a stranger. 'So just because she's had some issues at school, you're suddenly saying Beckie isn't a nice kid? You're looking at her now and thinking that's her Johnson genes coming out, that's the real Beckie –'

'No, of course not!'

'Is it any wonder Beckie's playing up at school, after being uprooted from her home and all her friends and not able to even contact them?'

'That's no excuse for cruelty.'

'Ruth. Every kid gets into arguments, scraps – Christ. I can't believe you're looking on this as evidence of Beckie's... what? Genetic original sin? Is that why you've been watching her like a hawk – not because of the Johnsons being a supposed threat but because you think she's some sort of danger *herself*?'

'You're the scientist. You know mental illnesses can have their onset around puberty or before... Of course I'm worried she might have inherited a predisposition... But no, that's not why I'm *watching her like a hawk*. The *supposed* threat from the Johnsons is actually the reason for that, believe it or not.' She set the glass down on the worktop, so abruptly that water sloshed over its rim, and pushed past him, making for the open doors to the garden.

This time, he didn't come after her.

She had to call Saskia. She had to get the Johnsons' address from Saskia, and go and speak to their neighbours. He wanted evidence? She'd get it. From the neighbours, and anyone else Saskia could point her towards, maybe other victims of the Johnsons, if they were willing to speak to her.

And then maybe she could persuade Alec that they needed to disappear again.

Where was her bloody mobile?

Not on the table or the loungers.

She returned to the family room, scanning the sofas, the coffee table... Neil had disappeared, thank God. She walked round the room, trying to think of where she could last remember looking at her phone.

Maybe she'd left it in the car.

She felt tears pricking at the back of her nose as she searched the car, the study, the front room, the bedroom – where the hell was her phone? All her numbers were in it, including Saskia's. She needed her *fucking phone*.

In the bedroom, she lay down on the carpet and flailed her hand around under the bed.

Nothing but dust and hair.

Sweat was trickling from her armpits down her sides.

She sat back against the bed and closed her eyes against the tears.

'Flora? Hey, Flora?' It was Caroline's voice, Caroline's steps on the stairs.

Flora took a big breath, opened her eyes and got to her feet, like an old woman, supporting herself on the bed. What now?

'In here.'

Caroline grinned at her from the door. Her hair was up in a jaunty ponytail and her face was flushed from the exercise. 'I'm just off... Hey, are you okay?'

'Still can't find my bloody phone.'

Caroline made a sympathetic face. 'Where were you when you last used it?'

'I've been trying to remember.' Flora sank down on the bed. 'I thought I had it in the garden. I thought I checked it and put it down on the table...'

'Have you tried ringing it?'

I'm not stupid! Flora wanted to snap. 'It's turned off.'

'Well, it'll turn up, eh? Gimme paper and I'll write my number down for you.'

Flora reached for a Post-it pad on her bedside table and opened the drawer for a pen. As Caroline wrote down her number, Flora said, 'Thanks for spending so much time with Beckie. It's – I know it really means a lot to her to be able to have fun with you. You're so good with her.'

Caroline smiled. 'Yeah, I'm just a big kid, let's face it.'

The great thing about Caroline was that she was so easy to have around. And somehow Flora knew she could trust her with Beckie. It seemed that Neil could have been right, and Caroline may well be the friend Flora needed. The difference in their ages didn't seem to matter at all.

'You don't need to thank me, Flora. I love hanging out with Beckie. She's a little sweetheart.'

Flora smiled and puffed out a laugh, feeling hysteria rushing up behind it. She clamped her lips together and turned away from Caroline to replace the pen and the pad, shoving the yellow Post-it with Caroline's number on it into the pocket of her jeans.

'Ahhhhhhh!'

The door behind Caroline was flung back against the wall and Jed-Bag burst into the room, legs flying out in front of him, sinister grinning Mr Blobby face wobbling. All she could see of Beckie was her trainers and some of her jeans behind Jed-Bag's. At his crotch, bits of flaky onion skin were poking out of the mesh bag, and the carrot was in bits.

'She's my *fucking granddaughter*, you *bloody buggering bitch!*' Jed-Bag jiggled across the room towards her.

'Beckie!' Flora said weakly.

'You have to hit him, Mum.'

Flora looked at Caroline, who grinned and shrugged.

She had always found Mr Blobby disturbing. She aimed a feeble punch at his shoulder.

'Go for his face!' came Beckie's muffled voice.

Flora whacked at the lipstick grin, sending the head on its thin neck bouncing around satisfyingly.

'Go for his balls!'

'Beckie,' she said again.

'Sorry,' Caroline muttered through her grin.

'The willy's broken but the balls are still good. Kick him in the balls! That's the best place to go for. Look Mum, he's *attacking* you!'

Jed-Bag flew through the air.

'That's my fucking buggery *granddaughter!*'

And as he sailed through the air towards her, all the rage that had been building seemed to whoosh through her and she was conscious only of her limbs flailing, of someone shouting, of jumping, of herself screaming, and 'Fucking old *bastard*' coming out of her mouth, and when she came back to herself she was letting go of Jed-Bag's ankles and he was flying in a centrifugal arc through the wide-open window.

Gasping, she stood in the rectangle of sun on the carpet and looked around her.

What had just happened?

Beckie was grabbing the windowsill to haul herself up and look down at the patio, shrieking, 'You've killed him!' in delight.

'Who?' came faintly back. Thomas.

'Jed-Bag!' yelled Beckie. 'My biological grandad! Mum smashed up his balls and his willy then she threw him out of the window! He's definitely dead now!'

Flora staggered to the window. Jed-Bag was sprawled on his back on the patio, legs and arms spreadeagled, the sorry collection of objects at his crotch pulverised beyond recognition. On the other side of the high wall, in next door's garden, Ailish, Iain and Thomas were standing staring up at them.

She waved weakly, shut the window, and sank down on the bed.

Beckie flung herself down full-length beside her and started to laugh, uninhibitedly, delightedly, and Caroline was peeking out of the window and saying, 'Her mouth is literally hanging open,' and then Flora was laughing too, and Caroline flung back her head and joined them, the three of them howling like a pack of wolves.

17

Rolliston Avenue was usually one of the best parts of the walk to school: leafy and quiet and genteel, with its high stone walls overhung by beech and magnolia and lilac trees, so you got a glimpse of the ground floors of the grand detached houses only at their gates. Number 6 was her favourite, with its brief view up the gravel drive to a wide, white-painted front door under an elegant fanlight, and wisteria growing around a sash-and-case window. You could almost imagine the door opening and a wasp-waisted Victorian maidservant appearing, a basket swinging on her arm, to do her morning shopping in the long-vanished grocers and butchers and haberdashers on Raeburn Place.

But today Flora didn't slow her pace at all as they passed the gate of Number 6.

She was cursing herself for not staying in the car and asking some nice passer-by for the use of their mobile phone. No matter how embarrassing it would have been to have to admit to running out of petrol, at least they would have been safe.

How could she have run out of petrol?

Had they tampered with the car? Had they been watching

her, following her on the route to school every day? Had they calculated exactly how much petrol to leave in it to strand them in this quiet street?

'Mum –'

'I said *don't* look round at them, Beckie.'

Behind, the yobs were barking like animals, scuffling with each other, laughing raucously, shouting sudden streams of obscenities.

'Are they the Johnsons?'

'No, they're just some silly boys.' She gripped Beckie's hand more tightly, and Beckie gripped hers.

But Flora was almost certain, the one time she'd looked back at them, that she'd recognised the one with the little fringe plastered to his forehead.

Travis Johnson.

When she'd looked round, he had grinned at her.

She scanned the street for potential saviours, but the pavements ahead to where the road curved were empty. She was walking so fast now that poor Beckie was half tripping along at her side and, despite what Flora had told her, kept swivelling her head to look behind.

'Mum, are –'

BANG!

A plastic bottle full of bright orange liquid exploded on the wall just in front of Beckie, spattering her hair.

'It's okay, Beckie. Just keep walking and *don't look round at them.*'

Distantly, she could hear the traffic on Raeburn Place.

But there was still no one in sight.

Should she turn in at the gate of the house ahead? Walk briskly to the door as if this had been their destination all along, as if she knew the people there?

But what if the Johnsons followed them into the garden, into the seclusion afforded by the high wall and the trees, blocking their exit to the street?

No. There would be people soon, surely, on the street if they just kept walking?

'Fucking snobs,' one of them shouted.

Beckie looked back again.

'Beckie!' Flora hissed furiously, tugging her arm and making her stumble. 'Would you *stop looking*?'

Now they were approaching the curve in the road. The street had never seemed so long.

'It's okay, darling, just ignore them.'

Beckie's face had closed, as if an expressionless mask had been pulled down over it.

What would she do if they made a grab for Beckie?

She would scream. She would fight. She would kick them in the balls.

She couldn't call 999 because she still hadn't found her fucking phone. Why hadn't she taken Neil's?

But they weren't going to do anything, not in public like this. Surely? When they got to the school she would call the police. Call Neil. At least this was the evidence she needed that the Johnsons really were a threat.

It seemed to take hours to reach the bend in the road. But at last the new vista opened up in front of them and there were people, a group of students slouching along, all skinny jeans and huge boots and ridiculous hair, crossing the junction with Raeburn Place.

Holding tight to Beckie's hand, Flora broke into a jog.

'Excuse me!' she shouted, and one of the boys – he looked like a giant insect, his limbs impossibly thin in black jeans and top, a pair of outsized, heavy-framed glasses on his pointed nose – stopped and looked at them.

'Excuse me!' she repeated, gasping, at last daring to look back as she approached the students.

The street behind was empty.

'There were some men,' she gabbled at them. 'Following us, shouting things...'

'It was the Johnsons,' Beckie said in a small voice. 'They're bad people, basically... It *was*, Mum – I recognised one of them from before.'

'Or it could have been someone who just looked a bit like one of them.'

'Wanna call the cops?' Insect Boy handed her a phone.

'Oh!' Flora took it gratefully. 'Thank you. I've lost my phone... Can we walk up the road with you while I call them?'

'Yeah, sure you can.'

She decided to call 101, the non-emergency number, rather than 999. She didn't want to seem as if she was hysterical and overreacting. She explained to the woman who answered what had happened, and she was put through to the local police station. She then had to explain it all again to a bored-sounding man, all the time checking the pavements ahead and across the road and behind.

She explained that the family of her adoptive daughter had been harassing them again, that there would be a record of the previous incident on file. The bored man said police officers would meet her at the school to take a statement.

At the school gate they said goodbye and thank you to the students, and then they were safely on the expanse of tarmacked playground in front of the school buildings, thronging with yelling children and groups of helicopter mums standing about talking with half their attention, the other half dedicated to tracking their children.

Beckie suddenly stopped. 'Why did you lie?'

'What?'

'It *was* the Johnsons. You just told the police it was them.'

'Well – actually I don't know for sure that it was...'

'Of course it was them, Mum. It was that big muscly one

from before. They're going to come back and try and like *grab* me or do something to me –'

'No, darling –'

'I'm not a baby!'

'They're not going to "grab" you. Dad and I would never let that happen.'

'Yes you would. You couldn't do anything to stop them. If they'd grabbed me just now, there's nothing you could have done about it.'

'Beckie –'

'I want to go home.'

'I'll tell Miss Douglas and Mrs Jenner what's been happening, and they'll keep you safe inside at break and at lunchtime – and Dad and I will both come and collect you in his car.'

'No, I mean I want to go *home* home. I hate it here. I hate this school. And I hate Miss Douglas and Mrs Jenner! They would probably *want* the Johnsons to take me! They're *fucking cows*.'

'Beckie!'

Beckie tugged her hand out of Flora's, and Flora grabbed it back and began pulling her towards the P4 extension where Beckie's classroom was. Beckie wriggled and struggled, tears and snot on her reddened face.

'*Behave yourself!*' Flora shouted.

And Beckie cringed away.

She cringed away and sort of ducked her head as if to avoid the blow that was coming.

Oh God.

Flora had never turned her anger on Beckie before; never once.

Her own tears coming, Flora folded Beckie in her arms. 'I'm sorry, darling. I'm so sorry.'

Beckie was stiff in her embrace.

Guiding her blindly across the tarmac, Flora was aware for

the first time of all the eyes upon them – children frozen mid-chase; groups of mums staring. And there was Ailish, in her usual prime position in the middle of the playground under the big horse chestnut, standing there in her high boots and swingy beige coat, muttering out of the side of her mouth to Marianne, her gaze fixed coldly on Flora.

That *bitch*.

Flora had seen her hurrying Thomas past on the street earlier as she and Beckie were leaving the house.

'Thanks a lot for your support, Ailish!' she shouted across at her, like someone on *EastEnders*.

She didn't wait for her response. She focused on the cheerful turquoise double doors of the extension, on the cut-out children's drawings of animals stuck to the safety glass, mutant deer and badgers and foxes.

Then she was pulling open the left-hand door and pushing Beckie inside.

The little lobby smelt of disinfectant and printer ink and glue.

She sat Beckie down in a chair and hunkered down in front of her, wiping her face with a tissue.

'I'm sorry I shouted at you. And I know it's very scary, darling, but Daddy and I both love you far too much to let anyone take you anywhere. We couldn't do without you, you know.'

She thought Beckie was going to stay mute – maybe she'd never speak to Flora again, and maybe she would deserve it – but then, without looking at Flora, she whispered, 'I couldn't do without *you*.'

Tears prickled again at the back of her nose, but Flora managed to smile and push Beckie's hair back off her face and say, 'Just as well I'm here, then, isn't it. And I'm not going anywhere. I'm going to speak to the policemen, and then I'm going to call Dad and he'll come and get us.'

'So I can skive off?'

'You can skive off. And if Mrs Jenner doesn't like it, she can lump it.'

They shared a little rebellious smile.

But Mrs Jenner was more than kind about the whole situation, insisting that Flora and the policemen use her office to take the statement while Beckie read a book in the outer sanctum where Mrs Jenner's secretary worked.

Ushering them into her office, she said, 'What a terrible stressful time you're having.'

Flora could only nod.

The ordinary sounds of the school could be heard faintly – a teacher's voice raised with calm, measured authority; the squeak of rubber shoes on polished vinyl flooring; a distant clatter.

Blinking her false eyelashes rapidly at Flora, Mrs Jenner murmured, 'We do take security extremely seriously – all schools must, these days, sadly. I'm afraid this sort of situation isn't unheard of – estranged parents threatening to snatch a child... We have systems in place.'

'Oh,' said Flora weakly.

Mrs Jenner nodded briskly. 'I'm with a class all morning, so please take all the time you need. And when you're finished, of course you can just take Beckie home – use the phone in my office to call your husband if you like.'

'You're so kind. Thank you.'

When Mrs Jenner had gone, the two young policemen looked at her rather helplessly, as if transported back to their own – not very far off – schooldays and a summons to the headmistress's office. Flora went round behind the desk and sat in Mrs Jenner's chair, hoping this might lend her an air of authority.

The policemen sat down on the other side of the desk, and

one of them produced a notebook to take down Flora's account of the morning.

But in this portentous setting, after all the build-up, somehow it fell flat when she actually began to tell them what had happened. Three youths had walked behind them on the pavement being loud and sweary and throwing a plastic bottle at a wall.

'So they didn't throw it *at* you or your daughter?'

'Maybe they did and missed.'

'They didn't actually speak to you? They didn't confront you?'

'They were shouting things – like "Fucking snobs".'

'And this was directed at you?'

'Well – yes, I'm sure it was.'

'But there was no actual confrontation…'

And then:

'And it was the same man you'd encountered earlier – it was Travis Johnson.'

'Yes, Beckie recognised him too, independently – of course I didn't tell her who it was. She came out with it; she said it was the same man as before. The muscly one, she called him. Muscles, tattoos and… a sort of little fringe stuck to his forehead. And he had a squashed nose, you know, like it's been broken… What will happen now? They were just cautioned about breaking the court order the first time, but now it's happened again despite the caution, what happens?'

'The Prosecution Service will review the situation regarding the court order, but it's likely another caution will be issued rather than an arrest being made at this stage, in the circumstances. Meanwhile, I think our colleagues explained about non-harassment orders? Now that there's been another incident, that's an option open to you. Or there's the option of an interdict through the civil courts, which is easier to apply for, but the penalties for breaking its conditions aren't as severe. To apply for either, you'll have to contact your solicitor. But there are victim support services that can guide you through it – my colleagues possibly have spoken to you about this already.'

'Yes. So basically, breaking the court order again is just going to get them a slap on the wrist. And even if we get a non-harassment order, they can't be arrested until they break it, or – or the whole thing escalates...'

The policeman sat back. 'That's up to the Prosecution Service. We'll let you know what's happening once the situation has been reviewed. Call us immediately, of course, if you see them again...'

When they'd gone, Flora picked up the phone, staring unseeingly at the Castles of Britain calendar on the wall as she waited for Neil to pick up.

It went to voicemail, and she left a message asking him to come home – she'd meet him there with Beckie. The Johnsons had followed them on their way to school, she said, and Beckie was really upset. 'We'll get a taxi. There's no way I'm walking her back.'

She put down the phone.

Tears threatened again, and as she rummaged in her jeans pockets for another tissue, a slip of paper drifted to the royal blue carpet.

She picked it up and saw it was Caroline's number.

Caroline answered immediately. 'Hi, Flora!'

'They followed us to school. The Johnsons.'

'Oh God! Where are you?'

'At the school. I can't get hold of Neil and I don't want to take Beckie home just the two of us...'

'Of course not! Have you called the police?'

'I've made another statement. They said we can take out a non-harassment order now...'

'What, they're not actually going to do anything?'

'They might give them another caution.'

'Oh whoopy-doo! Listen, Flora, don't move. I'm coming to get you. Where's the school?'

'THERE'S YOUR NEXT-DOOR NEIGHBOUR AGAIN,' said Beckie from her station by the window. 'Mr Hewson. That's the third time he's been to look in his wheelie bin. I think he's maybe suspicious. He could be, like, in league with them.'

'You reckon?' Caroline joined her to squint through the wooden Venetian blinds that she'd pulled almost closed against the bright light of the street. 'How about a break from surveillance for a peanut butter and jam sandwich?'

Beckie wrinkled her nose. 'Really?'

'Hey, don't knock it till you've tried it.'

'Disgusting enough that you probably *will* like it,' Flora smiled.

Beckie shot her a wary look.

Oh God.

She hadn't meant that as a criticism.

Beckie turned back to Caroline. 'What kind of jam?'

'Well, I think I have a choice. Can't remember exactly what of...'

'I'll come and help you.'

Two peanut butter and apricot jam sandwiches later, Beckie sat on the sofa glancing occasionally at the window but more often looking curiously at the huge jigsaw spread out on a special mat on the coffee table. All the pieces were set out, and some of the edges had been started. It was full of bright colours, and Flora thought she could make out eyes and feathers on some of the pieces, but it was impossible to tell what the picture was yet.

'It's one of my sad and completely useless hobbies,' said Caroline. 'Want to help?'

'Yes please. Where's the box?'

'Beckie!' Caroline pretended shock. 'You don't mean to tell me you look at the *picture*?'

'Um – yes?'

'Confirming your status as a complete amateur. You, my girl, have a lot to learn about the wonderful world of jigsaw freaks.'

'Okay!'

With Beckie hunched happily over the jigsaw, Flora and Caroline cleared away plates and cups to the kitchen. Closeted there, Flora gave her a proper rundown on what had happened.

'And that bitch Ailish was there in the playground. Looking down her nose at the spectacle we were making... What?'

Caroline grimaced. 'Nothing. But that explains the cryptic post on The Chipmunk Show.' She opened the laptop that was sitting on the kitchen table amidst folders and Post-it notes and documents with laminated covers. The desktop wallpaper was a photograph of a sunset over a beach, silvery waves lapping at a long stretch of sand and two colourful rowing boats tied to a quay in a tiny harbour, seabirds rising up from two tall stacks of rock further out to sea.

'That's lovely,' sighed Flora.

And now it was gone as Caroline quickly clicked on the Facebook icon, and an odd look flitted across her face. Was it somewhere Caroline used to go with a lover? The love of her life, maybe, lost to another woman?

It was none of Flora's business.

'Scroll down past all the Jasmine ones...' said Caroline.

Ailish had posted 'Just witnessed #MegaParentFail. Nope, shouting and screaming at your child until she cries is not parenting' and an inspirational quote:

YOUR CHILD MAY NOT REMEMBER THE WORDS YOU SPEAK, BUT ALL HER LIFE SHE WILL REMEMBER HOW YOU MADE HER FEEL

'Bitch,' said Flora as tears threatened. Ailish was right – Beckie would probably remember that awful scene in the playground all her life... the way she'd been made to feel... The way Flora had made her feel.

'Oh God, Flora, don't worry about it – it's *Ailish*. Everyone knows what she's like. Take a look at the Jasmine one above it.'

This was a photograph of Jasmine in yet another slutty outfit – a tight black dress with a cut-out over her stomach that dipped so low it was almost indecent. The comments under it, finally, made Flora smile.

Marianne Reiker: `Stunning! She's gorgeous, Ailish. ☼☼☼`

Tamsin Smith: `Beauty.`

John Fraser: `Crikey! Fifteen going on twenty-five. Does she go out in that?`

Ailish Young: `Dad, this is what they all wear now. It's fine, LOL. She's off out with her boyfriend.`

Marianne Reiker: `Lucky guy!!`

Ailish Young: `He's a keeper — just told me I'm way cooler than his mum!`

Katie Henderson: `Coming from a teenager, isn't that a bit of a worry?`

Ailish Young: `Katie, LOL, I don't think it's too much of a worry. I think Chris meant I don't`

sweat the small stuff and take it out on my
daughter, unlike some we could mention…

John Fraser: I thought her boyfriend was called
Jamie. Jasmine goes through boyfriends like
we go through Rich Tea biscuits! We'll have
to start calling her Liz!

Ailish Young: Dad, this is only her second ever
proper boyfriend. I don't think little Ricky
in P2 with the eye patch who used to leave
icky sweets in her bag counts!!!

'At least the dad sounds nice,' said Caroline, reading over
Flora's shoulder.

'Yes. At least Jasmine and Thomas have him. Those poor
kids.' She pushed the laptop away.

'I mean, the irony – Ailish is MegaParentFail in action
twenty-four-seven, and all her thousand-plus Facebook friends
know it.'

'Do they, though? Perceptions are so different, aren't they?
One person might look at a particular family and see Parent-
Fail, but another…' And Flora found herself telling Caroline all
about Saskia, about her hurting the children, hurting Beckie, to
get them removed from the families she thought were bad for
them.

'Oh my God,' Caroline kept saying, standing looking at
Flora with an expression Flora couldn't read – horror was there,
of course, but something else too, something like – blame?

But how could it be their fault, what had happened before
they even knew of Beckie's existence?

'I didn't find out until a few days ago,' she said defensively.

Caroline sat down in the chair across the table from her

and shut the laptop, running her fingers over the gunmetal grey surface as if removing nonexistent marks.

'Neil thinks this changes things,' Flora said. 'That we should maybe think about an open adoption, letting the Johnsons have contact with Beckie, but –'

'Oh God, no!' Caroline burst out, eyes flashing now at Flora. 'You can't do that! They're a load of nutters!'

Relief flooded through her. 'I know. That's exactly how I feel, but Neil – he's led such a sheltered life, you know, such an easy middle-class life, up to now, obviously... So he tends not to see the dangers.'

'And you haven't led a sheltered life?'

Flora shrugged.

'Sorry – didn't mean to pry.'

'No, it's okay.' In fact, the temptation to confide in this tough, pragmatic woman was dangerously strong. She was pretty sure Caroline wouldn't judge her as others might. 'I had a nice middle-class upbringing too, only Mum and I had a bit of a hard time after Dad died. And Mum and I, we didn't really get on... And she was killed in an accident when I was at uni. She was run over by a milk float, of all things.'

'Oh my God.'

Caroline's eyebrows shot up, but her mouth didn't even twitch. And for some reason Flora was suddenly remembering Pam's reaction to this piece of information.

Pam had smiled.

She'd repressed it almost immediately, but she had smiled.

'I'm sorry, Flora.' Caroline touched her hand, her face full of nothing but sympathy. 'How fucking awful.'

And Flora found herself blinking back tears. 'What about you?'

'Oh, I'm a council house girl. Not that it was exactly mean streets of Dunfermline. It was one of those 1930s estates with lots of grass and trees and corner shops. People looking out for each other. Pretty sheltered too, really.'

'No Johnsons.' Flora managed a smile.

'Definitely no Johnsons.'

'I have to try to make Neil see that the Johnsons are a threat to Beckie. That we should be doing everything in our power to keep them away from her, not thinking about initiating contact.'

'Surely after this... At least you can get things moving now with a non-harassment order.'

Flora looked at the leafy shadows shivering on the wall behind Caroline as a breeze whipped at the lilac tree at the window, sending its branches dipping and dancing. No doubt Neil would agree that doing things by the book was the way to go. But was it? With people like the Johnsons, what protection, really, did the justice system offer them?

18

They've pulled the curtains closed, aye, but there's a wee gap where I can get my neb in. And there's Bekki, sitting between they bastards on the couch in their fucking Grand Designs kitchen, playing a game on her iPad and chucking crisps in her gob.

The brass neck of Mair, making out like I was too *obese* and addicted to chicken fucking nuggets to look after Bekki, and here's that fat fucking bitch feeding her crap. The bitch puts her hand on Bekki's head and strokes her hair.

That's our wean.

That's our couch she should be on and that's my chebs she should be coorying in to.

There's some rocks in a circle under a tree with faces painted on them that're going manky with dirt and green shite. I get one of them, a tarty Miss Piggy face with rosy cheeks and big red lips and yellow hair, and airch it right at the patio doors.

Bang!

Bounces off the fucking safety glass.

I get it again and airch it at the same bit.

This time there's a kind of a crunching and then a tinkling as all the wee bits of glass round where it hit shower down.

Ya dancer!

Out of pure badness I get another, a wee pirate with an eye patch, and airch it at the other door.

And then I get my arse outta there.

FLORA STARED AT THE POLICEWOMAN. 'Well, even if they do all have alibis... they could have got someone else to do it.' The Johnsons were all at a wedding, apparently, and had been there since three o'clock that afternoon. 'And it was definitely Travis Johnson this morning. Beckie and I both recognised him.'

The policewoman smiled patiently. 'Travis Johnson's whereabouts have been established from 8:30 am to 1:30 pm today. He was working in a garage – he works there on a casual basis doing tyre changes and so on. There are a dozen witnesses attesting to his having been at the garage all morning – both staff and customers.'

They were back in Caroline's front room yet again, she and Neil and the policewoman; Beckie was asleep – Flora hoped she was, anyway – in Caroline's spare room, with Caroline watching over her. In the morning, a team would be out to process the 'scene' of the 'incident' on the patio.

Caroline's centre light fitting, a cheap branched thing in yellowy brass, cast a flat, harsh light over the room, turning the beige walls a stark white and bouncing off the glass of the one picture, above the fireplace, of wishy-washy poppies.

'What garage?' asked Flora.

'I can't tell you its name. But it's a branch of a well-known dealership.'

Neil was looking not at the policewoman but at Flora. 'You were pretty sure it was Travis Johnson.'

'Yes, because it *was* him. The Johnsons have obviously got a hold of some sort over the people at the garage, if they're not in cahoots...'

Neil raised his eyebrows. 'All of them? And their customers?'

Whose side are you on? she wanted to yell at him.

'I wouldn't be surprised,' she said tightly.

The policewoman stood. 'The team will be round to process the area around the patio in the morning. Please don't touch anything there. They'll phone to let you know they're on their way. You're not staying in the house tonight?'

'I am,' said Neil. 'Flora and Beckie will sleep here.'

He had been adamant about this. Flora had felt awful for resenting him earlier in the day for not being here for them. When the patio doors had suddenly exploded, he had leapt into action, bundling her and Beckie into the loo with his mobile and telling her to lock the door and call the police, while he, despite her protests, had gone to investigate.

He'd been pretty good in this particular crisis.

Then, after the police had arrived and they'd decamped to Caroline's, he had said he'd arrange for CCTV in the morning and take a few days off work to get it all set up.

At least, that had been the plan. But maybe the doubt sown by the Johnsons' 'alibis' was going to change that.

When they'd shown the policewoman out, Caroline appeared in the little hallway.

'She's fine. Sleeping like a baby on benzos.'

But neither of them could take her word for it. They tiptoed into the darkened room and bent over the bed. Under the covers, in the big king-sized bed, she was so *little*, hardly there at all.

Flora gently smoothed the covers over her.

Back in the sitting room – Caroline had tactfully disappeared into the kitchen – Neil said, 'Right. I'd better get back.'

'I think you should stay.'

He shook his head. 'I'll be fine.'

'What, because you don't believe the Johnsons had anything to do with it? You believe their so-called alibis?'

'The police seem to think they check out, Flora.'

'So it's all just coincidence? Some random yobs, one of them the spitting image of Travis Johnson, decide to harass us in the street after my car mysteriously runs out of petrol, and another random yob decides to lob rocks through our doors?'

'Well, you know, it *could* all be coincidence. I was thinking – remember the tulips getting vandalised a while back, and you suspected Mia? Maybe you were right. And maybe she thought it would be a laugh to throw stones at the glass doors. Or, I don't know, how about Mr Rapist-Hyphen-Serial Killer? Wouldn't put it past him to lurk in people's gardens, getting up to mischief. We mustn't automatically assume that anything bad that happens is down to the Johnsons.'

'So I suppose this means no CCTV? And you'll be going back to work tomorrow as if nothing has happened?'

'No. I'm not going back to work, and of course I'm going ahead with the CCTV... Beckie's pretty freaked out, isn't she?'

'Given that her psychotic biological family have just tried to force their way into our home, that's hardly surprising.'

He sighed. 'Nobody actually tried to get in... Look, I don't think it's a good thing to fill her head with –'

'With what? Hysterical nonsense?'

'I'm going back to the house. I'll have my camera at the ready for any more dramas, don't worry. And we'll get the CCTV.'

'Be careful,' Flora managed to say as he left the room.

She almost hoped that something *did* happen tonight, that the Johnsons *did* come back while Neil was alone in the house... Almost, but not quite.

She took her phone from her bag, which she'd left perched

on the arm of Caroline's sofa. She'd had to buy a new phone – her old one had never turned up.

She would call Saskia and ask her if the Johnsons had ever used a garage before to provide them with alibis.

Caroline's head appeared round the door. 'I'm having a nightcap – a brandy. Want one?'

Three brandies and several unanswered calls to Saskia later, she was feeling woozy and weepy and all she wanted to do was go to bed and cuddle her little girl and forget about everything else.

Caroline made her a hot water bottle and gave her a hug as they said goodnight.

She had thought she'd drop straight off, but she had restless legs and arms and had to get up in the end so as not to wake Beckie with all her tossing and turning. In the harsh light of the sitting room she paced, back and forward in front of the fireplace and round the coffee table with its half-finished picture of a flock of parakeets; to the darkened window and back to the door. What was Neil doing, five doors down? Was he sitting up waiting for something he knew wasn't going to happen? Or had he just gone to bed?

She was going to find out.

The front door was locked and she didn't know where Caroline kept the key.

Back door?

Fumbling on the wall for the kitchen light switch, she banged a shelf and something fell off it to the floor with a clatter.

Ten seconds later Caroline was in the hall in ninja mode, eyes wide, hair on end, feet spread ready for action. Flora giggled, and then found she couldn't stop.

'Sorry,' she gasped, as Caroline flicked on the light.

'God's sakes, Flora.'

The polka dots of the pyjama top Caroline was wearing

were doing funny things to Flora's eyes. She looked away. 'I need to go back to the house. Just for ten minutes. Can you let me out?'

'You must have had more brandy than I thought. Are you drunk?'

'No!'

'What do you want to go home for? Can't it wait till morning?'

'I want to see if he really is sitting up.'

Caroline folded her arms with a stern expression. 'Oh, right. So if he is, you're going to give him a heart attack. If he isn't, the two of you will have another row, and where will that get you? Both of you zonked out tomorrow and no use whatsoever to Beckie.'

Flora could only nod.

'Sit down. I'm making you a hot chocolate. Okay?'

Sitting down suddenly seemed like a very good idea.

It wasn't a nice table. It was one of those cheap varnished orangey pine ones, and there was a sticky patch of something under the palm of her hand. Caroline wasn't what you'd call houseproud – better things to do with her time. There was dust all over the shelf in the bathroom and mouldy grout in the shower, although the loo was clean enough.

The smell of the hot chocolate made her feel sick, but she smiled at Caroline as she handed Flora the steaming mug and sat with her hands around it.

'Ailish was right,' she said. 'I am MegaParentFail.'

Caroline spluttered into her hot chocolate. 'Like a character in a cartoon. *This is a job for MegaParentFail!*'

'No, but really – I lost it with Beckie this morning. I just lost it. As if things aren't bad enough for her already.'

'Give yourself a break, Flora. You're a good person in a really difficult situation.'

'But I'm not! That's the whole problem – I'm *not* a good person, I'm –' She stopped herself just in time.

'You're what?' Caroline put her slim, elegant hand over Flora's podgy one.

'I – when I was young...'

But she couldn't tell Caroline. She couldn't tell anyone. If the Johnsons found out –

'We've all done mad things when we were younger.' Caroline made a face. 'Don't tell Ailish, whatever you do, but I've got a conviction for drunk and disorderly. Apparently I was actually dancing on the roof of this poor bastard's car. In stilettos. Knickers on display. Can't remember a fucking thing about it, but there is photographic evidence in a dusty police file somewhere. Whatever you did, it can't be as bad as that? Can it?'

Flora stared at her, this wonderful friend she had somehow made. She felt closer to Caroline, already, than she'd ever felt to Pam. *Could* she tell her? If she swore her to secrecy?

'Eh, Flora?' said Caroline gently.

She shook her head. No.

She just couldn't take that risk.

She made herself smile, and the lie came smoothly: 'Well, no, nothing I did ever resulted in a conviction.' She pulled her hand out from under Caroline's and stood. 'Sorry. You must be so sick of us and all our dramas.'

'Don't be daft. You can talk to me, you know, any time. If you want to. About anything.'

'Thank you. You're... I don't know what we would do without you.'

Caroline stood too. 'Everything seems a hundred times worse than it is at 2:15 in the morning. Look, why don't you go and see your GP tomorrow and they can maybe give you something – just for now, just to help you sleep and stuff. I'm guessing you've not been sleeping much.'

'Not much.'

'You're going to get through this, Flora. You're –' She stopped, staring past Flora's shoulder.

Flora whipped round, scanning from window to door –

'What?'

Caroline shot round the table to the back door, cupping her hands round her face to peer out through one of the glass panels in its upper section. 'I thought... I thought I saw...'

'Oh God. You saw someone out there?' Flora went to the window, but all she could see was a reflection of herself, a madwoman with staring eyes in an old towelling robe. She pressed her face up against it, but it was too dark out there. The light from the kitchen illuminated only a few square feet of weedy concrete slabs.

She rested her palm on the cool glass: single-glazed, as all the windows in these listed old houses were. No protection at all.

'Just something moving,' said Caroline. 'It was probably a fox. Little bastards seem to be making themselves at home in the jungle I call a garden.' She expelled a breath. 'God, what are we like? Jumping at shadows. Come on, back to bed with you. You don't want Beckie waking and wondering where you are, do you?' But Flora noted that she turned the doorknob and pulled at the door to check it, and then removed the key that had been left in the lock.

lora was virtually certain that the yob sitting across the waiting room staring at her was a Johnson, or a Johnson's minion. She knew she'd seen him before. He had a long neck and a little head and a big Adam's apple like a turkey, and sharp little eyes fixed on her.

There were three other patients in the room, but they were all elderly women. They'd be no help if he went for her. And Sheena, the receptionist in the little office behind the glass window, probably had a non-intervention clause in her contract that meant she would sit there watching if one patient decided to attack another in front of her.

He was definitely looking at Flora.

Thank God Beckie wasn't here.

Neil had driven Beckie to school while Flora walked to the Health Centre. She'd felt the need for exercise, the need to get rid of all the pent-up energy inside her. She had expected Neil to object, to worry that it might be unsafe for her to walk even three streets to the Health Centre in broad daylight.

But he hadn't.

He'd just said, 'Can you pick Beckie up this afternoon?'

And the energy was still inside her, still making her legs twitch, her heels jig up and down on the carpet as if she was some hyperactive child come for her Ritalin.

The waiting room was smaller than she remembered.

A lot smaller. She felt as if she could reach out and touch the wall opposite, reach out and punch that yob right in the Adam's apple – he'd better watch it, she was ninja trained – oh God, Ailish's face when Jed-Bag had gone flying out of the window!

And then suddenly the yob was up and out of his chair and coming for her, out of nowhere, and she caught a huge gulp of air and jumped up and yelled something, and she was kicking out at his crotch and he was yelling too, and he was staggering back, away, and '*Bastard!*' she was shouting, and now, thank God, there was Dr Swain and she was telling him what had happened and the Johnson was whining and denying it, 'I never touched her,' and she was screaming, 'Keep away from me, you fucking *bastard*! Keep away from *my daughter*!'

HER HEAD FELT enormous and fragile, like her brain had swollen up and her skull was a thin bony balloon and all the nerves inside it were being squashed up against it and soon the whole thing was going to burst open. It hurt to open her eyes. She was lying down on something that felt funny – a piece of paper of all things, a giant piece of paper. She was on one of those narrow beds in a consulting room.

She could hear Neil's voice and another man's, talking too quietly for her to hear.

'Neil?'

'It's okay, Flora. You're okay.' Her hand was squeezed tight. 'You've had a sort of panic attack, the doctor thinks... Do you remember?'

.   .   .

IN THE QUEUE of traffic up Inverleith Row, she sat on the passenger seat, clutching her bag in her lap and looking out at all the people strolling by on the pavement, all the people with nice safe normal lives.

'I'm not going mad,' she finally said.

Neil, always a nervous driver, gave her a distracted look. 'Of course you're not. No one's suggesting that.'

Dr Swain had told her he thought her 'panic attack' had been a result of a combination of stress and sleep deprivation. He'd written her a prescription for an SSRI – just a short course of it, for a month. Then she was to go back and see him again.

'Neil, that man –'

Neil grimaced. 'Yeah, he's not pressing charges or anything. I explained our situation –'

'Oh, I imagine he already knows all about our *situation*. They're messing with me, Neil. Trying to make out I'm mad and an unfit mother so they can get Beckie back. He *did* try to attack me. Surely the other people in the waiting room could confirm that?'

'Apparently he stood up, tripped, and you – you went for him, basically. He didn't *attack* you.' His eyes were back on the road, on the brake lights of the white van in front.

'Okay, maybe he didn't actually touch me, but he wanted me to think he was about to. So I'd react. So I'd look like a nutter.'

'He's not a Johnson.' His voice was wearily patient. 'In fact, we know him – Darren, dunno his surname, but he's the lad who works with Bill Allen.'

Bill Allen was the builder who'd done their kitchen extension last year.

'His apprentice?' Neil prompted. 'Shy young lad? But nice – he made Beckie that wooden hamster from an offcut. The one she has on her windowsill.'

'Oh God.'

'He said he was wondering whether he should say hello or not. He got up to go to the toilet and tripped on the leg of the play table and sort of lurched forward – in your direction – and that's when you...'

'Kicked him in the balls. Oh God.'

'I think he saw the funny side. Said he wouldn't be suing you – didn't fancy producing the evidence in court.'

'But – okay, so maybe it was this Darren boy, but how do we know he's not in league with the Johnsons? Maybe that's how they found us – maybe he's a cousin or something –'

'Flora, they finished the extension a year ago. If that's how they found us, how come they've only now shown up? Of course Darren isn't involved.'

'You don't even believe it was them yesterday, do you? The Johnsons are all sweetness and light and it'll be lovely when they're part of Beckie's life – Let's throw them a party, in fact, let's have them all round for a barbeque and get this open adoption rolling!'

Neil didn't say anything. He indicated left, pulled over onto a double yellow line and stopped the car.

'Okay. So what do you want to do?'

'Right. For a start, can we expedite the CCTV installation? Pay them extra to hurry things along? We need to get firm evidence of the Johnsons harassing and intimidating us, and as soon as possible. Enough evidence to get them put away, ideally.'

He nodded. 'Evidence would be good.'

'And we need to be writing everything down, like the police said.'

'Yep, and also... Flora, if we're ever going to end up appearing as witnesses against the Johnsons in court... We need to be... um... well, credible. We need to hold it together.'

'No more kicking random people in the balls.'

'That would help.' He was drumming his fingertips on the

steering wheel. 'And we'll also need other, independent witnesses against them. I've been Googling their criminal trials and found out their address. Thirty-four Meadowlands Crescent. I was thinking we might go round there and talk to them, but –'

'Whoa! What would be the point in *that*?'

'*But*, I was saying... *But*, okay, if we're going down this road, what I'm thinking is we could go round there and speak to the neighbours. See what dirt we can dig up, if any.'

She ignored that *if any*. 'Yes! I thought of doing that too! And I was going to ask Saskia if they've got a history of using this garage for alibis... And we need to know which of the neighbours to approach – which ones we can trust.'

'Saskia would know that too,' Neil nodded. 'We could go and see her again – talk to her.'

One thing about Neil – he was a scientist through and through. It was all about the evidence. And no matter what theories he might hold, he was always open to changing his mind if the evidence led elsewhere. He knew Saskia was rabidly anti-Johnson, obviously, but he was prepared to listen to her. He was prepared to be open-minded.

'I've been trying to get through to her.' Flora found her phone in her bag and tried again. 'Still not picking up.' She frowned out of the window, at the sun dappling a bank of bright yellow and red tulips in the front garden opposite. 'But Neil. I don't think there's anything we can do to beat them. They're criminals. They're psychopaths. I think we're going to have to disappear again.'

'No,' he said at once. 'We can't keep running away from this. We can't spend our lives wondering when they're going to find us again. Beckie can't spend her life that way. Especially if... Let's face it, Flora, we don't *know* that they're a danger to us. Maybe we'd be running from something that doesn't even exist.'

'Oh, so you're just humouring me here? You're thinking that all this evidence gathering is going to come up with a big fat zero and then I'm going to have to concede that the Johnsons are no threat? I'm going to have to let them see Beckie? That's not happening, Alec. Not while I have breath in my body.'

'Hey, I'm not the enemy here, Ruth. If it looks like the Johnsons *are* a threat, don't worry, I'm prepared to do whatever it takes. And I mean *whatever* it takes to stop them getting to Beckie.'

She looked at him, this man who was her husband, as if seeing him properly for the first time. The typical beta male. The typical nerd. A ten-stone botanist who couldn't swat a fly without tripping over his own feet and knocking his front crown off on the edge of the coffee table.

But, 'Good,' was all she said.

And as he took her hand, sitting there in their bubble as the lunchtime hubbub of everyone else's nice normal lives swept past them, she made the same promise to Beckie.

Whatever it takes.

'OH, HI, RUTH!' Neil's sister Pippa's voice across nine thousand miles sounded unbearably cheerful. In the background there were other happy voices – she was probably in a bar somewhere. 'I was just thinking about you! How're you all doing?'

Where to start?

'Not great.' Flora was standing in the garden in the rain, the landline handset pressed to her ear, watching a man in an orange jacket up a ladder, positioning one of the tiny hidden CCTV cameras under the eaves. The glass doors had been replaced that morning and the glaziers had swept up the broken fragments of glass. She could see a few tiny mosaic-sized pieces, though, along the edges of the paving. She pushed at them with the toe of her shoe.

'The Johnsons have found us.'

'Oh – fuck!'

'Yep. They've been harassing us, and I'm terrified they're going to do something... Try to take Beckie.' She told Pippa everything that had happened.

'Fuck, Ruth! Fuck! Surely the police can do *something*?'

'The problem is, the Johnsons are wise to all the dodges. They've set up alibis for the times the incidents happened – quite honestly, the police don't seem to have a clue. We're getting CCTV put up around the house, but... It's just not safe to stay here now. I'm going to try to persuade Alec to leave, to disappear again, but he's saying we should stand and fight. Which is ridiculous, obviously – I mean, they're a family of hardened criminals, murderers...'

'But there are much stricter laws now, aren't there, about harassment? The police will have to do something once you have evidence. CCTV is a great idea. Once you get them on that...'

'They'll probably just get given another caution. And there are so many of them – even if one of them did get convicted and locked up, that would still leave half a dozen more...'

'But, Ruth... Say, worst-case scenario, they did take Beckie... they'd have to give her back. There's no way they're coming out of this the winners. If they keep harassing you, they're going to get into trouble, and the police will have to stop them somehow – tag them and stuff like that to stop them coming anywhere near you. They can put electronic detectors on people's houses now so that if the tagged person comes anywhere near it an alarm goes off...'

Fleetingly, it occurred to Flora to wonder how Pippa knew all this. Some of the men she'd hooked up with in the past had seemed a bit dodgy, to put it mildly. And she suspected that Pippa herself might have had a few brushes with the law.

'But what if they attacked us in the street again, not at the house?'

'They can probably put the detector on a person as well as on a house. And why *would* they attack you? That's not going to get them anywhere.'

'I don't know if they're that rational.'

'If they're setting up alibis for themselves, they sound pretty rational to me.'

Flora puffed out a sigh.

'Much as I hate to say it, I think Alec's right. You can't keep running away from them. You have to sort this. I know, easy for me to say...'

Flora waited for Pippa's offer to come back and help, but of course that didn't materialise. Under the friendly charm, Pippa was one of the most selfish people she knew. Flora finished the call with a vague promise to keep Pippa updated.

'And thanks a lot,' she muttered as she strode back to the house to break open the Hobnobs for the CCTV men.

IT WAS no good tackling Neil directly about leaving. She would have to be more subtle than that – make him think he'd come round to the idea on his own. So over the next two days she didn't even mention the possibility, pretending she was satisfied now they had the CCTV and continuing to bombard Saskia with voice and text messages which went unanswered.

Just before bed on Wednesday night, sitting with Neil on the sofa in the Family Room watching a Danish series on BBC Four, she mentioned, casually, that she'd called Pippa.

'Oh? How's she doing?'

'She seemed fine. She was talking about this new tagging system where the perpetrator wears an electronic tag that sets off an alarm if they come near the person who's being targeted, or their house...'

Neil's expression became irritatingly patient and courteous. 'Uh-huh?'

But he was saved from having to humour her further by the door flying open.

Beckie erupted into the room in a blur of purple pyjamas and flying hair. 'There's a man!'

Neil bolted from the sofa. 'Where?'

'In the garden!'

'Flora, get into the loo! Got your phone? Call 999.'

Hugging Beckie to her, Flora locked them both in the downstairs loo, which had the twin benefits of a lock on the door and a tiny high window. Flora had decorated it in a bright quirky yellow and hung the Larson cartoon of the two crocodiles relaxing after dining on canoeist in a prominent position above the towel rail. How could she ever have found that funny?

Beckie looked up at her as she tapped the nine on her phone. 'It was him again. It was that man. I heard someone shouting and I looked out and that man was there!'

20

'And then there's Mr Bean running at me like a spastic that's shat itself.' Travis takes another swally of lager and puts his other hand up the inside of Mackenzie's thigh. She's on his lap, wriggling against him like he's her fucking hero. 'And then he's tripping on a stane, flat on his fucking face, and I cannae get up the wall for pissing myself. And he's all "Stop right there, my man" and I make like I'm gonnae jump back down and he's bricking it.'

Connor's in the kitchen making us coffees, but he's earwigging, and I can see him through the door having a wee chuckle to hisself.

'Magic,' goes Jed.

I point at Travis. 'You'd better no have frighted Bekki.'

'Bekki wasnae there.'

'And no touching they bastards. We want them bricking it, aye, but no so they're gonnae up and go.'

'I didnae touch no one!'

Connor comes in with the coffees, lattes for him and Carly and Mandy, flat blacks for Ryan and Jed, a wee cappuccino for me. Mackenzie's on the ginger.

Connor's put a wee bit Flake on the side. I dip it in the foam and lick it. That coffee machine's barry so it is. 'Right Connor, me and you's off to St Andrews the morn.'

Connor sits on the floor with the dug, his back against Mandy's chair, and Mandy pats him on the heid like he's a dug an' all. 'Thanks Wee Man.' She's eating a packet of prawn cocktail with her latte, the mad cow.

'Cannae do the morn,' goes Connor. 'I've got my shift.'

'Pull a sickie, son.'

Connor's got a foam moustache on him. He doesnae lick it off like Travis would, he gets a bit tissue out his pocket and dabs it. 'Cannae. I'm already on a verbal.'

'What for?' goes Carly.

'Absenteeism.'

'Oh, *absenteeism*,' goes Travis.

'You can get cream for that,' goes Ryan.

'Who cares about your fucking job?' goes Carly. 'By the time they get round to a written warning, you'll be *Bye bye wankers* any road. Fucking numptie.'

'Aye, but.'

'Carly's right enough,' I goes. 'For once in her fucking life. You're wasted on they fuckers, son. Get me the Flora shite.'

Connor gets up and goes to the sideboard and gets out the red folder. He printed it all off of the internet – the newspaper articles about Flora's maw's death. How many folk are there in Scotland, in the fucking world, so shite-for-brains they've got themselves run over by a fucking milk float? There's only one Connor could find in the UK – Elizabeth Innes in St Andrews, back in 1989, address 24 Turner Drive.

So the bitch was Ruth Innes before she married Alec Morrison.

Whatever it is that bitch is hiding, we're finding it.

Then Connor goes, 'Motor,' and Ryan's up next him at the windae.

'Well, wouldn't you know,' goes Ryan. 'Mr Bean hisself.'

'Right yous.' I hear a car door slam, not real loud, like it's across the street maybe. 'Yous laddies dinnae move. Carly-hen, get out there. Connor, film it on your phone, aye? He's gonnae assault you, darlin', right? Connor, get that windae open for sound, and get filming.'

Mandy joins Ryan and Connor and me at the windae, still shoving prawn cocktail in her gob. Mr Bean's crossing the street and Carly's got her fat arse down the path to the gate, blocking his way, and he's all 'Let me past please' and he tries to breenge past and Carly shouts out like he's just shoved a knife in her chebs and falls back against the gate like a right hammy cow and then she's lying on the ground holding her belly giving it 'The babby! The babby!'

'THANKS, FLORA, THAT WAS LUSH,' said Caroline, bringing the empty soup bowls and the plates over to the sink. 'You're such a feeder.'

'The least I can do is feed you. Other than that I'm all *take take take.*'

'Hey, don't be daft. Happy to help. Give it a few months and it'll be me having some kind of crisis. Tony lining me up as his next victim, or oh God Flora, you won't want to know me when I'm in a dysfunctional relationship – I'm well overdue falling for a bastard – over here crying on your shoulder every five minutes. Being fed homemade soup and bread, hopefully.'

Flora smiled. Thank God for Caroline. 'I think that could be arranged.'

She squirted washing-up liquid into the sink.

Caroline twitched a tea towel from the rail of the Aga. 'It might not even come to court, you know.'

'But what was he thinking going over there in the first place? What did he think it would achieve?'

'He was angry.'

She'd never seen him so angry. At himself, she thought, as much as anything – at the way that yob had taunted him in their own garden. At the effect it had had on Beckie. After the police had arrived and he'd given his statement, he'd disappeared off in his car – to cool down, she'd thought, to take himself off away from Beckie so as not to upset her any more than she was already. Never mind Flora. Never mind leaving her to deal with the fallout, to explain to the police why he'd taken off like that.

She'd been furious with him even before she'd found out what had happened at 34 Meadowlands Crescent.

But actually getting charged with *assault*?

She clattered the cutlery into the sink.

Assault of a *pregnant woman*?

'It's almost like they planned it, eh?' Caroline mused. 'It's almost like they've been taunting you, trying to get you to react...'

'That's what Neil thinks too. But are they really that clever?' She swirled the little brush around a soup bowl and, without bothering to rinse, banged it down on the draining board.

Caroline picked it up, shaking off the suds. 'Maybe not. They probably just made use of the opportunity when Neil appeared at their door...'

'But – the bloody cheek of it! *They've* applied for a restraining order against *us*?' She slammed the other bowl down. 'And the CCTV didn't even pick Travis Johnson up – the cameras at the back don't cover that bit of the garden, next the wall at the bottom. All you see on the footage is Neil running across the grass like a maniac... It's almost as if they knew where the cameras were – as if they've been watching the house, watching where the cameras were directed...'

'I suppose that's possible,' Caroline said doubtfully.

'We need ammunition against them. We really need it!'

'Saskia still not answering?'

Flora shook her head.

'Maybe there's a problem with her phone. It sounds like, the state she's in, she could have lost it, or stopped paying for it, or it's muffled under a pile of dirty laundry or whatever. Do you have any other way of contacting her?'

'Nope, other than just turning up at her flat.' She stared at Caroline. 'And why haven't I just done that? What's stopping me driving over there now...'

'Well, you have to collect Beckie from school in...' Caroline consulted her watch 'about an hour. But you could get over there tomorrow, couldn't you? I could pick Beckie up.'

'Would you?'

'No problemo – I'm working from home. And it's always good to spend time with the Beckster.'

'Thanks, Caroline. Thank you so much.'

'And look, I wouldn't worry about these charges against Neil – any sheriff worth his or her salt is going to see through them. And I doubt the restraining order will be granted either. That little minx probably has a record as long as your arm. She's probably accusing people of assaulting her all the time.'

'Maybe.'

'Now – let's have a look at this CCTV. I want to see myself on camera.'

The bank of screens had been set up in Neil's study, ranged above his desk like he was Mr Spock in the Star Ship *Enterprise*. The screens showed the front and back gardens from various angles, and also views of the house, every door and window covered.

'Wow,' said Caroline.

'It's all very state of the art, apparently.' She sat down in Neil's swively chair and keyed in the password. 'See, we can switch any of the cameras off and on...' She clicked on the one looking out onto the street, and the screen went blank. She clicked on it again and the picture was back. 'And change the direction they point in...' She swivelled it to look off down the road. 'Either using this computer or our phones.'

'Excellent! And cute little bonsai trees.' Caroline was looking at Mimi's tank on the windowsill.

'Mm, that's...' But Flora didn't have the strength to explain Mimi the Mycorrhiza. 'Botany stuff. Okay, so footage of the front door about an hour ago...' She navigated through the menu, and on the screen there appeared a shot of Caroline, hood up against the rain, opening the gate and coming towards the front door, and running her tongue over her teeth before ringing the bell.

'Oh God – look at me checking for remnants of Jaffa cake!'

She looked as attractive as ever – and as if Jaffa cakes never passed her glossy lips.

'And you can see Ailish's house!' Caroline pointed at the screen on the far left showing the current feed for the front door. 'As if The Chipmunk Show wasn't more than enough exposure!'

The camera in the hedge covering the front door also gave a partial view into Ailish and Iain's front garden. Right on cue – she did her main shop after lunch every Thursday – Ailish's car had just pulled in at her gate. They watched her get out and open the boot, then turn and stare at the camera as if she'd suddenly seen it – but surely that was impossible? It was tiny, and hidden in the hedge.

And then the view was obliterated by something large and pink.

It receded from the lens and resolved itself into the rear view of a fat girl in a black skirt and, despite the rain, a short-sleeved pink blouse. And next to her an even larger woman in a black raincoat and leggings. They were swaying up the path to the door.

'Who's *that*?'

The bell chimed.

Flora opened the door to two unsmiling, fleshy faces blinking at her.

'You're Flora, aye? You're wee Beckie's new maw?'

Oh God.

She wanted to slam the door on them, but Caroline put a hand on her arm and said, 'And you are...?'

'I'm Lorraine Johnson. You'll have heard of me, aye? Beckie's gran? This's my daughter Carly.' She had a voice like a foghorn.

Flora couldn't help it – she took a step back. The woman was a formidable presence – a solid chunk of flesh, twenty stones at least, with rolls of fat under a determined, jutting chin. And clever little eyes that seemed to see right into Flora's heart.

The daughter blinked at Flora with a sad face, the rain glistening on her curly hair and round rosy cheeks and making dark splotches on her blouse. She was very pretty, with a sweetness to her expression that reminded Flora, horribly, just a little, of Beckie.

'We didnae mean to get your husband in trouble, aye?' Lorraine Johnson shouted. 'We didnae want him charged or nothing, we just wanted to make sure he didnae come back and hurt Carly again. She could've lost the wean. She's seven months pregnant, right? She's no in any condition to be getting assaulted and that. But we thought they'd just give him a caution.'

In the sudden silence, footsteps on gravel in Ailish's garden could be heard just the other side of the hedge.

Oh God.

'Now hold on just a minute,' said Caroline. 'It's you who've been harassing Neil and Flora. Neil only wanted to talk to you. He never meant to hurt anyone.'

'He didn't *assault* her,' said Flora.

'We've got it on camera, hen.'

'He just pushed her to get past – he didn't mean her any harm –'

'We know he was angry, aye,' Lorraine Johnson bellowed, tears now in her eyes, 'but he shouldnae have taken it out on a pregnant lassie, eh? We dinnae want no trouble. We're no here to see Beckie. We know we're no allowed. You've taken her off of us and that's broke our hearts, but it'll finish us, so it will, if anything happens to this wee one.'

And she placed her hand on Carly's massive stomach.

'*Please!*' she wailed. 'Just leave us *alone!*'

Flora opened her mouth.

'Oh for God's sake,' said Caroline.

'I'm that sorry about the other day, eh?' the ghastly woman continued, chins wobbling with emotion. 'Jed's in bits about Beckie, all he wanted was to get a wee deek at her, a wee glimpse, but when he saw you slapping her, he lost it...'

'*Slapping* her?' said Caroline.

'We know we've no say in how Beckie is disciplined now. Only – please, Flora. Dinnae hit the bairn.'

'But – I've never hit Beckie! I don't know what he thought he saw...' She turned, desperately, to Caroline, her mouth so dry she could hardly get the words out. 'You were there, in the street, when they... I didn't hit Beckie, did I?'

'Flora would never hit Beckie,' Caroline said at once.

'But you were *there* – you *know* I didn't!'

But of course Caroline didn't know any such thing. She'd only arrived on the scene after Jed Johnson had started shouting.

Caroline, though, was nodding. 'I was there,' she agreed. 'Flora was *hugging* Beckie while your husband and sons were threatening her. She wasn't *hitting* her.'

Rage filled Flora.

'How dare you come here accusing me of God knows what on the say-so of *that man*? A *convicted killer*! Your husband is a *convicted killer*, and thank God Beckie doesn't have to live with him any more, or any of your nightmare of a family! You're not the victims here!'

'And you know what? You're in breach of the court order just by being on this property,' Caroline added.

'So just *fuck off*!' Flora flung out a hand to point past them to the gate. '*Fuck off*!'

The girl took a tottering step back, and Lorraine Johnson put an exaggeratedly protective arm round her. 'No need for that, eh?'

'I think you'd better leave,' said Caroline calmly, reaching past Flora to shut the door.

'SHE'S GOT a gob on her, right enough,' goes Carly.

'Aye,' I goes. 'The brass neck of her. Giving it "You're not the victims here." It's our wee lassie's been taken off of us for no reason and we're no the fucking victims?'

Jed shuffles his arse in the La-Z-Boy, and he doesnae open his eyes, but random sounds come out his gob. He's fleein' so he is. There's a damp bit of piss on his joggers. Good job that La-Z-Boy's wipe clean.

Travis goes, 'Aye Da, my thoughts exactly' and the kids are all 'Aye, Father Jack,' the cheeky wee buggers.

The dug grabs a bit pizza off of Jordaine's plate, and she grabs it back and shoves it in her gob, and Mackenzie's like that: 'You wee minger!' and I'm biting my tongue but Carly doesnae hold back, she's 'Dinnae you call your wean a minger, that's gonnae undermine her confidence' and Mackenzie's: 'Go and take your face for a shite Carly, and maybe come back when you've popped that wean and ken what the fuck you're on about.'

I goes, 'Shut it yous. When Bekki's back I dinnae want none of this *shite this* and *fuck that*, aye? That wee lassie's gonnae show all yous up so she is.'

Mackenzie makes a face, and Corrigan goes, 'Aye, cos Bekki's a fucking wee angel.'

'Corrigan!' I yell. That boy hasnae quit giving me grief since he took his first fucking breath, wickit wee red face yowling and looking at me like he was: *Aye Lorraine, here's me, another fucking mad Johnson bastard.*

I'm needing outta here. I get my arse in the kitchen with the wee pay-as-you-go I bought yesterday. I put in the number for Social Services at Glasgow City Council.

'Oh, hello,' I goes when I'm through to the right fucker. 'This is Lydia Ross from Police Scotland – I'm calling in connection with the Saskia Mair investigation?'

'Oh. Right...' And you can hear the bint thinking: *Christ, am I in the shit here? What are they wanting to speak to me for?*

'I'm not sure if it was you or your colleague I spoke to yesterday?'

'That must have been Teresa.'

'Okay, well, no matter. We've just been to interview Saskia Mair again, but it seems she's no longer at the same address, or at least that was the story – could you just check and see if the address at Bielside Road is her current one, please? We're outside the property now, so if you could do that now, that would be great.'

'Yes, of course.' Relieved it's no her arse in the shit. 'Could you just hold on one second while I call up the file?'

Candy from a bairn.

'When's Bekki gonnae be here?' says wee Kai when I get back in the lounge. He cannae wait. God love him, he asked me the other day if Jordaine was gonnae get swapped for Bekki, like he was hoping.

Bairns!

'In a wee while,' I goes.

'I'm gonnae save this for Bekki,' goes Kai, and he lifts up the slice of pizza he's piled pepperoni on that he's picked off of the slice he's eaten. Kai doesnae like pepperoni. It all falls on the carpet and the dug hoovers it.

'She willnae want pizza,' goes Corrigan. 'Bekki only eats organic shite made by beardy wankers cos she's saving the fucking planet, the fucking wee snob.'

'Travis!' I goes. 'Are you gonnae just sit there and let him aff wi' that?'

Travis is on his tablet. He doesnae even look up, he just goes, 'Shut it ye wee bass.'

Looks like Travis and Mackenzie are maybe getting back together, and I'm no sure how I feel about that. It'll be barry seeing more of the weans, and they need taking in hand right enough, but that wee minger Mackenzie, I hate her fucking guts. She's a shite mother. Puts Jordaine in wee crop tops and lets her wear make-up and Jordaine's only five year old. Films her doing sexy moves, grinding her wee hips in time to Beyoncé. Gives me the boak. Gonnae end up a tart like her maw if we dinnae nip that in the bud.

Carly goes, 'Do you reckon Ailish heard?'

'Oh aye, darlin'. She heard all right.'

Timing was spot on. You could set your watch by that Ailish bint. Back home 2:30 every Thursday with her weekly shop from Marks and Sparks. So she's out there unloading for two, three minutes, and no way is that nosy cow not earwigging when two gobby bitches roll up at the Parrys' door.

'Flora was bricking it,' goes Carly.

'"But I never hit Bekki!"' I goes.

Ryan and Travis are pissing themselves.

'You were ace, Maw,' goes Carly. 'Here, if I have this wean preterm, I could maybe sue those bastards, eh, make out like it was the assault caused it –'

'Jesus Chutney! Dinnae even think about it!'

'I'm joking you!'

Aye, but is she? God's sakes, this fucking family.

And now Travis is going, 'Aw Christ, look at the state of it,' because Connor's at the lounge door in his funeral suit, and Mackenzie's cackling, and Corrigan goes, 'Put a suit on a bampot, it's still a bampot' and Travis is leaning over to high-five the wee shite, and I'm, 'Corrigan!'

'Aye Corrigan,' goes Connor. 'You'll maybe wannae reflect on the fact that when I was your age I could spell my own fucking name, aye? So if I'm a bampot, what does that make you?'

Corrigan's giving him evils.

'He's fucking *dyslexic*?' goes Mackenzie.

'Aye, and the rest,' goes Ryan.

Connor eyeballs me. 'You ready, Maw?'

'Aye son.' I get up off my arse. 'Aye son, let's us get outta here.'

I PARK on the street opposite 24 Turner Drive. It's a nice area, a posh wee street with bungalows and gardens for folk that's got nothing better to do than go at their lawns with nail scissors, and bonnie blossom trees, and it's a right bonnie evening with the sun hitting the blossom, still as anything, and at the end of the street you get a wee keek at the sea with the sunlight dancing off of it.

I need a jobbie. Fucking pizza lying heavy.

We start with Number 22 next door, but the place is dead and no bastard answers. Number 26 but, a wee wifie comes to the door carrying a yappy wee dug, a manky Scottie with brown scliters down its gob.

'I'm sorry to bother you,' I goes in a polite wee voice. 'My name's Susan Marchbanks and this is Kenneth Brown – we're from a company called We-Locate that searches for heirs of people who've died intestate and left a sizeable estate...'

'As featured on *Heir Hunters*,' goes Connor.

Aye, and that's got her attention right enough. 'Although it's mainly our Solihull branch features in the programme.'

She's nodding along, pound signs dancing across her fucking eyeballs.

'It's Ruth Innes we're looking for,' I goes.

It's pure comical so it is – the trip to the Canaries and the new smart TV gone for a Burton.

'The last address we have for her is 24 Turner Drive,' goes Connor.

I says, 'There's a monetary reward for information that allows us to trace an heir. Any information you can provide about Ruth Innes or her family could qualify.'

'Oh? What kind of... monetary reward would you be talking about?'

Connor opens the folder he's got with him and makes like he's checking. 'Given the value of the estate, we'd be looking at a sum in the region of one thousand three hundred pounds.'

She's back interested. 'Well, I don't know if what I can tell you would be of any help...'

'You'd be surprised. Mrs...?' I smile.

'Campbell. Jean Campbell.'

'Would you like to talk to us now, or...'

'Yes, that's fine. Please come in.'

She shuts the dug up somewhere ben the house and comes back in the front room with a tray with mugs and biscuits. Connor's got the form he printed out last night, and he sits there on the Parker Knoll and starts reading out questions – name, date of birth, all that shite, then it's, 'Do you have a current address for Ruth Innes?'

Wifie: 'No, I'm afraid not. After her mother died and the bungalow was sold, I didn't see Ruth again.'

Me: 'Did you know the family well when they lived next door?'

Wifie: 'Not to say *well*, but she was a good neighbour, Liz Innes, especially after my husband died. We'd have morning coffee together now and then, and go for the odd walk.'

There's something she's no saying. There's something here right enough.

Connor: 'And did you see much of her daughter Flora?'

The wee diddy. 'You mean Ruth, Kenneth.' I roll my eyes at the wifie. 'I think you're getting mixed up with Flora Adams from a previous case.'

'Oh aye. Aye. Sorry, Maw.'

Fucking hell.

'Susan,' he goes, a right beamer on him.

I shake my head and give a wee giggle. 'They call me "Ma" in the office because I'm always asking if they had enough for breakfast and telling them to wipe their feet – and this one's getting a clip round the ear in a minute! Ha ha ha!'

Wifie smiles, but like she's thinking *Eh...?*

'So,' I goes. 'Did you see much of Ruth?'

Wifie: 'No, Ruth wasn't home much. She was at boarding school, you see, and then university.'

'So they weren't close, then, Mrs Innes and her daughter?'

Wifie sucks in her cheeks. 'I wouldn't say they were close, no. It was odd, actually – I always thought it was odd that she hardly ever mentioned Ruth. I'm always blethering on about my two boys and the grandchildren, you can't shut me up, but Liz – if you asked her how Ruth was doing, she'd just smile and say, "Oh fine," and change the subject.'

I knew it! I fucking knew it!

'She was a cold woman in a way. Perfectly nice, but... not much warmth to her. On the few occasions Ruth was home, I never saw them go out together to the shops or anything. They seemed to live very much separate lives, which I thought was sad. Ruth was a lovely girl. She used to take Molly – my old Westie, Dee-Dee's great-grandmother – for walks, and she'd come in and feed her and cuddle her and groom her. Lovely. I wondered – even before the accident, I mean – I wondered if maybe Liz was depressed.'

I goes, 'This is the accident with the milk float you're talking about?'

Wifie: 'Awful. It really was. I saw it happen, you know. I was potting up plants at the front door... Primroses, I think. No – no, it was pansies. Liz was crossing the street – the milk float had been parked at the kerb, but then it started reversing. Liz – she seemed rooted to the spot. I shouted at her and dropped a pot onto the slabs, and it smashed, and then the milk float hit her and she went under the wheels. She could have got out of the way, but she didn't even seem to try. I almost got the impression – as I said at the time – I almost got the impression that she couldn't be bothered moving. I know that sounds ridiculous, but the way she just stood there sort of slumped... As if she was in a daze...'

Connor: 'That must have been hard for Ruth.'

Wifie: 'Oh, terrible. But I had to speak out, you see, at the fatal accident inquiry, for the sake of the poor driver. Yes, he should have looked in his mirrors before he started reversing, but it wasn't as if she couldn't have got out of the way.'

I goes, 'So what you're saying is that it was... to all intents and purposes... suicide by milk float?'

Connor snorts.

Wifie gives him evils. 'You could almost say that. The driver was convicted of dangerous driving nevertheless – got a few months in prison, poor man. He was devastated.'

'He must have been,' I goes.

'Hell of a thing to happen.' Connor makes like he's consulting his notes. 'And Liz and Ruth came to live next door when?'

'Oh – it would have been about 1983, I suppose.'

'They moved here from Australia, aye?'

'Well.' Wifie purses her lips. 'That was their story. Liz had an Australian accent, yes, just a slight one. But Ruth didn't. And when I would ask Ruth about Australia, she used to contradict what Liz had told me. About where they lived in Sydney, for one thing – Liz told me they lived in a suburb a lot like on *Neighbours*, and when they left to come to the UK, there was even a street party in the cul-de-sac to wish them *bon voyage*, but when I asked Ruth later if she enjoyed watching *Neighbours* because it reminded her of her old home – this was when *Neighbours* had just started and everyone was watching it – she said, "Oh, but we lived in a flat in the city, it was nothing like *Neighbours*." I told her that Liz had said they did live in a similar suburb, and you could see her thinking fast, and then she came out with, "I was too young to remember – we moved to the city when I was five." But Liz had told me they had that street party in the cul-de-sac when they left for the UK. That's when I knew they weren't telling the whole truth about it. And there were things Ruth didn't know about Australia – like where Darwin was. Any child growing up in Australia would know that, surely?'

'Aye,' I goes, 'that's a bit strange. So you think maybe Liz was Australian but Ruth was brought up somewhere else?'

'That was my suspicion. Although why they'd lie about it, I don't know.'

Aye, that was the question all right. That was the fucking question.

'Well, this is all very useful information, Mrs Campbell. Thank you.' I goes to stand up.

'And the monetary...?'

'We'll be in touch if the information you've provided facilitates the location of Ruth Innes,' goes Connor.

'And before we go,' I says, 'would it be possible to use your lavatory?'

21

'I don't think Edith will want to come, though,' said Beckie through a mouthful of muesli.

Flora took a swallow of tea. 'Well, maybe if you ask her really nicely, she will.'

'I'm already giving her like half my lunch and she still hardly speaks to me.'

'Beckie, you do realise that your own lunch is exactly the same size as ever? I hope you *have* been giving the extra food to Edith, and not eating it yourself.'

Beckie sighed. 'Yes! But you know how seagulls swoop down and snatch your food and then they disappear? Edith's like a human seagull. She's suddenly *there*, and then after I've given her the food, she's gone. I've asked her if she wants to play with us but she doesn't.'

Flora bit her lip. She had passed on to Mrs Jenner her concern about Edith not getting enough to eat, and Mrs Jenner had said she'd look into it, but according to Beckie, Edith still seemed desperate for the extra lunch Flora was now packing, which included ever more calorific – and presumably tempting to Beckie – items such as Snickers and homemade flapjacks. *Was* Beckie handing it all over?

She'd have to speak to Mrs Jenner again.

'If she does come to the party,' added Neil, 'you're going to treat her like a princess the whole time she's here. That'll be a good start to making it up to her.'

Beckie sighed. 'I know, but Edith hates me now.'

'I'm sure she doesn't,' said Flora weakly, although this was all too likely.

She waited for Neil to back her up, but he was intent on the screen of his laptop, breaking his own 'no screens at the table' rule.

As she got up and walked to the sink behind his chair, she saw that he had a table of data up on the screen – catching up on the work he'd let slide since the Johnsons had reappeared. Getting back to normal life. Carrying on as if nothing had happened.

They'd had another argument in bed this morning. Neil had decided that the Johnsons' whole strategy must be to persuade the authorities to review the adoption; to cast doubt on Neil and Flora's suitability as adoptive parents by provoking them to violence.

'Or to make us *appear* violent,' he'd added. 'I hardly even touched Carly Johnson.'

'They've got you on camera pushing her!'

'I didn't *push* her. I just tried to get past, and she deliberately fell to the ground. She's a pretty good actress, as you found out for yourself yesterday.' He'd sat up in bed and glared at her. They had intended taking the footage of Lorraine and Carly Johnston coming to the door to the police as evidence of their breaching the court order, but on playing it had discovered that the camera angle, from behind Carly, made it look as if Flora flinging out her arm to tell them to 'Fuck off' was an attempt to hit the girl, who had staggered back on cue. Flora had argued that Caroline would back up her version of the encounter, but as Neil had impatiently pointed out, a friend was hardly an independent witness – and what if the Johnsons had realised their nosy neighbour next door had been listening and told the police to go and ask Ailish? What might Ailish not say, just to land them in it?

Flora had sighed. 'We could just give the police the bit that shows them coming to the door. Truncate the footage at the point where I open the door...'

'Don't be stupid, Flora. The Johnsons would counterclaim that you tried to assault Carly again, and the police would ask to see the whole interaction and maybe interview Ailish.'

'But if we wiped the footage after the point where they come to the door...'

'We can't wipe it, it's all kept securely for six months on Eden Security's system. If the Johnsons do make another complaint off their own bat, and the police ask to see the footage, we're in trouble. We've seriously underestimated them. We've been stereotyping them as violent thugs without a brain cell between them who've been making a series of incompetent attempts to snatch Beckie, or possibly just harassing us out of malice – but they've obviously got another agenda. They're trying to make out *we're* the bad guys. And so far they're doing a pretty good job. What we have to do is remember that it's all bluster – that they're not going to actually *do* anything. They're not going to hurt us or snatch Beckie. We have to just turn the other cheek. Not let them provoke us again.'

'So you're saying they're not really dangerous at all. That they're harmless, like – like kids using naughtiness to provoke a reaction. And that we should stop stressing about it and just ignore them?'

'Exactly. Everything they've done has obviously been designed to provoke us into doing something stupid, so a lawyer can argue that *we're* the ones who are unfit to have custody of Beckie.'

'But we know that they *are* dangerous. They're hardened criminals. We can't afford to let down our guard, especially not where Beckie's concerned. Maybe that's what they want us to do. Maybe they want us on the back foot, maybe they're counting on us relaxing and thinking "As long as we don't react, everything will be fine", and that's when they'll strike.'

'If they were going to "strike", they'd have done so by now. If snatching Beckie has been their aim, let's face it, there's nothing much we could have done to stop them, "hardened criminals" as they are.'

She'd felt the bed rock as he'd pushed himself out of it.

'I'm going to Glasgow to see Saskia,' she'd said.

'What good's that going to do?'

'I thought you agreed that we should speak to her? Find out which of the neighbours to approach...'

'That was before it became clear what the Johnsons are up to. And anyway, we can't believe a word that woman says.'

Breakfast had been strained to say the least. But Flora knew she was right about this: they had to get as much on the Johnsons as they could from Saskia, and pick her brains on how to tackle them. Maybe Saskia would know something about the garage that had supplied Travis Johnson's so-called alibi; and she might let Flora have the names and numbers of the neighbours who had been prepared to talk and had described the Johnsons as a 'family from hell', so Flora could call them and maybe arrange to meet at a café or something – because no way were either of them going anywhere near Meadowlands Crescent again.

The landline started ringing on the side table by the TV.

She picked it up. 'Hello, Flora Parry here?'

'Oh, hello, Mrs Parry. This is Karen Baxter. I'm a Children's Reporter with the Scottish Children's Reporter Administration.

I'm calling to ask if it would be possible to arrange a time when I could pop round and see you and your husband and Beckie, just to check that everything's okay?'

Still smiling at Beckie, she pulled open the glass doors and took the call outside. 'What do you mean, to check that "everything's okay"? Scottish Children's... what?'

'Scottish Children's Reporter Administration. We deal with child welfare and protection in Scotland. We've had a referral from a member of the public with a few concerns about Beckie. I need to just pop round and see you. Would after school on Monday be convenient – say, 4:30?'

Flora shut her eyes. Breathed in the fresh, early morning scents of the garden. '*Concerns? What kind of concerns?*'

'We can talk about that when I see you.'

'But that's not necessary!' She crossed the patio to the expanse of grass, wanting to take this call as far from Beckie as possible. 'Beckie's fine, there's no –'

'We have a duty to investigate every referral made, Mrs Parry – if, as you say, everything's fine, no further action will be taken. But we do have to carry out an investigation, as I say, once a referral has been made.'

'This is the Johnsons. Beckie's biological family.' The grass was still dewy, moisture soaking into her pumps. 'It's meant to be a closed adoption, but they've found out where we live and they've been harassing us. It's the Johnsons, isn't it, who've made the referral?'

'I can't discuss that with you.'

Oh God. Neil, of course, was going to see this as support for his theory that the Johnsons were basically harmless, out to discredit them and nothing more; to make out that they were unsuitable parents for Beckie.

'No. Of course. All right. Tomorrow at 4:30, then. I suppose you have our address?'

.   .   .

THE PLACE IS a fucking disgrace so it is, fucking needles and that lying in the close and a big jobbie that looks fucking human.

Ryan's pulling on the white forensic suit over his shirt and the wee cushion he's got strapped to his belly, and then he's putting on the tabard with 'Environmental Health' on the back like I'm wearing. When he's done, I lean on him to put on the blue plastic covers for my trainers, and he's leaning on me to do the same, then we're pissing ourselves when we're getting the showercap whoogies on us over the wigs, and pulling up the masks, like we're dealing with fucking Ebola here.

Aye well, what we are dealing with isnae any less virulent, eh?

I make sure the false neb's still in place under the mask. Ryan got it off of the internet and it's that realistic wee Kai didnae even know me when I was practising with make-up and that, the poor wee bairn was 'Hello?' and his wee face was *Who are you and where's my Nana?*

I pull on the gloves and buzz the buzzers at the door. I've got my story all ready – we're from the Council, Environmental Health, here to get the place cleaned up – but I dinnae need it, the door buzzes open. Fuckers cannae even bother their arses to ask who's there?

Candy from a bairn.

Mair likely thinks she's safe enough in this dump.

Ryan's whistling his way up the stair, taking it two steps at a time.

I like to see a man happy in his work.

At Mair's flat door I do a *rap-tap-a-tap-tap* nice and cheery, and I go, 'Hi, Saskia, it's Claire from the ground-floor flat, can I have a wee word?' Mair isnae gonnae know anyone in the stair. 'It's about the wee lassie in Flat 2, she's in the hospital and I've got a card going round…'

There's sounds from inside the flat. Footsteps.

I've got the dishcloth I've brought with me over the peephole.

'Just take a sec for an autograph,' I goes, so fucking cheery it would make you boak.

There's scraping and clunking and then the door's opening and Ryan's breenging against it and Mair's 'Uh! Uh!' like she's a fucking chimp, and then we're in with the door shut behind us and I'm 'Hello Saskia-hen' and she's making a run for it to the bog and Ryan's got her by the arms and he shoves her back against the wall.

I can tell he's grinning away behind the mask.

I shove the dishcloth in her gob.

She's a fucking mess so she is, like she's no brushed her hair for a fucking month, and the stink off of her!

'Aye hen,' I goes. 'You fucked with our wean and now we're fucking with you. That's justice. That's fucking justice, eh?'

Mair's shaking her head.

'You hurt our Bekki. You took her whole fucking family off of her and gave her to fucking randoms. Her whole fucking family, that loved her to pieces and that she loved right back.'

Mair's pure white and she's shaking like an alky.

'Saskia-hen – I can call you Saskia, aye? Saskia-hen, it's payback time. Me and the family have been having a wee conference about what all you can do to make it up to Bekki. That right, son?'

Ryan smacks Mair back against the wall and goes, 'Aye. We've had what you might call some constructive interfacing around the whole issue and we have come to the conclusion that you, hen, are a piece of shite needs wiped off the arse of the fucking planet.'

Mair's going, 'Oh go... gay gay-eh-eh!'

'What's that, hen?' I goes. 'We're no gonnae get away with it? Oh, we're gonnae get away with it, because unlike you we're professionals. We're not in fucking forensic suits for a wee joke, eh?'

'It's not fucking Hallowe'en!' chuckles Ryan.

'Ee-ee gi-ee,' goes Mair.

'Eh?'

'CCTV, hen?' I chuckle. 'There's no cameras in the close – what bastard's gonnae bother? Two in the street that maybe cover the entrance, but the boys dealt with they ones last night.'

'Like Maw says, we're professionals.'

'It's a wee shame though, eh, what it's gonnae do to your kids? Hard on them, growing up without their maw. But maybe you shoulda thought about what kids' families mean to them before you started fucking with their lives, eh?'

'But check it, Maw.' Ryan waves a hand. 'Check the place. Check this bitch. Her weans come and bide, they're gonnae get septicaemia off of all this crap, and maybe while she's high on her drug of choice they're gonnae give it a wee try? We're doing they weans a favour.'

'You're right, son. We're practically Child Fucking Protection.'

Ryan chuckles. 'No word of a lie.'

'When I think,' I goes, real quiet, in Mair's face, 'when I think of you and that so-called *Doctor* Fernandez cooking up that pack of lies... The two of yous go for a wee coffee at Starbucks, aye, when yous was supposedly round ours carrying out a rigorous professional assessment of our ability to care for our wean? Sit there making up shite about low IQs and depression while you sipped your skinny lattes? Do I look like a fucking eejit, doll? Do I look like I'm depressed?'

THE GREY, dirty, dingy little courtyard wasn't just deserted – it felt abandoned, as if no one could possibly live here. No one, surely, could open that battered, graffiti-covered door and think 'Home'?

Flora couldn't remember which flat number Saskia was, so she pressed all the buzzers and waited.

No response.

It must have rung with voices once, this little close, with all those barefoot Haghill children, their lives spilling out of the single-ends down the stair and into the close and the street, all mixed up together in happy, heedless communal poverty. She'd heard them on TV programmes, these children, saying in old age: 'We didn't *know* we were poor, you see – sixpence to spend down the shop and we were millionaires! Deprived? Not a bit of it! None of us felt *deprived*. We all looked out for each other, you know? If you were out playing and you were hungry, you could chap a door and ask for a piece and like as not get it, though you'd maybe to put up with "Aw, Davie, the state of you!" and getting your face scrubbed and a comb through your hair. We were surrounded by folk that cared about us – how were we *deprived*, eh? Happy as the day is long.'

Did Saskia hear those children's ghosts, she wondered, their high voices echoing up the deserted close? Did they haunt her? Reproach her for what she'd done?

She tried the array of buzzers again. This time, a crackly voice said, 'Aye?'

'Hello. I'm here to see Saskia Mair in one of the top flats.'

'Okay dear.' And the door buzzed open.

Her shoes on the worn stone steps rapped out a rhythm as she climbed, clop clop, clop clop, echoing off the hard surfaces.

Saskia's door was open, just slightly. Maybe the neighbour had told her that Flora was on her way up. She knocked nevertheless.

'Saskia?'

No response.

Could she have popped down to the communal garden or into a neighbour's flat?

'Hello, Saskia? It's Flora.' She pushed open the door.

The place stank of stale air and drains. There was a pile of dirty clothes against the wall, and something dark and wet had been spilt on the carpet.

Not a pile of clothes.

'Saskia!'

That was blood.

Hands shaking, Flora knelt to push the hair off Saskia's face, to feel for a pulse at her neck.

No pulse.

She felt warm to the touch, but that could be because Flora was, suddenly, so freezing cold herself. Was she still warm?

'Saskia,' she said again, stupidly.

Vital signs.

She'd been a nurse, for God's sake.

Vital signs.

She found her sunglasses in her bag and held them, shaking, under Saskia's nose, peering at the dark surface for signs of condensation.

Nothing.

Shoving the sunglasses back in her bag and fumbling for her phone, she turned on the flashlight app. Her hand steady now, she lifted Saskia's right eyelid. The eye under it was rolled back slightly, as if already turned to heaven. She shone the light into the eye.

No constriction of the pupil.

She lifted one of Saskia's arms – surprisingly heavy for such a thin person – and shone the flashlight onto the skin under the forearm. It was reddened in mottled patches.

The first, definitive signs of lividity.

So no CPR.

She must have been dead for at least half an hour.

And then all Flora could do was kneel there as Saskia's blood soaked from the carpet into the knees of her jeans. The source of the blood, the nurse's part of her brain noted, was Saskia's chest – the front of the green T-shirt she was wearing was one huge dark purple stain.

Saskia Mair had been stabbed to death.

She needed to call the police.

She tapped 999 on her phone and then stopped.

She couldn't.

If she called the police, she would be scrutinised as a possible suspect. They would dig into her past. They might find out that Ruth Innes died at the age of six and was reborn as a teenager in 1983. They might find out about Rachel.

No one had seen her come in here.

She needed to just go.

She could find a phone box, disguise her voice, tell the police she was a concerned neighbour who didn't want to give her name, but there had been yobs hanging about the stair and she thought they might have got into Saskia's flat.

Or she could just go.

She dropped her phone back in her bag and stood.

'Sorry,' she mouthed to Saskia.

The knees of her jeans were sticky with blood. But they were dark navy denim and it wasn't too noticeable. She was parked just round the corner. All she had to do was get to her car without attracting attention.

But the police would be asking people about anyone they'd seen. There might even be CCTV in the street.

There were four doors off the tiny hall. The second one she tried was a cupboard, with some coats hanging up and others in a pile on top of various boxes. She found a raincoat which was way too small but which, tied round her waist by the sleeves, flapped over her knees and concealed the bloodstains.

Now she needed something to hide her face.

A hat?

She couldn't see one.

She opened another door – a bathroom, smelling of mould and uncleaned toilet, a grey tidemark all round the bath. And another – a chaotic bedroom – clothes all over the bed and floor, a furring of dust on the cheap pine dressing table.

She had her hand on the wardrobe when she realised: fingerprints. DNA.

She grabbed a dirty pink T-shirt from the floor and used it to wipe the door of the wardrobe, then the door handles in the hall. Had she touched anything else? Had she touched Saskia? Would her DNA be on Saskia's body?

She thought she had maybe touched her face.

Her neck, definitely, when she was feeling for a pulse.

Then, she had touched her with the tenderness of one human confronted by another who'd been hurt, who needed help. Now, it was like being a butcher prepping a slab of meat as she wiped the T-shirt flinchingly across Saskia's dead forehead, cheeks and neck.

Then she returned to the wardrobe and used the T-shirt to open it.

No hats.

There were a couple of hoodies badly folded on a shelf, one of which, a pale grey one, looked roomy enough to fit her. She grabbed it, wriggled it on over her top and pulled up the hood, feeling the need to hide her face immediately. It smelt of sweat and sickly deodorant. Her throat contracted and she gagged.

She folded her arms, hands tucked away so she wouldn't accidentally touch anything else, and stepped carefully from the bedroom to the hall – she didn't look down again – and to the front door of the flat. It was still standing slightly open.

She stopped just inside it and listened, but there were no sounds coming from the stairwell. Quickly, before she lost her nerve, she stepped onto the stone landing and, tugging the sleeve of the hoodie over her hand, pulled the door almost shut.

Her mouth dry, her pulse thumping in her ears, she made herself walk, not run, down the stone steps, onto the landing below, past the two doors there, onto the next flight of steps, the raincoat flapping against her legs.

On the next landing down she could hear voices behind one of the doors, the scruffy black one. What if the door suddenly opened and they saw her?

Grabbing the bannister, she flung herself round the curve of the stairwell and down two steps at once – and jolted to a halt.

Idiot!

She'd touched the bannister with her bare hand.

She pulled the thin wool of the hoodie's sleeve over her hand and ran it back up the bannister to where she'd grabbed it. She was going to be sick. Sour bile was rising at the back of her throat again –

If she was sick, could they get DNA from it?

Swallowing and gasping, she somehow made it down the last flight of stairs to the dingy passage that led to the main door.

Her footsteps clopped along it, echoing up the stair as she heard a voice on the landing above; a harsh laugh.

She ran.

Pulling the sleeve back over her hand, she wrenched open the heavy door and ran out into the air, up the narrow close to the street, to the litter and the traffic and the run-down shopfronts and the people walking by – an old woman's sharp little eyes on her –

She stopped running – slowed to a normal pace, her legs almost buckling under her, as if they'd forgotten how to do it, how to move normally.

She looked down at her feet as they moved, one past the

other, at the grubby pavement with its pockmarks of chewing gum, its fag ends and its broken paving. It had been raining, and where the slabs had sunk and cracked, dirty brown puddles had formed in random geometric shapes. Even the puddles here had hard edges. The pavement had a sheen on it, and her right foot came down on a disintegrating scratch card stuck to its surface.

All around her was the sound of people, potential witnesses – so many cars swishing past, so many bodies passing by, looking at her, probably, this strange woman in the hoodie walking with her head down.

But it had been raining, so maybe that was okay.

She risked a glance up to get her bearings. There was the newsagent on the corner with dusty windows behind metal grilles, a stark contrast to the aggressively smiling, doll-like celebrity couple on the sandwich board outside.

She waited for a break in the traffic, hood pulled well over her face, and when it came she ran across the road, ran up the side street where she'd left her car.

The tears came, for some reason, as soon as she caught a glimpse of red behind the broad rear of a silver four-by-four. Her little red Ka. For some reason, it was at this moment that she was no longer able to hold back the image of Saskia's little boy in his mother's arms, the arms that had held him as no one else ever would again.

I just wanted to see you.

Fumbling the key from her pocket, she pointed and pressed the rubbery button and the car winked its lights at her and she hauled open the door and dived inside.

22

The internet was full of Saskia, although her name hadn't yet been released.

While Beckie and Neil ate breakfast and argued about whether cats were too intelligent to be trained (Beckie) or not intelligent enough (Neil), Flora sat on one of the sofas with her laptop, trawling through the newsfeeds, trying to concentrate through the pulses of pain just above her eyebrows.

With the sound muted, she watched an STV reporter standing on the street outside the entrance to the close, while in the background a little crowd of people had gathered and a policewoman stood in front of the 'Police – Road Closed' sign, hands behind her back, face impassive. Behind her, blue and white police tape was stretched right across the road, and between the Road Closed sign and the tape there were white vans and police cars parked and people milling about, some in black police uniforms, some in white forensic suits, some in plain clothes.

She closed the page and did another search for 'Glasgow woman dead'. A BBC article was the first hit. It said that a woman had been found dead in a flat in the Haghill area of

Glasgow and police were treating her death as suspicious. And that she was understood to be a former social worker who had recently been suspended from her post with Glasgow City Council pending an inquiry into her conduct.

She closed her eyes.

'Mum?' said Beckie. 'Can we?'

She looked up. 'Hmm?'

'When Mia's cat has kittens, can we have one? Dad says we can if you agree.'

'I didn't say that, Beckie,' Neil said quickly, aiming an appeasing smile at Flora. He thought she was still angry with him – about the 'assault' on Carly Johnson and/or his new *laissez faire* strategy. He thought that was why she'd burst into tears when he'd started apologising again about it as they were preparing breakfast. He thought that was why she was so touchy and trembly and snappy.

She wished she could tell him about Saskia. But she couldn't. She couldn't tell him why she hadn't called the police.

Instead, she'd told him she hadn't gone to see Saskia after all. That she'd decided he was right, and they couldn't trust her. That she would ask Deirdre about the Johnsons instead.

'So can we?' Beckie persisted.

'No we can't.' She sighed. 'Beckie. Do you really think getting a kitten is a good idea?'

Beckie's face became expressionless. 'Because the Johnsons might kill it?'

'Oh, no darling, I just meant – kittens are a lot of work...' She shut the laptop and came over to the table and draped her arms round Beckie's neck. 'The Johnsons aren't going to do anything bad to us. And even if they try to, the police will arrest them.'

'They already tried to and the police haven't done anything.'

'Well, they've cautioned them. So if they do anything else,

they'll be in big trouble. And now we've got the CCTV, we'll have them on camera if they come anywhere near the house.'

What if she'd been caught on CCTV at Saskia's? What if even now the police were on their way here to arrest her?

But if she was on CCTV, surely whoever had killed Saskia would be too?

The Johnsons.

She wasn't going to kid herself that anyone else could be responsible.

They'd killed Saskia. They must have found out that Saskia had been suspended from her post for hurting children. And they'd managed to track her down and kill her.

And if they were capable of that, what might they do to Flora and Neil and Beckie?

'They can't do anything to us, darling,' she finished lamely. 'And now we're going to forget all about them and have a really fun day. After we've been to Cairn Hill, how about we have lunch at the Bistro?'

'Okay.' Beckie wriggled out from her arms and stood. 'I have to brush my teeth.'

When she'd left the room, Neil said, 'Are you okay?'

'Why on earth would you tell her she can have a kitten?'

'I didn't. But would it be such a terrible idea?'

'Do you really think I have the energy at the moment to cope with a demanding small animal? Because it would be me dealing with it, wouldn't it?' She sat down at the table opposite him and rubbed her forehead. 'Beckie can have her tablet in the car, just this once, so I can get some sleep.' It was the only thing guaranteed to keep her quiet.

'We shouldn't be inconsistent about these things, Flora.'

'I've got a really bad headache and I need to sleep in the car, okay?'

Neil raised his eyebrows – *Whatever* – and left the room.

· · ·

CONNOR'S SITTING in his PC World uniform with his laptop, reading all about Mair's tragic and untimely demise, and he's like that: 'What if there's another CCTV camera that yous didnae clock?'

Ryan rolls his eyes at me and he's all, 'Dinnae you have a cow, Wee Man. We was in wigs and that, eh, and I had a right fat belly on me, and the neb on Maw – you wouldnae have picked us out a line-up yoursel'.'

Connor's no happy. 'The motor, but?'

'Stolen fucking motor with false plates?'

'Aye...' goes Connor.

'Aye,' goes Ryan. 'So shut it with your fucking whinging. We covered all the bases. Gold stars all round. We're no in perfor-mance-below-acceptable-standard territory here, eh?' And he's chuckling away to hisself.

Connor's on another verbal at his work for performance below acceptable standard. They get in the shite if they just sell the punter what they're wanting without any of they crap extra care plans and add-ons and that, and the manager's telt the wee diddy he'd better start pushing the crap or else.

Jed wakes up and goes, 'That bint's motor's gonnae be picked up in the vicinity though, eh? She's no gonnae have false plates. Get on the polis, son, and get clyping on the bitch. You saw this bird looking suspicious and you got the plate.'

I roll my eyes at Ryan and he rolls his eyes at me. Are we the only ones in this fucking family with any fucking sense?

'Naw Da, no yet,' goes Ryan. 'The plan, aye?'

'The plan? The plan? Away and shove your fucking plan,' goes Jed, and falls back asleep, the prick.

23

Flora was woken from a heavy doze by Beckie's whine at the bedroom door. 'I want to say goodbye to Mum.'

'Mum's asleep – we have to let her rest,' came Neil's voice.

'It's okay, I'm not asleep,' she called, and Beckie shot into the dark bedroom and wormed into the bed and pressed her cool little body against Flora's side.

'I don't want to go to school,' she said. 'I want to stay here with you. Can I?'

Flora's heart turned over. 'I'm sorry, darling, but you have to go to school. You have to give out the party invitations, don't you?'

God. This bloody party.

'I should stay and look after you.' Beckie's fingers stroked Flora's arm.

'Well, darling, really I think I just need to sleep.'

'The doctor said it was nothing serious?' Beckie had asked her this about three times since Flora had been back to Dr Swain about her tiredness and headaches and general – well, he'd said it was depression and upped her dose of the SSRI, but it would be a couple of weeks until she felt any effect. Meanwhile, it was a struggle to get out of bed, let alone cope with the nightmare their lives had become.

'It's definitely nothing serious, Beckie. I promise you. The best thing you can do to make me feel better is go to school so I know you're with your friends and teachers having a nice time.'

'I won't have a nice time though.'

'Beckie,' said Neil gently, and Flora lay passively as he eased back the covers and lifted Beckie out of the bed. They'd all regressed in the last few days, Beckie behaving like a much younger child, and Neil and Flora treating her as such.

Things had got a lot worse after the Children's Reporter's visit. Although, as Neil said, the visit itself couldn't have gone better – Karen Baxter had been a nice woman, lovely with Beckie, and had reassured them as she left after her private 'chat' with Beckie that she had no concerns and no further action would be taken – Beckie was far from stupid and had realised what it all meant. That Karen had been there to check that Beckie was being well treated by her parents; that Karen had the power to take Beckie away from them, like she'd been taken away from the Johnsons.

Ever since, she'd become incredibly clingy, only happy away from Neil and Flora when she was with Caroline – who'd been wonderful, taking Beckie after school sometimes to give Flora a rest.

A much-needed rest.

She didn't even have the energy to keep tabs on the investigation into Saskia's death. Neil was doing that off and on, although, of course, he wasn't convinced that the Johnsons were responsible.

Saskia was all over the media now – she'd even been on the national news. Murder of disgraced social worker. Because, of course, the details of her disgrace had been leaked. And the police were now saying it was murder and were appealing for witnesses.

Someone was going to mention a strange woman in a grey hoodie, walking along with her head down. Maybe they'd be found, the hoodie and the raincoat, at the side of the road where Flora had flung them from the car window.

And her DNA would be on them, along with Saskia's.

What more damning evidence could there possibly be?

She could hear Neil and Beckie now downstairs in the hall, Beckie whining about something or other, Neil's voice patient, gentle. Neil was such a great father. He'd taken two weeks off work and did all the morning stuff, including making the extra lunch for Edith – she'd have to call Mrs Jenner again about Edith – and he drove Beckie to school every day; and because Beckie was nervous about being at school ('What if the Johnsons come and get me?'), he then waited in the car outside until lunchtime – parked where Beckie could look out of her classroom window and see him – and then he drove her home for lunch, then back to school, where he waited until the school day was over.

He was prepared to humour Beckie's fears, but not Flora's.

Neil and Caroline thought she was completely overreacting to Saskia's murder, that any number of people could have had a motive, given what Saskia had done – or that it could have been a motiveless stabbing by someone hanging about the close out of their skull on drugs. All of which was true, of course, looking at it objectively.

But Flora knew the Johnsons had done it.

She just knew.

The Johnsons were capable of anything.

So what was she doing lying here? What kind of a mother was she, not even able to get out of bed and protect her own child, when they were facing God knew what threat from a bunch of murdering psychopaths?

Clever murdering psychopaths.

Neil had engaged the services of a solicitor specialising in criminal law. Charles Aitcheson had advised them to record everything, to make sure their phones were charged at all times so they could film any further breaches of the court order by the Johnsons, any further threatening behaviour or trespass... Unfortunately there was insufficient evidence, in his opinion, to secure a harassment conviction as things stood, and Neil himself had 'compromised' their case with the 'assault' on pregnant Carly which, he had warned, was likely to end in a conviction when it came to court in three months' time, given that the incident had been caught on camera.

At least Flora hadn't been.

It had come out that the CCTV cameras on the street outside the close had not been operational at the time of Saskia's murder, and that no one had seen anyone acting suspiciously at the relevant time. The police were appealing for information about a woman who had buzzed one of the neighbours to get into the building to see Saskia, and were appealing for this woman to come forward.

But no one had yet come forward to say they'd seen her.

She drifted into a confused, repetitive dream in which she was endlessly climbing the stairs to Saskia's flat, knowing what she would find there but somehow unable to stop and turn and go back down the stairs. Endlessly buzzing to get into the stair.

No, she was awake, and someone was ringing the doorbell. Ringing and ringing.

Caroline.

Caroline had promised to come round.

She managed to roll to the edge of the bed and stand up, her head swimming. She managed to get out of the room, and down the stairs, and to the front door.

'Oh God, Flora,' said Caroline.

Flora couldn't look at her. Head bent like a naughty child,

she studied the pattern of tiles in the vestibule, studied her own bare feet, and the toenails that had grown too long.

'Come on, love.' And Caroline's arm was round her, and Flora was suddenly crying, suddenly howling in her friend's arms, and Caroline was closing the door behind her and saying, 'Let's get you sorted, eh?'

'I'm not sortable!' Flora wailed.

Caroline was brisk. 'We'll see about that.'

THE BOTANIC GARDENS had always been a favourite place of Flora's. It had been the house's main attraction, having the Botanics right opposite. She used to love to just stroll along the paths, touching the leaves of the plants, reading the Latin names on the labels, sitting on the grass with a book while Beckie lost herself in one imaginary world after another, bringing Flora leaves or blades of grass to hold that featured crucially in the dramas going on inside her head.

Today there was no Beckie, of course; nothing to capture her attention. Everything seemed flat, dull, one tree very much like the next, the late spring borders with their blocks of colour so painting-by-numbers ordinary that she couldn't understand why Caroline was bothering to stop and admire them.

'Coffee?' said Caroline brightly.

'What is wrong with me?' Flora blurted. 'What am I even doing here? The Johnsons are out there, they're planning God knows what – They've got it in for us just as much as they had it in for Saskia –'

'Flora.' Caroline took her arm. 'Come *on*. Even if the Johnsons did kill Saskia, which is pretty unlikely – I mean, how would they even know where she was? – they had good reason to hate her after what she did. I'm not saying it would justify *murdering* her... But the point is, they can't have anything against you and Neil personally, not like they did against Saskia. It's not your fault, what happened with Beckie.'

Flora breathed. She knew Caroline was wrong. She knew the Johnsons hated her. But she couldn't explain it. 'Okay, maybe not, but that doesn't mean they won't try to get Beckie back. Beckie needs me, and I'm a useless wreck.'

'Coffee,' Caroline said firmly, pushing Flora in the direction of the tearoom.

They chose a table outside in the sun, and while Caroline went in to buy the coffees and cakes, Flora sat and looked across the expanse of lawn to the Edinburgh skyline. Even that looked wrong, like a hackneyed illustration in a tourist brochure, not a real city, not somewhere real people lived real lives.

Oh get a grip.

She closed her eyes.

When she opened them again, the sun hitting her retinas made it difficult to see, washing out the colours of the lawn, and the shivering bright leaves, and the tall shape of the man standing under a tree looking at her.

He levelled his hand at her, holding it with his other hand as he mocked firing off shots, his hands kicking up with the recoil.

And something in her snapped.

Leaving her bag on the table, she ran towards him as he slipped away round the tree. Behind her she heard someone shouting her name, but she didn't stop, she kept going under the huge shadowed canopy, jumping over the slippery black roots in the grass, running to the path beyond –

Which way?

There were two elderly ladies on the path in one direction, a family with a buggy in the other –

No Ryan Johnson.

'Flora!' Caroline came skidding up. 'What are you *doing*?'

'It was Ryan Johnson.'

Caroline was holding her by both arms. 'Flora –'

'He was pretending he had a gun, pretending to shoot me... But I was too slow, and I – and now he's gone and –'

'And what do you reckon you're going to accomplish by chasing after him?'

She felt all the energy, the adrenaline, draining out of her.

'Let's go back and get those coffees down us, yeah?'

'He must have been following me. They must be watching the house.'

'Okay, so maybe Neil can fix up a camera pointing at the street. And Flora, instead of running after him, maybe you should have got out your phone and filmed him?'

Flora stared at her. 'What would happen to Beckie if we died? If Neil and I died...'

'God, Flora! That's not going to happen!'

'The Johnsons would get her back, wouldn't they?'

Caroline shook her head, taking Flora's arm like she was ninety years old and guiding her back to the tables. 'Of course not. The courts would hardly hand Beckie back to the family responsible for the murder of her adoptive parents.'

Flora stopped walking. 'But what if they made it look like an accident or... or suicide...?'

'Even then...' But was there a hint of uncertainty in her frown?

'Beckie was taken from them in a miscarriage of justice. While we're still alive, yes, the courts aren't going to disrupt Beckie's life by giving her back to them, but if we were dead and there was no one else to take her...'

'Someone in your family would take her. Look, if it would set your mind at rest, why don't you appoint a guardian to look after Beckie if anything happens to you?'

Flora looked up into the canopy of the tree. Two birds were squabbling, flying at each other, beaks stabbing.

'Our only close living relative is Pippa, Neil's sister. She's not exactly...' She grimaced. 'She's into having adventures, back-packing, rock climbing...'

'But she would put all that on hold for Beckie. I bet she'd do anything for Beckie.'

'Pippa's hardly had anything to do with her. A few flying visits, the odd five minutes on Skype...'

'But blood's thicker than...' She stopped. 'Sorry. I mean, she's family, isn't she? She'd step up?'

24

'Here it's, Maw,' goes Connor, and chucks an envelope at my chebs. I'm lying back in my chair with a family-size Galaxy waiting for *Bargain Hunt* to come on.

''Bout fucking time,' I goes, and I rip it open.

It's the copy of the death certificate we ordered from the National Records of Scotland for Flora's maw: Elizabeth Innes, died in St Andrews in 1989. I unfold it and me and Connor eyeball it.

Seems like Elizabeth Susan Innes died aged fifty-three, cause of death 'Motor vehicle accident'. But the interesting bit's no her death – it's her maiden name. Hertz. That's barry because it's no exactly common, eh?

'Right son. Get online at Scotland's People and see what marriages you can find for some bastard Innes and Elizabeth Susan Hertz.'

'If they really were Australian, I'll have to get on the Australian site.'

'Aye, get on that an' all.' I turn up the telly and sit back with my Galaxy. Fuck the fucking diet.

All through *Bargain Hunt* and the news, Connor's tapping away on his laptop. News is all shite about Brexit, just a ten-second update on Mair on *Reporting Scotland*, saying the police enquiry is continuing and a neighbour has been taken in for questioning. Stupid fuckers havenae a fucking clue.

Literally.

That's worth sharing so it is. 'Havenae a fucking clue, eh son?' I goes.

Connor rolls his eyes.

Neighbours starts and I'm onto the ginger and then Connor's bringing me the laptop with a wee smile that's no fooling no one, and I'm all 'Cracked it son?' and he's trying to play it cool but he cannae, he goes, 'God aye!' and he dumps the laptop on me and goes, 'Here's a Scotland's People entry for Elizabeth Susan Hertz, right, getting married to Alan Clark, in Peebles in 1968. Must be her, aye? That's the only marriage listed. Doesnae give the details online, you have to send off for the certificate if you're wanting it. Then there's another record for Rachel Elizabeth Clark, born 1969 in Peebles. That fits with Flora's age, eh? And an Alan Clark died in Peebles in 1975.'

'Get us copies of they certificates, Connor. Elizabeth marry again to some fucker Innes?'

'Naw.' Connor's grinning all over his spotty wee face. 'I'm thinking Rachel and her maw must've changed their names, right, because when I Googled Rachel Clark... Check it!'

He brings up another screen. A *Daily Record* article.

'There's loads a' hits!' He's peeing his pants. 'Hundreds. But this's it in a nutshell.'

I'm looking, and my gob is hanging open. 'Christ on a cheesy biscuit.'

'Aye. And that fucking bitch has Bekki.'

'No for much longer, son. No for much longer.' I'm reading down the article and God, I'm raging. Those fuckers gave Bekki to this bitch? I'm wanting to get out my chair and get round there and snatch our wean, but I cannae. This changes every-thing, aye, and it changes nothing.

'Looks like we're having us another wee road trip the morn, son.'

'To Peebles?'

'Naw, to the fucking moon.'

FLORA KNEW they were talking about her. As Beckie gobbled her lunch and Flora sat at the table pretending to listen as she outlined her latest plan to get Edith to like her, she could see Neil and Caroline standing in the garden – ostensibly looking to see where the Johnson thug had got over the wall in case he had left any evidence – but she knew they were talking about her: poor pathetic Flora falling apart.

Neil was grimacing, and Caroline was touching his arm.

'Isn't it?' Beckie said.

'What, darling?'

'Mum! You haven't been listening!'

'Sorry, I'm just tired, Beckie.'

Beckie's little face was suddenly heartbreakingly serious. 'I know. *I'm* sorry. You don't want to be bothered by all this, like, stupid kids' stuff. I don't want a party anyway.'

'Of course you do! I'm fine really, and it'll be good for me to have something nice to concentrate on.'

'Let's just cancel. No one's going to come anyway. It's going to be shit.'

'Beckie, don't be ridiculous! And please don't use that language.'

'Sorry.'

'Of course people will come. You've got lots and lots of friends.'

'But they're not allowed,' said Beckie slowly, looking down at her bowl and scraping at the last of the soup.

'Not allowed to come to the party? Why not?'

'Thomas says his mum has been spreading these... rumours...'

Flora sighed. 'What *rumours*?'

'About Dad being violent to a pregnant woman and you having... mental health issues and hitting me. And... that you and Dad are psycho and... stuff like that...'

'Oh, Beckie!'

Beckie looked up at her with a tight smile. 'It's okay, Mum, anyone with half a brain knows it's not true. Thomas says he's been telling everyone that his mum is just a stirrer and that you and Dad are like really nice and fun. And that everything that's happened is just because of the Johnsons twisting everything round on you when it's them who're the psychos and –'

The glass doors to the garden came open and Neil and Caroline came breezing in with false bright smiles for Beckie.

'Beckie's not going back to school this afternoon,' said Flora, getting abruptly to her feet. 'We need to speak to Mrs Jenner – Beckie has been on the receiving end of some very nasty – very nasty rubbish about us being violent and –'

'Mum! I don't mind. It *soooo* doesn't bother me.'

'What?' Neil was at the table in an instant, crouching down beside Beckie and putting an arm round her thin shoulders. 'What have they been saying?'

'I've not even really been listening. They're all like "Blah blah blah" and I'm like "Whatever!" Really, Dad. I could. Not. Care. *Less* what those losers say.'

'They've been saying we're violent?'

'Ailish,' said Flora. 'It seems Ailish has been spreading stuff.'

'That bloody woman!' said Neil.

'Language, Dad,' said Beckie.

Neil grinned and gave her a little squeeze. 'Sorry, Beckster.'

'Stress of the moment.'

'Indeed... So, would you like to stay off school for a bit?'

'Nope, it's fine. I've spread this rumour of my own about Ailish. You know how she's always on about how she was the best team leader ever at the Bank of Scotland, before she became the best mortgage advisor ever in the whole of Edinburgh, or maybe the UK? And there was this guy Malcolm in her team who she's always making fun of in a like really nasty way, saying he smelt and stuff and she gave him Sure deodorant in the Secret Santa? I've been telling people that Malcolm has just got the courage to come forward and accuse her of like discrimination against people who sweat a lot because they've got something wrong with them, and he's suing her for ten thousand pounds.'

'Oh wow, Beckie,' chortled Caroline. 'That's... very wrong.'

Beckie was smug. 'Ailish is maybe going to jail and that's why she's spreading rumours about other people – she's hoping everyone will stop talking about her and –'

'Beckie.' Neil shook his head, his mouth twisted in an effort not to laugh. 'Spreading lies about people is never the right thing to do.'

'It certainly isn't,' said Flora.

Caroline was grinning. 'Ailish obviously doesn't know what she's up against.'

'She started it,' Beckie agreed. 'But yeah, Mum, I know, two wrongs don't make a right.' She stood, wiping her hands on her napkin. 'Anyway, I'm going to just leave it there because if you go on too much, people don't believe you. And when people ask him about it, Thomas is going to say, "Yeah she's maybe going to jail but I can't talk about it."'

'Oh,' said Flora weakly. 'That's –'

'Really disturbingly Machiavellian,' finished Neil.

'I know! Let's go, Dad!'

'No,' said Flora. 'I don't want you going back to school. You can stay here with me. This is all getting... out of hand.'

'Honestly, Mum, it's fine. Dad, I'll just go to the loo?'

'Okay, Beckster.' And when she had left the room: 'Let's not make a big thing of this.' His voice strained to stay light, unconfrontational, in front of Caroline. 'She's fine to go back to school, and I think that's for the best. You can take it easy and chill this afternoon.' And his eyes lingered on her. 'Maybe – relax in a hot bath or something.'

She knew she looked a mess. She knew she probably whiffed a bit. 'Let's just keep her off today and then see about tomorrow. I'm not going to be able to "chill" if I'm worrying myself sick about her –'

'This isn't about you, though, is it?'

Caroline was edging towards the door. 'Okay guys, see you later.'

'Yes, thanks so much, Caroline.'

A charged silence until they heard the front door close. 'How dare you?' Flora spat at him. 'How dare you say I'm making this "all about me" when it's you saying Beckie being at school will give me a chance to "chill". As if I'm going to be able to "chill"!'

'Well, for Beckie's sake, Flora, if for no other reason, you're going to have to try to do *something* to...' He flapped his hands in the air. 'The last thing she needs is a neurotic mum to worry about on top of everything else. School is the best place for her at the moment, a normal environment –'

'Oh, it's *normal*, is it, to be ganged up on by a load of little bastards taunting her, saying her parents are psychos –'

'She's not being ganged up on! I'm there in the car watching, remember, when she's in the playground, and she's got plenty of friends. There's no problem that I can see –'

'That you can see. That *is* the whole problem, Alec!'

He opened his mouth; closed it. He moved to touch her, but she stepped back. 'Okay. We can talk about this later.'

. . .

Flora was lying on a sofa in the family room, drowsily watching the *Ten O'Clock News*, when Neil came back into the room. 'Asleep. She's amazing, isn't she? The way she's taking all this in her stride.'

'But *is* she taking it in her stride, or is it an act to keep us from worrying about her?'

He sat down on the arm of the sofa. 'Maybe a bit of both.'

'I don't want her going back to school. It's only a couple of weeks until the summer holidays; it's not as if she'd miss much...'

'She'd miss out on the class trip to the watersports centre, and she's been looking forward to that for ages.'

'We could take her there in the holidays.'

'Hardly the same.'

'I don't want her going back to that school. Don't you think... If we're going to move, now would be a good time to do it?'

'*Move?*'

'We're never going to be safe from the Johnsons unless we do.'

'No. I'm sorry, Flora, I know all this has really freaked you out – freaked *us* out, I should say... given that I was the one charged with assault.' He attempted a weak smile. 'But there is no way we're moving again. We have to get some perspective here. What have they actually done? Nothing, other than indulge in a bit of low-level harassment –'

'*Low level?*'

'But I agree, of course, that it's sensible to take reasonable precautions.'

'A few CCTV cameras and some self-defence tuition from an HR consultant?'

'If they were going to do anything –'

'They're toying with us! Ryan Johnson in the Botanics today – They're enjoying it, they're enjoying making us suffer before closing in for the kill! You weren't there. You didn't see the way he was looking at me –'

'Flora... Caroline didn't see anyone.'

'What, so I'm hallucinating now?' She got up; put distance between them. 'They *killed* Saskia! What's to stop them killing us? A few CCTV cameras? What would happen to Beckie then? Who would look after her?'

He just shook his head at her wearily.

'You have to wake up, Alec. Seriously.'

'I –'

'And the first thing we have to do is appoint someone to be her legal guardian in the event of our deaths. We have to make sure she'll be okay whatever.'

'Flora –'

'It's hardly ideal, but I guess that person has to be Pippa.'

He breathed. 'Okay.' Making a Herculean effort, it seemed, to humour her. 'If you want. I guess that's something we should have sorted years ago anyway.'

'Let's call her now.'

'Now? It's the middle of the night where she is.'

'If she agrees, we can at least get the legal stuff moving.' She reached for the landline handset and held it out to him. 'Put her on speakerphone.'

Pippa answered groggily. 'You do know what time it is here?'

'Sorry,' said Neil. 'We've, um... We've got something to ask you, Pip.'

'Is everything okay?'

'Yes, well, more or less...' He sighed. 'You know what's been going on with the Johnsons... But no, we're fine. It's just that... Flora... We're thinking we need to appoint someone as Beckie's legal guardian – not that we're thinking anything's going to happen to us or anything, but all this has concentrated our minds and, well – Would you be okay with being next in line to look after Beckie?'

Several hundred miles of static.

In that second's, two seconds' pause, Flora knew that it was the wrong thing. She knew it before Pippa's 'Sure, of course'; the false note in her voice.

'No, Pippa, actually it's fine,' she said quickly. 'It's not fair to ask you. You don't want a child in tow – what were we thinking? I mean, I hope you'd still be part of Beckie's life, just not – in a parenting role.'

'It's all hypothetical anyway,' said Pippa sleepily. 'Come on. Okay so these people are bad news, but they're not going to *murder* you. *Come on.*'

'Yeah, I know, sorry... Sorry to wake you,' said Neil, giving Flora a *What the hell?* look. And as soon as he'd ended the call: 'For Christ's sake, Flora!'

'Pippa would be a terrible guardian for Beckie. Last time she saw her, she got Beckie drunk.'

'It was a few sips of wine.'

'Beckie was staggering around giggling, and Pippa thought it was hilarious. She couldn't understand why I was so angry.'

'Mm.' Neil grimaced. 'But Beckie does love her.'

'She hasn't seen her for three years.'

'But still.'

'Beckie loves her because Pippa lets her do whatever she wants. I know she's your sister, and I'm really fond of her, but...'

Neil stood abruptly. 'This was *your* idea, remember? But somehow it's been turned back on me, as usual.'

'Pippa's not the right person.'

'Okay. So who else do you want to phone up and badger with a bizarre and frankly really disconcerting request in the middle of the night, before changing your mind and insulting them by pretty much coming out and saying they're not parenting material? Who else is there, Flora? Because let's face it, we don't really have any friends any more, do we?'

'There's Pam and James. Now the Johnsons know where we are, there's no reason not to contact them. We could ask them...'

'After disappearing on them like we did?'

'They'll understand if we explain it to them.'

'Right. "Hi, Pam, remember us? Yeah, sorry about that, sorry about dropping you like hot potatoes, but we had to disappear because Beckie's psychotic biological family were after us. If they murder us, you'll take her on, won't you? Okay so you might have to move to Alaska to avoid the same thing happening to you..." Look – Pippa's family. I know she's not ideal, but if you're intent on appointing a legal guardian for Beckie, we can't ask anyone else to do it.'

'I'm phoning Pam in the morning.'

'Oh, okay, fine. Do whatever the hell you like, Flora, and as usual I'll grin and bear the consequences.'

She blinked at him. 'What?'

'It's always about what *you* want, isn't it?'

'Alec, we wouldn't be in this situation in the first place if you hadn't been conned by Lorraine Johnson into giving her your name and address back in Arden. They probably found us this time because of something you did too, some absent-minded professor stunt –'

'Yep, let's play the blame game. That's really helping. That's really constructive. I'm trying to do what's right for Beckie, but you keep coming up with these mad schemes, like we just up sticks and move again –'

'It's *mad* to want to do everything possible to keep our daughter safe?'

'We should never have moved from Arden in the first place! We had a good life there, Beckie was happy – We should have dealt with this then, instead of running away.'

'And you're "dealing with it" now how, exactly? What do you think would have happened if we'd stayed in Arden? We'd probably be dead and Beckie –'

'Oh *Christ*, Ruth! We wouldn't be *dead*! I'm "dealing with it" – with the hypothetical "it" – by consulting a solicitor and going to the police and putting up cameras to catch them if they try anything. Excuse me for being halfway rational about it!'

And he banged out of the room like a four-year-old.

25

'Right son,' I goes to Connor, parking up outside the newspaper office. 'Let me do the talking, aye? Keep it zipped.'

Connor goes, 'Can I no do the bit about the lawyers? It's wrote down here.' He taps the documents on his clipboard.

'No you cannae. Maybe you can say it's a nice fucking day but that's it. This bastard's an old pro and he's gonnae be scrutinising every fucking word comes out our mouths. Nice day, nice wee town, nice wee paper. That's it. Right?'

Connor gives me evils.

He's smart in his funeral suit. He's getting to be no a bad-looking laddie apart from they fucking Johnson ears. I'm in a wee sleeveless green and white silk blouse and a navy pencil skirt and heels. We get out the motor and in that fucking office.

There's no a receptionist or nothing, just a poky wee room with copies of the paper spread out on a table and posters on the wall for jumble sales and rabbit shows and shite. There's a door with a keypad and a bell. I get my thumb on it.

In a bit, this long streak of piss comes through the door and gives it, 'Good morning, how can I help?' He's no much older than Connor. This cannae be the man.

'Good morning,' I goes. 'Jessica Stuart and Kieran McKay from Making Waves. We've an appointment to see Mr Roberts at 11:30?'

'Ah, yes, hello. Please come up. I'm Chris.' He huds the door open.

'Nice day, eh?' goes Connor. 'Sweating like a pig's knackers so I am in this fucking suit.'

I goes, 'Kieran, too much information,' with a chuckle. 'So you're Chris Mason? I read your piece on the controversy about local authority spending in the area. Great piece of journalism.'

He looks back down the stair at me. 'Oh, thanks!'

Oh aye, I've done my research.

He takes us up to a dark wee lobby with glass doors off of it. Old bugger comes through one giving it 'Ms Stuart?' and hudding out his hand.

I smile. 'Mr Roberts. Thank you so much for taking the time to see us. We do appreciate you must be busy.'

The wee blouse shows a fair bit cleavage and he's on it.

'Pleasure's all mine.'

'This's Kieran MacKay, one of our trainees.'

He shows us into his office. My God, there's no an inch of wall space left without a framed photy on it of yokels on the bevvy, or a charity bint meeting Camilla, or a dug that's pulled some fuckwit wean out a river. Roberts shuffles across the room. He's eighty if he's a day, more hair growing out his neb and his lugs than on his head.

I wave a hand at the walls. 'All of life is here, eh?'

He shrugs, pulling out chairs for us. 'All of life in Tweed-dale, anyway – which amounts to the same thing.'

I cross my legs. 'Can I just say before we start – reading *The Borderer* for background has been a joy. In my work I have to plough through a lot of column inches, and really, most of it these days, you're thinking to yourself, a ten-year-old could do better. It's genuinely been a joy to immerse myself in good writing.'

'Well, thank you.' He sits himself down behind his desk, a big brown bastard the size of a fucking tanker with piles of paper all over it, and raises an eyebrow. There's hairs sprouting off of his eyebrows in every fucking direction and I'm having a hard time no staring. 'Don't get me started, Ms Stuart, on standards in modern journalism.'

'Please, it's Jessica.'

Bit more chit-chat and then we're down to business. 'So,' I goes. 'I think I outlined in my email that we've been commissioned by BBC Scotland to produce a three-part series on kids who kill – although it won't be called that, obviously. This is the BBC we're talking about. They're giving us the Wednesday nine o'clock slot on BBC 2. Provisionally.'

He's nodding along. Maybe he's Googled Making Waves, but that's fine – it's a genuine TV production company operating outta Glasgow. Long as he hasnae contacted them, we're good.

'We're planning on the first episode focusing on the Tricia Fisher case. What I'm hoping you can supply us with is any details, any extra colour that didn't make it into print.'

'Aye,' goes Connor. 'And –'

I hold up a hand with a wee smile. 'Okay, Kieran, hold your horses, I'm sure Mr Roberts –'

'Jeff,' he goes.

'I'm sure Jeff is aware that it'll all be picked over by the lawyers before filming starts. Nothing with even a whiff of *litigious* will get past the grey men in suits, believe me!'

Jeff raises an eyebrow.

I'm no too keen on that eyebrow right enough. It's like he's maybe onto us. Maybe the old bugger's contacted Making Waves after all and they were all 'No, there must be some mistake.' Maybe he's just seeing what crap we're gonnae come out with.

'But I like to just ask people to speak freely, and worry about all that later. Obviously, as I said in my email, you'll be recompensed for your time, and if we film you for the production there'll be further remuneration, but...' I make a face. 'As I said, this is the BBC, so don't go booking any holidays in Barbados, Jeff!'

'Or even Largs!' goes Connor.

Jeff chuckles. 'But I think we can run to a cup of tea and a biscuit.' He turns to the door. 'Chris!' he yells. And when the young guy appears he gives him our order, and then we get down to it.

'You have to remember this was nearly forty years ago,' he goes, leaning back in his chair. 'No mobile phones, no internet. The first I knew of it was a call from one of my several contacts in the police force, tipping me off to get my behind over to Lomax Road in Kelbinning where a tragedy was unfolding – kids messing about with a bow and arrow and an accidental fatality was what we were led to believe.'

Now I'm relaxing. He's an old-school bastard likes the sound of his own voice. Too much of a fucking ego to maybe wonder why emdy making a documentary for the BBC would want to hear it. He's no questioning nothing.

I goes, 'This was on the actual day it happened?'

'Yes. The sixteenth of June. When I got there, though, there wasn't a whole lot to see. They didn't close off the road as they would now. There were just a couple of panda cars and an unmarked car I recognised, parked on the driveway of Number 7. The road's still very much as it was then – you'll get some good shots of it. It's a road rather than a street, just a few big houses on it before it leaves the village and winds off up into the hills. House is a big Edwardian detached job with what an estate agent would call "extensive policies". Very nice part of a very nice village. The Fishers still live there, as I assume you know?'

I nod. 'They've agreed to talk to us later.'

'I parked on the street and walked up. Young bobby I knew gave me the lowdown. It seemed that these two twelve-year-olds, Tricia Fisher and Rachel Clark, both from well-off middle-class families, had got themselves a reputation at the village primary school as bullies. It seemed they'd asked a girl in their class, Gail Boyle, if she wanted to come and play in Tricia's garden.

'Things soon turned ugly. Tricia and Rachel tied Gail to a tree and Tricia fetched her brother's bow and arrows. In those days, of course, kids did play with lethal weapons more or less willy-nilly.'

'Those were the days, eh?' goes Connor.

Jeff blanks the wee fuckwit. 'So there was nothing odd about a fourteen-year-old boy possessing such a thing. When Tricia returns with the bow, she's put on a pair of gloves. She fires off an arrow into the branches above Gail – nowhere near her, but Gail's terrified, poor kid. She's struggling to get free of the ropes they've used to tie her up. She can't scream for help because they've gagged her.' He shakes his head. 'Tricia takes off the gloves and gives them to Rachel, and hands her the bow, and tells her to "Shoot the little cow". Those were the exact words, apparently.'

I've got a dry mouth so I have. He's on a roll. He's loving it.

'Tricia is goading Rachel. She's saying, "Do it!" and, "It'll be two against one, they'll have to believe us and then he'll go to jail!" It seems Tricia and her brother had had a massive falling out the day before over something trivial – he'd spilt Ribena on Tricia's favourite dress, I think, and she was convinced he'd done it on purpose, and things escalated from there, culminating, unbelievably, in the girl deciding to frame him for murder. She's screaming at Rachel to *Do it*, she's saying Rachel is a wimp and a waste of space and that if Rachel doesn't do this Tricia will never speak to her again. Rachel lifts the bow and –'

'You'd think someone would hear them, eh?' goes Connor.

'Tricia's parents and brother were inside the house,' goes Jeff.

'How was she gonnae frame her brother if he wasnae there?'

'It seems he spent all his time in his room listening to records. The parents were in a different part of the house. They didn't know where the kids were or what they were doing.'

I'm grinding my teeth. 'Sorry, Jeff. Rachel's got the bow...'

'And she fires an arrow at Tricia's face, point-blank range. It goes through her eye and into her brain, killing her instantly.'

THE HOUSE IS like something off of *Pride and Prejudice*. But at least they've got new windaes in and it's all modern inside, big grey leather sofas and abstract shite on the walls like a wean's been chugging paint and boaked it on a bit paper.

Mrs Fisher's a shrivelled wee wifie keeps rubbing her arms like she's cold. Mister's a big old bastard doesnae say much. I'm in sympathy mode, giving it, 'Such an awful thing,' and 'I know Rachel Clark was just a child, but it must have been hard that she wasn't really... well, this is only my personal opinion, and of course we couldn't say this in the programme, but it seems to me she wasn't really properly punished.'

Mrs Fisher's blinking away. She's sitting next Mister on the sofa opposite with her knees together and her right hand on her left arm, stroking it like it's a wee dug.

'That was what we felt.'

'That girl should have been locked up for life,' goes Mister. 'God knows where she is now and what else she's done. They moved away, of course. It's our understanding they went to Australia – that's where the mother was from.'

I raise an eyebrow. 'Oh no, Rachel's still in the UK. She's changed her name of course. New identity. I don't think even her husband knows about her past as Rachel Clark. She has a husband and a little girl. Her husband's a university lecturer and they live in a big house in a very desirable part of Edinburgh. Tea and crumpets on the lawn kind of style.'

Mister's raging. But if Flora was here right now, if she walked through that fucking door, it'd be Missus got to the bitch first, no question.

I goes, 'We're planning to confront her on the programme.'

'She should pay for what she did!' goes Mister. 'For murdering our daughter! Oh, she pulled the wool over the judge's eyes all right, but that wasn't manslaughter. *She was shouting at me and I just did it! I didn't mean to kill her!* How do you *not mean* to fire an arrow into someone's brain?'

I nod. 'Of course, we're duty bound to give both sides. Gail Boyle gave evidence at the trial that Tricia had been goading Rachel to shoot Gail. That she wanted Rachel to kill her, and then the two of them would say Matthew did it. His prints would have been on the bow and arrows...'

Mister makes like he's gonnae jump up and pagger me, but Missus grabs his arm and goes, 'That Gail – she was in on it, I'm sure she was. She wasn't just an innocent witness. If she was tied to a tree, how did she get free? It was Gail who came and got me. She said that after it happened, after Tricia... She managed to pull her hands free and run to the house. But she was obviously in on it. That *nonsense* about Tricia telling Rachel to shoot Gail was obviously a *complete fabrication*. I mean, really – to suggest that Tricia wanted Rachel to *kill Gail* in order to frame Matthew for *murder*? It's *completely absurd!*'

'Your son also gave evidence for the defence...'

'Matthew was troubled,' says Mister.

'It was a tremendous shock for him,' says Missus. 'Losing his sister like that. He was fourteen years old.'

I nod. 'But he told the court that Tricia was violent. That she enjoyed inflicting pain...'

'That's rubbish. Yes, they fought sometimes, but what siblings don't?' She turns to Connor. 'Have you brothers or sisters?'

Connor nods. 'Aye, sibling rivalry's what you'd call a weapon of mass destruction in our house, eh M–'

'Thank you Kieran,' I goes. 'So what Matthew was referring to was really just the normal rough and tumble of family life?'

Missus gives me a grateful wee smile. 'Yes, that's exactly it. Tricia was a lovely girl. Very warm, very kind and considerate. All this nonsense about bullying – that was all Rachel. Before she became friends with Rachel, Tricia had never been in any trouble. Not really.'

'So you had concerns about Rachel before the –'

'Oh, call it what it was!' goes Mister. 'Murder! It was murder! How could that evil little monster have possibly *not* meant to kill Tricia?'

I nod. 'You'd concerns about Rachel from the get-go?'

'Yes, we did,' goes Missus. 'She was a mousy little thing, quiet... watchful, in a very unsettling way... She'd sit watching me while Tricia burbled on. She was polite, she always said please and thank you and offered to help with the washing up... but I always thought there was something... not quite right about her.'

My feelings exactly. My fucking feelings exactly.

26

Thank God for bad mothers, thought Flora, watching Selina Wright, elegant in white shirt and skinny jeans, Mulberry bag hanging from one elbow, light up a fag behind the *Forsythia* before bolting for the garden door and freedom. Her brood of five – or was it six? – were screaming their heads off at the bottom of the garden with Beckie and the only other three kids who had turned up to the party. Selina's daughter Miranda was in Beckie's class and had been invited, but her numerous siblings hadn't been. This was an opportunity, though, for Selina to unload responsibility for a few hours, and no way was she passing it up just because Beckie's parents were reputed to be violent towards pregnant girls and children.

It was the same story with the hyper little boy, whose parents were obviously just grateful for the respite. And Mia's mum, Flora suspected, was taking full advantage of the opportunity to rile Ailish. 'Sorry Ailish is being such a bitch,' she'd even grimaced as she'd unloaded Mia from a Land Rover that looked like it had just returned from a war zone.

The only other kid who'd turned up was Edith.

Her mother Shona hadn't come in with her – she'd turned

away from the door without once making eye contact, but Flora had told Edith to go through and find Beckie's dad, and followed Shona down the path to the pavement.

'Sorry Shona, can I have a quick word about... well, about Beckie and Edith?'

The other woman, pulling her bag up her skinny shoulder, had shot her a sideways look.

'I'm so sorry about the bullying – I hope there haven't been any more problems?'

'Oh no.' A nervous smile past Flora's left shoulder.

Flora smiled nervously herself. 'The thing is... I'm concerned that another child might be bullying Edith and stealing her lunch.' This was, after all, a possibility. 'Has she said anything to you about that...?'

Shona shook her head, her gaze now on the pavement.

'Right. It's just... I'm a bit of a "feeder", as my friend calls it, and I always pack far too much lunch for Beckie, and Beckie says Edith has been eating the extra food and seems... well, really hungry. So I think there's something going on there. I've mentioned it to Mrs Jenner, in fact...'

Shona's eyes met hers for a millisecond. 'I – thank you.'

'No no – there's no need to thank me. As I say, I'm such a feeder! But –'

'I suffer from depression and I'm not always...' The poor woman was twisting the strap of her bag. 'I'm not...'

'Oh, I'm so sorry.' Flora touched her arm.

'I'm not always able to look after her properly, I know that, I know Edith is suffering for it. Her dad wants custody.'

'Oh Shona. Would you like to come in for a minute? I – I do understand, I think, a bit. I... Recently, I've had some problems myself. Please, come in and have a coffee... or maybe some iced tea?'

For a fraction of a second Shona hesitated, and then, like a frightened deer, shook herself and backed up. 'Thank you, no, thank you, I have to...' And she turned and half-ran away down the pavement.

Oh God. Poor Shona.

Poor little Edith.

Edith hadn't stopped smiling nervously since she'd got here. Flora had taken Beckie to one side and told her that Edith's mum was having problems and wasn't well, a bit like Flora hadn't been well, and Edith didn't have her dad at home like Beckie did, so poor Edith wasn't eating properly and wasn't being looked after very well. But Beckie mustn't tell anyone. 'Because Edith might be taken away from her mum?' Beckie had immediately realised, and Flora, after a moment's thought, had nodded. 'Edith is having a really hard time at the moment. I don't think the problem is that she doesn't want to be friends with you – I think she's just very sad and, as you thought, lonely and maybe scared. I think she really needs someone looking out for her at school.'

Beckie had frowned, and nodded.

Now, Beckie was standing with Mia on one side and Edith on the other, and all three were poking at something in the grass with sticks, laughing. Edith poked her stick down too hard and it snapped, leaving her with a stump in her hand. Beckie, seeing this happen, swooped under a tree and returned with another stick, so big it was almost a branch, hauling it behind her with exaggerated effort until all three girls were in hysterics. Edith, accepting it from Beckie, pretended to stagger backwards, her face flushed.

Good girl, Beckie.

But what was she going to do about the whole Shona problem? Speak to Social Services? Karen at the Scottish Children's Reporter Administration? But what if that meant Shona losing Edith? But maybe that would be the best thing for Edith?

She would think about it later.

When this damn party was over.

Neil, when he'd eventually deigned to start speaking to Flora again, had said they had to put everything with the Johnsons aside for one afternoon and give Beckie a fun birthday. For the sake of peace, Flora had pretended to agree, but she'd no intention of letting down her guard. The fact that Neil was in denial meant she had to be doubly vigilant. And it didn't help that all the other mums of the kids that were here had bailed. She kept scanning the top of the wall, the trees, the bushes, expecting any moment to see one of the Johnson thugs. She kept wishing the kids would be quiet and not draw so much attention to themselves.

Should she even have let them out in the garden?

But it was a glorious, boiling hot July day. What possible reason could she give for not letting them play outside? As long as she was super-vigilant and never took her eyes off Beckie... At least Beckie was easy to spot. She was adorable in a hideous rainbow top and bright green leggings, jumping up and down and shouting. And now, in that dizzying way kids had at this age, she suddenly broke off what she was doing and raced across the grass towards Flora – and carried on past to the patio doors.

'Caroline!' She flung her arms round Caroline's waist. 'I thought you might have forgotten!'

'Forget the social event of the year?' Caroline had got into the party spirit in a short 1970s-style dress with swirly orange and brown and white flowers on it that showed off her slim tanned legs, and she'd gone the whole hog with green eye shadow and pale pink lips.

She looked sensational.

'Is that my present?'

'Maybe.' Caroline grinned at Flora. 'Sorry I'm late – bit of a work crisis.'

Flora hugged her. 'Thanks so much for coming. But if you've got stresses at work –'

'Hey, thank *you*. A whole afternoon with the Beckster? What could be better de-stress than that?'

And she grinned at Beckie, and Beckie grinned at her.

'Here you go then, sweetheart. Hope you like them.'

Beckie ripped into the paper. 'Ooh, Gazelles!' She pulled out the box and set it on the table. Her eyes wide, she slowly opened the lid.

Inside was a pair of pink trainers.

'Oh my God, they're *the ones*! They're the ones I *really wanted*!'

'Yep, somehow I kind of gathered that.'

'Thank you,' said Flora. 'You shouldn't have, though.'

'Because they're too expensive and I'll grow out of them in like ten seconds.' Beckie's face had fallen comically. 'It's a waste of money.'

'Hey, you think I care about wasting money on unnecessary clothing? I mean, hello?' And Caroline did a graceful twirl.

Beckie giggled. 'Your dress is like really weird.'

'Thank you,' Caroline smiled.

'Beckie!' Neil appeared from the family room with a large bottle of Appletiser, condensation already forming on the outside, and a glass with ice in it. It was a strictly alcohol-free party.

'In a good way,' Beckie said quickly.

'Say thank you to Caroline for the lovely present,' said Flora.

'Yes, thank you thank you thank you!'

'It's my pleasure.'

'Can I put them on?' She looked from Neil to Flora.

'Of course you can,' said Neil at the same time as Flora said, 'No, you'll get them dirty playing in the garden.'

'Mum's right,' Neil said at once. 'You can wear them tomorrow for your last day of school.'

'Okay.' Beckie put them carefully back in the box. 'I suppose

I would probably mess them up playing with those skanky kids.'

'Beckie!'

'They are. I mean, look at them. They totally smell. And the little one dropped a turd. Me and Mia and Edith got sticks and dug a hole and buried it, but – gross. You have to admit?'

'Oh.' Flora peered down the garden. 'Little – what's his name? The one in the blue shorts?'

Beckie shrugged. 'It's Kanga or Konga or something like equally random. And there's snot coming out of his nose the *whole time*. Mia reckons he should be called Bogie Turd Boy.'

'Now, he's only little. I'd better see if he needs cleaned up.'

'He so does. And all of them. But they won't. I said to Miranda she should get that little Turd Boy cleaned up but she said he was fine, and he so isn't.'

Neil handed Caroline her drink.

'Oh, lifesaver. Thanks.' She looked at Beckie. 'Tell you what... You've got a garden hose, yeah?'

Five minutes later all the kids were squealing in terror as Caroline chased them with the hose, turning it on and off unpredictably. The game seemed to be a complicated combination of tag, capture the flag and some sort of elimination element. Little Turd Boy was soon eliminated, much to his annoyance, and while Beckie took over the hose, Caroline swept him up and carried him inside to get 'dried off' with the promise of a biscuit to follow.

They re-emerged, hand in hand, the child wearing a pair of Beckie's pants and munching happily on a chocolate digestive.

'I've washed these out,' said Caroline, handing Flora his little shorts and pants. 'They'll dry in the sun in about thirty seconds.'

'Oh, thank you!'

Turd Boy crammed in the last of the biscuit and ran to join the others in ganging up on Neil, who was, inevitably, soaked from head to foot. Even Edith seemed to have lost her inhibitions, giggling manically and shouting, 'He's getting away!' when Neil made a break for it.

'Haven't had this much fun in ages,' grinned Caroline, stretching out on a lounger and closing her eyes against the sun.

'You're a natural with them.'

'Being with kids is kind of like reliving your own childhood, isn't it, and letting them share it? Only you're allowed to pick and choose the best bits for them.'

Flora looked down at her. 'Beckie loves you,' she found herself saying.

Caroline opened her eyes; raised her eyebrows. 'Aw. I love her too. You lot moving here is the best thing that's happened to me for – well, ages.'

'Do you want kids yourself?'

She shrugged. 'Sure, but it's the old cliché – never met the right guy to settle down with. Not that I'm looking that hard, to be honest. Kind of been focused on my career. But being with Beckie, well, it's making me re-evaluate that, you know?'

'Would you be Beckie's guardian?'

Caroline sat up. 'Eh?'

'I know you've got your career, and you probably wouldn't want to... I mean, playing with her for an afternoon is one thing, but having her full time – And all the stuff with the Johnsons, it's not fair to ask you...' Humiliatingly, tears were choking her. 'Sorry, I should never have even... Sorry.' She turned away.

'Hey, hey, Flora.' Caroline's arms were round her. 'Shh. God, I'd love to, but you don't want to give me that kind of responsibility! You hardly even know me.'

'I do know you.' Flora sniffed, pulled away, smiled shakily. 'I feel like I've known you forever. Please, Caroline? *Please?*'

'Okay, yes, of course, if you're sure... That's... God, Flora, I feel so honoured. Of course.'

'Thank you. Oh Caroline, thank you.'

Caroline pulled her back into the hug. 'Flora, I – oh-oh!'

Flora whipped round. 'What?'

But she could see what. Beckie, Mia and Edith had slipped their leggings (or in Edith's case, badly fitting jeans) and pants down at the back and were wiggling their bare bums in a row, screaming with laughter. Then Beckie turned and stuck out her tongue.

Flora looked up.

Ailish, her arms full of laundry, was standing at the first-floor landing window next door, mouth open.

Flora marched across the grass. 'Beckie, get inside! Neil! Look at them!'

Neil blinked.

'*Look at them!* Girls, pull up your clothes and get inside. All of you, get inside. *Now!*'

Ten little faces gaped at her.

'Come on guys, enough is enough,' said Caroline firmly. 'Beckie, what were you thinking? That's unacceptable and you know it.'

Beckie had gone bright red.

Neil was blinking, rabbit in the headlights.

'Come on you lot, move it,' said Caroline, and as she shepherded the kids across the grass towards the open glass doors, Flora let fly at Neil.

'I don't believe this! Can you not be trusted to supervise the kids for the five seconds I look away because I'm at the end of my tether taking all this on *my* shoulders because *you* have abrogated *all* responsibility? But no, I can't even have five seconds to cry on someone's shoulder, someone who actually understands my concerns –'

'And who would that be?'

'Caroline, who else? I've asked her to be Beckie's guardian.'

Long, tense silence.

'And you never thought to consult me about it?'

'As if you'd be interested!'

He flung up his hands. 'How can you say that? Of course I'm interested in *anything* that affects Beckie, let alone something as important as this!'

'Well, you've been doing a very good impression of someone who doesn't give a fuck!'

Then she remembered Ailish.

She was still there, the cow, staring down at them. Childishly, Flora made a face at her and stormed off up the garden.

Flora and Caroline had just got the kids settled round the table with juice and cake when the doorbell went.

'Neil, can you please get that?' Flora said tightly. 'And remember to check the CCTV before you open the door.'

Too much to hope that it was Selina Wright?

A few seconds later, Neil called out, his voice higher than usual and odd-sounding: 'Flora?'

She hurried out of the room and into the hall.

In the vestibule – he'd actually let them into the house? – stood Lorraine and Carly Johnson. Neil was holding onto the door between the vestibule and the hall as if for support.

'Get out of here,' she said. 'Get out or I'm calling the police.'

'Sorry hen, we know it's Beckie's birthday and you're busy and that, and the last folk you want to see is us, eh? But we just wanted to leave these for Beckie?' Lorraine Johnson rummaged in the carrier bags she was carrying and lifted out some shiny, nylony material. 'Wee Elsa and Anna costumes. You dinnae need to say where they came from. But we'd like Beckie to have them, aye?'

Neil looked round at Flora. 'Thank you, but –'

'As if we're going to let Beckie have anything from you!'

'Aye Maw,' said Carly. 'Maybe this wasnae such a good idea?'

The woman just stood there holding the hideous costumes.

'Let's go, eh?' The girl put a hand on her mother's arm. 'Sorry.'

Lorraine Johnson looked straight at Flora, sharp little eyes filmed with unshed tears. 'What that Mair bitch did was terrible so it was, but dinnae you think we had anything to do with what happened to her cos we didnae, we didnae even know what she did to Beckie till after she was dead and all the shite hit the fan, and I'm no saying I'm no glad the bitch is dead but we didnae touch her. And none of that was down to yous, eh, and we get that, we're all victims here by the way, and I'm no wanting trouble, we're gonnae withdraw the complaint about your man here assaulting Carly, it's no fair on yous, that was down to us so it was.'

'Oh,' was all Flora could find to say.

'And we'll no come near yous again and we'll leave yous and Beckie in peace but I just have to know, right, I just have to fucking know that you love her. You love our wee lassie, aye?' The tears, now, were dripping down her jowly cheeks and splotching on her thin white top.

'We love her very much indeed,' said Neil. 'You can be sure of that.'

Flora just stared.

Gently, Neil took the dresses from the woman's hands. 'Thank you. Beckie will be thrilled with these.'

'We love her more than anything,' Flora was finally able to choke out.

'Aye!' Lorraine half-sobbed, half-wailed, 'Aye, I know yous do!'

Carly was bawling too. 'She's that lucky to have yous!'

'God, look at me, a right traichy cow!' Lorraine swiped at her face with her hands. 'We're sorry about all the shite. Jed and Travis – they're no right in the head, eh? But I can promise you this, hen, I can promise you this – they bastards are no gonnae be coming near you and Beckie ever again.' And she looked straight at Flora, and Flora's gut lurched and her heart seemed to contract in her chest.

And the woman reached out a hand and touched the shiny material of one of the dresses Neil was holding, then took her hand away, and drew in a long breath, lifting her chin, facing it.

Facing her loss.

Her irrevocable loss.

Flora swallowed. 'That – that's good to know.'

'We're that sorry,' sobbed Carly. 'Yous are decent people.'

'I think you probably are too,' said Neil quietly.

'Naw, we're just traichy wee schemies,' sobbed Lorraine. 'Beckie's better off wi' yous right enough.' And she waved a hand as if to encompass Neil and Flora, the Victorian tiles of the vestibule, the pretty pictures on the walls, the antique pew, and under it Flora and Neil's expensive walking boots and comfy slippers lined up neatly next to Beckie's miniature versions.

The whole of Beckie's life.

Their child's life.

And she didn't know quite how it happened, but Flora found that her arms were round Lorraine Johnson and the big sweaty chest was pressed against Flora's.

'Do you want...' Neil coughed. 'Do you want to see Beckie?'

In the hot, rather ripe embrace, Flora stiffened.

'Naw, you're all right,' Lorraine muttered, pulling back from Flora and folding the carrier bags once, twice, again in her hands, looking down at them. 'You're all right.'

As Flora and Neil stood together at the door watching the two ponderous figures make their way down the path to the gate, Flora felt Neil's fingers close round hers. Behind them through the house came shouts of laughter, and Edith's high, delighted squeal: 'Beckie! It's all in his hair and everything!' The little birch tree by the gate swayed in the breeze, casting dappled shade across the geraniums and the lavender and the now empty path.

'God,' said Neil. 'Have we stepped into a parallel universe or what? Did that just happen?'

'Probably some sort of ruse,' said Flora. 'To – I don't know. Lull us into a false sense of security...'

'Mm,' Neil agreed. 'Let's just see if they do withdraw the complaint.'

Flora couldn't stop seeing Lorraine Johnson's face, the tears coursing down it as she clutched the pathetic nylon dresses Neil was now holding.

But: 'Yes,' she said. 'Let's just wait and see.'

27

ONE MONTH LATER

'Oof, you'd think we were going for a week,' said Caroline, lifting the cool box off the table.

'Let's go for a week!' said Beckie, surveying the junk-food drawer. 'We could take a tent and camp out!'

Flora was scanning the room. 'Has anyone seen my phone?'

Beckie groaned. 'What is it with you and phones, Mum?'

'I know, I'm hopeless.' She'd better not have lost this one too or she'd never live it down.

'Can I take my tablet? I want to show Edith that video of the hamster sneezing.'

'No, no screens – you can show Edith the video another time. And I think we've got enough crisps, Beckie.' She couldn't be bothered searching for her phone now. She'd just have to use Caroline's if she needed to call Neil for any reason. 'Come on.'

'Edith might not like cheese and onion.'

'Okay, choose one more flavour.' Flora followed Caroline into the hall.

'Bye, you lot,' came Neil's voice from the open study door. 'Have a good one.'

'Yeah, you too!' Caroline yelled back, lugging the cool box through the vestibule.

Flora, encumbered by two tote bags and three large beach towels, put her head round the door. 'Would you be able to get double cream, and rasps and strawberries and blueberries, or whatever there is, and I can make a summer fruits trifle?' Beckie's favourite.

Neil looked up abstractedly from his screen. 'Yeah, sure.'

He would probably forget.

'See you later, then.'

'Mm, see you – have fun. Don't forget the sunblock.'

'When have I ever forgotten the sunblock?'

The only time Beckie had ever got burnt at the beach was when she was with Neil.

She was struggling with the door to the vestibule when Beckie appeared and shoved three packets of crisps into the tote bag.

'Say goodbye to Dad, Beckie.'

'Bye, Dad!' Beckie yelled in the direction of the study before scooting out into the sunshine.

'Bye, Beckster,' came Neil's reply.

The heat hit her as she stepped out of the vestibule into the sun. She swung the larger beach bag off her shoulder and rummaged under hats, cardies and a packet of wine gums until her hand closed over the smooth plastic of the sun cream.

But by the time they'd picked up Edith and got to Yellowcraigs, and had lugged all the stuff from Caroline's car to the beach, it had clouded over. The view across the Firth to Fife was still spectacular, though, and the wide expanse of beach stretching all the way to North Berwick was virtually empty at this time in the morning – just some brisk walkers and dog owners, and a few other families with kids.

Flora held a towel round Edith and then Beckie as they wriggled out of their clothes and into their costumes, and plastered them with sunblock despite Beckie's protests that 'There's not even *sun*,' and then they were off, running at the sea.

'Just paddle until we get there, girls,' Flora called after them.

Edith was still thin but no longer worryingly so, Flora had reflected when she'd been putting the sunblock on her. The biggest difference was in her face – her cheeks had filled out into two sweet, pink little apples and there was a healthy glow about her. She was like a different child, as Shona had said the other day.

Shona had gulped: 'Thank you so much, Flora, for – for *saving* us. You really have *saved* us.'

Flora, her own tears threatening, had shaken her head. 'Maybe I've been the catalyst, but everything that's happened, it's all been down to you.'

All Flora had done was make Shona see that she needed help. It had been Shona who had found the courage to ask for that help: from her GP, from a charity that provided support to parents in difficulty, and, most importantly of all, from her ex-husband. She'd told Edith's father about her depression and how much she was struggling, and they had come to an agreement whereby they shared custody, Edith staying with her dad four days a week.

And Edith was blossoming in front of their eyes.

The two girls were fast friends now, and Beckie was touchingly protective of Edith. Shona had even been round a couple of times for lunch, and though the first time had been hard going, the second time she had seemed to relax more and had even made a few quite amusing remarks which suggested a lurking sense of humour.

Was it possible that Flora was making another friend?

Caroline was saying something.

'Sorry, what?'

'Are you getting changed some time this year, Flora?'

Caroline's swimming costume was a stylish navy one-piece; Flora's consisted of Lycra shorts and a long T-shirt. Not that she ever did much swimming. The only reason she ever went in the sea was to supervise Beckie.

But Beckie and Edith hadn't got anywhere near the water yet. They'd been sidetracked by a little dog that bounced around them excitedly while the couple who obviously owned him stood some way off down the beach, looking back. Beckie was giggling and running backwards towards Flora and Caroline, the dog jumping after her and then running to Edith, who was swishing a disgusting length of old seaweed temptingly across the sand.

'Beckie, I think his owners are wanting him to come.'

Beckie, grinning, dancing on her toes, shook her head. 'Nope, he's ours now. Look, he luuuves us! You luuuve us, don't you?' She squatted down and the dog planted his sandy paws on her lap and pushed his face towards hers.

'Don't let him lick your face –'

'– or I'll get a disease and my insides will turn to mush. It would be so worth it.' But Beckie put her hands over the dog's face and cupped his little head to stop him reaching her face, the surprisingly bright red tongue darting between her fingers. 'Ooh, tickly! Oh! He's so cute! Edith, do this! It's amazing!'

The man, resignedly, had started walking back towards them.

'Well what can they expect,' Beckie pre-empted Flora's next remark, 'when they've got a dog this cute?'

Edith, giggling as the dog licked her hands, said, 'If they didn't want people to pay their dog any attention they should have got like a Rottweiler or something.'

Beckie laughed. 'Or like a *wolf*!'

'A *lion*!'

'A *bear*!'

But Beckie jumped up and took off across the sand towards

the man, the little dog and Edith running after her. She called, 'Sorry, we had to play with him or our heads would have like exploded because he's too cute! What's his name?'

The couple were both smiling, and Beckie launched into a conversation as the dog cavorted happily.

'God, she's such a great kid,' said Caroline. 'She's really brought Edith out of her shell.'

'Mm, she's redeemed herself there. Just about.' Flora smiled. 'She's a handful.'

'No, but that's the thing – she's got all this energy and exuberance, and that witty sense of humour of hers that comes out of left field... but then when you tell her to do something, she does it.'

'Sometimes.'

'And she's happy as a pig in sh... in clover, just sitting reading a book for an hour.'

Flora smiled. 'Again, sometimes.' As they stood and started across the sand after the girls, Flora looked at her friend. 'Thank you so much for agreeing to – to be her guardian and everything. It's really taken a weight off our minds.'

Neil had come round to the whole idea, eventually. They'd been over at Caroline's for lunch last Saturday, which had been a great success – Beckie and Caroline had made a bizarre salad with pears and cheese which Neil had pretended to sick up behind a rhododendron but which had actually been quite nice.

They had met their solicitor a couple of days later and changed their wills to appoint Caroline as Beckie's guardian in the event of their deaths.

And it was weird, but just completing that paperwork had made Flora feel differently towards Caroline. She was more than a friend now. It was as if Caroline being officially Beckie's guardian had made her virtually family.

Caroline waved a dismissive hand. 'Hey. It's all hypothetical.'

They hadn't seen or heard of the Johnsons since the day of Beckie's party. The Johnsons had withdrawn the assault complaint, and the charges against Neil had been dropped. She was starting to hope that Lorraine Johnson had been sincere when she'd said they would leave them alone. That Neil had been right all along about the Johnsons not representing any real threat.

Even relations with Ailish had improved, after Neil had gone round and had a man-to-man talk with Iain about everything they'd been going through. Thomas and Mia had been round to play with Beckie, and vice versa. And Beckie was becoming a lot less clingy. Two weeks ago she would never have run off to speak to two strange people on the beach, cute dog or no cute dog.

Caroline was starting to run. 'Come on, girls, last one in's a scabby crab!'

AHEAD OF HER on the stairs, Beckie's pink Gazelles skipped from step to step as she continued to harp on the theme she'd been worrying since they'd got out of Caroline's car.

'Caroline probably thinks the raisins in a Fruit and Nut are like one of her five a day! She'd be like "It's practically health food." You know that pie chart with the amounts of things you should eat? I'm going to email her that.'

'That would be a bit cheeky, Beckie.'

'Could save her life?'

'I really don't think Caroline's got a problem. She's a very fit and healthy person – much more so than I am.'

Beckie ran across the landing to her room. Her voice, muffled, came floating back to Flora. 'She's slim and everything but that doesn't mean she's getting a healthy diet, Mum. She never cooks apart from pizza.'

Flora pushed open her own bedroom door, wondering if she should have a shower now or get dinner started first. A pizza was looking like an attractive option.

Neil was lying on the bed.

As if from another time, Beckie's muffled voice burbled on: 'And I suppose toast. When we were making that salad there was like nothing to put in it, and I mean *nothing*.'

His face was huge and purple.

There was a chain, a big metal chain, digging into his neck and his eyes were open and red. His legs were drawn up and over to one side.

This couldn't be what she was seeing.

Everything had to go back a second. Stop and go back.

'Not even lettuce,' said Beckie's voice.

Now Flora was on the bed, wordless sounds at the back of her throat, her fingers pulling at the chain, his eyes staring through her.

Vital signs vital signs vital signs.

She clutched him and put a hand to his awful purple neck to feel for a pulse, repeating, stupidly, the whole time: 'It's all right, it's all right, it's all right.' Repeating it even as she felt the coolness, the slight stiffness under her hands.

Rigor mortis.

Just the first signs of it.

Oh no no.

No no no no.

'Alec,' she said, and put both hands to his swollen face; willed his eyes to look back at her. 'Alec. I'm here. I'm here now.'

Beckie's steps on the landing. 'Mum, can I –'

She had never done anything as hard as leaving him, as taking her hands from him, as going to the door, getting the other side of it and pulling it shut. Meeting Beckie's eyes. 'Can you what, darling?'

The evening light was a hot, elongated rectangle stretching across the landing carpet. Beckie stood half inside it and Flora found she couldn't quite focus on her, she couldn't make her eyes rest on Beckie or anything else; her gaze was darting about the landing, to the window with its sunlit green vista of tree canopies, to the Greek key-patterned cornice, the Victorian table with a vase of roses on it, and a blue and white Chinese lamp, and a bowl of marble eggs.

It was as if there was something important she had to find, something that would anchor her to the old reality and stop this from happening, stop everything sliding away.

No no no Alec.

This can't be, you can't be in there dead with a chain round your neck you have to come back and what happened, the Johnsons came and one of them grabbed you and you couldn't fight them, you're just like you say a 'weedy wee guy', you're not strong enough and they –

What did they do?

And you must have been thinking Ruth *and* Beckie *and you were all alone when –*

'Can I just give her this?' Beckie held out a colourful booklet with a photograph of broccoli, a tomato, a carrot, an aubergine, an orange and grapes on the front and the title *Ten Tips for Healthy Eating* in big green letters. 'I got it from the Health Centre, remember that time I had that funny thing on my tongue but we had to wait like an hour or something before Dr Swain could see me?'

When she'd sat with Beckie in the Health Centre waiting area – and meanwhile Alec had been in a lecture theatre or a student laboratory or his own research lab, setting up an experiment or analysing data, or making coffee for himself and his fellow geeks in the grubby kitchen, or cracking some appalling, esoteric joke only another biologist would appreciate, and at the same time managing to send Flora twenty text messages reassuring her that he was a hundred per cent sure it was just an ulcer, but at the same time bugging her to let him know what was happening as it was happening.

'Mum?'

I won't let them hurt her I'll never let them hurt her.

'Yes, good idea,' Flora said brightly. 'Why don't we go round to Caroline's and give it to her now, before she starts her dinner?'

Beckie looked doubtful. 'Like, right now this minute?'

'And you can take an inventory of her fridge and cupboards.'

'And I can be vicious but fair?'

'Exactly.'

'Okay!'

In fact it was possible to pretend, it was possible to stay bright and upbeat and respond normally to Beckie as they left the house and walked the few steps down the street to Caroline's. It was possible right up to the point Caroline opened the door and looked at her.

'Thanks, Beckster!' Caroline took the booklet Beckie was brandishing. 'Right enough my eating habits need healthied up!'

'Can we do an intratory... an invertary of what's in your cupboards and your fridge? Then we can see what stuff you need to get.'

'Okay-doke, I'm up for it. You go through to the kitchen.'

As soon as Beckie was out of earshot, Flora said, 'Alec's dead. He's dead.'

Caroline just stared at her.

Then: '*What?*'

'He's dead.'

Still staring at Flora: 'You carry on for a minute there, okay Beckie? Me and your mum are doing boring grown-up stuff.'

'Okay!' came Beckie's voice from the kitchen.

Caroline shut the sitting room door behind them. 'Flora, what –'

'I found him just now, he's lying on the bed with a chain round his neck, he's been – strangled – he's –'

'He's definitely dead?'

'*Of course he's definitely dead!* Do you think I would fucking be here if he wasn't, do you think I would have left him –'

'Okay –'

'I was a *fucking nurse*, of course I know he's *fucking dead*! The Johnsons have killed him! They've waited till we let our guard down and then they've – they've *killed Alec*, Caroline! They've killed *Alec*.'

As the words were absorbed into the fabric of the room, Flora stood staring stupidly at Caroline.

'They've killed Neil.'

Here was where Caroline had to laugh and say, *Don't be ridiculous, Flora*. Because it was ridiculous. Because it couldn't be true.

But instead:

'Oh God, no. Oh *Flora*... And they've left him on your bed?'

All she could do was nod.

'Oh Christ – to incriminate you?'

But Flora couldn't summon the energy to care. She couldn't do anything, she found, but sink to her knees on the carpet, sink to her hands, to all fours like an animal, and *No no no no no* repeated in her head, and Caroline had her by the shoulders and was speaking to her but what did it matter, what did anything matter now and –

I'd do anything to keep her safe.

It was Alec's voice in her head and as waves of loss rushed through her they brought him, they carried him to her and she was screaming in her head at him to *fight, fight*, even as she knew it was over, his fight was over, Alec's fight was over except in this one way, in this one thing, in the strength that he had always given her.

She pushed herself up, got herself to her feet, shakily, a hand on Caroline's shoulder, and straightened. She stood straight and said, 'Yes. Yes. To incriminate me – That's why they – they strangled him. If they'd used a knife or a gun, the pattern... the forensics would clear me, because there'd be no blood on me, but... Using a chain to strangle him with, there'll be nothing to clear me, and I touched it –'

'Whoa. Let's just call the police and ambulance, first off, and then –'

'We can't call the police,' she said, quite calmly, 'because they'd arrest me. And how would Beckie even begin to cope with that? Her mum arrested, and taken away from her, for killing her dad?'

'God's sakes! Of course they won't arrest you. Their number one suspects are going to be the Johnsons, obviously –'

'Not if they've set up alibis again. And they will have. They're going to arrest me because I spent two years in a Young Offenders' Institution – when I was twelve I killed this girl, and they're going to go into all that and they're going to find out I'm Rachel Clark and I was there right after Saskia was murdered.'

Caroline was gaping at her.

'We can't call the police because I will be their number one suspect.'

For a long moment Caroline didn't speak. Then:

'Okay. Okay.' She was frowning off. 'Right. We have to think. We have to not panic. What are we going to do?'

Flora stared at her. 'I don't know.'

Caroline's eyes widened. 'Wait a minute though! The CCTV! The CCTV will show the Johnsons getting into the house, won't it?'

'Yes! Yes, it'll show the Johnsons –'

Leaving Beckie in the kitchen, where she was happily

arranging the contents of Caroline's kitchen on the table into their food groups, Flora and Caroline left the flat and ran down the street to Number 17.

With her hand on the front door, Caroline stopped. 'What if they're still here? Did you check the house?'

Flora shook her head. There had been no space in her brain for anything other than the huge, impossible fact:

Alec's dead.

Caroline grimaced. 'But I guess they're not going to be hanging about, are they? We're probably safe enough.' She pushed open the door and headed through the vestibule and up the stairs. 'Get the CCTV footage up. I'm going upstairs to – look at him, okay? To check...'

Flora just stood in the hall as the waves pounded her, the waves, the tsunami of *Alec's dead, Alec's dead, Alec's dead.*

'Flora? Get into the study and get up the footage for today. Fast-forward through it and check the Johnsons are on it, right, then we'll call the police. It doesn't matter what you've done. It doesn't matter what the police find out about you. If the Johnsons are on camera breaking in to the house today, that's them banged to rights.'

In the study she breathed him in. The pine shower gel he used and that faint outdoorsy botanist's aroma that he must pick up from spending hours in the lab around plants and soil. On the desk were a glass of water, the glass filmy from not being washed between refills; a mug, a plate, his untidy piles of paper.

How was it possible? This morning she'd been asking him to get fruit and double cream for dessert, and now she was standing here having to look at CCTV to try to get evidence against his murderers?

How could that be?

She didn't sit down in his swivel chair, she stood with her palms flat on the desk as the computer booted up.

When Caroline appeared she was staring at the screens, at the beautiful summer's day flashing past her eyes, like a time-lapse sequence in a nature programme on BBC 2. Trees shivering in the breeze. Birds shooting like bullets across the endless blue of the sky. Shadows moving, on the different screens, across the sandstone of the house, across rippled panes of Victorian glass, across the expanse of the glass doors.

Was he alive then – or then? Did he look out of the window and see those birds flying past? Was that when they were putting the chain round his neck, when he was fighting to stay a part of the life he could maybe see through the bedroom window, going on, just as normal, rushing on past as his time stopped, all at once and forever? There it was in front of her, his time flying past and then at one moment – maybe *then*, as a cloud crossed the sun, or maybe *then*, as a leaf flipped up in the breeze – coming to a stop. Reaching its limit. And then *that* and *that*, all the moments afterwards happening without him, without his ever knowing about any of it, second after minute after hour after day after year.

'Got them?' said Caroline.

'What?'

'Are the Johnsons on there?'

She shook her head.

'Fuck.'

The camera angled towards the street had captured a stream of humanity, vehicles, cats and dogs and birds, but from Flora and Beckie and Caroline leaving in the morning until their return, no one had approached the house, at either the front door or up the drive to the side.

As she shut down the screens, Flora was conscious, in a distant part of her brain, of Caroline looking at her.

'I didn't do it,' Flora said flatly.

'God's sakes, I know that! It's just weird that the cameras

didn't pick them up. They must have come in a window that wasn't covered, I guess.'

There wasn't any such window. Alec had made sure, in his thorough, nerdy way, that every single window was covered. But:

'I suppose so,' she said.

'Let me have a look.'

While Caroline checked from screen to screen, Flora stood, numb, staring at her back, at the pink sweatshirt she was wearing.

'Okay,' said Caroline. 'Every door and window is showing up on here except one – the window in the kitchen, the one over the sink. I guess because the obvious way for someone to break into that room is through the glass doors.'

'Oh.'

'They must have got in through that window. But we'd better look and check.'

The family room was full of warm afternoon sun. It bounced off the grey granite worktops, the never-opened jars of artisan pasta shapes and coloured pulses on the slatted shelves above, and the shiny white porcelain of the sink, pristine and gleaming.

The window above was intact.

There was no broken glass, no grubby footprints, nothing knocked over.

Caroline was frowning. 'That's weird. Is it still locked?'

Flora approached the sink and peered at the window catch. 'Yes.'

'Fuck. So how did they get in?'

'I don't know.' Suddenly it was impossible to stand up any more. Flora pulled out a chair from the table and sank onto it. The table was tidier than usual, with just a couple of plates and glasses on it, and one of Beckie's *Diary of a Wimpy Kid* books. And there was Flora's missing phone on top of the book. Alec must have found it somewhere. Down the back of one of the sofas? On the bathroom windowsill? In a kitchen drawer? She'd never know now.

She'd never know.

'I don't know,' she repeated. 'I *don't know*. Alec...' She got to her feet. 'I have to – Alec –' She had to go to him.

Caroline caught her arm, so tight it hurt. 'We don't have time. You obviously need to call the police, but first we have to think this through. If no one's been caught entering the house on the CCTV since you left, and the only window not covered by it is *fucking locked*, the police are going to look at the evidence and see no suspects *except you*. The Johnsons have set you up good and proper, Flora.'

'But how did they get in, if that window's still locked and the CCTV –'

'No idea. But the police are going to look at the footage – it's kept on the server on a cloud thing, yeah, at the security company, so we can't wipe it?'

Flora nodded.

'The police are going to take one look and come to the conclusion pretty fucking fast that no one else could have done it. No one else has been in the fucking house.'

Flora shook her head. She couldn't think. She needed to *think*.

'I'm going to jail. Beckie –'

Caroline caught her in a quick, fierce hug. 'No you're not!'

Flora grabbed at Caroline's sweatshirt. 'Beckie, you have to look after Beckie –'

Roughly, Caroline pushed her away again, holding her by the shoulders and saying into her face: 'You're not going to *fucking jail*, Flora! We've got time, right, to sort this before you call the cops. We need to make it look like someone got in from outside.' She nodded to herself. 'Yeah, a break-in... We get a hammer or something, open the window, and reach out to break it from the other side... We won't be caught on CCTV, not if we do it from the inside, because none of the cameras are trained on this window...'

Flora nodded. 'Okay.'

Caroline released her. 'Right then, great –'

'*Great?*'

Caroline took a long breath. 'Sorry.' She reached out and took Flora back into a hug. 'Oh God, Flora, I'm so sorry... We both have to hold it together for the next few hours; then we can have a complete fucking breakdown. Right? But you have to get moving. Get a hammer or whatever and break the window while I get back to Beckie. Then call the cops. Here's what you tell them, right? You found Neil dead and came round to mine with Beckie. Then we both came back here... We didn't look at the CCTV. We were both in a right state, crying over each other, we were both in shock. Then we were, "Beckie, we've left Beckie on her own" and I ran back to her. Meanwhile you were still in shock – so it took you a wee while to call the police. Took you a wee while to notice the broken window. Right?'

'Right.'

'Okay. I know this is a fucking nightmare and you're barely functioning – but you have to get a grip and do this, for Beckie's sake if for no other reason, right? That wee lassie – she needs you. She's going to fucking need you like never before, and what's going to happen to her if you're in the jail?'

Flora took in a huge gulp of air and nodded.

'You can do this. Yes?'

'Yes.'

But like a child she trailed Caroline to the front door, the sun through the stained-glass windows flooding the vestibule with coloured light, painting their feet in their sandals alternately green and yellow and red as they crossed the tiles to the door. When Caroline had gone, Flora just stood there shivering. It was always cold in the vestibule, even in the height of summer. She remembered wondering aloud about it to Neil when they'd first moved in.

Because she'd known it would rile him, she'd speculated that maybe the ghosts of the previous occupants of the house lingered here, about to go out or come in. She'd been holding the stepladder, because Neil couldn't be trusted to climb it to change the light bulb without somehow contriving to collapse the steps in on themselves and catapult himself head-first through one of the stained-glass windows, like something from Laurel and Hardy.

He had looked down at her with that disbelieving-but-gullible expression that always brought out the worst in her. She'd elaborated on her theory. The vestibule probably hadn't changed at all since the house was built. If there was anywhere ghosts would linger, it would surely be here.

It was easy to imagine a Victorian or Edwardian gentleman, she'd said, taking off his hat in here. Didn't he feel some kind of... presence?

'You can't *seriously* believe in *ghosts*,' Neil had finally spluttered, clattering down the steps to stand facing her, his chin lifted slightly. He was an inch shorter than her. 'Ruth –'

Her grin had faded. 'You mean Flora.'

'I mean Flora,' he had agreed, grimly.

And from somewhere the words had come out of her mouth: 'Do you believe in the ghosts of Ruth and Alec Morrison?'

Sometimes she used to imagine those ghosts, the ghosts of the people they had been, still living in the cottage at Arden: Ruth and Alec Morrison sitting out in the garden on a summer's evening, reading and talking and laughing, as Hobo swished his tail in the paddock and Beckie called down from her bedroom window that she wasn't sleepy and could Daddy come and tell her a story?

And Neil had looked around the vestibule, and started on

about how doorways had always had cultural significance; about how the Romans had worshipped Janus, the two-faced god of thresholds, one face looking back and one forward. The god of transitions, of endings and beginnings.

It had irritated her so much. Typical of him, she'd thought, to gloss over the personal and lose himself in contemplation of ancient history. But then:

'Let's not look back,' he'd said. 'Let's think of this as a beginning, yes? Not an end.' And he'd pulled her to him. 'Yes, Flora Parry?'

Oh God oh God oh God.

In the hall, the grandfather clock Alec had inherited from his actual grandfather ticked placidly on in its placid Victorian way.

She'd never met his grandparents, but he'd talked about them a lot. He and Pippa had spent happy summer holidays with them on the west coast, running wild along the shore, up in the hills... It was where Alec had developed his interest in nature. In *the natural world*, as he called it. She'd seen photographs of his grandparents, Granny a beaming, friendly-looking soul, Grandad a sterner prospect in shirtsleeves and waistcoat and wide 1940s suit trousers.

She shook her head.

Took a breath.

She had to do this. She had to hold it together, as Caroline had said, for just a few hours. For Beckie.

She could do this.

A hammer.

She needed to get a hammer.

WHEN IT WAS DONE, when she'd made the 999 call and the operator had told her that she must stay inside with the doors locked and that the police and paramedics would be there as soon as possible, she stood in the kitchen trying to think. She should be with Alec. But she had to *think*, and she couldn't do that in the bedroom with – with –

What would Alec have said?

It's not me *up there, it's just my body. This is more important. You have to get your story straight, Flora. You have to* think.

If the police found out that she was Rachel Clark, if they found out she'd killed before – what kind of implausible coincidence was it going to look like?

She felt as if all the Russian-doll layers of her life were being pulled apart to reveal the little hard solid core of her, that very last, tiniest, crudest doll which you knew was the last one but always twisted anyway, hoping it would open to reveal something better inside.

That hard little core that was Rachel Clark.

She had to convince the police that she was just what she seemed – a woman devastated by her husband's brutal murder. An innocent woman.

When they arrived, she would bring them in here to the family room. The heart of the home, full of their ordinary lives – Beckie's pictures on the corkboard, her puzzle books on the coffee table, Flora's new green cardigan from White Stuff chucked over the arm of one of the sofas. A book on hamsters and some DVDs in an untidy pile under the TV.

A nice ordinary family room.

That was what the architect had called it when they'd had the extension put on. The 'Kitchen/Family Room'. She could remember the words printed across the plans, in a friendly, arty font.

Yes. She would bring them in here to the family room rather than the more formal sitting room at the front of the house. She would sit them down and they would look around them and see the handmade kitchen, the cosy sitting area with all Beckie's things, the smiley photographs of them all, Flora and Neil and Beckie, in happier times.

She would tell them all about the Johnsons and the harassment and –

And they would look again at Saskia Mair's murder because of the connection, and they would ask Flora where she'd been –

But not today.

They weren't going to ask her that today. She could think about it later. And anyway, who remembered where they'd been weeks, months ago? She could just say she didn't remember.

But today.

They would be here any minute.

She would tell them where Alec was and then she'd say she had to go to Beckie. She had to go back to Caroline's and tell Beckie...

Oh God.

She had to tell Beckie.

28

I t wasn't the police who came first, it was the paramedics – two tall men in bulky green and black coveralls who told her to stay where she was as they headed upstairs. But she followed them. She had to follow them into that bedroom.

Alec was still on the bed.

Of course he was.

His face was turned towards her, grossly inflated, purple and red, and as one of the paramedics bent over him the ludicrous thought went through her head that maybe he wasn't dead, maybe they could actually help him.

'He's dead,' she said, and the paramedic must have heard the question in her voice, because he turned to her and said:

'Yes, he is. I'm sorry.'

The other man put an arm across her shoulders. 'I think you –'

But the doorbell was jangling again. She fled from the room, stumbling as she negotiated the stairs, arriving in the vestibule breathing heavily.

'Mrs Parry?'

She nodded and stepped back to let them in: two middle-aged policewomen. She had expected men. Surely, if a violent crime had just been committed, sending two women was taking political correctness too far? Alec would say...

Alec *would have said*.

What? What would he have said?

'The paramedics are upstairs. He's – he's dead. My husband. He's dead. I have to – my daughter... She's with my friend... Just down the street. Can I go to her? Please?'

'Of course you can,' the blonde one said at once, touching her arm. 'Why don't we do that while my colleague stays here and does what's necessary?' And she raised an eyebrow at the brunette, who nodded.

'Flora, isn't it?' the policewoman said as they left the house. 'I'm Sue.'

Flora nodded.

Round and round her head were going the questions: How can I protect Beckie from this? How can I make it okay for her? How can I make it right? But they were questions with only one answer:

I can't.

'I'm so sorry.' Sue had a hand under her elbow. 'Do you think you can manage...?'

'Yes. Yes. Thank you.'

But her legs had gone all wobbly, she found, as Sue guided her along the pavement like an old woman. This was good, though. Sue could see she was genuinely in shock, surely? But she had to hold it together. She had to hold it together for Beckie.

BECKIE DIDN'T CRY.

She just sat there on Caroline's sofa, in the circle of Flora's arms, passively resistant, her little face stiff, her eyes vacant. As if she had retreated somewhere Flora couldn't follow. As if all the years of being their daughter had been wiped out, at a stroke, and she wasn't Beckie Parry any more, she was Bekki Johnson, that traumatised little toddler who knew not to trust the world or anyone in it.

'Oh darling, darling.' Flora hugged her close, breathing her in, fruity shampoo and warm skin and a faint mineral sand-and-sea tang from their day at the beach.

Such a little bird she was, thin little ribcage fragile under her hands.

If only Flora could shelter her from it, if only she could wrap herself around Beckie's little body so that nothing could touch her, so that all the pain, all the grief, all the hurt that had come for her could fall instead on Flora's own shoulders.

She swallowed. Her mouth was so dry. Her throat. Weirdly, she'd never felt further from tears herself. She felt as if she'd been hollowed out, all her insides, leaving just a stupid trembly dry shell of skin and bone that wasn't her proper body, that wouldn't obey her instructions.

Beckie pulled away and got up from the sofa and said, not looking at Flora, 'Where has that policewoman gone?'

'She's gone to get us some things from the house that we might need.'

'Like what?' Beckie went to the window and stood looking out.

'Pyjamas and things. Toothbrushes. A change of clothes.'

Sue had got her to make out a list, with instructions on where to find things. Before she'd left, Lara, a family liaison officer, had arrived and would, Sue had reassured her, keep her updated on what was happening.

'Are we staying here tonight?' said Beckie.

'Yes. Caroline has very kindly said we can stay as long as we like.' Caroline was in the kitchen with Lara making sand-wiches. Lara had not, Flora realised, left Caroline and Flora alone for a second. Presumably so they couldn't collude before their statements were taken, which would be happening in the next hour or so, Lara had told them. Someone would come here to do it, so Flora didn't have to leave Beckie to go to the police station.

'Was it the Johnsons?' said Beckie.

Oh God.

'What, darling?' she stalled.

'Did the Johnsons kill Dad?'

Flora drew in a breath. 'Nobody knows yet what happened.'

And then, in a tiny voice: 'Is he *definitely* dead?' And Beckie turned, at last, and looked into her mother's eyes.

Flora nodded.

Beckie ducked her head, covering her face with both hands.

But still she didn't cry.

Flora flew across the room and gathered her up. Beckie clung to her, arms tight around her neck, legs wrapped around her hips, like she used to as a small child, as if she were trying to press herself inside Flora, into the empty space inside her.

Flora subsided back onto the sofa, cradling Beckie on her knee, rocking her.

Beckie said, in the same tiny voice: 'If you hadn't adopted me, Dad wouldn't be dead.'

Flora squeezed her close. 'We can't know that. We can't know what would have happened if we'd not had you. Dad loved you *so, so* much, Beckie. So terribly, terribly much. You made him happier than anything else in his whole life. I know for a fact that nothing... nothing that's happened could have made him not want you as his daughter.'

Silence. Then, whispered: 'You could have had another little girl.'

'But she wouldn't have been *you*, darling. She wouldn't have been you.'

29

Jed's getting right on Ryan's tits. Ryan's got on his old jeans and T-shirt and him and Connor are in the garden at the newbuild planting up the bonnie flowers and that from the garden centre, doing a wee bit chillaxing, but Jed's following Ryan round like a fucking Labrador giving it 'Wee spastic must have been bricking it, aye?' and 'Did he shite hissel'?'

Fucking psychopath willnae let it go, but Ryan's no giving him nothing.

'Gies that trowel Da, aye? And if you're wanting to make yourself useful you can get Connor that begonia while you're at it.'

'Aye, fuck off.'

I've had it. 'Right you.' I get in Jed's face. 'Get your arse back to our bit. There's a million fucking things to do and you're pissing about getting in the boys' road?'

'Oh yes, they're doing vital work here right enough,' he goes in what he thinks is his posh voice. He flips a limp wrist at Ryan. 'Fucking wee poofs.'

When he's gone I'm like that: 'Connor son, get us some cold

beers, aye? Should be some wee packets of crisps and that an' all in the cupboard.'

Connor gives me evils. He stands up and wipes his hands on his jeans. 'And take my time about it, aye? Dinnae worry Maw, I'm no wanting to hear it. I'm no fucking wanting to hear it.'

'Is that right?' Ryan's got a smile on his face. He's taking hisself for a wee stroll in Connor's direction. 'Is that right, Wee Man?'

Connor's backing up.

'You no wanting to hear it?' Ryan's all conversational. 'You no wanting that? Cannae have the Wee Man hearing something he's no gonnae like, eh? I cannae provide the sand, but there's some nice earth there, look, if you're wanting to bury your fucking head in it. You're happy enough taking a wee road trip to Peebles or St Andrews and sitting round drinking tea and eating fucking crumpets, you're happy enough on the fucking net getting us shite, long as some other fucker's doing the dirty work, eh? Long as you dinnae have to hear it?' Ryan's in his face. 'Do me a favour, aye, and spare me the fucking hypocrisy?'

Connor's eyeballing me.

'Okay boys, play nice. Get us those beers, son.'

Connor goes to Ryan, 'Aye, Mair had it coming right enough, but this guy... There could've been some other way, aye?'

'Oh is that right? Like what?'

Connor's shaking his head. 'Could've just snatched her.'

'And how long before the polis would be on our tail? Christ! Just as well mastermind here isnae calling the shots, eh Maw?'

'Aye son,' I goes. 'Snatching her, that's straight out your Da's book of shite.'

And that's Connor's arse out the windae, and Ryan's patting his cheeks and going 'Dinnae have a cow, Wee Man,' and

Connor's heading off inside. 'We're cool, aye?' Ryan goes, and Connor's like that: 'Aye Ryan, no worries.'

I cannae lie, they two are my favourite weans and I'm no happy when they're butting heads. Ryan takes a seat at the table under the parasol, and I go and join him. 'He doesnae mean nothing by it.'

'Thinks I'm a fucking psycho like Da?' Ryan's rattled so he is.

'Naw son. Naw.'

'It's no like I was thinking *Barry, I'm gonnae top this fucker* – it's no like I got any fucking pleasure out it, eh? No like Da would've.'

'Naw son. Naw.' I push the pay-as-you-go across the table at him. 'Let's us make that wee call, eh, then I'm outta here. Wannae do it?'

Ryan calls 101 and when he's put through to the right fucker he goes, 'The woman that got murdered in Haghill, aye? I'm no wanting to leave my name or nothing, I've got a wee shop on the street and I'm no wanting involved, I'm no wanting reprisals, get me?... Aye, I've got information that's maybe pertinent. Saw someone acting suspicious right when it must have happened.'

After we topped Mair, we staked out the entrance to the close in the motor, in the bit where the boys knackered they CCTV cameras. Clocked Flora arriving. Then here she's coming out 'disguised' in a hoodie, the daft bint.

'We've been getting hassle with shoplifters and that.' Ryan's winking at me. 'All of us with shops on the street have been getting hassle, so we all try to keep an eye out, eh, coordinate our response? And this woman walking by the windae, she was acting suspicious so she was, so I tells the wife, "Gonnae go and check that bitch out," and she goes and follows the bitch... Eh? Aye, she was a fat bitch in a hoodie, a grey hoodie, pulled right up over her face and she's got her head bent over while she's walking, right, like she's no wanting seen?... Aye... About average height for a woman. Fat aye, but no massive... About the wife's size, size sixteen maybe? Think her hair was maybe light brown? She goes round the corner of Quarryfield Lane and she gets in a car – red Ford Ka, wife got the registration number if you're wanting it?' He tells them Flora's number. 'We didnae think it was relevant, eh, when yous had arrested the neighbour, but now he's been released without charge we're like that: Let's us do our civic duty and call it in... Aye... Naw, have you got cloth ears by the way? I said I'm no giving my fucking name cos they fuckers round here are mental, aye? It gets out I've called yous and I'm fucking dead.' And he ends the call.

Connor's back with the beers. 'Looking good, eh?' he goes, sitting back admiring the wee border they've been planting up.

'Aye, magic,' goes Ryan. 'Magic.'

'JUST THROUGH HERE, FLORA.' Sue opened the door to a bland, pale blue interview room. 'The DI will be with us shortly. Can I get you a tea or coffee?'

'Thanks, a coffee would be good. Sue – how long is this going to take? I need to be with Beckie.'

'It shouldn't take long. There's just a few things the DI wants to go over with you.'

That was what Lara, the family liaison officer, had said too. 'Just a few things.' But Flora, left alone in the bare little room, wasn't sure she could do this. Giving her statement yesterday had been hard enough.

She didn't seem able to get enough air into her lungs. Was there even any ventilation in here? But she told herself that it didn't matter that she was breathing as if she'd just run a marathon, that her hands were sweating, that she couldn't sit still.

It wasn't as if they could charge her with 'looking guilty.'

Sue came back with the coffee and two men in suits with ID cards round their necks on blue lanyards, who introduced themselves without smiling. DI McLean was a big man with a shaved head. Like Kojak. His suit was well cut and looked expensive, and he was carrying a laptop. DI Murray, in contrast, was a '70s throwback in a worn suit and beige tie, grey hair straggling over his collar. He slumped down on one of the chairs.

Two DIs, just to ask her 'a few things'? Did she need a lawyer?

But to request one would probably look really suspicious.

When she was only three years older than Beckie, she had had to sit in an interview room just like this in Peebles police station with Mum and two policemen. Only no one had had a laptop, and the walls there had been grey. And everything anyone said, everything she said, had had to push its way through the scream inside her: *I killed Tricia, I killed Tricia, I killed Tricia.*

And she had found herself saying it out loud:

'*I killed Tricia!*'

And the grey walls had come in on her, blotting out the policemen's blank faces, Mum's mouth open in a huge O, voices receding suddenly until there had been nothing at all but grey.

She was an adult now, though. An adult with a daughter who was depending on her to get through this. There was no reason to think the police had penetrated her identity as Ruth Innes.

Their fake identities, hers and Mum's, had been set up for them by the fraudster father of one of the girls she'd got to know in the Young Offenders' Institution. For a price. Back then, before electronic records, it had been relatively straightforward. He'd found a family of 'ghosts', as he'd called them: the Innes family, who'd died in a house fire in Melrose. He'd chosen them because the mother and daughter were the right ages, and the mother had the same Christian names as Mum – Elizabeth Susan. And he'd somehow been able to discover that the mother had never had a National Insurance Number, as she'd never either been employed or claimed benefits – she'd married her husband straight out of school and had her family very quickly, so she'd spent her short adult life as what had, in those days, been termed a housewife.

It had been a simple process for Mum, in the name of Elizabeth Susan Innes, to order copies of her marriage certificate and the birth certificates of herself and her daughter Ruth from the National Records of Scotland. Then Mum had used the certificates to apply for a brand new National Insurance Number. The fraudster had supplied them with fake school records which had allowed 'Ruth Innes' to attend high school and then university.

Their new ghost identities were solid enough to allow them to do anything they needed to do, with one exception: it was too risky to apply for passports, so foreign trips and holidays had been out of the question. But that had been a small price to pay to allow them to leave Rachel Clark and what she'd done behind them.

Ruth had, though, made a terrible mistake. When she'd registered Mum's death, she had given her real maiden name of Hertz. She'd been in shock, she supposed, and not thinking straight. But the discrepancy wasn't something that anyone was going to pick up, surely? And if they did, they'd just assume – and rightly so – that Ruth had made a mistake under stress.

She laced her hands together on the table in front of her and made eye contact with Kojak.

'It was the Johnsons,' she said. 'It must have been the Johnsons. They must have killed him.'

He looked away to the screen of his laptop and, as if she

hadn't spoken, said, 'How were things at home, between you and your husband?'

'They were fine!'

That had sounded so forced. So unconvincing.

'This business with the Johnsons. I understand that, two years ago, after a mistake by Social Services led to the Johnson family learning your names and address, you changed your names, your husband found a new job, and you moved here. But they found you again. Cautions were issued to Jed, Ryan and Travis Johnson concerning breach of the court order in respect of the closed adoption. They were harassing you. That must all have been extremely stressful for both you and Neil.'

Flora nodded. 'It was. But we were coping.'

'Your husband was charged with assaulting Carly Johnson. A pregnant woman. How did you feel about that?'

Flora took a breath. 'I'm sorry, but I don't see the relevance... I thought I was here to talk about... about what happened yesterday?'

Alec is dead.

He was actually *dead*. Gone.

Forever.

All he would be from now on was a list of *nevers*. The papers he'd never write, the students he'd never inspire. The wife and daughter he'd never see, never speak to, never hold in his arms again.

Never never never never.

Alec.

'We'll get to that, don't worry. How did you feel about Neil's assault on Carly Johnson?'

'Neil... He'd just gone round there to their house to talk to them, and this girl stood at the gate blocking his way, and he just sort of tried to push past... It wasn't an *assault*.'

'Did you have a difference of opinion as to how to deal with the Johnsons?'

Who had they been speaking to? Ailish? What might Ailish have heard, over the garden wall?

'Neil was always inclined to give people the benefit of the doubt. I was... I suppose I'm more of a cynic. I didn't trust them.' Her voice broke. 'But I'm not exactly ecstatic to have been proved right.'

'So you argued about it?'

'Yes, we disagreed, and we did argue about it when the Johnsons were hassling us. But they haven't been near us for months. There was no reason for us –' And she stopped, realising the huge mistake she'd just made.

'The Johnsons hadn't been near you for months. Okay. Now, do you have anything to add to the statement you made yesterday?'

'No... No, I don't think so.'

'You've told us everything that happened, from when you got home from the beach to when the paramedics arrived?'

'Yes. I think so. Everything I can remember. I was – some of it's a bit hazy, as I think I said yesterday. I suppose I was in shock.'

He gave her a long look. 'Okay then, Mrs Parry, thank you. I do have some more questions, but first I'm going to hand over to DI Murray. All right?'

Flora nodded.

And it was DI Murray's turn to lean forward in his chair and make eye contact. He was saying he was from Haghill in Glasgow. And he was talking about Saskia.

Not Neil.

Saskia.

'A witness, a shopkeeper, saw a woman matching your description on the day in question, walking along Renfrew Road in a westerly direction at the relevant time, turning into Quarryfield Lane and getting into a red Ford Ka. The witness has also been able to give us the registration number.'

All Flora could do was stare at him.

'Mrs Parry?'

'Yes.'

'Were you that woman?'

And before she could do anything about it, the silence had stretched on too long for a denial.

'Yes. I – I'd gone to see Saskia, to ask her some questions about the Johnsons. I tried the buzzer, I tried all the buzzers, but I couldn't get a response. So... I just came home.'

'I see. And why didn't you come forward with this information?'

She swallowed. 'Because I didn't see anything. There was no point. And – to be honest, I didn't want the hassle. We had enough to deal with, so...'

'You weren't at any time in Saskia Mair's flat?'

'No. Well, I was before. Neil and I went to see her after we found out she'd been suspended, and why.'

DI Murray leant back in his chair. 'Okay, here's our problem with that. The witness who saw you getting into your car says you were wearing a grey hoodie. And there's a grey hoodie, according to Mr Mair, missing from Saskia Mair's wardrobe.'

Silence.

Flora looked from him to Sue, sitting alongside him taking notes on another laptop.

'I found her!' she blurted. 'Okay, yes, I was in the flat, I found Saskia... I found her dead! I'm a nurse – I used to be a nurse, I knew she was dead, I knew there was no point calling an ambulance...'

DI Murray nodded at her, a little smile of satisfaction tweaking at his mouth. 'But surely that would have been the normal thing to do? Call 999? Ask for the police, if not an ambulance?'

'I couldn't! The Johnsons – the Johnsons were obviously trying to set me up! Why would I kill Saskia?'

'Saskia Mair hurt your daughter.'

'Yes, but only so she could get her away from them! If she hadn't, Beckie would still be with those monsters! It's the Johnsons who hated Saskia. It's the Johnsons who had a motive for killing her, just like they've killed Neil – surely you can see that? The Johnsons *must* have killed both him and Saskia. They're – they're criminals.' *Not like me.* 'They're psychopaths! They're trying to set me up for Saskia's murder *and* for Neil's!'

DI Murray raised an eyebrow.

30

'You've been *ages*,' Beckie accused when Flora walked into Caroline's living room. She jumped up from the sofa, where she'd been sitting with Caroline watching TV, and clamped her arms around Flora's waist.

Flora stroked her hair. 'I know, darling. I'm sorry.'

'Why were you so long?'

'Well, there was a bit of waiting around. And then the police had some more questions.' She kissed Beckie's hair. 'They're being very thorough, trying to find out... well. What happened.'

'Do they know it was the Johnsons?'

'No darling, no one knows yet exactly what happened. We have to just let the police deal with that now, and concentrate on trying to... trying to do what Dad would have wanted us to, don't you think? Of course we're very sad and we miss him so terribly much – but that doesn't mean we can't still do normal things. He wouldn't want us to be miserable the whole time, would he?'

Beckie said nothing.

'What do you think Dad would have said?'

'I don't know.'

'I think he'd have given you a big hug... like *this*... And he'd have told you how much he loved you, and that he wanted you to be happy again just as soon as you could be. And you know what he was like – he'd probably have asked you something about food after that. Maybe: have you had lunch, and what did you have?'

'Lara made tomato pasta but I could hardly eat it. It was all funny in my mouth.'

'Oh, darling, I know. It's what happens when you're really sad – you don't feel like eating and any food you do eat tastes funny. But we have to eat to keep our strength up, don't we?'

'Do you think Dad would have said that?'

'Definitely.' She looked over Beckie's head at Caroline. 'Where is Lara?'

'In the kitchen,' said Caroline, getting up and taking Beckie gently by the shoulders. 'Why don't you go and help her wash up, Beckie, after she was so kind making us that pasta?'

'Okay.'

When Beckie had left the room, Caroline opened her arms and Flora walked into them.

When she could speak: 'They think I killed him. And Saskia. They know about Saskia, they know I was in her flat right at the time she was killed, I just blurted it out like an idiot... And they kept asking things like *Were you rowing about the Johnsons?* and of course I had to say yes, I had to tell the truth because they'd find out, wouldn't they –'

Caroline eased her down onto the sofa. 'That's hardly a motive for murder. And where's your motive for killing Saskia? There's no good reason why you would kill either Saskia or Neil.'

'But the way they were looking at me... It's usually the spouse, isn't it?'

'Aye, when it's the man's killed the woman. Other way round's surely pretty rare. Would you even have the strength to strangle him? They're just fishing. You stuck to the story, yeah?' She rubbed Flora's arm.

'I tried, but... It was going on and on and on... They kept asking me the same things again and again, in different ways... I must have been in there for hours. They took my fingerprints and everything, they said they needed to eliminate them for the forensics in the house... They need you to go in and give yours too this afternoon, and Beckie...'

'I can take her, no problem, while you get some rest, yeah?'

Flora nodded. 'Okay. Thank you... Oh God, Caroline, it was *awful*. In the end I couldn't think straight. They made me go over the whole of yesterday again, and they kept asking me about what I said in my statement... Like I forgot, when I was giving the statement, that we'd picked up Edith before driving to the beach – How could I have forgotten that?'

'But that's not a problem. Who's going to remember every little detail of any particular day? It would be more suss if you had everything off pat. Why would you want to miss out the bit about picking up Edith when she's part of your alibi, for God's sake? It's actually good that you got muddled up about that, when it's obviously not something you'd need or want to lie about. It'll make any other mistakes seem more innocent.'

'The only lie was about the window... I don't think I should have done it. Broken the window, I mean. It wasn't –'

'Listen, Flora, those fuckers are trying to frame you for murder, right? What's wrong with trying to protect yourself from that? Chances are they've been extremely careful not to leave any forensic evidence behind that puts them in the house, and what with the CCTV not showing anything... That broken window is crucial. It's the evidence the police need to put the Johnsons in the frame – without it you'd be fucked.'

'But Caroline –'

'You've got to get yourself into the mindset of an innocent person. You're convinced the Johnsons did it –'

'They *did* do it! You believe that, don't you? *You* believe I didn't do it?'

'I know you didn't, Flora. I know you didn't. And we're going to get through this, okay? They can't have enough evidence against you or they'd have charged you by now. It's going to be fine.'

Flora stared at her, at this woman who for some unknown reason seemed to think she was worth saving. 'Thank you. Thank you. I don't know how to thank you.'

Caroline pulled her into a hug.

IT'S A LOVELY WEE SCENE, so it is: a granda bonding with his grandkid. Jed's in his La-Z-Boy with my tablet and Corrigan's leaning over him eyeballing the screen. He's, 'What's that word?' and Jed's, 'Bile... Biligist... Bio-lo-gist,' and Corrigan's wrinkling his face just like Granda, and then he's, 'What's *that* word?' and Jed's, 'Strangled.' Right back in his comfort zone.

'That's no appropriate for a wean,' I goes. 'You fucking prick. What is it any road?'

Jed gives me evils.

'A bit on that blog *Edinburgh Crime Scene*,' goes Corrigan. 'But there's no even any photies of the body.'

I puff. 'Course there's no.'

'When's that bint getting arrested?' goes Jed.

'What bint?' goes Jordaine.

I goes, 'Connor son, get Corrigan and Jordaine a lolly in the kitchen, aye? And yous can take the dug an' all.'

Connor sighs. He and Jordaine have been making a wee card for Willow, Carly's babby, and there's pink fucking glitter all over the coffee table, the carpet, the settee, Connor, Jordaine and the dug. Jordaine's put a massive sticker of a Labradoodle on the dug's heid and he's going mental so he is.

'Can I get a strawberry mivvi?' goes Jordaine.

'If Corrigan hasnae had them all.' Connor picks the sticker off of the dug.

'I'm wanting two lollies, minimum,' goes Corrigan.

Connor gets up. There's a bit of pink card glued to his arse with 'KIK HEAR' written on it in black marker pen. Corrigan's giggling away, the wee bastard.

When they're out the room, I snatch the tablet off of Jed and have a wee look at the article. There's a photy of Neil and Flora's house with police tape across the driveway and the gate, and a polisman standing doing fuck all. Article goes on about how Neil was a respected scientist and worked at Edinburgh University. There's quotes from his colleagues about what a nice guy he was. Quotes from DI McLean saying they're pursuing several lines of inquiry, blah fucking blah. And then a bit about 'a source' saying that Mr Parry may have been strangled.

By an intruder.

Fuck.

Polis have been round interviewing Jed and the boys, right enough, and searching the place, but they found fuck all. Alibis are fucking solid. What are the bastards playing at? They cannae be thinking *intruder.* That's just some eejit mouthing off on the internet. The polis have got to like Flora for it. How can they no?

Jed's spot on for once in his fucking life – why have they no arrested the bint? Ryan keeps on about how the polis have to have their ducks in a row, but they fucking ducks are lined up ready and waiting. What is their fucking problem?

31

'Okay, darling. We're here,' Flora said unnecessarily.

She pulled in opposite Caroline's. There were still two police vans parked at the gate of Number 17, and tape across the entrance to the drive. Beckie had glanced at it all as they passed their old house – Flora was already thinking of it as their old house – but she hadn't said anything.

Beckie hadn't cried, not once, in the four days since Neil's death. She had acquiesced to all Flora's suggestions about how to fill their days. This afternoon they'd been at Shona's, and Beckie and Edith had played quietly on the carpet, threading beads to make necklaces and bracelets, while Shona had talked – so Flora didn't have to – about her new job in a florist's and the awkward customer she'd had yesterday, a man who'd insisted on pulling all the plants out of their pots to check their root systems. Beckie had hardly said a word, and she had stayed within a few feet of Flora the whole time. But Shona had succeeded in persuading her to eat a blueberry muffin, a very nice one with huge juicy blueberries in it, which Beckie had seemed to enjoy and had almost managed to finish.

Now she was sitting in the passenger seat, fingering the

bright pink and blue plastic beads on the necklace Edith had insisted she keep.

'We're here,' Flora repeated.

She got out of the car and opened the passenger door. She unclipped Beckie's seatbelt and lifted her out, as if she was still a toddler, and for a moment Beckie clung to her.

Caroline's front door opened and Lara appeared. Behind her was DI McLean, his face stony, and Sue.

DI McLean looked at Beckie, and fixed on a smile. 'Hello there. Beckie, right? We just need a word with your mum for a minute, okay?'

And now, thank goodness, here was Caroline, taking Beckie's hand, pulling her inside, and Flora was being herded after them, into Caroline's front room, where there were three cups on the coffee table and a plate of digestive biscuits.

'What are you doing here?'

Sue grimaced. 'Mrs Parry –'

Not Flora any more, then.

She took a breath. 'Why haven't you arrested the Johnsons?'

DI McLean just looked at her. 'Mrs Parry, I am placing you under arrest for the murder of your husband.' A pair of handcuffs were suddenly in his hands. 'You are being detained under Section 14 of the Criminal Procedure, Scotland, Act 1995. You have the right not to say anything other than giving your name, address, date of birth, place of birth and nationality, but anything you do say will be noted and may be used in evidence. You have the right to see a solicitor. Do you understand? Mrs Parry?'

'My daughter!'

'Do you understand?'

'Yes, I understand, but please – let me see her... Let me see her without...' She looked down at the handcuffs. '*Please!* Her dad's just been murdered, and now...'

The police officers exchanged glances. 'Okay. But please keep it brief.'

In the kitchen, Beckie was sitting at the table, staring at a slice of bread and jam. She looked up at Flora, at the police officers behind her, with a blank expression.

'Beckie. Darling... I have to go with the police now. There's... there's obviously been a misunderstanding, but it'll all get sorted out, so you don't have to worry, okay?' Flora squatted by her chair. 'I'm not sure when I'll be back, but Caroline will look after you for now.' She shot a pleading look at Caroline, who was standing propped against the sink, her face very pale.

'Course I will,' Caroline said at once, attempting a smile.

'Where are you going?' said Beckie.

'To the police station. I – the police think... They think I had something to do with Dad... with what happened to Dad... But Beckie, I *promise* you I didn't, okay?'

'Something to do with it? What do you mean?'

Flora couldn't say it. She put her arms round the thin, stiff little shoulders. 'It's going to be okay.'

'You mean –' Beckie pulled back. 'You mean they think *you killed Dad*?' And suddenly she was up and away, backing from the table, and Flora's words caught in her throat, she couldn't get them out, she couldn't move, like one of those terrible dreams where all powers of speech and movement are denied you.

Beckie was staring at DI McLean. 'She didn't,' she said, quite calmly. 'My mum didn't kill him.'

'But they have to... They have to ask me questions...'

'Are you arrested?'

Flora nodded. And at last she was able to go to her, to put her arms round her and pull her close, and Beckie was saying, 'It's okay, Mum, it'll be okay because you didn't hurt Dad.' But she wasn't hugging Flora back, she was just standing there.

It was the shock.

Of course it was the shock.

'Mrs Parry –'

Flora pulled away; put both hands either side of Beckie's face. 'You're going to have to try your hardest not to worry about me, Beckie, because I'll be fine. It's a mistake and it'll be sorted out. I'll be back before you know it, but in the meantime you'll be fine here with Caroline.' She smiled. 'Remember you have to eat to keep your strength up, okay? And probably soon they'll let Caroline pick up some more of your things from the house... Anything you want...'

Beckie's lips moved in an approximation of a smile. 'Okay.'

And then suddenly she was having to leave her, and how was Beckie going to even begin to cope with this? She wanted to hold her so tight and never let her go but she couldn't, all she could do was say 'Thank you' to Caroline, and then she was out of the kitchen, Beckie was gone, the cuffs were around her wrists and hands were on her upper arms and she was walking down the path to the street.

'This is fucking ridiculous!' Caroline said behind her. 'There's no way Flora... How can you think she killed Neil? This is a huge fucking mistake and you're getting your arses sued for this!'

Flora turned.

Caroline was trying to push her way past Sue.

Flora caught her gaze and held it. 'Look after her.'

It seemed to stretch on, the moment in which she stared into Caroline's eyes, wordlessly beseeching.

'God, yes, of course I will, Flora, don't worry about that for a second... Are you proud of yourselves, are you, for traumatising a nine-year-old child, taking her mum away from her when she's just lost her dad?'

'Ms Turnbull, please go back inside.'

'Don't worry, Flora! Don't you worry, okay, we'll sort this out!'

IT WAS the same pale blue interview room. This time her solicitor, Charles Aitcheson, was sitting next to her, a calm, reassuring presence. He had told her to make no comment to anything they said. They had to wait and see what 'evidence' they had against her before they formulated their response.

That made sense.

But what evidence could they possibly have against her?

She hadn't done it.

She hadn't killed Neil.

Could they know? Could they know she was Rachel Clark?

DI McLean was accompanied, this time, by a male colleague in uniform who was making notes on a laptop. DI McLean sat opposite Flora. He also had a laptop, and a blue card-covered file on the table in front of him.

He opened this, removed a photograph, and pushed it across the table. 'This is a photograph of the chain used to strangle your husband. A partial print has been recovered from it, and it's a match for the thumb of your right hand. How do you explain that?'

'I told you. I touched it when I found him. When I – when I tried to get it off him, when –'

Charles put a hand on her arm.

But she didn't need to say 'No comment' to that, because the explanation was so straightforward and obvious.

'Okay.' The policeman took back the photograph; returned it to the file.

She turned her head away. She didn't want to see anything else from that file.

'Mrs Parry, I'm going to ask you to have a look at some CCTV footage obtained from Eden Security, the company that stores footage from the cameras installed at your residence at 17 Gardens Terrace.'

'Okay.'

'Before you do so, I have to tell you that the post-mortem findings include an estimation of time of death of between 8:45 and 10:30 a.m. on the day your husband died. Until the arrival of the paramedics at 6:28 p.m., no one appears on the CCTV footage for that day apart from yourself, your daughter and your neighbour Caroline Turnbull. The three of you leave the house at 9:19 am. You and your daughter return at 5:38 p.m. and then leave again at 5:46 p.m. You said in your statement that your priority was getting your daughter out of the house to safety. That's why you didn't call the emergency services straight away.'

She nodded.

'Is that correct, Mrs Parry? Please speak for the audio.'

'Yes.'

'You and Ms Turnbull return to Number 17 at 6 p.m. precisely. Why? If you felt so unsafe in the house, why take that risk?'

'Because Caroline – She thought I might have made a mistake about Alec being dead.'

'Why didn't you call 999 from Ms Turnbull's house before returning to Number 17?'

'I – No comment.'

He nodded, as if satisfied by this answer. 'In her statement, Ms Turnbull has said that she assumed you had already called 999 when she returned with you to your house. Is there any reason for her to have assumed this?'

'No. I don't know.'

'Ms Turnbull is shown on the CCTV leaving the house at 6:09 p.m.' He sat back and looked at her. 'Your call to the emergency services was registered at 6:21 p.m. What were you doing, Mrs Parry, between the time Ms Turnbull left the house and that call? The two of you have just established that your husband is dead – murdered – and Ms Turnbull has run back to her own house to be with your daughter Beckie. Why delay *still further* before calling 999?'

'No comment.'

He turned the laptop sideways on the table so they could all see the screen.

'I'm going to ask you to look at this footage, Mrs Parry.'

On the screen was a sharp image of the back garden. Alec had insisted on state-of-the-art cameras and had spent hours adjusting them to get the pictures as sharp as possible. She could see the individual lavender flowers, and the little weeds between the stone slabs of the patio. And then a figure appeared on the patio, a pale-faced, wild-haired woman with the kind of fixed expression you saw on people filmed during earthquakes, or gun massacres, or famines.

She watched herself run across the patio, along the gravel path to the shed. Fumble with the combination padlock. Dive inside, and reappear with a hammer swinging from her hand. Run back down the path to the patio, and disappear off the edge of the screen.

DI McLean reached across the keyboard and tapped at the keys. The scene on the screen changed to the side wall of the house. The kitchen window – Oh God, the kitchen window was visible! Right at the edge of the screen.

Caroline had been wrong.

The CCTV *did* cover that window!

She watched in dismay as she appeared behind the glass. She had stood on a chair to enable herself to reach far enough over the sink to get her hand out of the window with the hammer... And there was her arm, her hand, the hammer... There was the glass shattering, her grimace at the noise of it...

DI McLean leant across the table. 'What happened, Flora? What happened in your house that day?'

She sighed. 'Okay.'

'Flora,' said Charles.

'No. It's fine, I need to explain... When we got back, Caroline and I –' But no. She couldn't implicate Caroline in this. If Caroline was also arrested, as accessory after the fact or whatever, what would happen to Beckie? 'When Caroline and I got back to the house, while she was upstairs... I checked the CCTV. I realised that it didn't show anyone breaking in to the house, I realised the Johnsons must somehow have manipulated the footage or something to frame me... But the kitchen window wasn't covered by the CCTV, at least that was what I thought, I didn't realise that that camera included it... So after Caroline had gone, I got a hammer and broke the glass...'

'Mrs Parry,' sighed DI MacLean. 'Even if the window itself had not been covered by your CCTV, in order to reach it, an intruder would have had to pass through the fields of view of at least two other cameras.'

'I – I didn't think of that.'

'Evidently not. Just how do you explain why no one was caught on the CCTV that day, in the time interval between yourself, Ms Turnbull and your daughter leaving the house, and yourself and your daughter returning?'

'Flora –' Charles shook his head.

There were grey splotches in front of her eyes. A buzzing, high in her head. But she managed to get it out. She managed to say:

'No comment.'

32

'H ello?'

'Mrs Fisher?' I goes in a polite wee voice. 'This is Jessica Stuart from Making Waves? The TV production company? You were kind enough to speak to myself and my colleague about your daughter Tricia a few weeks ago?'

'Oh. Yes. Hello.'

'It seems that Rachel Clark, or Flora Parry as she's calling herself now, was arrested today for the murder of her husband. I've just had a tip-off from a journalist. And she's also under suspicion of the murder of a social worker.'

Wifie's gasping away.

I goes: 'I'm sorry to be telling you this over the phone, but I didn't want you to find out from the media. It should hit the news tomorrow morning... Mrs Fisher, are you all right?'

'I – yes. Sorry.'

'The police are unaware, however, of Flora's real identity.' So how come this journo fucker tipped me off, eh? How come the journo knew Flora Parry was the Rachel Clark I was making a documentary about? It's no adding up, but I'm counting on Wifie no thinking straight. 'Rachel covered her tracks extremely well, and... Anyway. The thing is, my professional code of conduct precludes me from going to the police and telling them who Flora is...' And that's a load of pish an' all. 'But you could do so.'

'I'll do it right now.'

'Aye, if you wouldn't mind, Mrs Fisher, holding off until her photo's in the press? Then you can pretend you recognise her from the photo. I shouldn't have told you who she was, you see. I just – I couldn't in all conscience *not* tell you, but if anyone finds out I've done so, I'll probably lose my job.'

'Oh, of course. After all you've done for us...'

'If you just call the police after her photo's appeared in the press, and tell them she's the bitch killed Tricia, that should do it.'

Aye, that should do it right enough.

I chuck the phone on the settee and do a fist pump like one of they tennis fuckers.

Out in the wee hall, there's that up-herself bint coming at me in her wee cropped jeans and white linen shirt, pulling at the waistband of the jeans because aye, getting a bit tight there, eh doll? Fuck the fucking diet, eh?

'Right then Caroline-hen,' I goes. 'Let's us get outta here.'

Behind the bint, there's wee Bekki. Thank God. She's been locked in the lavvy for a fucking hour, poor wee bairn.

I turn and go, 'Okay sweetheart?'

'Who are you talking to?'

I chuckle. 'Talking to myself like a mentalist.' I wave at the mirror down the end of the hall and the bint waves back. Next her, Bekki's standing there giving it rabbit in the headlights.

It's fucking crazy but, like something out one of they halls of fucking mirrors – I'm rabbit in the headlights an' all, I cannae believe it, eh, there's me and there's my wee darlin' next me. Wee Bekki. I coorie her in to my chebs and in the mirror the bint Caroline's coorying her, and I'm going and she's going, 'It's okay, sweetheart. It's gonnae be okay.'

I PULL up in the drive outside the newbuild. It's a barry day, not a fucking cloud in the sky, and I'm thinking picnic lunch in the garden with all the wee treats we've got in for Bekki, they wee samosas and that, and Marks and Sparks salads with weird beans and shite.

'Here we are then, Bekki!' I goes, all cheery. 'That window up there's your room!'

Bekki doesnae say nothing.

And aye it's a lot for a bairn to take in, eh? When we stopped on the way for a wee poke of chips I went, 'This house where we'll be staying, it's where my kids live. Carly and Connor.'

And she goes, 'You've got *kids*?'

'Yes, Bekki, had you forgotten? Connor helped your mum sort her laptop when she had problems with it, remember?'

Wee Bekki's shaking her head.

And I pull out my phone and show her the photy of Carly after she had Willow in the hospital, with Connor sitting on the bed next her grinning like a daftie. 'There's Connor. Actually, maybe you were at school when he came over... but I'm sure Flora and I were talking about him when you were there. You don't remember? And that's Carly and wee Willow, her baby.'

Bekki's rabbit in the headlights.

'Carly's carrying a few extra pounds. She could benefit from your healthy eating plan, don't you reckon?'

'She's really pretty,' Bekki whispered, the wee darlin'.

Now I'm getting out the motor and going, 'Come on then, Bekki, let's go,' and here's Connor coming out the door and the wee diddy's all choked up, and I goes, 'Right then Connor, here's Bekki' and I give him evils because Bekki's gonnae be thinking *Why's that dowfie wee bastard trying no to greet?*

And he's 'Hiya Bekki' and Bekki's eyeballing him and going, 'Hi,' and then we're in the lounge and Carly's got Willow through and she's going, 'Wannae hold her, Bekki?' and Bekki's 'I don't know how. I might drop her' and Carly's 'Dinnae you worry, hen, I'll soon learn you, eh? Connor hasnae dropped her yet, and if that wee fuckwit –'

I'm 'Carly, mind your language please!' and Carly's 'Sorry. Here, Bekki, you sit down on the settee and then if you do drop the wean she's gonnae get a soft landing, eh?' and Bekki's got Willow in her arms and she's looking down at the babby and the babby's looking right back at her, and it's no happening just yet because Willow cannae and Bekki's sad, eh, but it winnae be long before they two's smiling and laughing together, and I'm that choked up I've to get outta there and through the kitchen and out the back to the garden, and I'm staring at they begonias and greeting my fucking eyes out.

33

F lora chose a table opposite the door as usual, so she would know straight away whether Caroline had Beckie with her. She never knew what to hope for – it was no place for a child, obviously, but she couldn't help hoping that Beckie would come this time.

An attempt had been made to make the Visit Room child friendly. The walls were painted sunshine yellow, and there were some pictures of smiling people bolted to them, and even some bright alphabet and number posters in the play area corner. But if a child used the play area, they had to be accompanied by a visitor, not the prisoner.

The prisoners had to remain seated at their tables at all times.

There were only three other women with this visiting slot today, as Flora had hoped. And they were all young girls whose presence was in no way threatening. Flora always waited until the last minute to book her visiting slot, just in case Beckie came, so she could find out who else had booked when, and avoid the hard nuts.

'Hey Flora,' said Danielle, twisting round at the table in front, knees jigging. 'God I'm needing a fucking fag.'

There was meant to be no talking among prisoners in the Visit Room, but Mrs Aitken, standing by the door, tended to turn a blind eye as long as the exchanges remained civil.

Flora smiled. 'It's a cup of coffee I want.'

Because they weren't allowed to leave their seats, they had to wait until their visitors arrived to get them stuff from the vending machines.

'It's shite,' said Danielle.

'But it's caffeine.'

'I'm wanting chocolate buttons. But they should let us fucking smoke. Should be a nonsmoking room and a smoking room for stupid cows like me cannae quit.' Her knees were jumping now. Danielle was cyclothymic, and currently in a hyper phase. 'Although I guess it's for the kids, eh. Don't want them getting passive smoking.'

'You don't *get* passive smoking,' said one of the other girls with a roll of her eyes.

'All right, ladies,' said Mrs Aitken.

'Sorry,' said Danielle, although the rebuke hadn't been aimed at her.

'Verbal fucking diarrhoea,' said the other girl.

'Aye, just because I'm bubbly and that –'

'And we wouldn't have you any other way,' said Flora. 'Although, when your brother arrives for your visit –'

Danielle grinned. 'Keep it zipped, eh?'

'Well, at least let him say hello.'

Everyone in the room smiled, including Mrs Aitken.

Flora had rediscovered the knack she'd acquired, all those years ago, in the Young Offenders' Institution of diffusing this sort of tension, the sort of tension that was inevitable when you put a group of troubled young women together. Sometimes it felt as if she'd never left it, as if the intervening years had been a wonderful dream, and now she'd woken up to reality.

Bail had been refused after it had come out that she was Rachel Clark and a 'flight risk', having already 'disappeared' with a new identity more than once.

As one of the older inmates, she had found that she was automatically afforded a certain amount of respect. But she knew how to avoid trouble. She knew how to deal with the other prisoners. Walk tall. Act confident. Be friendly, but not too friendly. Be generous with food and possessions, but don't be a doormat. Don't initiate eye contact with the hard nuts, but if you sense them looking at you, look back, hold their gaze, maybe greet them casually by name.

She'd been helping Danielle and some of the others with literacy and numeracy, and yesterday in the gym Wendy, one of the hard nuts, had taken her aside and muttered that she'd be 'grateful' if Flora would help her with her reading. 'Never went much to the school, you know?'

Now that she was in with Wendy, she was home and dry.

And she was hating every minute, every hour that Beckie had to be without her.

But she was innocent and she was going to prove it, no matter what doom and gloom Charles Aitcheson came out with. There must be evidence, somewhere, that the Johnsons did this. She would be found innocent, and Beckie would believe it, and everything would be fine. She and Beckie would go far away and make a new start.

And now the door was opening and Danielle's brother was beaming at his sister, and behind him Caroline was shaking her head apologetically.

No Beckie.

'Sorry Flora,' Caroline grimaced through a nervous smile. 'She still doesn't want to come. I told her about the Family Hub and the wee garden and everything, I said it didn't even seem like a prison, but –'

Flora nodded. 'It's fine. It's maybe better she doesn't come. I –'

'Coffee, yeah? And a Kit Kat?' A smile still fixed to her face, Caroline hooked her bag over the chair opposite Flora's.

'Thanks, that would be great.'

'I'm really sorry, Flora.'

'Don't worry about it. I think it might be better to concentrate on persuading her to agree to Skype. Or even just to write to me.'

'She just needs a bit more time. She'll come round. She's just...'

'She's confused and angry and scared.' Flora breathed. 'Of course she is.'

Watching Caroline making her selections at the drinks vending machine, glancing first one way and then the other over her shoulder, as if expecting to be jumped at any moment, Flora reflected that it was as if they had swapped places. Flora seemed to have acquired all the assurance Caroline had lost. It was obvious that Caroline hated coming here, that it unnerved and disturbed her. And where Flora had lost weight and toned up thanks to hitting the gym for four hours every day, Caroline's figure had expanded and softened, the fabric of her white jeans sausage-tight across her bum and thighs.

The coffee was as terrible as ever. And she found she didn't even want the Kit Kat.

'Are things any better at school?'

'Not much. She and Edith have fallen out again.'

'Oh no.'

'She's... I think the word is *volatile*. She's really volatile. You don't know what's going to set her off. The headmistress and the teachers have been great, but...' She shrugged. 'And living a few doors down from her old home... It's not easy for her. What

I'm thinking is it might be better if we moved away. There's this nice wee house in Bearsden for rent... I used to live in Bearsden a while back and I think Beckie would like it there. New house, new environment, new school...'

'Oh, but Glasgow... That's where the Johnsons live.'

'I doubt whether the Johnsons ever frequent Bearsden! Practically a different planet from Meadowlands Crescent.'

'But I can't ask that of you. To uproot yourself...'

'Oft, no problem. I can work from anywhere, eh?'

'But you must let me give you the money for the rent. I'm going to get a bridging loan on the house. I've been advised not to sell until... well, until the murder has faded from the collective memory. But... I'm so sorry, this is so disruptive for you. Caroline, I don't know how to thank you, for everything, for taking such good care of her. Really.'

'I love the Beckster, you know that. And we still manage to have fun. She's really into jigsaws now. On Saturday we went into town and she chose three two-thousand-piece numbers. Kittens, the Taj Mahal and an underwater scene.'

'And let me guess – you're doing the kittens first?'

'Course we are.' Caroline took a slug of coffee and made a face, looking for a moment like her old self. 'That is foul. If you're not going to eat that Kit Kat...'

Flora pushed it across the table. 'The good news is that I'm not being charged with Saskia's murder. The neighbour who buzzed me into the stair apparently went across the landing to Saskia's door to tell her she had a visitor, and saw her dead on the floor. It took her a while to come forward because she was plucking up courage – frightened of repercussions from whoever was responsible.'

'Aw, that's brilliant, Flora!'

'The bad news is that Ailish has made a statement about the quarrels she overheard between me and Neil.'

'Bitch.'

'And not just Ailish. Pippa too – it seems Neil called her a few times to talk about his worries about my "weird behaviour". And Dr Swain has also made a statement. About my "disturbed" state of mind when I went for that Darren boy in the waiting room.'

'Oh Christ. But you thought he was attacking you.' Caroline snapped the Kit Kat in half.

'But he wasn't. That's the point.' She sighed. 'And there's just no evidence that the Johnsons were anywhere near the house on the day Alec was killed. That's a huge problem.'

Caroline grimaced. 'And what about the drug issue? Any further forward on that?'

Methamphetamine had been found in the blood sample taken on her arrest, and she had no clue how it got there, unless the Johnsons had somehow managed to put it in her food – but how could they? Her solicitor was working on the assumption that there had been a mix-up with the samples. 'The police are insisting the chain of evidence is intact. But I know I never took methamphetamine. I wouldn't even know how to go about getting hold of it. Charles says it could work in my favour if I said I'd taken it, it could explain my "paranoia", but why do I need to explain it? The Johnsons were harassing us. That wasn't just me being paranoid – you were there, that time on the pavement. They've got your statement and everything.'

Caroline was munching Kit Kat, looking down at the silver foil, rubbing it with her finger.

She flicked a look up at Flora. 'I'm really sorry, but I think I've messed up big time as far as that's concerned... They had me in to give another statement. They've got a witness to what happened on the street that day – I'm thinking it could be Ailish. This witness corroborates what the Johnsons are saying, that it was just Jed going a bit mental, that at no time was Beckie threatened, or either of us... And you know how they are, how they ask you the same thing again and again but in a slightly different way, so you have to give a slightly different answer, till you're not thinking straight? I think... I think I might have given the impression that it *was* just Jed, and that the two boys were just trying to get him away from you. Sorry, Flora.'

Damn. 'It's okay, Caroline, I know how they twist what you say...'

'Aye, but that's not all. That's not the worst of it.' Her gaze was back on the Kit Kat foil. 'They've taken a statement from Beckie.'

Flora couldn't speak.

'Apparently they asked her what happened before we left the house, and she said she called out "Bye Dad" to Neil without waiting to hear his reply. She's beating herself up about that, poor wee soul. And she also told the police that I just called "See you, Neil" or something, and he didn't reply to me either. Which contradicted my previous statement – I'd told them that both Beckie and I had said goodbye and he'd replied. So second time round – in the second statement – after what Beckie had said, I had to admit that I didn't see or hear Neil that morning.'

'But – that's wrong.' Flora could feel her palms moistening. 'Maybe Beckie didn't wait for a reply, but you heard him speak to you as we were leaving – Beckie was still in the kitchen, so she couldn't know how the exchange went, she must be misremembering... We were both in the hall, and Neil called out "Have a good one" or something, and you said "You too." We were both there. You must remember that? And then you went out and I had a conversation with him about...' She swallowed. 'About getting ingredients for a trifle.'

'Oh God. Sorry, Flora, yes, you're right. I *did* hear him say that. Oh God, I've really fucked up. They were messing with my head, I wasn't thinking... I'll go back and make another statement, set the record straight.'

'Okay. Thanks.'

But it was too late.

The damage had been done.

The prosecution would have a field day with Caroline's three different versions of events. So now there was no credible witness to Neil still being alive when Flora had left the house.

'It probably doesn't matter anyway,' Flora said. 'The main problem is the complete lack of evidence against the Johnsons. First and foremost, there was no sign of a break-in to the house – other than the window *I* smashed – and no one was picked up on the CCTV that day apart from you, me and Beckie. Charles says it's going to be really tough getting round that.' She sighed. 'He thinks I did it. I'm sure Charles thinks I'm guilty.'

'Sack the bugger.'

'No, it doesn't matter what he thinks, he'll do his best for me. He's good. Better the devil you know…'

'True enough. Flora, the thing you've got to remember through this is – you didn't do it. You're innocent. Yeah?'

Flora nodded. 'So they can't have enough evidence to convict me. I know. That's what I keep telling myself.'

I'M on my mobile to Ryan, walking up the wee cul-de-sac to the newbuild.

'She's in the shite and she knows it. She's all "Surely there must be some evidence against the Johnsons" and I'm "Aye, surely" but there isnae, right son? Travis got the gear you was wearing lit down the back of the Unit, aye, and the chain's in the fucking Clyde?'

'Aye, no even Travis could fuck that up. Dinnae you worry, Maw. Dinnae you worry.'

'How am I *no* gonnae worry, eh son, with shite-for-brains

weans giving me fucking grief twenty-four-seven? Aye, and another thing: Wendy fucking Burns is in that gaff.'

'Fuck. She clock you?'

'Naw. She was in the wee bit garden having a fag when the screws was herding us down the corridor to the Visit Room. She was too busy mouthing off to another bint to pay us any notice. But even if that fuckwit had of clocked me – which she didnae – she wasnae gonnae go *Here, that's fucking Lorraine Johnson*. All she'd be thinking as I walked on by in Caroline's white Jigsaw jeans that cost seventy-five fucking quid and her wee Joules top and jacket would be *Fucking up-herself bint*.'

'Aye, likely,' Ryan chuckles. 'But next visit, how about wearing shades and that, eh Maw?'

'That mentalist fucking slag isnae gonnae rumble Caroline, son, shades or no fucking shades.'

Even my ain grandkids have a hard time getting their heads round how their Nana's gone anorexic and wearing snobby crap. No way Burns is gonnae rumble Caroline.

But I'm no happy.

Wendy fucking Burns.

I'm no fucking happy.

Now I'm in the door, and I've no even got my jacket off and here's Bekki coming down the stair giving it, 'Did she like the card? Did she read my letter?'

I kick off my boots. Hall carpet in the wee newbuild's dead gorgeous, a wool blend in barley with a pile that thick you could use it as a fucking trampoline. After three fucking hours in they fucking fashion-victim boots, my feet think they've died and gone to heaven.

'Sorry, sweetheart.' I open my bag and take out the bits of ripped-up green card. And the letter, still sealed in the envelope.

Bekki takes the bits like they're wee hurt animals, the poor darlin'.

'Aw, come here, Bekki.' She lets me coorie her but she's no leaning in. 'I'm sorry. She says she doesn't want to see you and she doesn't want to have any contact with you. It's not your fault, sweetheart, okay, it's nothing you've done.'

'But why…' It's a wee whisper.

'What's that, sweetheart?' I'm stroking her hair.

'Why doesn't she?'

'Aw Bekki, I don't know. She's under a lot of stress at the moment and probably not thinking straight. But I'm here. I'm always going to be here for you.'

'I want my mum!' And she's pushing me away and running back up the stair.

Connor's coming down and he catches her and goes, 'Whoa, Bekki, where's the fire?' and she's going, 'I want my *mummm!*' in his face, and he's 'Aye, I know, hen,' and she's pushing past him.

'Dinnae you start,' I go as I puff past him up the stair.

But I'm no feeling great about it neither. It's a wee shame for Bekki so it is, and if I'm honest, if I'm a hundred per cent fucking honest with myself, I'm feeling bad for fucking Flora. Me and that bitch, in another world maybe, in another fucking universe where bairns dinnae get taken off of folk for no reason, maybe me and that bitch coulda been pals.

'What's up?' Carly yells from through the house, and then her fucking wean's bawling.

God's sakes.

'See t'your fff… Please see to Willow, Carly!' I yell back.

If the social worker could see us now, eh?

Had a wee visit from the bint a week past, checking on Beckie Parry's welfare. Caroline's decided to move back to where she's from, Bearsden, because after everything that's happened, both she and Beckie need to get away from Gardens Terrace. Beckie's attending the local primary. Caroline's two children have moved back in with her, and they're one big happy family.

Checks on Caroline all came back fine, thank God – I dinnae know who the real Caroline Turnbull is and where she's at now, and I dinnae want to know, but looks like Ryan's contact Skeeter's done barry getting us a clean identity there.

'Can I come in, Bekki?' I goes, and I push open the door to her room.

She's lying under the *Frozen* duvet, greeting her wee eyes out, coorying that fucking lemur. I cannae see Shrek. On the windowsill there's the tank with the wee trees in it Neil had in his study. When I asked her what all she wanted to take with her, that was top of the fucking list.

I sit down on the bed and touch her back.

After a bit I leave her be, and she's up in that fucking room all afternoon, but then five o'clock comes round and I've fired up the fryer and Connor's got burgers on the go, and here's Bekki coming in the kitchen giving it 'I feel sick.'

'Aw, course you do sweetheart, but don't you worry, everything's going to work out fine.'

She's looking at Connor. He's got a face on him like he's chewing a wasp.

'Isn't that right, Connor?' I goes.

'Aye Maw. Fine and dandy. You want a chicken burger or a hamburger, Bekki?'

'I don't want anything, thank you.'

'Just some chips?' I goes. 'Or how about a milkshake? Got to keep your strength up.'

'Okay.'

'Banana or strawberry?'

'Banana, please.'

Aye, it's all *please* this and *thank you* that with wee Bekki, the wee darlin'.

And then suddenly it's coming out her: 'Will I have to go and live with the Johnsons now that Mum's in prison?'

I get out the mixer and a pint of milk. 'You don't have to do anything you don't want to, sweetheart. If you want to stay here with us, then that's what's happening.'

'But the Johnsons might try to get me back again.'

I get the nicest banana out the bowl. 'You don't need to worry about that, Bekki. The Johnsons aren't bad people.'

'They must be, or I wouldn't have been taken away from them, would I?'

I sit down at the table. 'Come here, Bekki.'

Bekki takes a seat next me.

'That was a mistake. Connor son, get the Mair sh... The press coverage of Saskia Mair's death.' While Connor's in the front room, I finish making the shake and pour it in a tall glass.

Bekki takes a big swally.

'Is that nice?'

'Yes, thank you.'

Connor's back with the Mair shite. 'Now, Bekki,' I goes, 'Saskia Mair was the woman who took you from the Johnsons, but the authorities have found out she was lying. The Johnsons never hurt you. See, it says here Saskia Mair admitted to hurting the children so people would think it was their families that did it...'

Bekki's reading the article on the laptop. 'One of those children was me?'

'Yes. The Johnsons never hurt you.'

'But they're still horrible! You were there, when they tried to grab me outside your flat!'

'But they didn't try to grab you, did they? They were just trying to talk to you, I think. I know I've got ninja skills and everything, but if they'd really wanted to grab you, how could Flora and I have stopped those big bbb... those big men?'

Bekki frowns. 'But... that old man was horrible.'

'Was he? What did he say to you?'

'He kept saying "Wee Bekki".'

'Well, that's not too horrible, is it?'

'But he *was* horrible!'

'In what way?'

'He was... dirty. And I think he was drunk.'

'Oh. Well, maybe he has problems. You know, like Edith's mum? Medical problems.'

'Like depression?'

I nod. 'Yes, maybe depression.'

'But even if he's got depression I don't want to live with the Johnsons! I want to stay with you, and Connor and Carly and Willow, until Mum gets out of prison!'

'Aw, and we want you to stay with us, more than anything, sweetheart! We're made up to have you living with us. And you know Flora and Neil made me your guardian in case anything happened to them, so it's all legal and everything. So don't you worry, Bekster, you're staying right here.'

Bekki pokes the straw in the shake. 'Burgers and chips aren't good for you.'

'All right, missie, you can have a nice salad if you want.'

'I mean for *you*.' She gives me a gorgeous wee smile.

'Oh, here we go, Connor, here's Miss Calorie Conscious on the case again.'

'Aw Maw, she's right enough, you're getting a right lard arse on you. You need to get back on that exercise bike.'

Bekki snickers.

'Huh! Less of your cheek, my lad!'

'It's less of your cheek we're needing – less of your bum cheek, eh?' And he's chuckling away and Bekki's choking on her shake, and I'm grinning all over my fucking face.

And when she's off washing her hands before tea, I'm like that: 'No happy? She's no happy?'

'Course she's no fucking happy! You're living in a fucking

dream world if you think she's fucking *happy* about any of this! Okay it's no so bad with just us, but what's gonnae happen when we're in Spain and it's *Here wee Bekki, here's fucking Psycho Granda, and aye Ryan and Travis are fucking mentalists but hey, they're no worse than that wee shit Corrigan, your wee shit cousin's gonnae be in your face twenty-four-seven, aye we're all living under the same roof, whoopy-doo.*'

'Your Da's sakeless so he is. Travis, aye maybe he has his moments, eh, but there's no malice in the boy.'

'He broke my fucking arm!'

'Bairns, eh? Yous were bairns. And Ryan's always looked out for you. What for are you calling him a mentalist?'

'He's a fucking murderer!'

'Keep it down, son! Aye, Ryan's no angel, but Christ on a cheesy biscuit! No fucker's ever messed with you cos they know if they do, Ryan's gonnae do them. He's always looked out for this fucking family and that's the thanks he gets?'

'Aye, okay, maybe he looks out for us and that, but how's Bekki gonnae react if she finds out he –'

'She's no *gonnae* find out.' I go and shut the door. 'Look, son. Right enough, it's gonnae be hard on Bekki to begin with, aye, but I know what I'm doing here. She's getting on fine with you and Carly and she loves wee Willow. I'm thinking tomorrow we can all go a wee trip to the zoo and Bekki can meet Mandy.'

Connor's got a right face on him.

'Right enough, it's best we wait till we're in Spain before she meets the boys and Jed and the other bairns. Wait till the bitch is convicted and the adoption's finalised and that. Get it all done and dusted –'

'Aye, wait till we've a legal fucking hold on her and she's in another fucking country where she cannae speak the language and she cannae run away to Edith's or Mia's or that. Aye Maw, that'll be ace. Bekki's gonnae be made up.'

'I'm no saying it's ideal, and aye, there's maybe gonnae be tears, but long term, it's for the best, aye?'

Connor rolls his eyes and I'm in his face.

'Get off my fucking case, son. We're in this together for Bekki, right?'

'Aye, whatever you say, Maw. Whatever you fucking say.'

34

SIX MONTHS LATER

M*y dear, darling Beckie*

I'm so sorry

SHE SAT BACK in the chair. The view from her window was of the wall of the block opposite, against which a slender birch tree grew. She had watched the tree – she thought of it as 'her' tree – lose its leaves, she had watched it agitated by November gales and worried for it, she had watched the snow delicately ice its branches, and now little fat buds were swelling at the end of every twig.

Beckie didn't want this letter.

She didn't want any contact with Flora.

And who could blame her?

Yesterday the jury had returned their unanimous verdict

that Flora was guilty of the charge of murdering her husband. And now it would be all over the press in every horrendous detail:

Rachel Clark has killed again.

Beckie was going to find out all about what Rachel had done.

She scrunched up the letter and dropped it into the raffia wastepaper basket.

The contents of the room were designed to offer as few opportunities as possible for violence. So the bin was raffia, not metal or even wicker. There were no drawers in the desk she was sitting at, only open spaces for your things. Drawers, even the kind that were anchored in place, could be pulled out and used to clobber someone.

'Flora, this fucking stinks. I'm that sorry.'

She turned in the chair.

Danielle was standing at the door, scratching at the side of her mouth where the skin was always dry.

'Thanks, Danielle.'

'Least you're no getting transferred to some other fucking hole for the rest your sentence, though, eh? Least you get to stay wi' us?'

Flora smiled.

Wendy appeared behind Danielle. 'You're gonnae appeal though, right?'

Wendy favoured cut-off T-shirts that showcased her muscly arms. Today it was a neon-green number with the slogan 'Blink if You Want Me' emblazoned across it in silver text.

Flora nodded. 'Actually, Wendy, I was going to ask you something.'

Most of the women didn't talk much about what had brought them here. Some not at all, and that was respected. Flora had told Wendy and Danielle what had happened, in general terms, not naming any names because you never knew what connections people might have in this place. But now she was desperate.

'Aye doll, go for it.' Wendy swung herself up onto the top bunk, trainers swinging perilously close to Flora's head.

'You're Glaswegian?'

'Aye I'm a Weegie, can you no fucking tell?'

Flora shifted her position in the chair. 'I'm wondering if you know a family called the Johnsons. Jed and Lorraine are the parents, and the kids are Ryan, Travis, Carly and Connor. And Shannon-Rose –'

'Aw fuck, Flora, you dinnae want to have nothing to do with they fuckers. They're fucking animals.'

'Well, yes, I know. They're the ones who killed my husband and set me up for it. They're Beckie's biological family. Shannon-Rose is Beckie's biological mother.'

Wendy's legs stopped swinging, and she whistled.

'The thing is, they have alibis for the morning it happened – provided by the mechanics at a garage who say Ryan, Travis and Jed were there the whole day, apart from lunch in a café where the staff and customers also vouch for them and say Lorraine was there all morning.'

'Aye, dinnae tell me, doll – Finnegan's Garage on North Castle Street, and The Cup that Cheers down past the Haghill Cemetery?'

Flora could only nod.

Wendy snorted. 'The Cup that Cheers – aye right, more like The Cup that'll Gie You the Dry Boak. Fat cow runs the place's about forty fucking stone with a leg ulcer on her you can smell from the fucking pavement? Never anyone in the place, but from the witness statements get read out in the High Fucking Court you'd think it was jumping every fucking day of the week.'

'Do you... You wouldn't be able to help me, would you? If you know anyone who could help break the alibis –'

Wendy held up her hands. 'Hold your horses, Flora. I'm thick as shite maybe but I'm no daft. I'm no going up against they fuckers, no way.' She narrowed her eyes. 'Christ. The fucking *Johnsons*?'

'They found out that we were the couple who adopted Beckie, and they've been targeting us ever since.'

'Fuck!' Danielle was wide-eyed. 'They topped your old man? Your pal that's got Beckie, she'd better make sure they cannae find her, eh?'

'Well, she's moved house.' Flora swallowed. 'But I don't think... The Johnsons can't actually have wanted Beckie back. They could have snatched her easily any time. I think they're just doing it out of... spite, I suppose.'

Wendy was shaking her head. 'Now you listen to me, doll, and you listen good. One hundred per cent, they're wanting their lassie back. Aye maybe they could've snatched her, but Lorraine's a smart fucking bitch, you know? What all she's planning I havenae a scooby, but she'll be planning some shite to get that lassie back, and getting your man out the way and you in the jail for it, that's likely step one. You'd better be sure that lassie is somewhere Lorraine cannae get to her. I'm no joking, Flora, that bitch is smart.'

Flora put a hand to her mouth as her stomach clenched and bile shot up the back of her throat. She pushed back the chair.

'I need to make a phone call.'

'Aye, you call your pal, wherever she's at, tell her to skedaddle cos they fuckers'll be after her, no question.' Wendy sucked her teeth. 'And Flora...?'

Flora stopped, impatiently, at the door.

'I can maybe no help you with the Johnsons, but there's this ex-polisman Brian MacLeod, right, a PI, if you're wanting polis evidence challenged, if you really didnae top your old man? Briefs use him for appeals and that. That wee girl Sienna Carmichael that was done for torching her ex's gaff and him in it? She didnae do it, right, but she got convicted and her brief got Brian on the case and he found a witness heard this fucker mouthing off that he'd lit the gaff. And Brian gets hold of CCTV shows the fucker filling up a can with petrol ten minutes before it happened? And his woman makes a statement that he came home that night with burns on his face and that. Sienna got off on appeal. I've got his number if you're wanting it.'

'Thanks, Wendy. That would be great.'

The phones in D Wing were in the next corridor along. Flora had to wait in the queue for an interminable ten minutes before she could snatch up the receiver, enter her pin number and dial Caroline's mobile.

'Hi, Flora.'

'Oh God, Caroline, I've just been speaking to another prisoner who knows the Johnsons, and she's saying they probably *are* going to try to take Beckie – you have to move, I'm sorry, but you really have to move away, somewhere they won't find you... You can't stay in Glasgow.'

'Whoa, Flora, okay. If they were going to snatch Beckie, wouldn't they have done it by now?'

Flora breathed. 'Yes, maybe, but... Caroline, I've been thinking... Unless there's some sort of miracle with the appeal – and let's face it, that's not going to happen. The evidence against me is just too strong.' She breathed again. 'I'm going to be in here for at least ten years. Beckie – She's cut herself off from me anyway. Even if I did get out... She's happy with you.'

She was pressing the receiver so hard against her ear it was aching. She concentrated on that as some detached part of her brain sent the words into her mouth: 'I'd like you to adopt her.'

'Oh, but Flora –'

'I want you to adopt her and move away. As far away as possible.'

· · ·

CARLY COMES up the road pushing the buggy. Bekki's dawdling behind, fucking adorable in her wee red puffer jacket. That snobby fucking school maybe can make the weans wear the school fucking skirt and jumper and tie, but I goes to Bekki in TK Maxx, I goes, 'You get whatever jacket you want, Bekki, they can't touch you for it.'

I get back from the windae and point the remote at the TV, and I channel surf until I get *Tracy Beaker*, and then I fold up the *Mirror* and push it down behind one of the cushions on the settee, but with Flora's face just keeking out, like I've tried to hide it, so I have, but in too much a fucking hurry.

'Well then, Bekki,' I goes when they're in the door, 'how was school today?'

She shrugs her wee shoulders.

She's been that depressed, poor wee soul, since the conviction. Sentencing was three days ago and the bitch got twelve year, but we're making out to Bekki that it's all fine, Flora's gonnae appeal and she'll be let go and then maybe she'll come and get Bekki.

'You wanting a juice and a bit of Battenberg? Or a wee piece of fruit? The fire's on in the lounge, it's all cosy in there and your programme's on. In you go and relax, eh? What're you wanting?'

'Can I have Fanta?'

'Course you can. Fanta and what all else?'

'Crisps?'

'Prawn cocktail or pickled onion?'

'Pickled onion, please.'

When Bekki's in the lounge, I goes to Carly: 'Right you, get that Fanta and crisps.' And I keek through the crack in the door. Bekki's got her wee slippers off and her feet up on the settee. And now she's pulling the cushion away and she's got the *Mirror* out and I can hear the poor wee bairn going, 'Oh!'

And she's reading all about it.

And my heart's breaking for her so it is.

Now she's got it open to where the story continues on page five, and here's Carly with the Fanta and crisps. I grab them off of her. I leave it a bit and then I'm breezing in the lounge, all cheery.

'Here you go, Bekster.' And then I'm: 'Oh, Bekki –' And I'm putting the glass of Fanta and the crisps down on the coffee table and grabbing the paper off of her.

Bekki's jumping up from the settee. Her wee face is white as a ghost. 'It says – it says Mum... There was this girl called Tricia Fisher that Mum was friends with when she was twelve, and Mum... Mum *killed* her. That's not true, is it? She didn't really kill Dad and she didn't really kill that girl either.'

I puff. 'I'm sorry, Bekki. I never meant you to see that.' I fold up the paper. The headline's barry:

FLORA PARRY WAS CHILD KILLER

It's all coming out now, eh, they couldnae report on her previous conviction until the sentencing and that, but now it's all over the fucking press.

'It's not true.'

I get my arse on that settee and pull her down next me. I smooth her hair where it's coming out the French braid. 'Sweetheart... You're going to have to be a really brave girl, okay? Because there's some things I have to tell you.'

Bekki's no leaning in. She's sitting there twisting the wee bracelet she got from Connor for her Christmas, made of lemurs all pulling each other's stripy wee tails.

'Flora... Last time I saw her, she told me... I'm sorry, sweetheart... Just remember that I'm always going to look after you, I love you to bits and nothing bad's going to happen to you, okay?'

She's biting her lip.

'I wish I didn't have to tell you this, but... You have to know.'

She's nodding. The wee soldier.

'Flora told me she killed Neil.'

Bekki's shaking her head. 'No. That's not true. Why would she say that?'

'She didn't mean to do it. She says they were arguing, and she just snapped.'

Bekki's going, 'No.'

I grab her hand. 'Bekki, you're going to have to be *really* brave... I wasn't sure whether to tell you this or not, but I think it's important to know the truth, isn't it?'

She swallows and whispers: 'Yes?'

'They were arguing about you. Flora wanted to give you back to the Johnsons, and Neil didn't.'

Bekki doesnae say nothing. She doesnae look at me.

I go to coory her but she pulls away.

'I'm so sorry, Bekki. I didn't believe it either when Flora told me, but the more I think about it... Well, the police are sure she killed him, and the jury were as well, and there had to be a motive, eh?'

'But she didn't kill him.'

'Aw sweetheart. She's been convicted, after all those smart people sifted through the evidence for months and months, you know? The justice system in this country, Bekki, the way it works, anyone who's really innocent isn't going to get convicted, or hardly ever.'

'But sometimes.'

'Aye,' I puff, 'but Flora *told* me she did it.' I'm no gonnae lose it with the wean. It's only natural, eh, that she's in denial. 'That appeal, sweetheart – that's not going to work out. Flora's going to be in that jail for ten years at least. You're going to be nine-teen years old by the time she gets out of there, and Bekki, I'm not going to lie to you, I'm not confident she's going to want to see you when she does get out. She kept going on about how you weren't hers. How you weren't her real daughter.'

Bekki's wee finger is stroking they lemurs.

I coory her. 'But don't you worry, sweetheart, don't you worry, because I'm here for you. I love you to bits. We all of us love you to bits. And there's one good thing Flora said.'

Bekki flicks her eyes at me.

'She said I can adopt you if I want. And I'd be that made up if I could, sweetheart, if you could be part of this family that would be wonderful, wouldn't it?'

Bekki doesnae say nothing.

I pat her wee leg. 'You have your Fanta and crisps, eh, and watch your programme.'

And then I leave her be. Comes round six o'clock, Connor's back from his shift and he's feeding wee Willow in her high chair in the kitchen, and Willow's girning away and I cannae blame her, wee soul, Connor boils up carrot and sweet potato and that and purees it for the wean and it's pure boggin' so it is. And now here's wee Bekki giving it, 'On the internet it says there was this little boy called Nathan and his mum died and the mum's best friend wanted to adopt him but they didn't let her. They might not let you adopt me.'

She's standing there so straight, God love her, like she's gonnae be a brave lassie, and she's breaking my fucking heart.

'Bekki, it's okay, no one's going to take you away from me. Now, I'm going tell you a secret, right, but it's really important you don't tell anyone, not Mia or Edith when you're Skyping them, right, and not anyone else?'

'Aw Christ Maw,' goes Connor.

'It's okay son, it's time. Right, Bekki?'

She's nodding.

'My real name's not Caroline Turnbull. It's Lorraine Johnson, and I'm your nana.' I can hardly get the fucking words out I'm that choked up. 'I'm your grandma, sweetheart, and you're our wee lassie that was lost and that we love to bits, and now you're back safe and sound, eh, and no one's ever gonnae take you away again.'

Bekki's giving it rabbit in headlights. 'You're – you're *the Johnsons*?'

'Aye, Bekki.'

'But you can't be. You're *Caroline*.'

'That's not my real name.'

And she's running, she's out the room and in the lounge and she's snatching up Connor's phone, she's going, 'I'm calling the police!' and I'm grabbing the phone and going, 'You call the polis and they'll put you in a children's home, and bad things happen to kids in children's homes, Bekki, *real* bad things. I don't want you going in one of they places. If you don't want to stay with us, you can go and live with someone else, maybe a friend of Flora's or a relative – as long as they're nice, as long as you're happy, I'm not caring. But I'm not having the polis taking you to a children's home. I'm not having you put in care like that wee boy Nathan, because kids in care get hurt. That's a fact.'

Bekki's gulping.

'Okay, you don't want to stay here, that's fine. You're breaking our hearts, but we just want what's gonnae make you happy, Bekki, and that's the honest truth.' I hold out the phone to her. 'Go ahead and call whoever you like, sweetheart, but not the polis because they'll take you to a children's home.'

She just stares at the phone. She doesnae take it.

'You can't be the Johnsons,' she goes. 'How can you be my grandma? You're not old.'

I've got out a tissue and I'm wiping at my face. I give a wee chuckle. 'Thanks Bekster, but I'm forty-two years old. Willow's my wee granddaughter, eh? And so are you. I was young when I had my kids, right enough, but I'm your nana. Eh Connor?'

Connor's standing by the door with a face on him. 'Aye, Bekki, Maw was just a lassie, fifteen year old, when she had your maw and R–'

'That's right,' I goes before he can say it. It's been hard

enough for Bekki getting her wee head round Carly and Connor being my weans, and now she's hearing I'm her nana? She doesnae need Ryan and Travis in the mix. No yet.

'The Johnsons are bad people,' she goes again.

'Is that right?' I give her a wee smile. 'When you thought my name was Caroline, did you think I was a bad person? I thought you and me were pals.'

Bekki bites her wee lip.

'Do you think Connor's a bad person?'

She looks at Connor. Then she whispers: 'No.'

'What about Carly and Willow?'

'No!' Bekki's greeting. 'You're not bad, but those men – those men who tried to snatch me, who followed us in the street…'

'They didn't try to snatch you. Jed – he's my husband. He's your granda. He's got mental problems, like I said. He's got depression. He didn't mean to scare you, just like Edith's mum didn't mean to not give her enough to eat.'

She takes in a massive breath and goes, 'I want to go home. I want Mum.'

Fucking hell.

'Home, is it?' I puff. 'This is your home, sweetheart, and we're your real family that loves you, right? Not Flora. Aye, it's gonnae be weird at first, but you and me and Connor and Carly and wee Willow, we're going to have a magic time. But you can't tell *anyone* about this, aye, especially not the police and not social workers, or you'll maybe get taken off of us and put in care.'

'Aw Christ Maw –'

'She needs to hear it like it is, son. Kids in care get treated like shite.'

Bekki goes, 'Is human resources even your job?'

What the fuck has that got to do with it?

But I dinnae lose it with the poor wee bairn. 'Not exactly, unless you count this lot as either human or any sort of resource, eh? But – okay so my name's not Caroline, but everything else about me – except the human resources shite – that's me, Bekki. I've not been putting on an act or nothing.'

'But you even speak differently now.'

I puff. Right enough, it's no easy being Caroline now I'm back with my weans and they're pushing my fucking buttons. 'It's what's on the inside counts, eh? And what's inside is that I love you to bits. When you were wee – you won't remember, but me and you, we were that close. Eh Connor? Bekki was my wee princess, eh?'

'Aye,' goes Connor. He goes and puts his arm round Bekki. 'You were our wee princess right enough.'

'Still are, sweetheart. You still are.'

'I want to talk to my mum. I don't believe you. I'm going to the prison to see her and you can't stop me.' And she's out the door.

'Right son, here we go.'

Connor's giving me evils.

'Right son?'

'Aye.'

I'm after her. 'Bekki. Bekki!'

She's putting on the puffer jacket, her wee face that determined.

The bairn's something else so she is.

'They don't let kids in the prison unless they're accompanied by an adult.'

'Connor can come with me. We can get the bus. I can use my savings to get the bus tickets.'

Connor's got a right face on him.

'That's not happening,' I goes.

'You can't stop us,' goes Bekki.

'If she wants to go, we should take her,' goes Connor, finally.

'Aye, and have her end up traumatised?'

'I won't be traumatised. If you don't take me, I'm going to go to Edith's and get Edith's mum to come with me.'

Bairns!

I says, 'Even if you're with an adult, they won't let you in the prison when you get there, because the prisoner has to be the one sets up the visit, not the visitor.'

I'm giving Connor evils.

The wee diddy's gone and forgot the fucking script.

'They won't let you in the prison,' I goes again, and I'm half turning towards the drawer in the hall table where the letter's been put.

'Aye,' he goes, finally, 'that's right enough, eh? But you could give Bekki that letter Flora wrote her, eh Maw? And Bekki could write her back?'

I puff, like this is the last thing I'm wanting to hear.

'Eh Maw?'

'A letter?' Bekki's eyeballing me.

'Yes, Flora wrote you a letter, and I haven't opened it, I don't know what it says, but I don't think... She's not in a good place, Bekki, and I don't think there's going to be anything good in it.'

'I want to see it! I want to see that letter *now*. *Please*.'

'It's best you don't. It's only going to break your wee heart, sweetheart.'

'No it's not. I want to read it. Where is it?'

I'm no saying.

'*Please*, Caroline.'

'You have to call me Nana now, Bekki.'

She takes a breath. 'Please, Nana.'

I'm choking up. 'Bekki, darlin', I can't let you put yourself through it. I can't let you do it. I'm not letting you do it to yourself.' And I get my arse up that stair and in my room with the door shut. Connor better fucking step up to the plate or so help me I'll swing for the boy. When I was typing the letter he kept giving it 'That's well harsh' and 'Naw Maw, you cannae' and I was 'That bitch's been turning Bekki against her own fucking family, her own fucking family that loves her to bits, for seven fucking year, bad-mouthing us and making her feart of us like we're fucking mentalists, seven fucking year, son, so dinnae you start, dinnae you fucking start on what I can and cannae do, right?'

Letter's a belter.

Dear Beckie

I'm sorry, darling, but I think it's for the best that we don't have any contact. You're safe and happy with Caroline, and it's better for both of us if you just accept that this is your new life now. I'm sure you're having lots of fun.

I tried to be a good mum to you, but the truth is that it didn't come naturally to me. I think nature has a way of deciding who should and shouldn't be a mum – Dad would agree about that, wouldn't he? And it wasn't right that we took you away from your real family, and I think we always knew that, and that's why Dad and I argued so much about you.

I've come to realise that you're better off with your real family – Caroline has told me who she really is, and although I was shocked at first, it's all making sense now. It's making sense why she had an immediate connection with you that I never had. She's your real family and you'll be happier with her than you ever were with me. It's just going to take time to get used to it. Remember when we had to move to Edinburgh? At first you were really sad, but soon you got used to it and everything was fine, wasn't it?

It's not as if we were ever a proper family. I know that and I think you do too.

You have to be a brave girl and try your hardest to be happy. I think it'll be easier for us all if you don't try to make contact with me again. I'm not a good person, Beckie, and I never have been. I get so angry – I don't know why. I did some terrible things when I was younger. And worst of all, I killed poor Dad. The prison doctor who's been trying to work out why I did it says that the strain of looking after someone else's child, when I'm not a natural mum, was probably what pushed me over the edge.

So please don't send me any more letters or cards. But I know Caroline loves your drawings – maybe you can make a card for her saying thank you for all she's doing for you. She's your real nana and she loves you so much, and I know you love her too.

Goodbye, darling.

Mum

AND HERE SHE'S running up the stair, and I've my door open giving it, 'Bekki darlin'!' and she's in my arms, wee wet face pushed in my chebs.

'It's okay Bekki my wee love, my wee darlin'. It's okay.'

35

Flora knew it was good news as soon as Charles came into the little room set aside for visits from lawyers. He probably thought his professional demeanour was intact, but his eyes were sparkling. Brian, the lugubrious PI, slunk in behind him as if he were attending someone's funeral, but Flora suspected he'd look the same if he'd just won the lottery. He was carrying a laptop under his arm.

'We've been granted leave to appeal!' Charles blurted out as soon as he'd sat down. 'They really couldn't *not* grant it, given the strength of the new evidence – but until you get the word, you can never be quite sure.'

Flora released a huge breath. 'Thank God. Or rather, thanks to you and Brian.'

'Ah, but that's not all.' He was practically rubbing his hands together. 'Flora, the even better news is –'

'Wait,' she said. 'Before you tell me...' Her leg was jigging under the table like Danielle's. She wanted to reach across and hug them both. Beckie. Soon she would be back with Beckie. 'Before you tell me whatever it is, I want to show you this.'

She pushed the letter across the table.

'I know it's got nothing to do with my conviction, I know it's not going to influence the appeal...'

Brian, sighing in a 'What now?' kind of way, started to read the letter over Charles's shoulder.

Dear Rachel

I was going to put 'Flora' because that's who you are now, but then I thought no, you haven't chosen to be Flora Parry, you had to stop being Rachel Clark because people hated her. And that's my fault.

I'm so sorry.

Really inadequate, I know.

I'm going to tell the police what really happened. But first I have to do something even harder, and that's tell you. Because I don't think you know. I think you went into shock and your brain shut down or something. Otherwise, you'd have told them the truth. Like I should have.

I know it's nearly 40 years too late. I know I could have put things right at any point in those 40 years and I chose not to. Why now? you're probably thinking.

It was seeing you on TV getting into that van outside court. The look on your face.

I don't believe you killed your husband. But how were you going to convince the police you were innocent when they knew you were Rachel Clark?

So I'm going to tell the police that Rachel was innocent then, and maybe there's a chance they'll see you're innocent now.

When Tricia gave you that bow and arrow and told you to shoot me, I knew you wouldn't do it. You were nasty to me, yes, and I hated you for it, but you weren't evil like Tricia. You were just acting out because your mum made your life a misery. You probably don't see it that way, even now, do you? You always made excuses for her, like she wouldn't let you come out to play and made you slave away doing housework because it was good practice for when you had your own home.

Anyway. When Tricia gave you that bow and arrow, I knew you weren't going to shoot anyone. You just sort of stood there frozen, while Tricia yelled at you to 'Do it!' and threatened all kinds of things if you didn't. Tricia was 'in your face' as my kids would say, and you backed up, holding the bow and arrow in front of you to stop her coming any closer, as a kind of barrier, but then you stumbled on a tussock of grass and let go the arrow and it went into Tricia's eye.

It was an accident.

I told the police you'd fired the arrow at her while the two of you were arguing, but that was a lie. I told them that because I hated you. I hated you for being horrible to me when we were supposed to be friends. But you didn't fire the arrow. You tripped and let it go.

And once I'd told the lie, it took on a life of its own and I didn't have the courage to take it back. Until now.

I hope it's not too late to put right some of the damage I've done. I'll go to the police a week after I've posted this.

So sorry

Gail

CHARLES LOOKED UP AT FLORA, his grin widening. 'But this is dynamite! You say it won't influence the appeal, and in theory it shouldn't – but I learned a long time ago that there's no such thing as impartiality. We need this all over the press so whoever hears the appeal can't help but be aware of it. This is great.' And he half reached across the table towards her hand. 'Write back to Gail, tell her how much this means to you – urge her to go to the press. And if she doesn't, we will.'

Flora nodded. 'I still can't believe it.'

'You never thought of contacting Gail yourself?'

'No. I suppose I just accepted her version of what happened because, as she says, I must have blanked it out... Well, I remember tying Gail to the tree, and Tricia yelling at me to shoot her, and I remember the arrow... I remember it going into her eye...' She swallowed. 'But nothing in between. Although –' She shrugged. 'I suppose I always felt it was wrong, that I wasn't the person everyone said I was, this – this psychotic girl called Rachel Clark. This monster. I couldn't think of myself like that.'

'Of course you couldn't.'

'By rights,' said Brian, 'Gail Boyle should be charged with perverting the course of justice.'

'Oh – I wouldn't want her to get into trouble.' Actually Flora didn't care if they locked Gail up and threw away the key – as Gail herself had said, she'd had forty years to put this right and hadn't – but it was almost as if Flora had been handed back her virtue. As if she had to live up to everyone's new idea of her.

'She was a traumatised child,' said Charles. 'They won't charge her with anything.' He grinned at her. 'So, don't you want to hear the best part?' He was like a favourite uncle about to present the birthday girl with the best gift of all.

She nodded.

'In the light of the evidence Brian's unearthed, the police are reopening the investigation.'

Flora could only stare at Brian.

Such an unlikely saviour.

'What evidence?'

Brian sighed, and opened the laptop on the table. 'Finally got the CCTV footage off Eden Security. The outfit who installed your system. And I've been through the lot, minute by minute, for the day of the murder.'

Brian turned the laptop round so Flora could see the screen. 'This is footage from one of the cameras covering the east side of the house. 9:42 a.m. on the morning of that day.'

The shock of seeing the house, their house, their home, on the screen was physical. The footage was of a section of the driveway and the side of the house facing the garage, with the window of what had been the old pantry and was now a store-room to the left, and the downstairs loo, and then the dining room which they never used. On the dining room windowsill she could see the dusty dried flower arrangement she and Beckie had made years ago, and through the frosted glass of the loo window, the vague shape of the 'Victorian' pendant light fitting.

At 9:42 Alec was probably inside, in his study, little knowing...

'Watch the dining room window... Now!'

The dried-flower arrangement suddenly jumped to the left.

Brian reached over to the keyboard and rewound the footage. 'Now watch the time at the top left... See? Jumps from 9:52 to 10:22. Same with the camera next to it. This system, which lets you switch the cameras on and off remotely, doesn't show a blank screen when the camera is off – the footage is continuous.'

'Oh my God. They switched off the cameras and got in at the dining room window?'

Charles nodded. 'And in doing so, accidentally moved the flower arrangement.'

Brian sighed. 'According to Eden Security, someone logged into the system at 9:52 a.m. and switched these two cameras off. Talk about negligence. Some PC Plod's had the footage from eight cameras to go through, right, and he's looking for an intruder, he's not looking at the time, he's fast-forwarding and he goes for a bite of Mars Bar and he's missed it. He's missed the outages from 9:52 to 10:22 on these two cameras.'

'But how could the Johnsons have switched the cameras off?'

'That is the problem. Your system's state of the art, right? Sure it's communicating over the net, but the data's encrypted like something out the bloody Pentagon.'

Charles shrugged. 'They must have hacked into it somehow. The lad Connor works at PC World. He'll be IT savvy.'

Brian looked mournful. 'A wee laddie from PC World up against programmers this good?'

'How else could they have done it?'

'Haven't got a bloody clue.'

'But however they switched off the cameras,' Flora said, 'we kept all the windows locked. And the police checked them all, and they were all still locked. Apart from the one I broke, obviously.'

Brian nodded. 'I'm thinking one of them must have got into the house at some point previously to unlock the dining room window. They could have remotely switched off the camera covering one of the doors, snuck in, unlocked the window, snuck back out again, and switched the camera back on. I've been checking through the footage for another outage and haven't found anything as yet, but I'll keep looking.'

'But how would they have got in? I was always careful to keep the front door locked, and the patio doors at the back.'

'What if you were in the garden? Very few people lock the door behind them if they're in the garden.'

'Oh. No, of course. If I was in the garden, I'd leave the patio doors unlocked.' She frowned. 'Okay, if they managed to sneak into the house at some point while I was in the garden, that would explain how they unlocked the window, but on the day that... after they'd... after they'd killed Neil, and got back out through the window... How did they lock it after them?'

'No idea.' Brian snapped shut the laptop. 'It's sometimes possible with the locks on these old windows to manipulate the mechanism through the gap between the sashes... Magician's trick kind of thing.'

'But however they did it, the important thing is that there's evidence of tampering with the cameras to create an opportunity of entry,' said Charles. 'And there's more. Jasmine Young has made a statement to the police to the effect that she saw a man in a boiler suit going in at your gate at approximately ten to ten that morning. Which dovetails nicely with the camera evidence.'

Flora blinked. '*Jasmine?*'

'Yes.' Brian sighed. 'I had a word with the neighbours, badgered them a bit maybe, went back to the Youngs a few times because I thought there was something there, you know?' He rolled his eyes as if to say *The people I have to deal with*. 'Last time, the daughter's saying "Mum, we should –" but the mum, Ailish, shuts her down. So I stake the place out and a couple of days later, Jasmine's coming out the door with her earbuds in, oblivious, and I follow her into town. Make like it's a coincidence when I bump into her in French Connection, buying a present for the wife. And I tell her straight: "Jasmine, if you know something that could get an innocent woman out of prison and back with her child, you have to go to the police."'

'Oh my God. So...'

'Seems that when the shit hit the fan and it came out Neil had been murdered et cetera, Jasmine told her mum she'd seen this guy at your gate on the morning of the murder, and the mother tells her to keep quiet and not get involved. Said it was probably your lover, your accomplice. But I put the girl straight. And she's done the right thing at last, been and made a statement and even picked Ryan Johnson out of a photo line-up, although he was wearing a disguise when she saw him – long curly blond wig in a ponytail and sideburns. Teenage girls might be the most bloody annoying sector of the population, but at least they can be counted on to notice every detail about a good-looking guy. In particular, in this case, thick black eyelashes and a tiny scar at the side of his right eye. She got a good close look – was walking past him on the pavement when he was opening your gate. Oh yes, she's going to be our star witness, no doubt about it.'

'What with the CCTV evidence and Jasmine's statement, the procurator fiscal considers there are grounds for a warrant to search the Johnsons' house again,' said Charles. 'Hopefully they might find physical evidence connecting them to the crime scene. Something stolen from your house, for example.' He was practically bouncing on his chair. 'But even without anything like that... Flora, you're getting out of here. The evidence we've already got is strong, and now the police are seriously focused on the Johnsons, they're likely to uncover more... You're getting out of here.'

I'M RAGING SO I am. 'Disguise, is it? Fucking disguise?'

Ryan takes a swally Coke. We're in the KFC round from the scheme. 'Dinnae have a cow, Maw. Fucking photy line-up? Brief'll pick that to pieces in three fucking seconds. And alibi's fucking solid.'

'Aye son, but the bitch was that confident. Her brief and that fucking PI have telt her her conviction's unsafe and she's getting out.'

'Aye, that's briefs. Fucking warrant, is it? Aye, be my guest, gents. They're no gonnae find nothing in the house.'

'You sure of that, son? It's your Da and Travis and Connor we're talking about here. Who's to say one of they fuckwits hasnae stashed away something incriminating?'

'Like what?'

I take a bite of my Zinger Stacker. 'Who the fuck knows? We're lighting it, son. Petrol through the letterbox. There's no shortage of candidates will be in the frame for an arson attack, eh? And then yous are outta here. Me and Bekki'll have to wait till the adoption's through, but the rest of yous is on that fucking boat and off to Sunny Fucking Spain, right?'

Ryan's set us all up with new identities and that. And a bastard with a boat so we willnae have to present our new passports at customs.

But he's no a happy bunny. He doesnae like it when we've to switch to Plan B. He's a Plan A kind of guy.

'Right, son?'

'Aye, Maw, right.'

36

Flora couldn't help it. Before Caroline had even sat down, she was asking her: 'You told her? You told Beckie?'

Caroline shrugged out of her coat. 'Yeah, sorry Flora, she's... She'll come round, I'm sure she will, she probably just needs time to digest it all, you know?'

'She won't know what to make of it all. If I could only talk to her...'

'I know. I'm working on it, trust me.'

'Sorry, it's just – everything suddenly happening, and I just need to see her, I need to reassure her that everything's going to be fine. Because it really is. Caroline – you're not going to believe this, I can hardly believe it myself, but the appeal's been accelerated, in view of the new forensic evidence, and Charles says it's just a formality, I'll be out of here in a week, two weeks at the most. It –'

'Oh wow Flora, that's brilliant!'

'I know! I can't believe it!'

'What new evidence? Do you want a coffee...?'

'No thanks. You go ahead though.'

Caroline shook her head. 'Don't keep me in suspense! What new evidence?'

'Well!' Flora wanted to jump up and move, walk, jump, run. Caroline was looking at her almost in trepidation, as if afraid Flora was getting her hopes up prematurely. 'The police have searched the Johnsons' property – not much to find in the house, obviously, it's basically been wrecked by the fire and any forensic evidence that might have been in there's been obliterated – but in the so-called garden they found a chain buried, wrapped in a boiler suit. And the chain matches the chain that was used to strangle Neil. Apparently there's tests they can do to match the metal and the way it's made... Anyway, the neighbours say they used a long chain to tie up their Rottweiler in the garden, after it jumped the fence and went for someone... But then the chain was replaced by nylon rope, right after Neil's murder apparently. So it looks as if they used a bit of this chain, and the idiots buried the rest of it.'

Caroline blinked at her. 'In their own garden?'

'I know, stupid or what? But that's not the best part. Ryan Johnson's DNA is all over the boiler suit, along with Neil's. It's conclusive. My conviction is going to be overturned, and Ryan Johnson is going to be arrested for Neil's murder!'

'That's – that's amazing, Flora. I'm sorry, I'm in shock here...'

'I know! Me too! Apparently there's probably going to be compensation as there's a question of police incompetence in that the initial investigation was incomplete, and Caroline, no arguments, I want you to have it. I want you to have the compensation money – you've more than earned it, you've been absolutely wonderful. I was going to ask you, though, for one last favour?'

'Aye?'

'There'll be a period of adjustment for Beckie. I wonder if it would be okay if we all lived together for a few weeks, just until she gets used to having me around again? Would it be okay if I joined you in Bearsden?'

'Course it would, that'll be great.' But Caroline looked shell-shocked. Not surprisingly. Flora had known for days that she was getting out, and she still couldn't get her head round it. This was really happening! She was going to be back with Beckie! It was all going to be okay!

'Oh, and we have to let the adoption people know that it's not going ahead.'

'I'll do that. I'll sort all that, Flora, don't you worry. Just you concentrate on your appeal. That's the important thing to focus on at the moment, yeah?'

'I'm thinking we'll probably move abroad. I can get a pass-port now – I'm going to legally change my name from Rachel Clark to Flora Parry by deed poll. I was wondering about New Zealand, where Pippa seems to have settled down with this new man of hers... But you'd still be part of Beckie's life, I hope? You'd come for holidays?'

'Ooh, New Zealand, eh? Try and stop me!'

I'M SHAKING so I am. I've got the case open on the bed and I'm shoving Bekki's clothes in it, and she's whinging on about they fucking wee trees, how she cannae leave them behind, and I'm going, 'Aye, we'll get they packed up and sent on, sweetheart, dinnae you worry.' Aye right. Oh dear, looks like they got lost in the fucking useless Spanish post.

Now she's going, 'But why do we have to leave tonight?'

'You know how Flora made you move house and get a new name and that, because she said we were bad people and you were in danger from us?'

Bekki gives me evils. 'She never said that.'

'Aye, but reading between the lines, eh? Well, she was lying through her teeth about that, so she was, cos how would we hurt a wee sweetheart we love to bits? You know what irony is, Bekki? Well, the *irony* is, we've having to do the same thing because Flora's getting out of prison because she planted evidence on us and the police are thinking one of the lads killed your dad, and you're gonnae see all sorts of shite on the net about that, but that's all it is, right? Shite. Because me and you, we know she did it. She telt me and she telt you she killed your dad.'

Wee Bekki's shaking her head. 'No. No way.'

'Now that mad bitch is getting out and who knows what she's gonnae do – who knows if she's gonnae come after you because she's telt you she killed him and she's feart you're gonnae shoot your mouth off. But you dinnae have to worry, right, cos we're disappearing, and we're doing it right. We're off to Spain! Off to Sunny Spain. It's gonnae be a magic adventure, and you've got a magic new name.'

'I'm not going.'

'Oh aye hen, you're going all right. Don't you wannae know what your new name is?'

She folds her arms. 'What?'

'Madison. Bonnie, eh?'

'That's a chav name.' And she huffs out the room and slams the toilet door.

Bairns! Christ sakes, as if I've no got enough on my plate without Bekki playing up. We're outta here, and when we get to Spain that lazy fuckwit Travis is fucking dead so he is for landing us in this fucking mess.

WENDY TOSSED Flora another towel from the clean laundry basket, and Flora folded it and placed it on the pile. That was another thing she would be glad to see the back of – the awful orangey-beige towels, the colour presumably chosen to hide a multitude.

And laundry duty – the airless, humid little room, the smell of sickly sweet washing powder and sweat.

'Reckon Shannon-Rose must be in this gaff,' Wendy said. 'You'd think she'd be in Carstairs, seeing how she's a fucking loony-tune. You'd better watch yourself, doll. Dinnae go telling folk *nothing* about your pal that's looking after Beckie. *Nothing*, aye? If her name or that gets back to Shannon-Rose, the Johnsons'll be on it like flies on shite.'

'But as far as I know, Shannon-Rose *is* in Carstairs.' Flora caught the next towel. 'What makes you think she's here?'

'Yesterday, right, I'm at the Rec Room windae and the visitors are coming out the Family Hub making for Reception, and one of them, I've seen her before visiting, right, but I didnae recognise the bitch – but that was before you telt me all the shite that's gone on with the Johnsons, you know? She's gone brunette and she's been to Weight Watchers or that, and she's had herself a fucking makeover. Thinks she's all that but she's still just a fucking Haghill slag. It's Lorraine fucking Johnson. She's got her arse in this navy trouser suit out Hobbs or shite and a wee flowery scarf, but she's putting the beef back on and I reckon that's how come I –'

And Flora was somehow sitting down on one of the hard chairs, and Wendy was saying, 'Flora? What's up, hen? Flora?'

And Flora was on her feet, she was dropping the towel on the floor, she was saying, 'I have to – I have to make a phone call – I have to call Charles *right now*.'

'Aye, okay, but –'

'*She's got Beckie!* Lorraine Johnson's *got Beckie!*'

Two hours later Flora was on the edge of her chair, both legs jiggling, as Charles swept into the room and dropped onto the chair opposite. His hair was standing up on one side where the wind had dishevelled it and he hadn't bothered to smooth it. His face was white.

'They've gone,' he said. 'I'm so sorry, Flora. The police went to the house in Bearsden, but they've gone.'

37

TWO MONTHS LATER

I t was a pleasant view at any time of day, but now, after sunset, when dusk shrouded the plastic rubbish bins and the litter along the high-tide mark and the blockwork walls, it was beautiful. The sky seemed to go on forever, streaked with orange and purple and a deep indigo it seemed to take from the sea, although of course it was the other way round. The waves lapping at the beach shimmered silver, and the two stacks of rock out to sea loomed up like sentinels, as if guarding the little cove with its jetty and solitary rowing boat bobbing on the swell.

But if she turned her head to look left from her window instead of right, the scene was just like any other along this coast: streetlights illuminating two more ugly high-rise hotels, some dusty cafés and tavernas and shops, and then a line of run-down orange and yellow apartments with railed balconies, metal-shuttered windows and satellite dishes. The beach, such as it was, on the other side of the road was a tumbled mass of rocks and a little strip of flat grey sand disappearing into a darkened sea. Between the apartments and the junction with the main coast road were half a dozen white, red-roofed 'executive' villas that looked like MacDonald's restaurants, and a few dispirited palm trees.

Fuerte Blanco, the place was called, although there was no sign now of the fort that had presumably given it its name. The original fisherfolk's houses had gone too, with the one exception of a little boarded-up stone building behind one of the cafés. Flora had never seen anyone use the boat that was tied to the jetty.

She got up from her chair and stretched.

Time to call it a day.

They wouldn't come now.

She lay down on the bed and shut her eyes.

Maybe tomorrow.

Maybe tomorrow would be the day Caroline – she couldn't stop thinking of her as Caroline – brought Beckie here.

It had taken Brian just three days to find the place, after Flora had described to him the scene Caroline had as her desktop wallpaper – the photograph of the beach and the little harbour and the two tall stacks of rock.

Fuerte Blanco, five miles along the coast from Malaga.

It had been a long shot, but the only one they had. Brian had come straight out here armed with photographs of them all – Jed and Lorraine Johnson and their offspring – and a bar owner had recognised Travis Johnson as the *bastardo* who'd punched him in the nose a couple of years ago. He wasn't likely to forget the face of that *matón*.

Brian had distributed the photographs around the bars and hotels and cafés, impressing on the staff the importance of keeping them hidden from the view of customers, with the promise of a substantial reward for information. Then he'd staked the place out and hired three local PIs to help with the enquiry. On the day Flora had been released from prison she'd joined him here.

He'd been the most animated she'd ever seen him as they'd

sat across from each other at a table outside Café Victor, piecing together the puzzle of Lorraine Johnson's masquerade. 'Incredible,' he kept saying. 'Bloody incredible.'

He'd discovered that the previous occupant of Caroline's flat on Gardens Terrace had been beaten up and told to leave – thus enabling new tenant 'Caroline' to move in. 'She played it cool,' Brian had said in admiration. 'Waited a whole three months before making your acquaintance at that party; let you get used to seeing her around. Smart. Very smart.'

And of course it had been Lorraine who had drugged Flora; who had stolen her old phone so that when, on the way to school, she had run out of petrol – presumably siphoned off by one of the Johnson boys – she hadn't been able to call for help, presenting Travis with the perfect harassment opportunity; who had unlocked and then relocked the window through which Ryan had entered the house; who had memorised the password for the CCTV system, and borrowed Flora's new phone to allow Ryan to log in using it, and switch the cameras off and on. Afterwards, Ryan must have left the phone somewhere – in Caroline's flat, maybe – and Caroline had returned it to the kitchen table while Flora had been in the study checking the CCTV footage.

'Inside job,' Brian had nodded, draining his espresso and gazing out to sea, a little smile on his lips.

For six weeks Flora had spent all day every day in Fuerte Blanco, while the PIs expanded the search in either direction along the coast and inland, and Brian returned to the UK to follow up other potential leads.

Every day she walked along the beach in a floppy hat and sunglasses, scrutinising everyone she saw. She sat in the shade of the awning at Victor's pretending to read books and magazines, an empty coffee cup at her elbow. But mostly she sat up here, at the window of her hotel room, scanning the beach and the road below with a pair of binoculars.

The hotel staff had been great, bringing meals and drinks to her room. They had even enlisted their friends and families in the search for Beckie. Her picture was all over the press and social media, both in the UK and in Spain, although Flora had tried to make sure the name Fuerte Blanco wasn't mentioned – she didn't want the Johnsons warned off coming here. She had been touched to see a batch of homemade laminated notices tied to lampposts and in windows of local houses, with Beckie's photograph and a plea to *'Encuentre Beckie'*. It had turned out to be lovely Sofia, the maid who cleaned her room, who was responsible, and Flora had felt awful asking her to take them down, explaining that if the Johnsons did turn up here, she didn't want them to see the notices and be scared off.

'But maybe they never come,' Sofia had said.

Flora wasn't even going to contemplate that possibility.

They would come, and when they did, she'd be ready.

The local police were primed to expect her call. She was paying Victor, café owner and former member of the *Guardia Civil*, and his two brothers a retainer of £300 a week each to be on hand in case of trouble, their phones always turned on, ready to receive her SOS.

Money wasn't an issue. She'd sold the Gardens Terrace house for three-quarters of its valuation, which had still netted her an obscene amount of money, and she had Alec's life insurance payout now too. Plus there would be the compensation, eventually, from the police for their incompetence and from the press for their slanderous coverage of the case leading up to her conviction.

She sat up and swung her legs over the side of the bed, drawn back, as always, to the view. Standing at the window, she trained the binoculars on the line of little cafés and bars strung out along the beach; on the people on the pavement; on two shadowy figures on the beach... Her breath caught in her throat, but a car turning in the hotel car park briefly illuminated two dark heads and slim figures in bikini tops and cut-off jeans. It was Sofia's teenage daughters, heads bent together over a match as they lit illicit cigarettes.

If Alec were here, he'd be down there presenting to them the evidence of how many people who smoked as teenagers ended up in an early grave.

She hadn't been able to think about Alec at all in prison – and when she had had to talk about him, to Charles, to Brian, to the court, she had always referred to him as Neil. But now, for some reason, he was ever-present in her head. She kept thinking how he'd react to this or that, and what he would say; she kept imagining his smile, his touch on her back, her face, her hand; she kept hearing him telling her that the Johnsons, despite everything, loved Beckie and wouldn't harm her.

How desperately he would want to be here.

How he would hate having had to abandon them.

Only, he hadn't. He was with her, as he would always be with her, as she was sure he was with Beckie, not just in her thoughts and her memories but in the very fabric of her being. In how she looked at the world.

With his scientist's knowledge, he had been able to show them layers and layers of life that most people never even imagined existed, let alone experienced. She smiled as she remembered the day, soon after that awful scene on the street with the Johnsons, when they'd taken Beckie to the Botanic Gardens and Alec had picked a leaf off a beech hedge and explained that two cells shaped like lips formed the pores that let gases and water in and out of the leaf. When the cells were swollen with water, they were like the lips of women who had had too much Botox and couldn't close their mouths: the pore was forced open. And when there was a drought, enzymes and hormones acted to expel potassium ions and water from the pore cells so that they shrank and closed the pore to stop water escaping.

'The world is a wonderful place, Beckie,' he had said. 'And when you take notice of something wonderful in it – how this leaf protects itself, or what a fossil inside a rock did when it was alive millions of years ago, or why a bird sings – you get a little bit of the wonderful to have for yourself, no matter what not-so-wonderful things might be going on in your life at the time.'

And then Beckie, of course, had wanted to know all about why birds sang, and they had gone round the Gardens listening out for robins as Neil explained that robins had territories all the time, not just in summer, so they sang all year round – except when they were moulting in late summer and felt vulnerable – in order to tell other birds to keep off.

Was there a robin where Beckie was, to sing for her? Did you even get robins in Spain? And Beckie would probably object: 'It wouldn't be singing for *me* anyway. It would be singing to tell other birds to get lost.'

She set the binoculars down on the windowsill.

Was she happy, with Caroline? Did she hate Flora now? Or was she wondering *Why*?

Why doesn't Mum come and get me?

Flora's hand went to her pocket, her fingers closing round the smooth length of the flick-knife Wendy's partner Sol had procured for her.

I will come.

I will come for you, my darling.

I will come.

38

'Corrigan!' I yell.

Wee fucker's jumped in the pool on Jordaine's head and she's yowling.

'Right yous, picnic's ready so get your arses outta there, aye? Ryan son, you coming?'

'Naw Maw, I'm gonnae hit the gym.' He's never out that fucking gym.

'Carly and Willow are gonnae be done at WaterBabies 12:20, 12:30 at the latest, but dinnae get there till one, aye? Place gets locked up so she's gonnae have to fry her arse out on that pavement. Maybe teach the bint a fucking lesson.' Princess Fucking Carly cannae drive cos why should she, she's got three fucking brothers chauffeuring her arse any place she needs to go.

Ryan chuckles. 'She'll be a wee ray of sunshine, eh?'

'Aye, and that reminds me, go and tell Madison she's fucking coming on this fucking picnic.'

Ryan sits up on the lounger and takes off his shades. I cannae get used to the shaved head and blue contacts. Aye, he needs to lie low, but Christ on a cheesy biscuit. He looks like a fucking skinhead.

'Can Connor no go? Or Mandy?'

'Better coming from you, son.'

He loves Bekki to bits and he's gutted she's feart of him and doesnae want a bar of him because of all the shite she's read on the net about Ryan being wanted for murdering her da. After all he's done for her, it's a kick in the fucking teeth. He cannae ever go back to the UK.

And aye, I've telt Bekki over and over that it's all shite, that it was Flora killed her da and she knows it, but just in case that wean's got it in her heid she's going to the polis and that? I'm 'Polis catch up with us, you're going into fucking care, Bekki, cos that fucking woman doesnae want you back, right?'

Ryan gets up and gets on his flip-flops but then here's Bekki running out the patio doors giving it 'He killed Dave!'

Dave's her hamster. She's got the wee fucker in her hand, and I can see from here it's an ex hamster right enough. Brains chirted out its wee heid.

'Aw Jesus,' goes Mandy.

I yell, 'Corrigan!'

'It wasn't Corrigan,' goes Bekki. 'It was that fucking old alky bastard!'

And there's Jed coming out the patio doors behind her, pissing himself laughing. 'It was an acccccc-ident so it was.'

'No it wasn't! I poured his vodka down the sink and he must have gone and got Dave out of his cage and stood on him!'

'Right you.' I'm in Jed's face. 'This is your last fucking warning, right? You leave the wean alone, and that includes all of her belongings, right? You leave her be or you're outta here, and you think I'm fucking joking? Aye, go to the polis then, you think we havenae got a contingency plan? They're never catching up with us but you go to the polis and that's your arse back in the Big Bar L before you can say *I'm a fucking fuckwit.*'

Jed's effing and blinding, shuffling back in the house.

'Sorry hen,' I goes, and I pull Bekki into my chebs. 'Poor

wee Dave, eh? But it would've been quick right enough. He winnae have suffered.'

'How do you know?' she's gasping.

'Aye,' goes Corrigan, coming out the pool and getting a good deek at the late lamented Dave. 'He was maybe going "Fuck's sake" when Granda's size ten was coming down on his heid, and then he's like that: "Where's my fucking brains?"'

'That's what you say every day, isn't it, Corrigan?' Bekki's back at him. She's pulling away from me, standing there with the manky dead hamster in her hand, chin up like the wee fighter she is. 'You know you were wanting a tattoo? How about that right across your forehead? *Where's my fucking brains?*'

Ryan and Connor and Mandy are pissing themselves.

'Da!' Corrigan goes to Travis. 'She cannae say that, eh? That's a fucking hate crime! I'm fucking dyslexic!'

'Aye son.' Travis is giving Bekki evils but he cannae think of a comeback, so he cannae.

'If it was a crime to hate you, Corrigan,' goes Bekki, 'they'd need to build like a hundred new jails because everyone who's met you would need locking up.'

'Belter,' goes Ryan.

'Shut it yous!' I goes. 'We're leaving in five, right, so get your shit together and let's get to that fucking beach.'

'I'm not coming,' goes Bekki.

'Aw Madison-hen, but you're gonnae like this wee place, right, there's a barry wee café serves Coke floats like me and Mands had when we was bairns, and there's a wee harbour and that.'

'I'm not coming.'

And she's running back in the house.

I give her ten and then I go to her room. She's got Dave's remains in a cardboard box that had biscuits in it, and she's got a wee pink scarf tucked round him.

'Aw, that's nice, eh?' I goes. 'Wannae have a wee funeral and bury him in the garden?'

She's no saying nothing.

'I'm sorry, doll. Jed's a f... a mentalist, eh? But he's no gonnae do nothing like that again, I can promise you that.'

'I want Mum.'

I puff. 'Bekki darlin', Flora's no your mum. She's just a fucking random, and if she finds out where you are, I'm no gonnae lie to you, hen, she's gonnae try and kill you an' all.' I'm in her face. 'So shut it about that bitch. We're your family that loves you to bits, and we're all you've got, so you'd better start fucking appreciating us and what all we've done for you, right? We've put it on the line for you, Bekki, we've had our lives turned upside down by that bitch but we'd do it all again for you in a heartbeat because we fucking love you, right? Now get your flip-flops and get your arse in that fucking people carrier.'

SHE STOOD, just for a moment, in the shadow of the harbour wall, in the tepid few centimetres of water lapping at the sand, and looked out to the horizon where a cruise ship was slowly crossing from right to left. Her first holiday with Alec had been to the Lake District, and they had stood like this looking out over Windermere as Alec had burbled on about how the lake had been formed by glaciers.

She had pretended to be interested. 'The glacier kind of scooped it out?'

And he'd opened his mouth and shut it again, and smiled at her, and said, 'Pretty much.'

She'd learned later that his mother had told him not to 'pontificate at the poor girl'.

She closed her eyes.

Beckie's voice said, 'Boats have barnacles. Maybe there's some on that one... Yes, look! Connor, come and see! If you lie here you can see them, you can see their tentacle things. They aren't actually tentacles, they're legs, but they don't need legs to walk so evolution has made them into swishers to swish the food into their mouths. See!'

'Aye, mad. Check that one, swishing like a bastard.'

'And they've got the longest – you-know-whats of any creature compared with the size of their body, so they can reach other barnacles and – you know.'

She couldn't breathe.

She wasn't imagining this. That really was Beckie's voice. And that must be Connor Johnson. The voices were coming from the other side of the harbour wall.

'Ex-rated, eh, Beckie?'

A silence. Then:

'I hate your dad, Connor.'

'Aye, well, join the club. Hey, Beckie. Hey, it's okay hen.'

And now Flora was running up the sand, running round the end of the wall and into the harbour and *Beckie*, it really was Beckie, lying on her stomach on the stone quay with her face pressed against her bare arm.

Connor Johnson was patting her back.

How had her legs got so long?

And her hair was cropped short like a boy's. And her ears – what had happened to her ears? They weren't pixie any more. They didn't stick out from her head at all.

It *was* Beckie?

Then the boy looked up and said, 'Aw Jesus' and the girl looked up and –

'*Mum?*'

And Flora was running along the quay towards them, saying '*Beckie!*' over and over again, and Beckie's face was alight and she was scrambling to her feet, but then the smile was gone and she was backing away.

She was actually backing away.

And the joy in her face had been replaced by –

Oh God.

Flora stopped dead. 'Beckie, darling! Listen – I don't know what they've been telling you, I don't know what lies they've told you about me but –'

'You killed Dad.' Her voice was carefully controlled.

'Oh Beckie, no! Of course not! That was Ryan Johnson. The police know that now. When they catch him, he's going to prison for what he did.'

'You *told* me you killed him. So don't lie.'

'I never told you that! You know I didn't. How could you think I would kill Dad?' She took a step towards her.

Beckie took another step back. 'You wrote me a letter and you said you never wanted me to contact you again and you killed Dad –'

'Oh, no, darling. *No.* I never wrote a letter saying that. Lorraine must have faked it.'

Beckie was still backing up, tears coursing down her cheeks. *'Don't lie!'*

The boy suddenly spoke. 'She's no lying, Becks.' He was a tall young man, in a blue T-shirt and dark jeans, with a gentle face. 'That was Maw. That was Maw wrote that letter, right enough, making out she was your maw. She telt you, Beckie, that your maw didnae want nothing to do with you, and she telt your maw the same thing about you, but it wasnae true. I'm sorry, hen. I'm that sorry, eh?' His face had gone bright red.

Beckie was crying.

And Beckie never cried.

She was crying and staring at Flora.

'So do you – do you – do you still want me really?'

'Oh darling!' And in three strides Beckie was in her arms and Flora was saying, 'My darling, my darling, I don't want anything else in the whole wide world.'

But now someone was shouting, footsteps pounded on

the stone quay and the boy was saying 'Aw Christ' and 'Let them be, Maw' and then she felt herself pulled back by the shoulders and oh God, how stupid she'd been, how stupid not to call the police, not to call Victor and his brother straight away, and then Caroline's face was filling her vision, Caroline's voice was saying 'Hiya Flora' and then she was being flung backwards, stumbling, and hard fingers closed round her arms and the stale stench of cigarettes and BO engulfed her as she twisted to come face to face with Jed Johnson.

He grinned at her.

'*Mum!*'

Caroline had Beckie trapped in her arms. A new Caroline, a flabby Caroline with dirty blonde streaks in her hair.

Lorraine Johnson.

'She's no your *Mum*, hen!'

Flora kicked back against Jed's legs and he grunted, and she managed to get her hand into her pocket, to close her fingers around her mobile phone, to pull it out –

It was snatched from her hand by soft white fingers.

A hugely fat woman was standing between her and Beckie and Caroline, smiling at her. 'Oops.' Without looking, the woman flicked her bloated fingers to toss the phone neatly into the water.

And the last piece of the puzzle fell into place.

It was the 'Lorraine Johnson' who'd come to the door at Gardens Terrace.

The family resemblance was striking.

'Please,' said Flora. 'Please, just let Beckie go.'

'*Please!*' mimicked Jed in her ear.

'Mands, get the weans in that wee café, aye, while we have ourselves a wee chat with this bitch? Connor son, get on the blower to that fuckwit Travis, tell him to get that fucking people carrier back here pronto cos we've got ourselves a wee situation, aye? Fucking mad bitch has only been and attacked Beckie.'

'She didn't!' Beckie wailed. 'You're just pretending! You're just pretending Mum is a bad person to make me stay with you but she isn't!'

With all the strength of her new prison gym-toned body, Flora stamped down on Jed's foot and drove her elbow back into his body.

'Fuckin' –'

And she thrust her hand back into the pocket of her jeans to pull out the flick-knife. She depressed the button and the wicked five-inch blade shot out of the casing and she lunged at Jed's tattooed naked torso.

The next thing she knew she was slamming into the stone surface of the quay, all the breath thumped out of her lungs, and the knife was bouncing away from her towards Caroline's foot. And a hard body smacked down on top of her, Jed's hands in her hair, pulling her head up as she gasped for the air she couldn't suck into her lungs.

Caroline looked down at her. 'Like Mands said: Oops. See that, Beckie-hen? That's a flick-knife and they're fucking illegal, but when you're a fucking serial killer that's no gonnae give you many sleepless nights, eh? What were you gonnae do with that, Flora? Stick it in Beckie?'

Flora gasped, desperately appealing to Beckie with her eyes: *Don't believe her, don't believe her!*

'What's a... a flick-knife?' Beckie sounded so scared.

'It's a fucking murder weapon, hen. See the blade on that?' Caroline nudged it with the toe of her flip-flop. 'Flora, Flora, what next, eh?'

And suddenly the weight on her back was gone. She rolled over to see the boy, Connor, wrestling with Jed. And a darting movement from Beckie, and then Beckie was standing with the flick-knife pointed, wobbling, at Caroline.

.   .   .

THE WEE DIDDY! He's rolling on Jed and Jed's like that: 'Fucking wee wanker!' and Bekki's pulling away and squatting and Jesus Chutney, she's only got the fucking chib, and that bitch Flora is getting up and I'm like that:

'Bekki-hen, come here to me hen, I'll no let her hurt you' and wee Bekki's looking at the bitch and then she's looking at me and she's got the chib in her hand and she's all, 'You're a fucking liar' and I'm 'Naw hen' and she's '*Mum* would never hurt me. You wrote that letter and you said really horrible things' and I'm 'Naw hen' and she's 'You said Mum told me she killed Dad but *how could you know that because I never told you what was in the letter and you couldn't have read it because I tore it up and put the bits in the bin*' and right enough, she's one smart cookie so she is, and I'm 'Aye, maybe there was a wee bit deception there but it was for your own good, aye? It's all for your own good, Bekki, it's all for you, my wee darlin', it's all of it been for you.'

And then the bitch is 'Come here, Bekki!' and Jed's roaring at Connor and I'm snatching at the wean and the chib, it's like it's in slow motion, eh, the chib's coming at me and it's in my fucking neck.

'I hate you!' Bekki's greeting, and I cannae speak, eh, and I'm on the deck and Connor's like that: 'Maw!' and the wee diddy's taken the chib out my neck and the blood's pouring out me and I get my fingers in the hole and I'm 'It's okay hen, it's okay.' There's grey circles in my eyes but I manage to say it:

'A wee accident, eh?'

Fuck it, but.

39

FIVE YEARS LATER

I touch each of the bonsais for luck – Pinkie, Perkie and little Podgie, who's the least valuable because he's got a funny bushy shape but he's the cutest. Then I put my finger on the glass over a bit of Mimi. 'See you guys later.'

They're on the windowsill with the best view. Both the windows on this side of my room look over the trees and two of our fields – I can see Marvin's big arse, he's chomping away on the grass as usual – and after the fields there's the dunes, and then there's the lovely blue of the Tasman Sea and I'm already thinking about tomorrow morning when Mum and Connor and Erin and I are going hacking to the beach on Brodie and Sam and Turpin and either Bindie or Marvin, depending on whether Bindie's leg is still giving her a problem, but Erin really loves Bindie so I'm hoping it'll be possible for her to ride her and Marvin's such an old slowcoach, he's not ideal for a hack.

Our house is a big old farmhouse up on a little hill, what they call a 'colonial homestead', and it's really desirable because there are hardly any old houses here, most of the houses are newish bungalows like the one Connor and Erin and Carly and Willow live in in Westport, which is still really nice but not *as* nice? Our house was built in 1896 and has massive gorgeous big rooms. My room is like something from a magazine, with sloping bits of wall and a fireplace where you can have real fires in the winter, if it's like *really* cold, and wooden walls that I painted myself in this colour called Mizzle. It's a kind of a pale greeny-blue?

Down from the window I can see the roof of the veranda where the two rurus were last night. They're way cuter than British owls. I was in bed and I heard them doing their *ruuuu-ru* call, like *really* close, so close I thought *Are they inside the room?!* and I tippy-toed out of bed to the window and there they were! Two of the little guys just sitting there side by side on the veranda roof right under my window! I could see their big golden eyes in the dark. They were the cutest! No sign of them now, but maybe they'll be back tonight.

Dad would have so loved it here.

Every time I look at Pinkie and Perkie and Podgie and Mimi I think about Dad but also that man Brian who rescued them from my room in that house because he knew they were special, after Bitch left them to die after she told me she was getting them posted to Spain.

Such a fucking liar.

What's really unbelievable, when I think about it, is I thought Connor and Carly would totally hate me after I killed their 'Maw' but they don't. Right enough, they think I didn't *mean* to kill her. They think I was so scared I didn't know what I was doing and I was just trying to keep her away from me. And I've pretended to be all guilty and everything and all sad that the ambulance got there too late.

Mum and I had gone by then so I didn't see Bitch actually die. Connor told us to just go, to run – he said he'd tell the police, and Mandy as well, that me and Mum had run off and then Jed had stabbed Bitch. And then Mum could call the police and make out like *We've just escaped from the Johnsons – Help!* as if she didn't know the stabbing had even happened.

So that's what we did.

And now Jed and Ryan are both in prison.

Result!

I get my bag from where I dumped it on the chair and run downstairs.

Mum's clearing the table. She's all 'My little girl's first date' and I'm 'Mu-uuum.' I'm not a little girl, I'm like fifteen?

'You look beautiful!'

I so don't. I'm just in old jeans and a shirt and no make-up, or hardly any, because it's no big deal.

Then she starts, 'Now, don't feel pressured to do *anything* you don't feel comfortable with' and I'm 'Mu-uuum!' and then I'm 'Relax, I'm not going to have sex or anything' and she's 'Well, that's a relief!' and I can tell she's trying not to laugh.

But sex is so gross. I'm not having it till I'm like twenty at least. Connor says he was twenty-one when he first had it. I know it's not cool to think sex is gross but it so is? Mibs, my best friend, she agrees. But I'm pretty sure Andrew doesn't, so I've laid down some ground rules, just to make sure everything's clear from the start, and now I'm telling Mum:

'He knows there's going to be no physical contact until the third date. Then holding hands and maybe kissing but that's it. He's cool with that.'

'I should hope so!'

'He's not a jock or anything, he's pretty much king of the super-nerds, and he's not good-looking so it's kind of I'll take what I can get, you know?'

'Beckie!'

Now we can hear an engine on the track and we go out onto the veranda to wave at Connor's car. He's driving me to

Andrew's house and then he's driving us both to the NBS Theatre in Westport, where Pippa works, to see the *Star Wars* film which is going to be mobbed by kids and nerds and Pippa will like probably sit with us, and Connor's picking us up right after the film, so even if I wanted to have sex how could I?

It's really nice and warm but not too hot on the veranda and there's a lovely breeze, and we sit on the swing seat and swing ourselves and breathe in the lovely piney smell of the trees.

'So what is it you see in this Andrew, then?'

'He's really funny? And super-smart. Bit like me.'

Mum laughs. 'And is he as modest as you are?'

'He's modest about some stuff and not modest about other stuff.' I grin. 'He's... He's a bit like, you know, Dad in that way? And maybe in other ways as well.'

And there's a bit of a silence, not exactly awkward, more like we're both thinking stuff and it's kind of sad and kind of happy.

'Like, I know he's going to be telling me all about game theory and evolutionarily stable strategies. It's his new thing. He thinks game theory can be used to solve pretty much all the problems in the world.'

'Not short on ambition, then.'

We both laugh.

'For example, war? Apparently there are these three different strategies, hawk and dove and crow. Doves are like really nice and kind, like peace activists and people, but the problem is that if everyone in the world is a dove the system's inherently unstable because the minute a hawk appears – hawks are like super-nasty and just want to exterminate everyone else? – if they're in a world full of doves they basically just go mental and pretty soon the world's fucked.'

'Beckie.'

'Sorry. I mean, like if the Nazis had won the war. Because the hawks know they can do whatever they want and the doves won't stop them. It'd be like Hitler or Putin or Trump somehow gets into Teletubby Land. Or like every country's Switzerland except for North Korea? Then the opposite scenario, a world full of just hawks, obviously that's f... that isn't going to work either because they'll all just kill each other. The only way for it to be stable is to have retaliators in the mix – crows. They're like doves except they're smart and they fight back if a hawk starts anything, like maybe James Bond? So everyone can coexist.'

Mum's smiling. 'Well, that makes sense, although I'm sure Dad would be up for a debate about it with Andrew.'

Connor's getting out of his car. 'Hiya!'

'Hi Connor!' Mum gets up. 'Thanks so much for acting as Beckie's chauffeur yet again.'

'You're welcome.'

'Yeah, thanks Connor,' I say on cue.

Mum hugs me. 'Have fun, darling.'

I hug her back. 'Thanks Mum. I will.'

'Looking good, Beckster,' says Connor.

I can see myself in the glass of the kitchen window and I'm thinking, yeah, I'm not bad. I'm not the prettiest girl in the class or anything but I'm okay. I'm tall and slim but I've got curves. Quite a few boys have asked me out before, so I can't be like a total minger, but I said 'Thanks but no thanks' because I only wanted to go out with Andrew Main but he was with Sherilyn, that skanky cow who called Mibs a retard just because she thought a caftan was a kind of cafetière. Sherilyn made Andrew's life hell, ordering him about and once when he got her the wrong yoghurt in the canteen she glooped it over his head and all her skanky friends were laughing and Sherilyn was yelling at him, 'You fucking know I hate strawberry!' and he just smiled his goofy smile and used his scarf to try and wipe it off his hair.

That girl is such a fucking bully.

Last week after hockey there was just me and her in the

changing room because she always takes forever in the shower washing all her skanky flab, and I waited behind pretending to have lost my scrunchy, and I told Mibs and them just to go ahead to our next class and explain to Mrs Hutchison why I was late, and then when Sherilyn came out of the shower I slammed her up against the changing room door and told her if she didn't (a) chuck Andrew and (b) stop picking on Mibs I was going to break her nose so fucking badly no fucking surgeon on the planet would be able to put it back together and how many boys would want to go out with her then?

She pissed herself and had to go back in the shower.

CONNOR'S GOING on about the wedding as usual – they're getting married at our house because neither Connor nor Erin is religious – and it's super-dull, so I ask him about Mrs Miller, the old lady who's the latest client of Connor's Computer Services.

'Aw Beckie, you should've seen the spread she'd laid out for me, right? We're no just talking scones and cake, there was like tuna and prawn rolls and wee pork pies and egg mayo sandwiches and that, and peanut butter ice cream and an oat and strawberry smoothie. It was pure amazing so it was.'

'And you scoffed the lot?'

'Only polite, eh? Mrs Miller thinks I need fed up or Erin's gonnae leave me for some big hunky guy she's gonnae meet at the pool.'

That's where Erin works. She's like a *really* amazing swimmer and she was nearly picked for the New Zealand Olympic team for breaststroke when she was fourteen.

'That explains all the protein.'

'Aye, she's maybe been Googling it with her newfound skills, eh? How to get muscles on a skinny wee fucker, she's maybe inputted.'

I snort. 'I bet Mrs Miller would be on my side in the Is-Willow-Too-Fat debate.'

'Aye, likely.'

Willow's six now and she's staying with us tomorrow night so Carly and Connor and Erin can all go out. Mum bans poor Willow from eating any sweets or crisps or ice cream or basically anything nice while she's with us because she says she's on the cusp of obesity but I love her chubby little cheeks and her chubby little arms and legs. She's so adorable.

I'm telling her Dad's Wanderer stories and she loves them.

'She wouldn't be so cute if she was thin. It's like cats – they're super-cute when they're really fat, but Mum says you should think about their health, and I know she's got a point, but when Willow gets back to yours she'll just stuff her face to make up for it anyway.'

'Aye, Carly needs to stop buying that wean crap. She needs to step up as a responsible parent, eh?'

I shrug. 'I guess. And talking of which – have you spoken to Ryan about Ailish yet?'

'No yet.'

'You don't think he'd do it.'

'Ryan would do anything for you, Beckie, you know that, he feels that bad about your da, eh? That's no the issue here. Do you no think it's maybe best to just move on, eh, and forget it?'

'Nope.'

Ailish needs to be punished. If she hadn't stopped Jasmine coming forward and telling the police she'd seen Ryan, they would have focused the investigation on him from the start and Mum would never have gone to jail.

But even more important than that is what's happening to Jack. Jasmine's little toddler Jack. While Jasmine's at work, Ailish is meant to look after him on Mondays and Wednesdays and she's all 'Just call me Super Gran' and posting photos on Facebook of stupid cakes she's baked for him and stuff. She hardly ever features Jack himself, though, and when she does it's always from the back. Mia's all over that Facebook page now – 'Quality niece and auntie time!' – because Mia's really *really* pretty, like a model. Ailish is always taking her photo without her knowing, so Mia can't mess it up by making one of her gargoyle faces. Mia says Ailish basically ignores Jack unless she needs the back of his head for a photo. Otherwise he's in his playpen the whole time apart from when he's being fed or changed, and if Thomas or Mia is there they have to do that.

Ailish basically despises Jack because he's got this eye problem and he's cross-eyed. Ailish keeps going on to Jasmine about how they should take him to Bulgaria or wherever to get it sorted because no UK surgeon will do the operation until he's older.

Until she can put him on Facebook and get 'Oh he's so gorgeous' comments, she doesn't want to know.

The evil, evil cow.

Mia and Thomas have tried telling Jasmine what she's doing, but Jasmine doesn't believe them because Ailish has brainwashed her. Mia was crying about Jack last time we Skyped, and I was too. Mum says we'd need evidence before social services would intervene and maybe Mia could set up a camera or something, but footage of a toddler in a playpen probably wouldn't cut it.

It's so not fair.

It's Thomas all over again.

This time, though, she's not getting away with it. Some people just shouldn't be around kids, and okay so Ailish isn't as bad as Jed and Bitch, but she's still pretty fucking bad.

'It's not like I'm wanting Ryan to put out a hit on her or anything. Although...'

Connor whips his head round.

'I'm joking! God, Connor! But I've been thinking maybe framing her for burglary isn't the way to go.'

All he says is 'Oh aye?' but he's obviously thinking *Thank fuck for that*.

'It would be her first offence, so she probably wouldn't even get a custodial sentence. But I've been thinking – what if she was filmed being super-neglectful and there were witnesses and she was convicted of child neglect?'

'We cannae hurt a bairn.'

'Of course not! But what I'm thinking is, one really hot day in summer when she's doing her Super Gran stuff, one of Ryan's goons can somehow give her Rohypnol and get her and Jack and the buggy and her car into town. Somewhere there's no CCTV. Park up the car, get a load of alcohol down Ailish, and leave her slumped on a bench or somewhere with the empty buggy and an empty bottle of Bailey's. Meanwhile, one of the goons, acting the concerned citizen, has to smash the car window to get Jack out of the boiling hot car before he dies of dehydration and heat shock. They wouldn't *actually* leave him in the car, but with no CCTV, who's to know? They take him to the nearest hospital and the police get involved. Someone else meanwhile secretly films Ailish as she's coming round, as she's realising "Fuck where's Jack?" and going mental, staggering around with the empty buggy looking for him. The footage goes up on YouTube, all her Facebook friends get sent the link, and she's trolled by a load of self-righteous bitches just like her. Then hopefully she's arrested for child neglect, and her life's basically over. And she never gets near Jack again.'

'Aw Christ Beckie.'

'Would Ryan be able to organise all that from prison?'

'Aye, but –'

'Ryan owes us big time.'

I can't wait to see Mum's face when I'm like 'Oh Mum look at this that Mia sent me!' and I show her the YouTube footage of Ailish and she reads all the troll stuff. She's going to be 'Oh that's dreadful' but secretly she'll be going *Yes!*

Andrew's right. One thing I've learned from all the shit that's happened to me is that being a dove just gets you fucked over. Like Mum and Dad were by Bitch. And like Mum was by that Tricia girl. If she had stood up to Tricia she would never have got into all that trouble in the first place.

I do kind of wonder about that, though. I mean, the bow and arrow. How is it possible to *accidentally* fire an arrow at someone? Even if you tripped up, wouldn't you just let go of the bow as well as the arrow and they would both just get dropped to the ground? And how could that Gail tell it was an accident?

But I so would not blame Mum if it wasn't.

Tricia had it coming. People like Tricia and Ailish and Bitch, they're hawks and they'll basically try to shaft you every time. You have to be a crow. You have to shaft them back.

'He'll be able to organise that, you reckon?'

Connor shrugs. 'Aye.'

'And you'll ask him? It's really not a big deal, is it, compared with the stuff he's already done? Compared with, oh, I don't know... *murdering my dad*?'

Connor looks at me sideways. 'Beckie –'

'Yeah yeah, heard it all before. Will you ask him or will you not, Connor?'

'Aye, okay then.'

And now we're turning into Andrew's road on the edge of Westport. It's called Abattoir Road which doesn't exactly sound like it's a brilliant address, but it's out in nice countryside with lots of grass and trees between the houses and there's a view of the mountains, and his house is nowhere near the actual abattoir. And Connor suddenly slows down and says, 'Check the fantail!' and he points up into a tree and there's a fantail jumping about in there flicking his tail and it really does look like a fan, it doesn't look real, and I'm 'Awww amazing!'

And now we're at Andrew's house and he's waiting at the end of his drive in a black T-shirt with the Crab Nebula on it and brown trousers that so don't go, and when he sees the car slowing down he waves in a really dorky way, like he's making a circle in the air with his hand, and he's grinning like Wallace out of *Wallace and Gromit*, and Connor's saying 'The wee fuck-wit' and oh my God I love my life.

FROM JANE

Firstly, I must thank *you* for enduring the Johnsons throughout this novel. That is quite a feat. My long-suffering friends and family have also had to put up with a lot – thank you, all of you, for humouring me when I bore you with all the (often) gory details of my latest plot idea, and for refraining from committing a real-life murder.

The only people to read *Watch Over Me* in its early stages were Lesley McLaren (www.mediterraneanpyrenees.com) and Lucy Lawrie (author of *Tiny Acts of Love* and *The Last Day I Saw Her*), my wonderful writer friends, who as always provided everything I needed, from the impetus to write it in the first place, to how to solve problems with the plot and characters, to the nitty-gritty of sorting out the text (yes, Beckie's original dialogue was *too annoying?*), not to mention endless encouragement and patience throughout the whole process. Thank you both for taking so much time from your own writing to help me – and for all the laughs!
Author Cathryn Grant was kind enough to offer very valuable advice, particularly about how much Glaswegian dialect the novel could take without becoming too incomprehensible to readers outside Scotland. Thank you, Cathryn!

I am hugely indebted to the team at Inkubator Books. Pauline Nolet picked up an embarrassingly high number of mistakes in her careful read of the manuscript. Brian Lynch and Garret

Ryan took a chance on a 'random' (as Lorraine would say) and made the scary process of preparing for publication not scary at all – in fact, it has been great fun! I am extremely lucky to have found a publisher that offers such excellent and intelligent help with all things editorial– from the big picture to the smallest detail – combined with an in-depth knowledge of marketing. Thank you so much for all your guidance and support, and for your enthusiasm for *Watch Over Me*. In Johnson-speak: belter!

Finally, reviews are so important to us authors. I would be very grateful if you could spend a moment to write an honest review (no matter how short). They really do help get the word out.

Leave a Review

Best wishes,

Jane

www.janerenshaw.co.uk

GLOSSARY OF SCOTTISH DIALECT & SLANG

aff off
airch to throw
alky alcoholic
aye yes
babby baby
bairn child
bampot idiot
bangsty mad
barry wonderful
bass bastard
baws balls
beamer blushing face
belter something very good
ben through
bevvy alcoholic drink; to drink alcohol
bint woman
boak vomit
boggin' disgusting
bonnie pretty
bowfin' disgusting and/or stinking

breenge to shove or barge
bumfled up bundled up (in clothes)
by the way actually (used for emphasis)
cannae can't
cauld cold
chap to knock
chebs breasts
chib knife
coorie cuddle
coup to tip or overturn
da dad
daftie idiot
deek to look or peek
diddy silly idiot
dinnae don't
dowfie stupid
dug dog
eejit idiot
evils a hostile look
fanny female genitalia (vulgar)
feart scared
fleein' drunk
flit to move house
gies give us/me
ginger sweet fizzy drink
girn to cry, whine or both
glaikit stupid
gob mouth
gobby loud-mouthed
gobshite rubbish
gonnae going to
greet to cry
gub mouth
hairy young woman of loose morals

havenae haven't
heehaw nothing
heid head
hen affectionate term for a girl or woman
hisself himself
hud to hold
hyter to stumble
isnae isn't
jagged jabbed
jakied inebriated
jobbie poo
keek to peep
laddie boy
laird landowner
lassie girl
lug ear
manky dirty or unsavoury
maw mother
minger dirty or disgusting person
minging dirty or disgusting
(the) morn tomorrow
-nae (e.g. isnae) -n't (e.g. isn't)
naw no
neb nose
ned lout
no not
numptie idiot
photy photo
piece sandwich
pish piss
podging overeating
polis police
pooch pocket
radge wildly angry

raging angry
rammie a fight
rare good
Rotty Rottweiler
runch to crunch
sakeless harmless
scheme a housing estate (often council housing)
schemie an inhabitant of a council housing estate
scliters dirty wetness
scooby clue
shite shit
shoogly unsteady or rocking (e.g. a table on an uneven surface)
shoosh be quiet
skelp to smack
slavers long strings of saliva hanging from the mouth
sleekit underhand
stane stone
swadging relaxing
swally swallow
swalt swollen
syping seeping
telt told
teuchter country bumpkin or Highlander
thingmae thing
trauchle to trudge or trail
wammling wriggling
wasnae wasn't
wean child (pronounced 'wane')
wee little
whoogie thing
widnae wouldn't
wifie older woman
windae window
windae-licker a person with a learning disability

wisnae wasn't
wouldnae wouldn't
ya beauty! excellent!
ya dancer! excellent!
ya you
ye you
yous you (plural)

Published by Inkubator Books
www.inkubatorbooks.com

Printed in Great Britain
by Amazon